Shots and Shutouts

Shots and Shutouts

Goshawks Hockey Romance #1
Dee Marie

Conceptual Images Publishing

Shots and Shutouts: Goshawks Hockey Romance #1

Published by Conceptual Images Publishing
PO Box 654
Clear Lake, South Dakota, 57226

All efforts have been made to ensure the accuracy of any Internet information and links, however, neither the publisher, nor the author may be held responsible for any inaccuracies or unforeseen URL changes.

Cover Design and Interior Illustrations © 2024 D. M. Haskell

ISBN: 979-8-9909182-2-1 Hard Cover
ISBN: 979-8-9909182-0-7 Paperback
ISBN: 979-8-9909182-1-4 E-book

Library of Congress Control Number: 2024911945

Printed in the United States of America

Portland, Maine Goshawks Roster

FORWARDS

Etan Eklund #56 Right Wing: Age19 – 5'11"/188lbs – Sweden
Chase Rutherford #7 [Captain] Center: Age 26 – 6'1"/199lbs – Maine
Finn O'Connell #63 Left Wing: Age 31 – 6'4"/220lbs – Canadian

Steve Sturman #74 Right Wing: Age 26 – 6'/188lbs – Czech Republic
Eddie Bennett #18 Center: Age 26 – 5'10"/181lbs – Michigan
Daniel Murphy #11 [Alt Captain] Left Wing: Age 25 – 6'/203lbs – Canadian

Henry Kennedy #21 Left Wing: Age 32 – 217lbs/6'3" – Massachusetts
James Thompson #39 Center: Age 25 – 178lbs/5'9" – California
Vavrin Pavel #91 Right Wing: Age 23 – 6'/210lbs – Czech Republic

Aidan Casey #17 Left Wing: Age 33 – 6'/203lbs – Florida
Zach Miller #38 Center: Age 31 – 5'11"/189lbs – Canadian
Lenka Divila #10 Right Wing: Age 26 – 6'3"/215lbs – Czech Republic

DEFENSE

Ryan Mitchell #73 [Alt Captain] Age 24 – 6'3"/200lbs – Canadian
Axel Berger #25 Age 19 – 6'3"/205lbs – German

Matthew Presto #62 Age 25 – 6'1"/209lbs – Michigan
Liam Armstrong #28 Age 30 - 6'3"/224lbs – Texas

Dylan Gallagher #27 Age 29 – 6'4"/224lbs – Canadian
Jake Carter #14 Age 24 – 6'1"/209lbs – New York

GOALIES

Hunter 'Ice Wall' Griffin #1 Age 22 – 6'2"/198lbs – Maine
Olaf 'Snowman' Svensson #30 Age 32 – 6'4"/220lbs – Sweden

Chapter 1

First Shot

April 5th

Hunter 'Ice Wall' Griffin, at twenty-two, was already a legend between the pipes for the Portland, Maine Goshawks. Tonight, in the locker room, surrounded by his teammates, he experienced a solitude that the chatter and commotion could not penetrate. He seldom lost a game, but when he did, the room felt more like a morgue than a sanctuary.

Slumped in his stall, eyes closed, head in hands, he replayed the last minutes of the game. The shrill echo of the final whistle, signaling not just the close of the third period, but more cutting, the end of their nine-game winning streak. Falling to a team ranked far below the Goshawks' standings made the sting of defeat even harsher. The chill of the loss bit deep, turning Ice Wall—a name earned through countless impenetrable performances—into a mocking echo of the fortress he embodied on the ice.

Each period had been a nerve-wracking showdown, as the other team clashed with the Goshawks in their quest for one of the last playoff wildcard spots. Every pass, every shot on goal, every save was a pulsating beat in the living entity that was the game. Like a throbbing heart, one wrong move, one miss, could prove fatal.

Hunter cringed as he recalled the sound of the puck hitting the ice, the skates carving through the surface, the hometown crowd's escalating anticipation. The crucial shot came like a sniper's bullet, a blistering drive. It soared through a maze of defenders, heading straight for him, straight for his net.

He could still feel his trapper hand outstretched, his pounding heart thundering in his chest. Around him, the fans in the arena had held their collective breath. Time stretched thin as the puck arced through the air. Fate, with a sardonic smile, let the puck graze the edge of his glove, deflecting into the net. Behind him, the red lamp had flickered to life, sealing the moment.

The disappointment was immediate and intense, like a punch to the gut. It wasn't just his failure; it was the team's loss, and this regular season—until tonight—the Goshawks had only lost ten games. A slap on his knee pads brought Hunter to the present. "Shake it off, Griffin." Olaf 'The Snowman' Svensson, the Goshawks' backup goalie, was always there with encouragement. "Next game you'll shut em out."

Ryan Mitchell, his best friend, and the Goshawks' defensive rock wasn't one for empty comforts. "We win as a team. We lose as one, too. We're all a part of this loss."

The rookies, Etan Eklund and Axel Berger hovered nearby.

"Yeah, man," Etan started, "You're the fortress, you know? One goal doesn't change that."

Axel nodded, adding in his thick German accent, "It's just one game. We'll fight again, yes?"

Hunter almost smiled at their attempts to lift the gloom. The camaraderie was a small salve, but the sting of loss remained raw. Every game mattered, even though the Goshawks had clinched the top spot in their division for the playoffs. The other team had proven hungrier. Still, the weight of the loss sat heavy on his shoulders.

The sweat on his skin cooled in the room's chill, but he couldn't bring himself to move. One by one, his teammates trickled out. Some clapped him on the shoulder, murmuring words of encouragement. Others wore tight-lipped expressions, mirroring his disappointment. Then, he was alone with only the quiet as his companion.

His gloves lay discarded by his side, the sturdy leather seeming useless now. They had failed him when he needed them the most. Or had he failed them? Still dressed in his gear, he picked up his phone. Scrolling through the angry posts left by fans on the official Goshawks Facebook page, a lone positive comment caught his attention.

Sage Photography: Tough loss … but Ice Wall stood on his head. Looking forward to the next game. I know he'll get a shutout.

There was something genuine about her words that compelled Hunter to check out her Facebook page. He paused at her profile. She was a stunning blonde. Although the camera blocked most of her features, her deep blue eyes piqued his interest.

He read her bio. Age: twenty-one. Profession: photographer. Home: Brookings, South Dakota.

Searching through her posting a series of photos caught his attention—sweeping landscapes, intimate portraits, moments of everyday life captured with a keen eye. Sage Larson wasn't just a fan; she was a gifted photographer.

He inhaled, then began typing a message to accompany his Facebook friend request.

Hunter Griffin: Hey Sage, this is Hunter, better known to my fans as Ice Wall. Read your comment on the Goshawks' page. Thanks for the support. It means a lot after a night like this.

His finger hovered over the 'send' button for a moment. "Why not?" he said. He couldn't help but hope this minor act would somehow mend the gaping hole tonight's game had left in his confidence.

Hunter never reached out to fans on social media; he kept a wall, not just on the ice, but between his public persona and personal life. Yet Sage's comment, a lone beacon of encouragement amid a storm of criticism, pulled at him. When he put his phone aside, there was a stir of something unfamiliar—a flicker of hope or perhaps the thrill of beginning anew. Peeling off his goalie gear, each layer lifted a fraction of the night's weight from his shoulders.

Stepping into the shower, he let the hot water cascade over him, attempting to cleanse the disappointment that had seeped into his bones. Amidst the steam and the solitude, Hunter smiled—genuinely smiled—for the first time tonight, with the thought of Sage's pending response.

His friend request was a simple gesture, but it felt like the first step towards something transformative. As the water washed over him, Hunter's thoughts weren't on the game lost, but on the possibilities Sage's reply might bring. What could one message change? Eager to find out, he experienced a sudden warmth against the lingering cold of defeat.

Chapter 2
Through the Lens of Doubt

April 5th

Perched at the open window of her apartment, nestled above the horse barn, Sage Larson found herself lost in the late spring night's celestial beauty. The expansive night sky, a canvas strewn with stars, offered a tranquil contrast to the residual adrenaline pulsing through her from watching the Goshawks' game.

Her passion for hockey stemmed from a high school romance with Joey, a new student, from Portland, Maine. Five years ago, watching the Goshawks on TV in his parents' basement defined their dating life. Though the relationship faded, her love for hockey, especially the Goshawks, endured.

Living on her family's sprawling cattle ranch on the outskirts of Brookings, South Dakota, Sage was worlds apart from professional hockey arenas. Though the Minnesota team was just a state away, ranch work and her budding photography career consumed her days, leaving no room for out-of-state road trips. Still, her love for hockey flourished, with nights dedicated to the game ... each check, save, and goal only experienced through televised broadcasts.

Her admiration was especially strong for pro hockey goalies, those lone guardians of the net. Among them, Hunter Griffin stood out. Watching him dominate the ice with his height of six feet two inches, with a presence that commanded attention, was mesmerizing. His expertise in the butterfly style, which rendered him nearly invincible, had captured her from the start. Hunter didn't just defend the goal; he turned it into an impregnable fortress, an 'Ice Wall' rarely breached by opposing teams. Tonight was an exception. He'd allowed a puck to slip past him at a critical moment. Sage ached with empathy for the man behind the mask.

She returned to her desk, surrounded by the smell of strong coffee and the occasional whiff of horses from below. She did her best to refocus on work. The glow of her computer screen cast her in a soft light as she glided her stylus across the drawing pad. Despite her intention to dive into the latest batch of photos from a recent shoot, her thoughts kept circling back to Hunter and the game's outcome.

The images on her screen showcased Sage's knack for capturing the extraordinary in the mundane. As the evening unfolded, her focus shifted from the photos to thoughts of icy arenas miles away. There, Hunter moved with a grace and power that Sage strived to encapsulate in her photographs. This alignment in their pursuits, capturing fleeting moments of perfection, whether on ice or through the lens, solidified her connection to the game and, by extension, to Hunter himself.

Several sharp chimes from her phone pierced the tranquility of the night. A message notification blinked on the screen. Her breath caught as she registered the sender's name—Hunter Griffin. Accompanied by a friend request. "No way. This can't be the real Hunter Ice Wall Griffin reaching out to me," she said aloud.

Yet, the message carried sincerity. It thanked her for the supportive comment she'd left on the Goshawks' Facebook page. Expressing his own disappointment about the game's outcome. Sage sighed, his words igniting a war between reality and deception.

Sage's first move was to scrutinize his Facebook profile. There, under his name, was a picture of Hunter Griffin in full Goshawks regalia. Yet, as she delved deeper, his feed was barren save for that single image, mirrored in his only other post. No verified badge, and his personal details were conspicuously missing—all red flags that set off alarm bells.

Haunted by previous encounters with creeps masquerading as pro hockey stars, she approached with warranted skepticism. Despite these doubts, a part of her held onto the slim hope that this time might be different. With cautious optimism, she engaged him, laying down a gauntlet for this supposed 'Ice Wall' to authenticate himself.

Sage Photography: Nice try, buddy. If you're the Goshawks' Hunter Griffin, then I'm the Queen of Denmark.

Pressing send, her heart raced. Turning back to her photo editing, Sage sought comfort in the familiar dance of shadows and light on her screen. Yet, the undercurrent of excitement at the thought of this being the real Hunter Griffin refused to be quelled, keeping her company as she worked late into the night.

Chapter 3
Proof in the Puck

April 5th

Returning to the solitude of his apartment, once more Hunter felt the night's weight settling around him. His footsteps echoed through the sparsely furnished space of his front room, each step resonating with the night's disappointment. The panoramic view of downtown Portland, normally a beacon of solace, now echoed his inner turmoil.

Dressed in the remnants of his professional façade, the fabric of his tailored suit felt like a constraint compared to the liberating fit of his hockey gear. Undoing his silk tie, he watched it slip through his fingers, like the game had slipped away. Draping his suit jacket over the back of the recliner, he sank into the nearby leather couch. The shedding of layers allowed Hunter to find a semblance of peace ... the stillness of his home wrapped around him like a comforting shroud.

Hunter's attention was drawn to the phone he'd tossed on the coffee table. A blinking notification showed a message from Sage. Her playful skepticism was a welcome contrast to the fans' criticism he'd read earlier. Her implied challenge ignited a flicker of warmth in the cold aftermath of defeat.

With a sense of purpose, Hunter retrieved a sheet of paper from a nearby printer, along with a thick black Sharpie. Debating, he settled on a direct 'Hi, Sage,' leaving out the royal title. Shirtless, his athletic physique on display—a testament to countless hours of rigorous training—he captured a selfie against the backdrop of his living room. The Goshawks' banner, hanging on the wall behind him, added to his authenticity. This photo, a blend of personal vulnerability and casual charm, was intended just for her. A tangible proof of his identity. He intended to delete the post as soon as he was assured she'd viewed it.

Uploading the picture to his Instagram story, Hunter captioned it 'For a special fan,' marking a departure from his typical guarded self. Most uploads to his social media accounts were done by Goshawks' interns. Although he was an avid reader of his fans' comments, he seldom posted anything. This act of openness, a personal connection with a fan he'd never met, was uncharted territory. He prided himself on keeping his hockey life and personal life separate.

Why now? Why this fan? These were questions he couldn't answer or fully comprehend. Something enticed him to Sage. Not unlike the pull that first drew him to hockey. Shrugging off his concerns, he sent a quick response via Messenger, along with a direct link to his Instagram page.

Hunter Griffin: Your Majesty, click on this link for identity verification.

"Short and sweet," he muttered, as he pressed the send button. A sudden wave of second thoughts washed over him, a rare occurrence for a goalie who faced down slap shots without flinching. The casual disarray of his clothes, left where they fell, mirrored the unusual disorder in his life tonight. In this moment, he'd shed the impenetrable Ice Wall persona ... breaking free from his sheltered existence, reaching out beyond the confines of a life dictated solely by his hockey career.

Hunter stood motionless, the silence of his apartment echoing back to his own uncertainty. From a young age, his parents forced him to build walls around himself, a fortress as impenetrable as his Goshawks' nickname suggested. Tonight, driven by an impulse, he'd extended a bridge across his guarded solitude to a stranger.

Making his way to the bedroom, the chill from the wood floors seeped into his bare feet, a stark contrast to the warmth flickering in his chest—a warmth kindled by Sage's unexpected intrusion into his world. Crawling into bed, he felt the sheets cool and crisp against his skin. In the room's darkness, he fought sleep. The flutter of anticipation for Sage's response, for that connection to someone who saw beyond the goalie mask, left him with a sense of excitement. He smiled, reflecting on the day's shift—from the sting of public defeat to the private thrill of a new connection.

When sleep won, his dreams were filled with the piercing blue eyes of a girl in South Dakota.

Chapter 4
Unexpected Faceoffs

April 6th

The sharp ping of Sage's alarm sliced through the quiet dawn in South Dakota, ending a dream that felt too good to leave. Grumbling, she reached for her phone, intent on silencing the day's first annoyance. Her fingers brushed the screen. A new notification from Hunter jolted her awake.

Opening the app, she read his post from last night. He taunted, offering proof by sharing a link to his private Instagram page. Without hesitating, she composed a message back.

Sage Photography: I don't have an Instagram account, and I'm not about to sign up for one. How naïve do you think I am? Opening a random link from a stranger? I think not.

Sage's skepticism was like a shield, one honed from too many online tales of deceit. The sliver of hope that this was the genuine Hunter Griffin made her pause. "No luxury to dwell on what-ifs with a busy day ahead," she mumbled. Photos waited for no one, and neither did her clients. Grabbing a breakfast bar and her camera bag, the unanswered question of the messenger's true identity lingered, a puzzle she didn't have time to solve right now.

Portland's morning silence was a stark contrast to the buzzing anticipation of game nights. Hunter, cocooned in the comfort of his darkened bedroom, was startled awake by his phone. 'Sage Photography' glared back at him from the screen. Rubbing the sleep from his eyes, Hunter's interest spiked as he read Sage's feisty comeback. His grogginess gave way to amusement at her blunt response. A smirk tugged at his lips—challenge accepted. Hockey battles were his domain, but this little digital spar ... had its own thrill. Capturing a screenshot of his Instagram proof, he made sure the caption "For a special fan" was visible, a direct hit for Sage's skepticism.

He shot back a message, his tone laced with the confidence of a goalie who never backed down from an opponent's breakaway shot.

Hunter Griffin: Who doesn't have an Instagram account?

Waiting for her reply, He moved on with his unshakable routine; sleep, eat, practice/games, repeat. His interaction with Sage was a welcome deviation from the early morning monotony. He was accustomed to game days and practice schedules, not this ... whatever this was. It was new, a bit unsettling, but undeniably invigorating.

Flipping an omelet onto his plate, his phone pinged. Taking a deep breath, he couldn't help but think he was getting a little too involved in this game of digital ping-pong. Opening her reply was akin to the anticipation of stopping a game-winning shot from entering his net.

Sage Photography: Not everyone has time to sit around all day scrolling through social media.

Sage recognized the snarkiness and falsehood of it. In her defense, the assignment she just shot had been a disaster ... an outdoor family portrait with a crying baby, a bratty toddler, and a grumpy husband ... then the storm clouds rolled in. Finishing before the torrential downpour hit, Sage sat in her SUV, messaging Hunter while waiting out the storm.

In the solitude of her vehicle, with the relentless rain drumming against the roof, Sage found herself in a standoff of sorts with her phone. The next volley from Hunter came quick, a cheeky retort that had her laughing despite herself.

Hunter Griffin: Ouch! That hurt.

The swift ping of his reply was a bright spot in the dreary aftermath of her photo shoot. A sense of relief washed over her. She was glad she didn't block him earlier. Whoever this person was, he knew how to wield humor like a well-aimed slap shot.

Sage Photography: So, I'm waiting for the proof you promised.

The ensuing silence, punctuated only by the ellipsis blinking in and out of existence, stretched longer than she expected. It seemed her challenger was in deep thought, crafting his next move. A mixture of apprehension and curiosity buzzed through her, making her more invested in the outcome than she cared to admit.

Hunter Griffin: Ta! Da!

His response came with the suddenness of a breakaway goal, followed by the screen grab image of his Instagram posting.

It took Sage several minutes before she noticed the 'Hi Sage' sign he was holding, as his tight abs, muscular arms, and cocky grin kept getting in the way. "Holy Crap," she blurted into the empty vehicle.

Sage's fingers trembled as she downloaded his image, saving it to her photos folder ... a memory for her digital scrapbook. Her reply was quick, words of contrition reflecting the roller-coaster of emotions she'd been riding since his initial contact.

Sage Photography: Touché, Hunter Griffin, you've brightened my gloomy day. I apologize for doubting you. I never thought Ice Wall would send me a shirtless photo ... or any photo, for that matter.

She hit send, her heart pounding. Just yesterday, her interaction with the Goshawks Facebook page was nothing out of her ordinary fan engagement. Now, she was in direct contact with the very foundation of her hockey fandom, trading barbs. Exhilaration coursed through her, yet caution whispered in her ear as she stepped onto the uncharted ice, uncertain of what lay beneath.

Hunter was about to take a bite of his toast when the quick buzz of his phone signaled Sage's response. Her playful acknowledgment coaxed laughter, a rarity in the solitude of his mornings. This back-and-forth was unfamiliar terrain for him; he was more at home on the ice than navigating the intricacies of social media banter.

He'd always kept fans at arm's length. He was content with the adulation from the safety of the rink or through the impersonal barrier of a screen. Direct messages? Unheard of for Hunter until Sage's skepticism nudged him into this novel exchange. The Goshawks' marketing team had been after him for ages to get more 'engaged' online. He'd reluctantly agreed, handing off the reins to Margret VanAlen, the team's PR guru, while he focused on what he did best ... guarding the net.

Hockey wasn't just a career for Hunter; it was his entire existence. The Goshawks were more than a team. They were the closest thing he had to a family, with his Russian coach, Viktor Volkov, standing in as a surrogate father. His private life, especially the dating scene, had always taken a back seat to the demands of his profession. Yet, here he was, venturing beyond the protective barriers for the first time, engaging with a fan on a personal level.

Sitting, phone in hand, Hunter pondered his reply with an intensity he reserved for game strategies.

Hunter Griffin: Alright, Sage, you caught me. I've never been driven to share a shirtless photo for a fan's verification before. Glad it hit the mark.

Sending the message, he felt a rare off-the-ice adrenaline rush. Sage's straightforward challenge had broken through the routine shield of his hockey life, igniting a spark of curiosity about where this new interaction might lead. His smile widened, even though he felt a mixture of anticipation with an edge of nerves. Unlike previous days ... this one felt charged with the possibility of something new, as thrilling as the lead-up to a game-winning shutout.

The sound of firm knocks and the front door opening, followed by the unmistakable tone of his friend's voice, snapped Hunter back to reality. Ryan's Canadian accent filtered through the room, a hint of impatience lacing his words. "Hey, buddy, you gonna make us late? I'm not keen on coach having us skate extra laps today, eh?"

"Yeah, yeah, give me a minute!" Hunter shouted back. He grabbed his phone, a final quick glance at the screen before tossing it into his gear bag. His thoughts were still with Sage and what her next message might hold. With a sense of anticipation bubbling inside him, Hunter joined Ryan, his usual ride to the rink. Today, the drive felt different, energized by the prospect of what awaited him after practice.

Chapter 5
Between Frames

April 8th

Sage's morning routine led her to the familiar ambiance of the Kool Beans coffee shop, where the barista greeted her with a knowing smile. "The usual, Sage?"

Grateful for the warm familiarity, she nodded. "Yeah, a large Butterscotch Toffee, to go. Thanks." The coffee shop, with its blend of aromas and the promise of her favorite brew, offered a brief respite from her hectic schedule.

"Big day ahead?" the barista inquired, handing over the coffee.

"Only an afternoon wedding shoot," Sage replied, securing the lid on her cup. With a quick exchange of pleasantries, she settled by the window, the sun inviting her to pause and savor the moment.

Sage rarely let her guard down, especially with online interactions. Since their initial contact, she'd experienced a whirlwind of emotions, all sparked by a surprising connection with Hunter Griffin. Yet, it had been two days since their last interaction. Her phone pinged. His message notification caught her off guard.

Hunter Griffin: Feeling the weight of tonight's game. It's crunch time, and the pressure's massive.

A brief pause before the ellipsis began its dance anew.

Hunter Griffin: Losses unnerve me. We've got the top spot secured in the playoffs, yet I'm still nervous. Every game counts. The team ... they're relying on me. I can't let them down again. The pressure is unbearable.

Reading Hunter's message, Sage sensed a vulnerability she hadn't expected from the stalwart goalie. His candidness broke through the image of the untouchable athlete, revealing a glimpse of the man behind the mask. Without hesitating, she responded, hoping to offer some comfort.

Sage Photography: It's one game, Hunter. Remember the thrill, not the fear. You've got this.

Hunter Griffin: It's more than a game to me. I don't expect you to understand. Hard to explain.

His terse reply hinted at a depth of commitment Sage admired but couldn't completely grasp. Yet, the connection they were forging compelled her to bridge the gap between their worlds.

Sage Photography: I may not get it, but I want to. Please share your world with me, and I'll do the same with mine.

The exchange was electrifying, pushing Sage to empathize with Hunter's plight. Recalling her own disappointment over a lost thumb drive of crucial photos, she understood the sting of letting others down. This shared vulnerability drew her closer to Hunter, igniting a curiosity about the man who lived and breathed hockey.

———— ◆ ————

Hunter laced his skates in the locker room. The icy anticipation of practice couldn't cut through his thoughts tethered to his phone's last interaction. The world of ice and pucks ... before his singular focus ... now shared space with thoughts of Sage.

Despite the physical distance, her words had bridged miles, connecting them in a way he hadn't expected. This new feeling of openness to share glimpses of his life, beyond the rink, was sparked by someone who recognized him as more than just a pro hockey goaltender.

Viktor's voice cut through his daydreaming. His goaltending coach, a stern reminder of the world he was drifting from. "Hunter, put down phone. Get on ice. Now!"

Hunter Griffin: Duty calls. Catch you later.

Shoving his phone into his gear bag, Hunter joined Viktor on the rink. The familiar chill of the arena enveloped him. Yet, as he glided onto the ice, a part of him lingered with the conversation. For the first time, he found his focus divided. Sage's curiosity about his world drew him towards thoughts of sharing his experiences, his fears, and maybe a bit of the joy he found in the game.

Viktor watched with an intense gaze, pounding his stick on the ice. He yelled, "Focus, Hunter. I need you here, on the ice. Get your head in game."

Practice was rigorous, pushing Hunter to the limits of his physical and mental stamina. Each drill, each save, was a battle, not just against the puck, but against the distractions pulling at the edges of his concentration.

As practice wore on, Hunter found his rhythm, the game reclaiming its central place in his thoughts. Still, Sage's words lingered, a reminder that a world existed beyond the ice, filled with possibilities, connections, and maybe understanding. A revelation, unsettling yet exhilarating ... his life could encompass more than the relentless pursuit of hockey excellence.

The session ended with Viktor offering a rare nod of approval, acknowledging Hunter's effort to return to form. As Hunter left the rink, the physical exertion had cleared his head, but the emotional pull towards Sage remained. A gentle tug reminding him of the paused but not forgotten conversation.

Hunter Griffin: Practice over. Survived another morning.

The message sent as he left the locker room was more than an update; it was an acknowledgment of the shift within him, a door opening to new experiences and, perhaps, a new friend. As he awaited Sage's reply, Hunter felt a keen anticipation, a curiosity about where this unexpected journey might lead, both on and off the ice.

<hr/>

After wrapping up the outdoor wedding shoot under the deep blue South Dakota sky, Sage felt a mix of professional satisfaction and personal contemplation. The ceremony had been picturesque, but her thoughts often side-tracked to Hunter and their recent exchanges. During the shoot, she'd left her phone in the SUV to avoid distraction. Now, with the last photo captured, she could no longer resist the temptation.

Opening the door to her SUV, she retrieved her phone with a mixture of antic-ipation and trepidation. She leaned on the bumper, opening the app. She was met with a short message. That was an hour ago, and nothing since. She contemplated the possibility of Hunter pulling back, and it pricked at her more than she expected. Compelled by a blend of concern and curiosity, she reached out.

Sage Photography: Hey, Hunter. Just thinking about our last chat. How are you holding up?

Hunter Griffin: Sometimes it feels like I'm carrying the weight of the team on my shoulders. Scared of letting everyone down, you know?

Reading his words, Sage felt a profound connection to his vulnerability. It mirrored her own moments of doubt, the fear of not meeting expectations. She knew too well the burden of responsibility, having navigated her own path through the competitive world of photography.

Sage Photography: I get it, more than you might think. But remember, it's that pressure that's shaped you into the incredible athlete you are. Don't let it crush you. Let it elevate you. You've got this, Hunter.

The dialogue between them, once light and flirtatious, had shifted into something deeper, a mutual exchange of fears and encouragements. Sage found herself invested in his struggle, eager to offer solace.

Hunter Griffin: Thanks, Sage. That means a lot. Just wish it was as easy to shake off the nerves as it is to talk about it.

The connection, though digital, felt real ... supportive. Sage pondered on their unique situation—two strangers, connected through circumstance, finding comfort in each other's virtual presence. She smiled. Her resolve strengthened by their shared vulnerabilities.

Sage Photography: Anytime, Hunter. And hey, if you ever need a distraction or want to chat, I'm here. You're not alone in this.

Hitting send, Sage felt a sense of purpose. She'd gone from a distant admirer to a confidante, a role she hadn't anticipated, but was ready to embrace. The challenges ahead for both of them were daunting, yet in this shared space between frames and face-offs, they'd found an unexpected source of strength.

Chapter 6
Breakaways and Shutouts

April 8th [Game Day: Maine]

In the Goshawks locker room, Hunter sat statue still in his stall, blocking out the hum surrounding him. Tonight, the Goshawks were matched against the Minnesota Blizzards. The Blizzards were one of three teams fighting for the last playoff wildcard spots. He knew they would be ravenous for a win. What the Blizzards didn't know, Hunter was equally determined to keep them from advancing.

Hunter was overcome by a strong feeling of déjà vu, which only strengthened his resolve. Staring into a void, Hunter visualized the game ahead. In his mind, he met each shot on goal with unwavering defense. He pictured himself making crucial saves, depending on his muscle memory to kick in, creating sharp, precise movements

Inhaling for a count of four, he held his breath for two counts, then exhaled slowly for eight. The controlled breathing steadied his heart rate ... cleared his mind. With each inhale and exhale the locker room noises faded, replaced by the rhythm of his breath and the images of success he painted in his mind.

"You ready to go, bud?" D-man, Ryan Mitchell, asked as he tapped Hunter's leg pads.

Hunter's body jerked back to the present. Looking at his best friend, he nodded, doing his best to keep his mental focus on the upcoming game. He opened and closed his fingers within his goalie gloves, ensuring the fit was perfect. Donning his mask, the familiar weight settled on his head, symbolic of his transformation from a mere mortal to goalie deity.

Leading his team to the ice, Hunter felt the cool air, heard the distant roar of the crowd, and embraced the surrounding energy. Not even a disgruntled fan, yelling, "Don't suck tonight, Griffin!" could penetrate his calm resolve.

"You've got this?" Chase Rutherford, the Goshawks' captain, clapped a hand on Hunter's shoulder as they skated onto the ice.

The fans' roar was deafening as Hunter skated to his crease, adjusting his water bottle on top of the net. He removed his mask, resting a hand over his heart as the National Anthem played. He pictured Sage in the stands instead of rooting for him from afar.

When the puck dropped, the battle began in a whirlwind of movement.

"Let's keep it tight, boys!" Chase yelled, skating past Hunter's net, maneuvering the puck to the offensive zone.

Hunter watched as the Goshawks' top line barreled down the ice, the Blizzards chasing them in hot pursuit. He was thankful for the brief reprieve. His focus stayed on the play, glued to the puck.

Throughout the first and second periods, Hunter's mind remained clear, his focus absolute. Every save he made was a calculated move of agility and anticipation. Yet, at the end of the second period, the score remained no goals for either side.

As the third period began, the puck bounced and weaved through players, becoming a tantalizing target for the opposing team. But Hunter was always there, even when the Blizzards ramped up their offense. He blocked their rapid succession of shots. Each save reinforcing his confidence. A glove in the right place, a strategic shuffle of his skates, a quick dive—he was a wall the other team could not breach.

"Hit 'em hard, boys!" Chase barked as the Goshawks' defense tightened. The Blizzards became relentless, desperate, as their forward charged, the puck sailing high. Hunter sprang up, his trapper snapping shut around the disc.

After the next faceoff, Ryan Mitchell shouted, "Watch your left!" His voice cutting through the chaos as he battled for possession in the corner.

The puck was deep in the Goshawks' zone, with the Blizzards pressing hard. Ryan managed to wrestle the puck away from the Blizzards forward, sending a sharp pass up the boards to Etan Eklund. Etan carried the puck through the neutral zone, dodging an aggressive forecheck, passing it to Chase Rutherford, who was streaking down the left wing.

The Goshawks' captain received the puck just before the blue line. With a quick glance up, he saw a gap between two Blizzards' defensemen. Chase accelerated. His powerful strides eating up the ice as he approached the offensive zone. The crowd's roar was a dull thrum in Hunter's ears, his focus on Chase's progress.

As Chase crossed the blue line, the Blizzards' defenseman, Jake Foster, lunged to poke check the puck away. Chase's stickwork was impeccable, lifting the puck over Foster's outstretched stick. In a blur of motion, Chase's skate appeared to cross the blue line a split second before the puck. The Blizzards' bench erupted, shouting for an offside call, but the linesman's arm stayed down. Play continued.

Now in the high slot, Chase wound up for a slap shot. The puck rocketed off his stick, a blur heading straight for the top corner of the net. The Blizzards' goalie, already set in his butterfly stance, barely flinched as the puck whizzed past his glove side, hitting the back of the net.

When the goal light flashed, the arena erupted. Both the Blizzards' captain and alternate captain surrounded the referees, vehemently arguing Chase was offside. With the play being reviewed in the Situation Room in Toronto, the referees huddled in the corner. On the big screen the replay showed Chase's skate a hair behind the puck. Waiting, the crowd held its collective breath.

After a tense few moments, a referee skated to center ice, clicking on his mic. "After reviewing the play. The call on the ice stands. We've Got A Goal!"

Hunter stilled himself in his net, steadying his breathing, attempting to deafen the fans' cheers and jeers. Searching the Blizzards' bench, he watched the players as they exploded in frustration, arms waving, sticks hitting the boards. The Blizzards' head coach's face, red with outrage. His arms crossed; cheeks puffed as he brutally chomped his gum.

Before the next puck dropped, the Jumbotron replayed a closeup of Chase as he crossed the blueline. Hunter knew it was a controversial call. But in the world of pro hockey, the ref's final decision always stood. Within the protection of his mask, Hunter's face was hidden. His lips twitched into a half-smile ... for once, the call had gone their way.

With the goal standing, the Goshawks had a crucial 1-0 lead. The Blizzards intensified their assault on Hunter's net, but embodying his 'Ice Wall' persona he denied them at every turn. Their goal, though fiercely disputed, shifted the momentum in favor of the Goshawks and proved to be the game-winner.

"Get it out, get it out!" Hunter's voice was raw from shouting, his focus unyielding.

With seconds left, the Blizzards pulled their goalie. The Goshawks fought to clear the zone. Hunter's heart pounded as a final shot came through traffic. He dropped to the ice, his body covering the puck. The final whistle blew. 1-0. Another shutout.

The arena erupted. Hunter skated outside his crease, raising his stick in victory. His teammates mobbed him, their congratulations a blur of sound and movement. Each head touch to his mask, each word of praise, was a testament to their unity.

"Hell of a game, Ice Wall," Finn O'Connell said, poking Hunter's chest. "Way to shut them down."

The atmosphere in the locker room was intoxicating. Although Hunter knew he would feel it in the morning, amid celebrating, the pain from the game's physical toll dissipated. As the players showered and changed into their suits and ties, the locker room talk changed from game plays to celebrating at the Frosty Nest.

———————◦◦◦———————

The Frosty Nest buzzed with excitement, the patrons welcoming the Goshawks with open arms. A communal understanding filled the air, a shared love for the game. Tonight, they weren't just fans and players; they were part of the same tribe.

Throughout the evening, in their blocked off VIP section of the bar, Hunter was at the center of the celebration. His teammates ensured his glass was never empty, their ribbing and jesting a testament to their bond. Conversation flowed, revolving around on-ice strategies, memorable plays, and debates on hockey trivia.

"You crushed it tonight, Griffin." Chase lifted his beer in a toast. Around him, the other players joined in, their drinks raised high in a silent acknowledgment of Hunter's shutout.

"Man, you were everywhere in that net, on a whole different level." Ryan draped an arm around Hunter in a gesture of brotherhood.

Through it all, Hunter kept checking his phone. He wanted to shoot off a quick message to Sage, but between the rounds of drinks and physical congratulations, it was becoming an impossible task.

Etan, ever the curious and spirited forward, leaned in with a playful grin. "Who are you texting?" he asked, making a grab for Hunter's phone.

Hunter, caught off-guard, laughed, pulling his phone out of reach. "I was attempting to send a victory note to someone special," his reply cloaked in mystery as he pocketed his phone.

Axel, standing nearby with a seltzer in hand, nudged Etan. "Hey man, looks like Ice Wall's sweetie outshines his thoughts about The Cup?"

Hunter shook his head, rolling his eyes upward. "Hey guys, this was fun, but I gotta go."

"You need a ride?" Olaf asked.

"Thanks Snowman. My Uber should be pulling up any minute." Hunter hated leaving so early, but the draw to Sage was strong. He yearned for a different conversation, a quieter moment away from the chaos—one where he could share his triumph with someone who'd only been there in spirit.

As he made his way out of the bar, he reflected on the game. Despite the aches and bruises, this was a night he would remember—a testament to their unity, their resilience, and their shared love for the game. For Hunter, the celebration marked a milestone. He sensed the approaching Cup playoffs, a stronger team connection. He enjoyed the Goshawks brotherhood. But right now, he craved a quiet bonding time with Sage in the solitude of his apartment.

Chapter 7

Cheers and Revelations

April 8th [Game Day: South Dakota]
O'Sullivan's sports bar on the outskirts of Brookings, South Dakota, was alive with a unique rhythm of its own—an orchestra of clinking glasses, raucous laughter, and sporadic cheers of an impending win. Collective groans would soon echo in the room whenever the referee called a penalty the fans disagreed with. The air was heavy, laden with the heady aroma of beer, sizzling wings, and the electric anticipation of the hockey match.

Tucked away in their usual corner, Sage, Jessica, and Patty were a beacon of contrasting loyalties, a lone island nestled in a sea of Minnesota fans. Their dedication to the Goshawks remained unwavering. Their enthusiasm was bolstered not just by Sage's infectious passion for the game, but also by their shared appreciation for the rugged, irresistible charm of the players.

On the TV screen, the camera zoomed in on Hunter as he glided to his net. Sage's best friend Jessica let out a low whistle. "I would do him in a heartbeat."

Her remarks sent Sage into a choking fit, beer spurting out her mouth. Patty patted her on the back. Jessica grabbed a handful of napkins, handing them to her friend.

Wiping the liquid from her face, Sage looked Jessica in the eyes and in a calm voice stated, "Ice Wall is off-limits."

"What are you talking about?" Jessica laughed. "I didn't know we were dividing up the team."

Patty clapped her hands. "Oh, if we're doing that, Jessica, you should call dibs on Ryan. I just Googled him and he's back on the market, fresh from breaking up with his skanky girlfriend."

"We are not dividing up the Goshawks. That would be barbaric," Sage said, licking hot wings sauce off her fingers.

"So, what gives? We all know you've had a goalie crush on Ice Wall since high school. But we've always shared a mutual admiration for all the players on the team."

Before Sage could explain, the bar erupted with cheers, as Minnesota won the first face off. Their star right winger, known for his wicked slap shot, was skating hard and fast towards the Goshawks' net. All three girls jumped from their seats to get a better view.

"He! Shoots! No! Score!" Jessica yelled as one of the Minnesota fans turned to stare. He shouted jeers at her mixed with a few obscenities.

Sage sat down first, followed by Patty.

"Good Grief! You'd think this was the first time we were in the bar rooting for the Goshawks," Jessica yelled, as she too sat down.

"It's been a long time since Minnesota played our team," Patty offered.

Several blocked shots followed by excessive celebration from the three girls. Luke, one of four bartenders on duty, sauntered over to their table. "How are you all doing tonight, ladies? Can I get you anything?"

"What are you offering?" Jessica cooed as she rubbed her hand up and down his arm.

"Words of advice." Luke removed her hand, adding, "celebrate with a little less enthusiasm, especially when your team blocks a Minnesota shot on goal."

"How about when the Goshawks score? Any advice for that?" Patty asked with a playful, innocent expression.

"Well, they're at the end of the first period. The score is a big goose egg for both teams. Guess we'll cross that bridge when we come to it." Ignoring both Jessica and Patty, he smiled at Sage. "I hope you ladies have a ride home tonight."

"Are you offering to be our driver?" Jessica leaned into Luke, sporting a flirty smile.

"Nope. But I am offering to call an Uber when the game is over." Staring into Sage's eyes, his lips teetered on a smile as he gathered their empty beer bottles.

"Can you get us another round?" asked Sage.

"Only if you all promise to heed my advice." He laughed as all three girls nodded in agreement.

When Luke was out of viewing and hearing distance, Sage beckoned her friends to move closer. "I have something to confess." Not waiting for their reactions to her announcement, she pulled out her phone. "The other day, after the Goshawks losing game, I posted an encouraging comment about Ice Wall on their team's Facebook page."

"And that's your big confession?" Jessica asked, her face crinkling.

"The fact he sent me a friend request, with a personal message, kind of is."

"Are you sure it was him? There are a lot of sickos out there that love to pretend they are celebrities," Patty said, arching an eyebrow.

"I had my doubts at first too, until he sent me this." Sage opened her phone to the Instagram screen grab, showing it first to Patty and then to Jessica.

"Wow, he has a pretty smile." Were the first words falling out of Patty's mouth.

"I think he might have pretty everything from the looks of those abs." Jessica pulled the phone away from Sage to enlarge the screen and get a better look. "Nice sign too."

"There was a sign?" Patty asked, reaching for the phone, which Jessica handed over.

Luke returned with their beers. He did a quick glance at the phone screen as it passed from one hand to another. "New boyfriend Jessica?"

"Yeah, very new," Jessica said, doing her best to keep Sage's secret private.

"You deserve a good-looking guy like that." He set the beers down, picked up their empty Buffalo Wings containers, wiped the table, and left.

"Thank goodness he didn't read the sign." Sage moaned as she reached out to Patty for the phone.

"What sign?" Patty asked again.

Sage took the phone, enlarging the image.

"Oh! Oh! THAT sign. Holy Cow, Sage, it really is him."

"Holy Cow indeed," Sage replied.

The second period remained goalless, as did the third. The game was shaping up to be a duel between the goalies, with both teams' goaltenders making numerous saves. Throughout it all, the girls had kept their promise to Luke; doing their best to keep their celebration of Ice Wall's saves to a joyous rumble, with silent raised beer bottles coupled with clandestine low-fives under the table.

The Goshawks captain, Chase Rutherford, took aim from the center of the ice as the clock clicked to two minutes. The puck lacing through skates and sticks, stopped hard at the back of Minnesota's net. The Goshawks scored, with a questionable goal. Minnesota fans screamed at the overhead TV screens as the bar went wild, waiting for the goal to be overturned. The refs, huddled in a corner, headsets on, scrutinizing the replay cameras. Did or didn't the Goshawks' captain's skate cross the blue line before the puck?

An eerie silence fell inside the bar as the referee skated to center ice. Reaching to his waistband, he clicked on his mic. With a dramatic pause, he waited for the arena to quiet before making his announcement.

"After reviewing the play. The call on the ice stands. We've Got A Goal!"

The speakers vibrated with the Goshawks fans cheering on their home team from the arena. In the bar, the Minnesota fans' jeers were just as loud.

With the exception of the corner table. Jessica couldn't refrain from standing up, waving her arms in the air, as if she were the referee, yelling, "Yesssss, we have a goal! Way to go Goshawks."

Sage looked to Luke and mouthed, "Sorry." Sporting her best apologetic smile. Luke shook his head as he continued to take orders.

The climax of their jubilation came when the final whistle blew. The Goshawks' victory confirmed. Only one corner of the bar exploded with cheers and high-fives.

When Luke's shift was over, he headed to the girls' table to join in on their celebration with a pitcher of beer and four glasses in place of their bottles. Setting the tray on the table, he took a seat in the chair between Sage and Patty.

"I don't suppose I can convince you gals to tone down your celebration just a little?"

"Not happening tonight, cowboy," Jessica said, her sly smile growing wider as she stared into Luke's eyes. "Our boy, Ice Wall, just earned his twenty-first shutout of the season. We've behaved throughout the last two periods. We've earned our celebration."

A burly man in a Minnesota jersey that barely covered his belly walked by. His face was a red mask of irritation and booze-induced courage. Stopping at their table, he sneered, "Hey, Goshawks puck bunnies, how about you pipe down? We've all had enough of your obnoxious girlie chirps."

Jessica, never one to back down, especially after a night full of hockey and beers, retorted, "Call us what you want, old timer. We're celebrating our Goshawks' victory. It won't be long before our team heads to the playoffs, and your team heads to the golf course." She smiled her sweetest smile before turning her attention back to her group.

Before things could go south, Luke intervened, stepping in front of the irate fan. Looming over him, Luke eased the tension with a firm yet friendly voice. "Look, Harry, we're all here to enjoy the game and unwind. Let's not ruin a good night over a little team rivalry, okay?"

The Minnesota fan grumbled, muttering something under his breath before shrugging. When he walked back to his friends, Luke rejoined the girls' table.

"My hero!" Jessica cooed, batting her eyelashes.

Luke laughed, nodding towards Jessica, but his gaze rested on Sage. "If you want to keep watching hockey here, you all have to promise to keep the cheering a bit quieter. Not everyone is a fan of your Goshawks. But you know that," he said, a teasing spark in his eyes.

Jessica opened her mouth, continuing her playful banter, but Sage beat her to it. "Deal, Luke. And ... thanks," Sage replied.

Luke's answering grin was soft, genuine. "No problem, Sage. I'll call you an Uber as soon as we finish this pitcher."

Sage nodded and smiled back, but her heart was still in the arena with Hunter. As her friends went back to their celebration, she took a moment to relish the excitement, the thrill of the victory, and the promising friendship she was cultivating with Ice Wall himself.

———◆———

Once inside her cozy apartment, the warmth greeted her like a soft embrace, Sage reached for her phone. Her mood turned sullen, finding no new messages from Hunter. He was likely caught in the postgame whirlwind, she reasoned, yet she had harbored a faint hope.

Pushing aside the sting of disappointment, she changed into her pajamas, the cotton fabric comforting against her skin. Crawling into bed, she nestled into her pillows. She tapped out a quick message to Hunter, her fingers brushing against the smooth screen.

Sage Photography: Incredible game tonight. You were phenomenal.

Her screen lit up immediately, its glow a beacon in her dark bedroom.

Hunter Griffin: Hey, Sage. Thanks, it was quite the battle.

Sage Photography: I can only imagine! You must be exhausted.

Her body vibrated with excitement, reading his swift reply.

Hunter Griffin: Bruised and achy. Puts a new meaning to the phrase, no pain, no gain. But the win made it worth it.

Laughter bubbled up from Sage, a warm sound filling the quiet of her bedroom.

Sage Photography: Bask in your victory. You deserve it.

Hunter Griffin: It's always fleeting, but yeah, I will. What about you? Did you watch the game?

Sage Photography: Absolutely watched. The Goshawks arena was rocking with some very vocal fans. My eardrums are still ringing from sitting between two equally rambunctious Goshawks' fans at my table.

Hunter Griffin: Fans in our arena get a bit excited. I'll have a word with them for you. Not much I can do about the ones in South Dakota.

The soft tapping of her fingers against the phone keys continued, their messaging weaving through topics for an hour: the game, their shared passion for hockey, and slices of their lives. It felt as natural and comfortable as old friends reconnecting, the digital divide between them narrowing with each exchange.

Hunter Griffin: Hey Sage, I should get some sleep. We're heading to Florida early tomorrow.

Sage Photography: I forgot about the Florida game. Sorry to keep you up so late.

Hunter Griffin: No problem. I can never sleep right after a game. It's tough on the body playing an away game the day after a home game.

Sage Photography: I can only imagine.

Hunter Griffin: We'll be flying back to Portland right after the game. A day off ... then we play Washington at home. Then it's off to Canada to play two days later.

Sage Photography: That's a brutal schedule.

Sage could only imagine the emotional and physical stress Hunter must be under playing so many games back-to-back.

Hunter Griffin: It is, but that's hockey for you. The best part, Canada is our last regulation game. Then we're off for three days before starting the playoffs.

Sage Photography: Wow, three whole days. What ever will you do with yourself?

Hunter Griffin: I'm sure I'll think of something. ;-)

Even though she couldn't hear it, Sage imagined Hunter's laughter ... deep and sensual ... the thought of it made her smile in the darkness of her room.

Sage Photography: Get some sleep. Safe travels.

Hunter Griffin: Good night, Sage. Thanks for being there for me.

Setting her phone aside, Sage sank deeper into her bed, the blankets a soft cocoon. Contentment washed over her, a novel feeling of belonging to a world she'd only observed from the sidelines. With Hunter as her newfound friend, that world seemed more thrilling. She drifted into sleep, the dreams that visited her filled with the roar of crowds and the steadfast figure of a goalie guarding his net.

Chapter 8
Turbulence

April 9th [Game Day: Florida]

Portland was shrouded in darkness as the team boarded their early morning flight to Florida. Rain pelted the windows, thunder growled in the distance. Flashes of lightning cut through the predawn sky. Inside the cabin, a different kind of storm brewed, emanating from Hunter in waves of frustration.

"Can't get a damn decent signal," Hunter cursed, poking at his failing phone. The battery life teetered on its last percentages—an ominous metaphor for his state of mind.

Olaf, the Goshawks' back-up goalie and Hunter's older, more experienced teammate, watched the younger man's mounting frustration. Standing six feet four inches tall and weighing 220 pounds, Olaf was a monster on the ice, but off it, he was a gentle giant.

"Is this about that girl?" Olaf asked, his impish grin splitting his bearded face. "The one you've been messaging like a love-struck teenager?"

Hunter sent Olaf a side-eyed glare. "I'm not love-struck."

"Sure," Olaf replied. He leaned back, stretching his long legs into the aisle. "You know, making them wait is not a bad thing. Adds a bit of mystery."

Hunter huffed a laugh. "You're now a love guru?"

Olaf raised an eyebrow. "No, but I've seen more seasons than you, kid."

Maneuvering over Olaf, Hunter grabbed his bag from the overhead compartment. Rummaging through it, he groaned. "I left my charger at home. Hey, do you have one I can use?"

"Nothing that would fit your fancy phone."

Accepting defeat, Hunter secured his bag once more in the overhead. He turned off his phone to conserve the last bit of battery, shoving it into his suit pocket. As he leaned his head against the window, he barely noticed the world outside beginning to brighten as the plane climbed above the storm clouds.

As breakfast service began, the flight attendant approached with a cart. Hunter perked up, hoping to restore some semblance of his routine with his game-day oatmeal. As he pulled down his tray, disaster struck again.

"Thanks for saving the last bowl of oats for me, Sally," Finn sang out.

Hunter looked back to see the Goshawks' enforcer slathering honey into a steaming bowl.

Sitting across the aisle, Axel looked from Hunter to Finn, then back to Hunter. Rummaging in his backpack, he retrieved a granola bar. "It's not oatmeal, but it's made with oats," he said, sporting a silly grin.

"Thanks, Axel." Hunter accepted the bar with a reluctant nod. As he unwrapped it, his mood darkened further. Each bite felt like a betrayal of his routine.

The team's flight touched down in Florida under a sweltering sun, a harsh contrast to the stormy morning in Portland. As they disembarked, the oppressive heat mirrored Hunter's growing frustration, magnifying the irritation of his disrupted morning. Without their usual stop at the hotel to regroup and relax, the team was shuttled directly to the practice arena.

"Griffin!" Coach Harrison barked, pulling Hunter aside as they entered the visitors' locker room. "You've got a game face like a badger with a sore tail. You need to shake whatever is eating at you."

Before Hunter could reply, the coach snatched the phone from his hand. "You'll get this back after the game," he declared, pocketing it to ensure Hunter's focus remained on the ice, not his disrupted rituals.

The loss of his phone, his only line of communication with Sage, hit Hunter harder than any puck ever had. His irritation gave way to an even darker mood.

As he strapped on his pads, then pulled on his blocker and catcher, Hunter felt the weight of his teammates' expectant gazes. They needed their goalie focused and unshaken ... at the moment he was neither.

Hunter's irritation seeped into the practice. His sharp reflexes a tad slower, his precise angles off. His teammates felt it too; their fluid movements became stilted, the easy banter replaced with an uncomfortable silence.

"Hunter, what the hell, man?" Ryan skated over, wearing a frown. "You're letting pucks through like you're made of Swiss cheese."

"I know, I know," Hunter snapped, smashing his stick onto the ice in frustration.

Back on the bench, he heard the coach lecturing the team, pumping them up for the game. The words becoming muffled, drowned out by the thunderous beat of Hunter's own frustration.

As practice wrapped up, Hunter seethed. His performance was off, way off, letting pucks slip by like he was a sieve. Hunter knew he had to shake it off and sharpen up. Right now, his head was a mess, cluttered with everything but the game. Lack of access to Sage was a missing piece, throwing him off balance. The Goshawks had a crucial match tonight, and he needed to get his head back in the game—fast.

First Period

Although the Goshawks had clinched their division's top playoff spot, it was a different story for the Florida Barracudas. They were in the fight for their lives to get one of the two final wildcard spots. The chance for their team to get closer to the playoffs, coupled with a weekend game, accounted for the packed arena.

The seats were a clash of color. Barracudas' fans in their red and gold jerseys contrasting with an impressive number of Portland fans in navy and powder blue. Both teams' fans expected a hard-fought game. It was a shared hunger fueling the fans and players. The tension rippling through the arena.

When the Goshawks filed from the visitor's tunnel, the atmosphere turned electric. The stadium echoed with the deafening voices of scattered boos along with wild cheers. Suddenly, the mood shifted, the crowd hushed. All eyes focused upward as the giant multi-screen scoreboard hanging ominously overhead flickered to life.

Standing at the edge of the rink, Hunter gazed upward along with the rest of the fans and players. His eyes widened in shock. Splashed across the screen, larger than life, was his Instagram picture. The 'Hi Sage' sign displayed over his bare torso greeted thousands of spectators. The crowd erupted in raucous laughter and wolf-whistles, pointing upward, then directing their amusement towards Hunter as he stood frozen in the open gateway leading to the ice.

Adding to the insult, the broadcaster's amplified voice boomed through the arena. "A special shout out to Sage, wherever you are, lucky lady."

The building became a rumble of noise filled with fans clapping hands and stomping feet. As quickly as it appeared, the image was replaced by the Kiss Cam, but the damage had been done.

Still frozen, Hunter's heart dropped into his skates, as he stood mouth open. *How could his private message be shared with not only the packed arena, but millions of viewers watching the televised pregame?*

A shove from behind propelled Hunter onto the ice, causing him to trip as he entered the rink.

"Move it, Griffin," growled Finn O'Connell.

"This really sucks." The irritation in Hunter's voice did little to erase his humiliation. A hot flush spread up Hunter's neck as he shuffled onto the ice.

Skating to his net, he noticed the Barracudas' pest, Chucky Trembly, leaning on the boards, leering in his direction. Over the past five seasons, Hunter had played, and won, hard fought games against Florida. Every game the Goshawks were hungry for a win, but tonight the Barracudas looked ravenous.

Only one team intimidated Hunter ... and Florida was that team. They played dirty, their defense and offense lines teeming with unyielding enforcers. Among them, the biggest pest in pro hockey, the notorious Chucky ... a player beloved by Florida fans as much as he was loathed by everyone else, fans and players alike.

Chucky was a terror on the ice. His actions evoked the raw brutality of the infamous doll he derived his nickname from. He had an annoying habit of always gnawing at his mouth guard, like a junkyard dog with a bone. His predatory position in front of the visiting team's net, along with his foul-mouthed chirps, made him a nightmare to goalies.

Putting his water bottle on top of his net, Hunter looked upward pleading aloud, "Please save me from this day getting any worse."

Hunter just made it through the first period. From the initial puck drop, Chucky invaded Hunter's blue crease. He constantly pushed and jabbed Hunter with his stick the second a referee or the linesmen had their backs turned, often after a whistle was blown. Hunter still stopped over a dozen pucks from entering his net. The only good thing about Chucky's presence ... he had no time to think about Sage.

With only minutes on the clock, Ryan passed to Chase. The captain roofed it into the Barracudas' net.

GOAL! Goshawks—Rutherford

———◦◦◦———

At the first intermission, Hunter was the last one off the ice. He shuffled his skates on the tunnel's padded floor, tossing his gloves to the equipment manager. With his cage in one hand and his stick in the other, he hesitated a moment, then entered the locker room.

"Take a seat Griffin," the coach's voice was soft, welcoming. Yet every player knew that tone was only used when trouble brewed. Coach Harrison walked in front of a now seated Hunter. Leaning over, his face inches away, he bellowed, "What the hell was that on the pregame screen?"

Hunter opened his mouth to explain that he didn't know how his photo ended up on public display. But he didn't get a chance.

"You have embarrassed not only yourself, but your team and this organization."

"Come on coach. He didn't leak the picture. He posted it as a prank on his private Instagram account," Chase said.

Harrison turned his anger to the team's captain. "You are as much to blame as him," he growled, turning to Chase, while pointing a finger at Hunter.

"How so?" Chase looked from the coach to Hunter, with a bewildered expression.

"As captain, you're responsible for the moral compass of this team." Harrison turned and once again directed his anger towards Hunter. "Remove that picture from your account before you get back on the ice."

"I would, but I can't," Hunter whispered.

"You dare defy me, boy?" Coach Harrison's face turned red.

Chase jumped in once more. "Coach, he can't delete the photo because you took his phone."

"Even if I had my phone, I still couldn't delete it. The battery is dead, and my charger is in Portland," Hunter blurted, before bending over, rubbing his face with his hands.

"Ten minutes before the second period," the equipment manager yelled, as he entered the room with the team's dried gloves.

Harrison glared at Hunter before storming from the locker room out to the arena.

"That ended well." Olaf chuckled as he walked to Hunter. Patting his fellow goalie on the back. "Shake it off, kid. Best part, you only have to hear the coach yell at you for one more break before the end of the game."

Hunter put on his mask and gloves. Picking up his stick, he led his team onto the ice. Walking down the tunnel, he imagined how gladiators must have felt entering the Colosseum.

Second Period

The game's pace during the second period was double that of the first. The puck glided and bounced like a pinball, bodies colliding into the boards with grunts and gasps, sweat, and icy air intertwining in a heady visceral dance. At one time, the Barracudas had three enforcers sitting in the penalty box. Still, the score remained unchanged.

Fifteen minutes in, Chucky flew down the ice in a breakaway. He stopped short, snowing Hunter. During the ensuing chaos, Chucky slid the puck through Hunter's five-hole. Resulting in a red light-the-lamp moment. The Barracudas' fans went wild.

GOAL! Barracudas—Trembly

"Looks like your wall is melting," Chucky taunted before he raised his stick, taking a victory lap around the rink.

Ryan skated to Hunter's side. "Shake it off, bud. Don't let him get under your skin."

Hunter nodded in response. Without turning around, he pulled up his mask with one hand, while reaching for the water bottle with the other. He sprayed his face, doing his best to wash the ice crystals from his eyes. Blinking, he pulled his mask on just as the puck dropped at center ice; the nightmare continuing.

He knew his defensemen would block Chucky from another breakaway, but he also knew Chucky was not finished with his non-sportsmanlike plays. Hunter didn't mind gritty players. It was part of hockey. But Chucky always took it one step too far, with an uncanny knack for knowing when the refs were busy looking elsewhere.

The rest of the game was filled with numerous penalties called against both the Goshawks and the Barracudas. Miraculously, most were called against Chucky, which gave Hunter some breathing room. Without the pest blocking his view, Hunter was back into his rhythm, using his moving butterfly skills to his team's advantage, blocking several more shots.

With six minutes to go in the second period, Chucky once more skated in front of the Goshawk net. "I'm baaack," he chirped over his shoulder in a sing-song voice, slamming his body into Hunter.

Hunter pushed Chucky to the side, doing his best to see who was in control of the puck, but Chucky held his ground.

"Why are you such an asshole?" Hunter yelled.

"You sure do a lot of whining for a goalie."

"Put your binky back in your mouth and get out of my crease." Hunter snarled as he once more attempted to shove Chucky out of his line of vision.

With the stealth of a ninja, Chucky sliced his stick backward, jabbing its butt-end hard into Hunter's midsection. "How's that butterfly stance working for you now, kid?"

Hunter caught his balance and was about to retaliate when a scrum broke out behind the Goshawk net ... the referee and linesmen focusing all their energy to break it up before it escalated into a full-blown brawl.

Chucky took the opportunity to face Hunter. Wearing a smirk, he whispered, "When I meet Sage, I'm going to teach her what it's like to be with a real man."

Hunter snapped. Shaking off his gloves, he grabbed a handful of Chucky's sweater with one hand, raising the other in a balled fist.

Chucky let out a maniacal laugh, egging Hunter on. "Go ahead, pretty boy. You'll get yourself suspended. I'm sure your team will thank you for getting us into the playoffs." Sticking half his mouth guard out, clamping down, he wiggled the plastic end in Hunter's face. Taunting him with a 'come and get me' smirk.

A linesmen skated up fast, as Chucky raised both gloved hands, palms facing Hunter, in a non-combative gesture.

Seething, Hunter ripped the guard from Chucky's mouth, tossed it on the ice, crushing it under his skate. The action blanketed the arena in silence, soon replaced by a deafening angry roar from the Barracudas' crowd.

The referee was beside them in an instant, his whistle shrill. "Griffin. You. Are. Out!" he commanded, pointing to the tunnel.

The ejection was met with a chaotic blend of cheers and boos as Hunter skated off. Passing his team's bench, he watched Olaf gather his goalie gear, heading to the net to warm up, as a fourth-line forward skated to the box to do the penalty time.

Hunter more ran than walked to the locker room. Once there, he tossed his gloves and mask into his stall. Skipping a shower, he changed into street clothes, knowing he would violate the rules by leaving before the second intermission. He'd had enough berating for one day ... for a lifetime. Leaving the arena, he hailed a taxi to the hotel.

Hunter sat at the far end of the hotel bar. Ball cap low on his forehead, he watched the third period of the game, cursing under his breath as the broadcasters replayed the disaster that unfolded after his ejection. Hunter downed two shots of vodka when they replayed the Barracudas scoring mere seconds after he left the ice. All because the Goshawks were shorthanded, coupled with Olaf coming off the bench cold. The final dagger dug deep when Chucky scored the winning goal.

He ordered two more shots when he listened in disbelief as the broadcasters heaped praise on Chucky for saving the day again for Florida. The Barracudas winning 1 to 2. Paying for his drinks, he went to his room; the loss weighed on his shoulders. He passed out on the bed, hoping when he woke, today would have been just a hellish dream.

Chapter 9
Cheers, Jeers, and Fears

April 9th [Game Day: South Dakota]

In Sage's apartment, it was almost game time. Jessica and Patty sat in the living room sipping beers, watching the large flatscreen TV, while Sage pulled an extra-large pizza from the oven.

"Come quick, Sage! You've got to see this," Jessica shouted.

Sage rushed into the room; the sizzling pizza pan secured in an oven-mitted hand. Placing it on the coffee table, she asked, "What happened?" Wiping her hands on the sides of her jeans, Sage plopped down in an overstuffed chair.

Both Jessica and Patty were bouncing on the couch, pointing at the TV. Hunter's grinning face and naked torso filled the screen, holding the 'Hi Sage' sign. The commentators were almost falling out of their seats, laughing, teasing each other about who the mysterious Sage could be.

Sage felt the blood drain from her face. "Oh my gosh," she whispered, staring at the screen in disbelief.

"Wow. I expected to see Ice Wall on the big screen today, but I sure didn't expect to see so much of him." Patty let out a giggle, followed by a snort.

Sage glanced at her, then back to the TV. "I ... I don't know how this happened. It was supposed to be a private joke," she stammered, feeling a strange mixture of embarrassment for herself, along with concerns for Hunter.

"Hey, don't let it bother you, Sage. Hunter's a big boy. He can handle it," Jessica said, as she pulled off a piece of cheesy pepperoni from her slice, shoving it in her mouth.

Patty gave Jessica a side-eye glance as she reached over to Sage, patting her knee. "How are you handling it? That's what I want to know."

"I'm not worried about me. It's Hunter who's being made a laughingstock." Sage took a long swig of her beer. Looking at a winking Jessica, it was obvious her friend was about to say something off the wall.

"Chucky's on fire tonight." Jessica leaned forward. Her eyes wide as she watched the first faceoff.

Blowing on her slice of pizza, Patty snorted a retort, "Sure, if by on fire you mean being a dink. He should take up residency in the penalty box, for all the times he's pushed and shoved opponents. You know his specialty is doing it when a ref's back is turned, and almost always after the whistle's blown."

Jessica shrugged. "That's pro hockey for you, Patty. If the referee didn't see it, it didn't happen." Jessica shrugged as she turned to her friend. "I still think he's hot."

Tossing a wadded napkin at Jessica, Sage managed a laugh. "You think all hockey players are hot."

"Well, you know it's true." Jessica teased. "Especially goalies. Now, they are smoking hot."

Patty looked upward, doing her best to pretend she didn't hear Jessica's comments. Just then, the camera zoomed in on Chucky. "Why does he always do that?"

"Do what?" both Jessica and Sage asked in unison.

"Chew on his mouth guard. How is it going to protect him, if it's always hanging out of his mouth like a cigarette? It's like wearing a jockstrap as an elbow pad."

Jessica laughed so hard she blew beer out of her nose. "Only you, a dental assistant, would worry about his teeth, let alone the placement of a jockstrap."

"Have you seen what hockey can do to your teeth?" Patty frowned. "Just look at Tyler Bertuzzi."

Jessica didn't miss a beat. "Yeah, but Bert is so hot. Gotta love his smile, missing tooth and all."

Patty and Sage shared a nod of agreement.

Once more, Patty turned her attention to the screen. "I think Chucky is dangerous. He has a blatant disregard for the unwritten rules of hockey."

Jessica shrugged again. "Chucky's a pest, but he's one of the best at what he does. That's what they pay him the big bucks to do."

As her friends verbally jousted about the virtues of hockey players and their protective equipment, Sage sat, meditating. Her mind drifted to her phone, dark and mute on the table ... a stark reminder that she hadn't heard from Hunter since last night.

The first period ended with a last-minute goal from the Goshawks' captain, putting the score at 1 to 0. Waiting for the next period to start, Sage stared at her phone, hoping Hunter could find the time to message her during the intermission, but the screen remained dark.

The second period ignited with a flourish of activity. Even with her big screen TV, the players appeared small and animated. Until the camera sought out and zoomed in on Chucky's face. His focus intense ... determined.

"Breakaway!" Jessica announced with a yelp, jolting from her lounging position on the couch. Patty barely secured the popcorn bowl on her lap from a disastrous fall, curling her arms protectively around it, stuffing her mouth with the buttery kernels. All three watched with wide eyes as the spectacle unfolded on the screen.

Sage felt her whole body respond to the growing tension. She sprang to her feet, her fists clenched. "You got this, Hunter!" she shouted with desperate conviction, her voice echoing through the living room.

On the screen, Chucky was a whirlwind of energy and momentum. His skates sliced the ice as he bore down on the Goshawks' net. He executed a sudden, dramatic sliding stop in front of Hunter, kicking up a veil of ice in a blatant attempt to blind the goalie.

"Dirty Move!" Patty spat.

Chucky took full advantage of the snow screen. With a swift, calculated shot, the puck flew between Hunter's knee pads, slamming into the back of the net. The flashing red light signaled the goal. Cheers from the Florida crowd erupted. The vibrations from the soundbar filled the apartment with a deafening roar.

Sage, still on her feet, face flushing with anger and indignation, screamed at the TV, "Where's the ref? That goal doesn't count!"

Patty, her face twisted in agreement, shouted, "Chucky needs to be put in the sin bin. He needs a misconduct. He needs to be ejected from the game ... for life!"

The three friends waited with bated breath for the referee's verdict. Their attention glued to the screen as the officials huddled in consultation. In the end, to their dismay, the referee signaled the goal was good.

Sage sank into the chair like a deflated balloon. Patty and Jessica remained silent ... eyes locked on the TV ... their faces mirroring Sage's disbelief.

The screen held the image of Chucky grinning victoriously, chirping at Hunter before skating away, holding his stick high. Hunter stood in the crease, mask up, flakes of ice falling on his chest. His face held an anger Sage had never seen ... a visible rage sent a shiver of unease down her spine.

Sage turned to Jessica, her anger simmering just below the surface. "How hot do you think Chucky is *now*?" The question hung in the air; a bitter jab aimed at the triumphant pest as he skated a second victory lap.

Jessica voice devoid of the usual humor, replied, "Not so very."

A cloud of resentment and frustration settled over the apartment, dulling their usual lively chatter. On the TV, the game resumed, with Chucky playing the antagonist in Hunter's on-ice drama.

Throughout the second period, Chucky continued to be a thorn in Hunter's side at every turn. The camera would occasionally pan over to the Goshawks' net, where Hunter stood, steadfast and focused. More than once, Chucky was captured giving a sharp sly poke with his stick into Hunter's belly.

Sage's body clenched at the sight, her hands balling into fists again. She felt a simmering anger towards Chucky, as the tension on the ice heightened with each push and chirp the pest delivered. Sage could also feel the energy in the room change as the girls watched the rivalry escalate.

When a scrum broke out behind the Goshawks' net, Chucky turned to face Hunter. Sage felt her breath hitch as she watched the exchange, her instincts telling her the situation was about to explode.

Jessica muttered, "This isn't going to end well."

No sooner had Jessica uttered her words than the referee's whistle shrilled. A hush fell over the living room when Hunter dropped his gloves, grabbing Chucky's sweater with one hand, a raised balled fist in the other.

"I'd give anything for Hunter to be mic'd up right now," Jessica blurted, echoing the collective sentiment in the room.

"Me too," whispered Sage, her voice trembling as tears welled in her eyes.

Chucky put his gloved hands up in a pacifying gesture, but his smirk and wiggling mouth guard said otherwise. In one swift move, Hunter yanked the mouthpiece free, tossing it on the ice. Chucky wore an expression of disbelief as he watched Hunter's skate slice over the discarded mouth guard, a definitive show of defiance.

A linesmen intervened, skating between the two players. Then a referee pointed first at Hunter, then to the visitors' tunnel. Jessica turned to Patty, her lips curving into a humorless smile. "Now, that's one way to fix Chucky's annoying habit."

Jessica and Patty shared a high-five. But Sage refused to find any humor in the situation. Tears trickled down her cheeks, blurring her vision as she watched Hunter skate off the ice disappearing into the tunnel. The sight of Olaf gliding into the net was a harsh reminder of what had transpired. Her head ached. She'd never felt so helpless.

"I've watched enough," Sage said, her voice choked with tears. She grabbed the remote, switching off the TV. The room fell silent, the only sound an occasional sniffle and the faint ticking of the wall clock. The game would go on, but without her ... or her beloved goalie.

Chapter 10
Penance

April 10th

The incessant pounding on the door dragged Hunter from the depths of a fitful slumber. He reached for his phone to check the time, then he remembered it was in its own sin bin. His mouth tasted like rotten, dirty potatoes. Staggering to stand, he noticed the hotel bed was still made, a single indentation of where he had sprawled. His suit barely wrinkled.

He never slept in his clothes. He rarely drank hard liquor. He never fought on the ice. He never broke the rules. Yet last night was filled with things he'd never done. His head throbbed louder than the pounding on the door.

"Damn it. I'm coming," he meant to shout, but it came out as a mumble, rubbing his temples as he staggered to discover his intruder.

Yanking the door open, he came face-to-face with the Goshawks' captain.

"How much trouble am I in?" Hunter asked, tucking in his disheveled shirt.

Chase grunted, stepping into the room uninvited. "Well, let's see," he said, sinking into an armchair. "You, our starting goalie, went MIA. The coach is out for blood. Oh, and we lost the game thanks to that grand show you put on ... I'd say you're up the creek, no paddle in sight."

Hunter shut the door, moving to perch on the corner of the unmade bed. "I know, I messed up big time." He ran a hand through his disheveled hair.

"You know I've followed your hockey career for a long time, kid. I've never seen you lose it like you did on the ice last night. You want to talk about it?"

Hunter took a deep breath. "I couldn't take one more second of Chucky."

"We all feel that way about him," Chase responded. "I just don't get it. You've played against the Florida team before. You've never let Chucky get under your skin like he did yesterday."

"I'm used to his physical abuse on the ice," Hunter confessed. "We all know that's what pests do, and for all his faults, he's one of the best. But it was his vile verbal chirps that got to me." He paused, one side of his lip curled into a half smile. "And I'd had enough of his binky waving in my face."

Chase couldn't suppress a smile. "Our entire team was rooting for you when you destroyed his pacifier." Then his expression sobered. "What did he say that pushed you over the edge?"

"It doesn't matter," Hunter declared. "I can handle him goading me, but when he starts spewing vulgarities about someone I care about, he crossed a line. I couldn't let him get away with it."

Chase nodded in agreement. "Get yourself cleaned up. Coach wants you down in the hotel's conference room ASAP."

Chase stood, giving Hunter a reassuring pat on the back leaving Hunter alone with his thoughts.

His head might be pounding, and his actions might have caused a storm, but he didn't regret standing up for the person he cared about.

Hunter walked into the hotel conference room, an arena of another kind. On one end of the imposing table sat a stern-faced Coach Harrison and Assistant Coach Frank Scott. Their glares were as icy as a fresh Zamboni groomed rink. Across from them, Chase ... his lone defender. Adding to Hunter's guilt, the unresolved issue of his disappearance after the penalty. He slid into the chair next to Chase, locking eyes with the coach.

"What happened last night? More important, where in the hell did you disappear to?" Harrison asked, a dangerous calm in his voice.

Chase began to interject, but the head coach silenced him with a raised hand. "You've already pleaded his case. Now I need to hear from Hunter."

Exhaling a heavy sigh, Hunter found his voice. "My only excuse ... the pressure got to me. But there are no excuses for my behavior, nor for my abrupt departure from the arena. I let the team down, and I regret that."

Harrison leaned back in his chair, arms crossed, chomping on gum, chewing on Hunter's admission. "That's not the story I got from your captain."

Chase shifted in his chair. Hunter shot him a sidelong look before turning back to the coach. "I can only control my words and actions. I let Chucky's actions and chirps get under my skin. I was wrong. I'm ready for the consequences."

Harrison uncrossed his arms, leaning forward, hands resting on the table. "Management had a long talk with the league. They handed you a misconduct for unsportsmanlike behavior. No game suspension. But they struggled with the fine. Apparently, there are no specific rules in the books for destroying an opponent's mouth guard."

A muffled laugh came from the assistant coach, abruptly silenced by a pointed glare from Coach Harrison.

"This is not a laughing matter," Harrison growled.

Hunter swallowed hard. "I take my behavior seriously, Coach."

Harrison nodded, settling back into his chair. "The real issue, your actions were the indirect reason we lost the game." He held up his hand, ticking off each infraction. "Loss of our starting goalie. Our back-up goalie had to go in cold. A major penalty, resulting in us being a man short for five minutes." He paused, letting his words sink in, and his anger to quell. "Your on-ice antics may have just gotten Florida in the playoffs." After a long pause, he added, "Was. It. Worth. It?"

Hunter flinched. Each word hitting him like a physical blow.

Harrison's voice lowered. "Well, was it? Was it worth letting your team down, tarnishing your reputation?"

"Enough, Coach," Chase cut in. "Hunter's only twenty-two. He's been with the Goshawks for five seasons ... never a single infraction. This is his first screw up."

Coach Harrison turned his stern gaze to Chase. "How many times do I need to say this? You're not an innocent bystander. As team captain, you bear responsibility for your team's conduct."

Chase gritted his teeth but remained silent.

Hunter spoke up. "Sir, I take full responsibility. It won't happen again."

Harrison gave a curt nod. "You're a valuable player, Hunter, I see that ... but if management doesn't, you could be playing elsewhere, or nowhere ... in a heartbeat."

Pushing his chair back, Harrison stood looking into Hunter's eyes. "Scott will give you the details of your fine. I had it doubled because you didn't stay in the arena and take your punishment like a man." Directing his attention to Chase, he added, "Make sure everyone is packed up. Our flight leaves for home in an hour."

Taking a deep breath, Hunter gathered courage to ask one last question. "Can I have my phone back?"

Coach Harrison shook his head. "You got a lot of nerve, kid." He reached into his pocket, tossing the phone on the table. "Get your head back in the game, boy, or you're going to lose more than your phone privileges." The room felt like the air had been sucked out as Coach Harrison exited.

"We'll get you a charger when we board the plane," Chase said.

Hunter nodded as he slipped the phone into his suit jacket pocket.

Chapter 11

Unsettled Feelings

April 14th

Entering Sage's parents' home, the warmth of the old farmhouse was a stark contrast to the crisp evening chill outside. A symphony of homey scents wafted to greet her, the comforting aroma of stew taking center stage.

"How'd your day go, honey?" Sage's mom asked, lifting the lid to the bubbling pot. "Excellent timing. The dumplings are done rising." The scents of simmering beef and vegetables permeated the kitchen, laced with the fragrant notes of rosemary and thyme. Stirring spoon in hand, her mother was the picture of comforting familiarity.

In the mudroom, Sage shrugged off her jacket, placing her photo bag with the worn leather straps, a remnant from her childhood, on the old wooden bench. "Not so great, Mom."

Lilly turned to face Sage. "You're still not moping around about that silly hockey player, are you?"

Sage sighed, "It's more complicated than that." Needing to change the subject, she asked, "Where's dad?"

"He's out of town on business. It's you and me for dinner tonight." Lilly dished up the stew, placing both bowls on the table. "Come, sit. Tell me what's bothering you, honey."

Sage took a seat across from her mom. She'd always been an open book to her mother ... tonight was no exception. "Mom," she whispered, "I haven't heard from Hunter since his last game in Portland."

Her mother paused, the spoon lingering over the bowl of steaming meat, veggies, and broth. "Oh," she said, allowing Sage to continue.

Sage took a deep breath. "It's not only that. I've been following the Goshawks' Facebook page and their official website. Hunter was not suspended because of his actions in Florida. I watched the Goshawks' next home game. Hunter was suited up but sat on the bench."

"Did the Goshawks win?"

"They did win, but it was a close back-and-forth game. One of the highest scoring games of the season." Sage's spoon chased a parsnip around her bowl as she spoke. "The Goshawks play again tonight, in Canada, yet there's no indication that Hunter will be in the net.

"When do they post a list of the players?" Her mom asked between bites.

"Mom, it's called the lineup, and the Goshawks are notorious for not posting it until right before the game starts." Sage took a spoonful of stew; she felt the need to chew on something.

"Oh Sage, are you listening to yourself? I don't pretend to understand the first thing about hockey. Other than Jessica can't stop talking about how hot all the players are, and Patty can't stop prattling about their teeth."

"Mom. You. Don't. Understand."

Setting her spoon in the bowl, and wiping her lips with a napkin, Lilly stared at her daughter before speaking. "First off, young lady, just because you are twenty-one, do not think you can take that tone with me."

"I'm sorry, Mom." Sage hung her head, mumbling, "I'm just so worried about him."

"For goodness' sake, Sage. You've only communicated with this boy a handful of times. And then, only online, he's never called you. For all you know, you could be 'finger-talking' to one of those artificial intelligent thingies that's all over the news now."

Sage could not help but laugh. "Mom, Hunter is not an AI. I have proof that the Hunter I've been messaging is a real flesh and blood person."

"Well, that's good. All teasing aside. You've never met him in person. He could have a girlfriend, be engaged, or worse, married." She pursed her lips. "Darling, this is not like you. I know how addicted you are to your little hockey games. But sweetheart, he's just a hockey player."

"He's more than that. Plus, I know a lot about his professional life. I've been following his career for five seasons."

Sage leaned her elbows on the table, cupping her chin with her hands. "Like I'm a fourth-generation South Dakotan farm girl, Hunter's bloodline is from Maine. From the time he could walk, he's lived and breathed hockey. I know he loves the thrill of winning, yet even a small game loss puts him in an irrational downward spiral."

"Well, at least you have one thing in common."

"What's that?"

"You're both prone to being moody when something doesn't go your way."

"I'm not moody. I'm concerned about Hunter's mental state." Sage did her best to fake a smile, knowing full well her mom could see right through her. She sat back, waiting for the forthcoming lecture.

"That's just another reason for you to not be moping about. It seems your goalie is an entitled east coast boy, with his heart and soul devoted to his first and only true love ... hockey." Lilly reached over, squeezing her daughter's hand. "Honey, you two live in different worlds. Distance is not the only thing between you. How could a pro hockey player fit into a world filled with horses, cattle, and cornfields? You were raised with small-town values. He's a city boy. What do you really have in common?"

"We have a love of hockey, Mom."

"Sage, he's just a boy, making a lot of money, playing a game he loves ... on skates."

"He's not just a boy on skates. Hunter has both brains and talent. He skipped eighth grade and became a breakout goalie on the high school team. Because of his talent, he was offered a full-ride scholarship to a prestigious Maine university. He played goalie at a Div. 1 college. The pro hockey scouts made it their mission to get him into the draft when he was age eligible."

Perking up, Lilly asked, "What was his major in college?" She broke apart a dumpling with her spoon, mixing it in the meaty broth.

"I have no idea. By the end of his freshman year in college, Hunter became eligible for the pro hockey draft. That same year, the Goshawks became a pro hockey expansion team. The Goshawks got the first-round draft pick and selected Hunter. Goalies, especially an eighteen-year-old, are rarely selected first overall. Let alone signed directly to a pro team. Everyone in the hockey world was talking about Hunter."

"So, he's a college drop out?"

"OMG, is that all you've taken away from what I've said?" Sage dropped her spoon into the bowl, her stew only half eaten. "Mom, he's not a silly boy playing a game ... he's a record setting phenom in the world of hockey." Sage wanted to add *... and until five days ago, I believed he was my friend.*

"It hurts me to see you get so depressed over someone you've never met in person." Lilly sighed. "So what if he hasn't contacted you in five days, or five weeks for that matter? You're not his girlfriend. You're not even in a serious relationship. He's a professional athlete. What I've gathered from you, hockey players have a rigorous and rigid schedule. What makes you think he owes you anything, let alone his precious time?"

"You're right Mom. I'm being selfish. I know I'm getting upset over nothing. Sometimes, it feels like ... like, I was being used."

"Oh, you mean because of that half-naked selfie he took? I bet his mom saw it and made him take it down." She smiled, plucking a piece of carrot out of her bowl with her spoon.

"Because the picture with 'The Sign' is plastered all over social media." Sage formed air-quotes with her fingers.

"Sweetheart ..." her mother started, but Sage held up a hand, shaking her head.

"I think that's why he's ghosting me. But I can't be sure. I'm so confused," Sage's voice faltered.

"How mortifying for both of you." Lilly frowned. Standing, she walked behind her daughter, giving her a hug.

Sage inhaled the warm scent of her mother, mixed with the lingering smell of homemade stew, but it provided little comfort. She ached talking about the infamous 'Hi Sage' photo, now being mocked on all social media platforms, with snide remarks aimed at Hunter.

"Sometimes I feel like I've been abandoned by Hunter. Like I'm an embarrassment to him."

"If that's the case, he's not worthy of your concern or worry. You're lucky to find out his true character ... before getting more involved."

"I'm more to blame than him. If not for me, Hunter would never have posted the picture. It would never have been viewed by millions. His reputation has always been squeaky clean." Sage paused, fighting back tears before continuing.

"He's beloved by Goshawks' fans, and even fans of other teams. Now, because of me, he's been turned into a laughingstock." Sage paused again, doing her best to gather the right words. "I thought we were on the verge of building a solid friendship." Despite the comfort food in front of her, her gut was twisting ... dinner barely touched.

"Not that hungry, hon?"

"Sorry Mom. Your stew is amazing as always, but I've lost my appetite. I want to get in my pajamas and crawl into bed with a good book."

"I understand. I'll send you home with a tub of stew in case you change your mind later." Lilly filled a plastic bowl, adding a couple of dumplings. Handing it to Sage, she said, "Please, promise me you won't spend a wakeful night stressing about that boy. Don't let his thoughtlessness take you to a dark place. You have so much going for you, it breaks my heart to see you like this."

"I promise." Sage hugged her mom, then picked up her things. Checking her phone for messages—nothing. The walk across the yard to her apartment felt longer than usual, each step heavy with her thoughts. The night sky, littered with stars, couldn't bring solace to Sage's troubled thoughts.

Pausing at her apartment door, Sage's fingers lingered on the doorknob. Her mother's words echoed in her mind, a blend of comfort and caution. Though she knew she needed to reconsider her feelings for Hunter, for now, all she wanted was the escape of sleep. Stepping inside, she yearned for the oblivion of dreamless rest, a temporary refuge from the turmoil within her.

Chapter 12
Confessions

April 14th

Sage snuggled in her bed, turning the crisp pages of her novel, sending a soft whisper through the silence of her room. The faint aroma of chamomile tea drifted from her bedside table. The steam dancing upwards did little to calm tonight's conversation she had with her mom.

As she was losing herself in the plot of her book, the insistent ping of her phone broke through the tranquility. She glanced over. Her breath hitched at the sight of a Facebook Messenger notification from Hunter Griffin.

Her pulse quickened, a tidal wave of emotions flooding. She was furious at his silence over the past five days. But overriding the anger was a curiosity that had her reaching for her phone. The teacup teetered on the edge of the table, but Sage's attention was fully captured by the screen's soft glow.

Hunter Griffin: Please Call Me.

His message was followed by a phone number.

The gravity of those words held her captive for a moment. She bit her bottom lip, her mind racing. Curiosity won. With trembling fingers, she punched in each number. Hovering over the last digit, she felt like she was about to have a panic attack. She could hear her heart beating. Closing her eyes, she hit the number, then the send button.

The cell rang for several seconds. When she was about to disconnect the call, a smooth, masculine voice answered, "Hello. Sage?"

His voice took her by surprise, even though she had heard him speaking over the past five years on tons of Goshawks after game interviews. Tonight, it sounded sensual, filled with mystery.

"Sage?" Hunter repeated.

Finding her voice, she replied, "Hunter?"

"I'm so glad you called. I was afraid you might block my Facebook account."

"I usually do block people who ghost me," Sage cut in, her tone a fusion of reproach and confusion. "I just left my mom's house. She reminded me you don't owe me anything, let alone an explanation for dropping me." Her face grew red. *Ye Gads. She sounded like her mother.*

"Man, Sage, you really know how to hurt a guy," Hunter replied.

"Sometimes the truth hurts. I know I was hurt by the reality of our recent online interactions. However, if you recall, you were the one who initiated first contact." She collected her thoughts, but only for a moment before continuing, not giving him time to respond. "Silly me. I thought our brief encounter was turning into a friendship."

"I know, Sage," Hunter admitted, his deep voice echoing with sincerity. "I messed up."

"No, Hunter. I messed up when I accepted your Facebook request."

"Please, Sage, take a breath and let me explain what happened." After a few seconds of dead airtime, Hunter continued, "It started the morning after our last game in Portland. I woke up late. Hurrying to pack, I left my charger in the apartment. Being the dumbass that I am, I forgot to charge my phone the night before. My battery died as soon as I got seated on the plane."

"I'm having a hard time buying your story, Hunter. You fly with nineteen teammates. A head coach, your goalie coach, along with several assistant coaches, and lord knows how many support people ... plus the flight crew. Are you trying to tell me no one on your private team plane had a phone charger you could borrow?"

The silence on the other end of the line was so thick it was suffocating. Hunter then let out a weary sigh. "You've never flown on a team plane. I asked Olaf if he had a charger, but he didn't have one compatible with my phone. It wouldn't have mattered. Everyone was having bad cell reception because of the storm. I thought I'd have time to get a charger from someone when we reached the hotel ... but we went directly to the visitor's practice rink."

Sage kept silent. Hunter sounded sincere. She wanted to believe his story. Yet, he knew from their first encounter how apprehensive she was. To make matters worse, her mom was right. She only knew Hunter from watching him play, his post-game interviews, and from reading Internet stories about him. She knew a lot about Ice Wall, the Goshawks star goalie. The truth hit her; she knew next to nothing about the man behind the goalie mask.

"Are you still there?"

"Yes, I'm still listening." Sage could hear his footsteps. Unsure of where he was calling from, she was positive he was pacing while talking.

"Good. I thought you might have disconnected."

Sage wanted to insert that she was not the one who had disconnected for five days without a word. Instead, she said, "I'm still here."

"Thank you." Clearing his throat, he continued, "After I got off the bus to the visitor's rink, I was busy getting dressed for practice when the head coach walked in. He saw me checking my phone's battery level. I was hoping it had enough juice to at least squeeze one quick message to you."

Sage could no longer hear his footsteps.

"The coach was pissed. He grabbed the phone out of my hand, yelling. Reminding me to keep my head in the game. Then he pocketed my phone, saying I wouldn't get it back until after the game."

"Yeah, well, the game was five days ago."

"It was over earlier than that for me."

"I know. I watched the Florida game."

"Then you know about the Instagram picture being plastered on the overhead screen?"

"Yes, I saw it." Sage wanted to shout, *on a repeated loop*. Instead, she remained calm. After all, Hunter was the one who had gotten the immediate backlash from the announcers and fans. "That must have been unnerving, especially right before a game."

"It was more than that ... it got into my head and shook my game the first period."

"It was just a silly picture."

"A picture blown up larger than life. I was naked from the waist up, Sage. I looked like a fool," he added. His instant pause gave the impression he regretted his words as soon as they fell from his mouth.

"If you felt so foolish, you shouldn't have posted the picture in the first place." Sage could feel her anger rise.

"I'm sorry you were hurt by having the world see your name plastered across my chest. I can only imagine how shocked you must have felt." Hunter's tone was laced with a sarcastic edge.

"Nobody knows I'm that girl." Sage did her best to defuse the situation. She took a sip of her now tepid herbal tea to calm her nerves. It didn't work.

"I hope the press doesn't find out."

"Thanks. I think." Sage had no idea if his comment was meant to be protective or spiteful.

"Trust me, you do not want the press hounding you. They can be your worst nightmare, all the while pretending to be your best friend."

"You know more about that than I do."

After a long pause, Hunter spoke again. "Towards the end of the first period, I was feeling better. I blocked a dozen shots on goal. During the first intermission, the coach jumped all over me about the image, and how I'd embarrassed the team and the whole Goshawks' organization. He demanded I delete the picture."

"Is that why you deleted your Instagram page?"

"Yes and no. Coach had my phone, so I couldn't do anything. The Goshawks' marketing team has my Instagram password. I didn't know they were going to delete my entire account."

"Apparently, they didn't get to it quick enough. Your picture's gone viral. I wouldn't be surprised if it's not on the sides of the Portland city buses by the time you get home." The bitterness in her tone surprised even herself.

"I hope you're wrong." Hunter let out a laugh, more of a murmur, barely audible over the phone.

"OMG, Hunter. Does the Marketing Team have the password to your Facebook account too? Have they read our conversations on Facebook Messenger?"

"They had my Facebook password, but I changed it as soon as I got my phone back the next morning. As far as I know, they only deleted the Instagram stuff."

"Is your Instagram picture the real reason you've ignored me for the past five days?"

"I'm so sorry Sage. You did nothing to deserve any of this. I apologize for not reaching out to you until now. I ... I just had to sort things out."

Sage could hear the sincerity in his voice. "Don't worry about it. I'll deal with the press if my identity gets leaked." She could almost picture him running a hand through his hair while pacing about again. She swallowed the lump in her throat. "I need to know, Hunter. What happened that led up to your ejection from the game?"

"You should know. You just told me you watched it unfold." Hunter's words came out harsh, laced with bitterness.

"Watching it on the big screen, and living the experience, are worlds apart. Please tell me what happened. I've followed your career since you were first drafted. I've never seen you retaliate."

"Chucky got the best of me."

"I saw that. But I still don't understand. It's not the first time you've played against him."

No response on Hunter's end.

"So, what did he do differently that game that he hadn't done before?"

There was a heartbeat's pause before he confessed. "I was already hot from being berated by the coach in front of everyone. Then Chucky was in my face, with his wiggling mouth guard, getting away with jabbing me with his stick while the refs looked the other way. Hell, I was blinded when he snowed me at the end of his breakaway."

"Chucky should've been kicked out of the game instead of you," Sage huffed.

"He's a pest. But he's the Barracudas' star player. He tends to get away with a lot of dirty stuff other players don't." Hunter's voice broke as he confessed, "Between the Instagram photo and Chucky ... he was trash-talking the whole game. I tried to ignore it, but he crossed a line. He said things ... things about you. I lost it. I snapped. The ejection was all on me ... no one else."

Sage's body tensed. She hadn't realized the extent of what had happened. Her voice softened. "I'm so sorry. I had no idea. Please don't beat yourself up about the penalty. You're not a machine. You're a human being with feelings. I still can't believe Chucky got away with what he did."

Hunter let out a humorless laugh. "Sage, as much as you profess, you're a super fan ... you know nothing about playing professional hockey. When I step onto the ice, I cannot afford to let emotions seep into my game. Once I no longer focus on the puck, the game is lost. That is precisely what happened in Florida. I let my team down, I let the Goshawks organization down. I let the fans down ... but most important, I put my career as a professional goalie in jeopardy. That can never happen again."

"I understand. Thank you for taking the time to explain what happened. It means a lot." Sage felt her mood change, her anger towards Hunter dissipate. She drew in a shaky breath. "I was worried sick about you. I felt so helpless. I wanted to comfort you after the game, but you just vanished behind your wall."

"I guess I earned my nickname."

"Guess so."

"Listen, I'm truly sorry you got caught up in my hockey melodrama. Coach thinks it's a good idea for me to stay off all social media until after the playoffs, which start in four days. He didn't tell me to stay off my phone. If you want to cut ties with me ... I won't like it ... but I'll understand."

"Listen, the Ice Wall has been an important part of my life for five years. Now I think it might be time to get to know the real man that guards the net ... if you'll let me."

"I've learned a lot these past days," he admitted. "Although we've just met, I want to see where this ... whatever this is ... will take us. I'm willing to try if you are. I want to make things right. Will you let me?"

His words hung in the air, leaving a silence filled with possibility. "Okay, Hunter. I too want to see where this takes us. I'm glad we cleared the air. I'm glad you got your phone privileges back. I've missed our online conversations."

"I've missed them too. I've missed you more than you know."

"Hey, it's getting late. I have an early photo shoot. Thanks again for reaching out to me."

"Thanks for not dumping me. I'll get back to you the first chance I can."

"Good night, Hunter."

"Night, Sage."

Sage shut her phone, turning off the light. She went over the conversation. Then she realized the one question she forgot to ask. She shot Hunter a quick text.

Sage: Which playoff team are you up against first?

Hunter: Florida!

Chapter 13
Pride and Punishment

April 17th [Game 1 of the First Round of Playoffs: Portland]
The Goshawks' home locker room was thick with tension. A heady cocktail of sweat, adrenaline, and focus permeated the air. The room hummed with the collective energy of men preparing for battle, the sound of taping hockey sticks and the zipping of bags lending to the hypnotic anticipation.

Into this charged atmosphere strode Coach Harrison. His eyes scanned the room, taking in each player's pregame ritual. The silence was absolute as they awaited his words, a potent mixture of nerves and determination filling the space.

"Gentlemen," he began, his voice echoing in the silence. He clapped his beefy hands together, the sharp noise cutting through the tension. "Tonight marks the beginning of our playoff journey. A journey we've been preparing for all season."

A murmur of agreement passed through the room. Hunter's gaze fixed on his skates. Coach Harrison paused, letting his words sink in before he continued.

"I don't need to remind you, but I will ... we've had an incredible season," Coach Harrison said. "Only twelve losses. But that success is in the past. Tonight, the slate has been wiped clean. The regular season stats, the previous scores, they may be in the record books, but that chapter of our season has closed." Once more, he slapped his hands together.

Harrison paced, being careful not to walk on the Goshawks logo. "Tonight, we write a new book. What matters is right here, right now. What matters is how much we want it." He paused, searching each player's face. "The question remains, how much do you want it? Let Me Hear How Much You Want It!"

"We! Want! It! All!"

The team yelled as one. The message was clear ... fight for every goal, every game. No room for complacency.

Coach Harrison continued, his voice resonating with each word. "Stay out of the penalty box. Keep your emotions in check." He looked at Hunter as he added, "We're here to win a series, not exact revenge."

The room's charged silence was shattered by a handful of deep bursts of laughter, offering a brief respite from the coach's lecture. The coach's gaze swept across the room again, focused and serious. Before leaving, he handed Hunter a folded piece of paper.

It was always an honor to read the starting lineup. Hunter walked to the front of the room, cleared his throat. Pointing to the first stall, he shouted, "Tonight, playing center ... like this is a huge surprise ... our captain, number Lucky 7, Chase Rutherford."

Hunter waited for the noise and laughter to subside before he continued. "His left winger, number 63, Finn O'Connell." He then turned, pointing to the player sitting next to Finn. "We are counting on you to live up to your Goshawks' name, right winger, number 56, Etan, quick shot, Eklund." The players stomped their feet as the rookie stood, taking a bow before sitting.

"Now for the goalie's best friends, the big D starters are ... number 73, Ryan Mitchell, and our other star rookie, number 25, Axel Berger.

Hunter looked at the last name on the list, at first disappointed, then elated. "Tonight, in the net, is none other than our favorite Snowman, the big number 30, Olaf Svensson."

A hush fell over the room as Hunter walked to his stall, taking something from his gear bag. He walked back to Olaf, handing him a miniature doll from their favorite horror movie. Patting Olaf on the back, Hunter sported a face-splitting grin. "I'm sorry you drew the start and have to deal with Chucky on the first night of playoffs." The locker room exploded with a celebration of hoots and howls.

With a final, resounding "Go, Goshawks!" the team stood, the energy in the room reaching a fever pitch. The sound of gear being adjusted echoed around the room as the players started towards the door.

The last of his teammates disappeared into the tunnel as Hunter took a deep breath. He felt a mixture of nerves, anticipation, and excitement course through his veins. The pressure of the playoff's first game was intense. The stakes were high, the atmosphere electric.

With that, he stepped out of the locker room, his heart pounding in sync with the distant chants of the crowd, along with the irritating pop songs from the DJ's booth. Time for the pregame warm up. Soon the Goshawks would be fighting for their lives.

First Period

The roar of the crowd was deafening as the Goshawks stepped onto the rink, with the Snowman leading them into the arena. The scent of ice mixed with anticipation hung heavy. Olaf's expression was one of surprise and gratitude, as the chant of "Snowman! Snowman!" reverberated throughout the stadium, echoing the unyielding faith the fans had in both their goalies.

On the bench, Hunter watched the starting players lineup for the national anthem. Each breath he tasted frost and adrenaline, coupled with the yearning to be between the pipes.

When the referee's whistle sliced through the noise, signaling the start of the battle, the puck dropped. The captain claimed it. Like a lightning bolt, Chase passed it to his left winger, Finn O'Connell. Finn charged forward with a thunderous unstoppable force, outmaneuvering the Florida team's defense as though they were standing still. With a swift, decisive pass back to Chase, the Goshawks took the lead.

GOAL! Goshawks—Rutherford

Goshawks' fans exploded, their joy ricocheting off the cold, hard ice and the steel girders above.

On the Barracudas' bench, Chucky Trembly glared at the Goshawk's captain as he skated by, pounded his stick against the boards. On the next exchange, he entered the fray with a new level of fury, pushing, prodding, and chirping with each Goshawks' encounter.

Chasing a loose puck, Chucky slammed Chase into the corner as he chirped, "Lucky goal Rutherford. Did your granny teach you how to handle your twig?"

Unfazed, Rutherford skated away, as if he were deaf to Chucky's taunts. Letting the Barracudas know the Goshawks were here to play, here to win. Unable to get under the captain's skin, Chucky drew a penalty out of an innocent contact with the Goshawks' rookie winger, Etan Eklund. Etan's stick barely touched Chucky, but the pest flung his body onto the ice as if hit by a sniper's bullet. The referee fell for the performance, sending Etan to the penalty box, leaving the Goshawks shorthanded.

The Snowman's net was breached by Barracudas' young forward during the power play.

GOAL! Barracudas—Banks

But it was a minor setback. Olaf was back in form, stonewalling the Barracudas' attempts to get through his fortress. The Goshawks stayed on the defense, giving room for their offense to score two goals in quick succession.

GOAL! Goshawks—Rutherford

GOAL! Goshawks—Eklund

The precision of the Goshawks' passes, expert stick handling and speed, left the Barracudas floundering. Each home team's goal was met with an uproar from the crowd, nearly shaking the foundations of the stadium.

The first period ended 3 to 1 in favor of the Goshawks. The arena was alive with the pulse of playoff hockey. It was raw and exhilarating. Above all, it was just the beginning.

Second Period

The next period proved to be a white-knuckle ride. The puck bounced back and forth like a pinball. Lending a rhythm to the madness; the crisp sound of skates slicing through the ice, bodies crashing, boards rattling. Matching the Barracudas stride-for-stride, the Goshawks were in a continuous battle of possession and position. Their hard-earned lead remained intact. The Snowman was a bulwark in the net, swatting away shots with an ease that belied the tension running through the game.

Florida players, growing desperate and reckless, started racking up penalties. The referees' whistles set to a constant trill. The Barracudas' coach's intense gum chomping visibly exhibited his frustration with the stream of interference and roughing calls on his players. Despite their disadvantage, the Barracudas' goalie also held firm. The Goshawks were unable to extend their lead.

With only seconds on the clock, Poston, the Barracudas' left winger, barreled down the ice, launching a vicious slap shot straight at Olaf. The Snowman didn't flinch, but the impact of the puck hitting his mask sent a shudder through the crowd. The puck ricocheted off Olaf, dropping in the crease, the goalie reeling from the blow.

Before anyone could react, Chucky was there, sweeping in like a vulture to a carcass, knocking the puck into the net's sliver of an opening. The arena erupted with protests, along with a smattering of cheers from Barracudas' fans, as Olaf crumpled onto the ice, unconscious.

GOAL! Barracudas—Trembly

The whistle blew, ending the period.

It took two men to help Olaf off the ice. He was now conscious but dazed. His departure marked the igniting of the powder keg that had been building.

A melee broke out among the remaining players on the ice. Both sides clashed, crushing each other into the boards, gloves dropped, fists flying. The linesmen, in the middle of it, did their best to douse the flames as tempers raged out of control.

On the Goshawks' bench, hockey sticks hit the boards, as angry slurs burst out from the players. Viktor grabbed Hunter by his sweater, preventing him from joining the fray.

Going into the locker room, the Goshawks still led, but the atmosphere was thick with unease. Losing their goalie and the violent free-for-all afterwards left resentment in both players and fans. The last period promised to be an all-out war.

Third Period

The howling winds of retribution, and the biting chill of retaliation, swept across the rink as the Goshawks took to the ice for the third period. Their every stride on the slick surface was a testament to the resilience etched deep into their bones. Each of the Goshawks' players involved in the previous fight wore his battle scars proudly. The badges of honor on their bloodied and battered faces, a stark reminder of their fallen comrade, Olaf. As a single force, they were ready to show the Florida team just whose house they were playing in ... which team ruled the ice.

Then there was Hunter, the Ice Wall. The man the Barracudas had humiliated by flashing his Instagram image on the scoreboard. He was back in the net, his heart beating like a war drum. He slid his mask over his face, his gaze sweeping across the rink. His icy resolve mirrored in his hardened stare was a clear message ... time for payback.

The whistle cut through the tension, followed by the renewed roar from the home crowd.

The Goshawks' bear of a defenseman, Liam Armstrong, set the tone early, hammering Barracudas' Poston into the boards with a check that would echo in the Florida forward's bones for weeks. With the puck wrestled from Poston, Armstrong drove towards the enemy's blue crease, the cheers of the crowd propelling him forward. The Barracudas' fans feeble protests were drowned in the deafening roar that erupted when Armstrong scored with a high puck to the upper corner of the net.

GOAL! Goshawks—Armstrong

Next, Chucky was caught in the eye of the storm when Goshawks winger, Finn O'Connell, and defenseman, Ryan Mitchell, descended upon him. During the double hit, a clandestine sharp elbow from Ryan found its home in Chucky's ribs, a message delivered with brutal precision. Chucky was left winded, the breath knocked out of him as justice was meted on the ice. Again, no penalty called.

Just after the line change, the Goshawks' second-line center, Eddie Bennett, received a call for high sticking. The referee's whistle was followed by Bennett skating to the box with a two-minute penalty.

Shorthanded, the Ice Wall earned his name. He formed a barrier the Barracudas could not penetrate, blocking 10 rapid-fire shots on goal. With only seconds left on the penalty clock, the Goshawks' captain picked the pocket of a Florida forward. Chase was having a razor-sharp game. He raced toward the Barracudas' goalie. With precision stick handling, the puck kissed the inside of the bar, sliding into the net.

GOAL! Goshawks—Rutherford

The Goshawks' fans stood in unison, hats raining onto the ice, as the crowd erupted with a thunderous roar. Their captain scoring a shorty and the first hat trick of the playoffs.

With only five minutes left in regulation play, both teams were on edge, both playing chippy. Florida released the Hounds-of-Hell, their top enforcers, in a last-ditch effort to change the tide. But the Goshawks remained unfazed.

The final buzzer rang ending the game. A deafening chorus of victory echoed throughout the stadium, along with a collective sigh of relief from the Goshawks' players. The first game of the playoffs was theirs. It was a testament to their unwavering will, and a dire warning to those who dare cross their path.

The Goshawks players cleared the bench to form a line in front of their goalie, to give him well-deserved praise. Each player touched the top of Hunter's mask with reverence. The final score: Goshawks 5 - Barracudas 2. This was not just a victory. It was a message, a declaration.

Hunter smiled. Victory never tasted sweeter. Leaving the rink to the shouts of "Ice Wall! Ice Wall!" Hunter tossed his stick over the glass to a young fan. For the Goshawks, the road to glory was just beginning. For Hunter, tonight was the first step on his journey to redemption.

In the heart of Portland, Maine, under the glaring stadium lights, a new legend was born. Tonight, the Goshawks were not just a team. They were conquerors, heroes of their city, the harbingers of a playoff run that promised to be unforgettable.

Chapter 14
Winners and Losers

April 17th [Game 1 of the First Round of Playoffs: South Dakota]
The pregame chatter echoed through Sage's apartment, bouncing off the walls, feeding off the adrenaline-laced anticipation. In the small living room, Patty sat on the edge of the couch, her knees bouncing. The energy in her body was contagious, infecting the room with an electric buzz. Patty picked up her phone, scrolling through the live comments streaming in on the Goshawks' official Facebook page.

"Guys, listen to this," Patty announced. "The whole hockey world is homing in on tonight's game. Everyone's talking about Hunter and the mouth guard drama when they last played Florida in the regulation season."

Sprawled on the armchair, Jessica declared, "It's all anyone can talk about. It's been ages since we've seen that kind of hockey drama. Chucky's wiggling mouth guard was his trademark. Let's see if tonight Hunter can keep his cool. We all know the Goshawks' first game of the playoffs depends on it."

Sage emerged from her bedroom. "Oh please, Patty, stop reporting the fan gossip. I'm already a bundle of nerves."

"I've checked the Barracudas' Facebook page too. Seems like their fans are urging Chucky to retaliate." Patty's eyes went wide. "Oh, My. Gosh. One fan wants Chucky to hit the Ice Wall so hard his mask flies off ... with Hunter's head still in it."

"Patty, put your phone away," Sage scolded.

She complied. "I'm sure the Goshawks' defensemen will keep the two apart."

"Ah, to hell with Chucky!" Jessica piped in, her eyes flashing. "All that drama over a mouth guard. Honestly, the things these macho hockey players will use as an excuse for a brawl."

"I keep reminding you, Jessica. Even though the league does not require pro hockey players to wear mouth guards, they're still a very important protective piece of equipment that every player should covet," Patty said, as she stared down Jessica.

Jessica sported an evil grin. "Look at you Patty. You've come a long way from calling the goalies' five-hole, a pie-hole. I can now dub you a member in good standing of the Goshawks fan club." She mock waved a wand over Patty's shoulders.

Patty stuck her tongue out at Jessica. "It was a logical mistake. After all, when a puck goes through the goalie's knee pads, it looks like it's going through the first cut of pie. Plus, I think it was mean of you two for not correcting me sooner."

"Geez Patty, are you sure you're not related to Betty White's character in the Golden Girls?" Jessica responded, nearly falling to the floor with laughter.

Ignoring Jessica, Patty continued to prattle, "The best part about everyone talking about Chucky's mouthpiece, it takes the focus off you, Sage, and the Instagram image."

"Way to go Patty." Jessica snarked.

"Sorry Sage." Patty walked over, giving Sage a hug.

"No problem. That's all behind us. Since announcing the Goshawks are playing Florida, no one has mentioned my name."

"Thank goodness for the mouthpiece controversy," shouted Jessica. Her high-five fluttered in the air, unanswered.

A knock at the door interrupted their speculation about the upcoming game. Sage and Patty exchanged glances.

Jessica jumped up and ran to the door. "That must be our ride."

Patty sported a confused look. "Since when does the Uber driver come to the door?" Jessica winked in response. Patty's eyebrows raised in surprise as the door swung open.

"Luke," Sage exclaimed. "What are you doing here?"

He lifted a shoulder in a half-shrug, his eyes flicking to Sage with a warm smile. "Jessica mentioned you ladies were heading to the bar to watch the game. Thought I might tag along if that's okay. I've got the night off. I can be your designated driver."

A flurry of excitement filled the room as the girls gathered their things. The moment of truth was just around the corner. Sage could feel the butterflies causing havoc in her stomach. Hunter and the Goshawks were on the verge of something monumental.

"I call shotgun." Jessica raced to the truck's front passenger door.

Luke hung back a second, shaking his head. Following Sage to his truck with the big double cab, he opened the back door. Picking her up by the waist, he lifted her inside.

"Thanks Luke. Getting in a monster truck is one of the downsides of being a short girl."

Reaching over to tighten her seatbelt, Luke whispered, "I've never known you to have any downsides."

"Ah, Luke, you always say the nicest things." Sage gave Luke a playful slap on the shoulder.

"Hurry up back there," Jessica urged. "This time we don't want to miss the pregame show."

Luke was someone Sage admired, someone who would never break her heart. Hunter ... Hunter was someone she could fall for ... and she was certain her heart needed protective equipment.

———————◆◆◆———————

The atmosphere in O'Sullivan's vibrated with the charged energy of the playoff season. Packed with locals, the crowd was a hodgepodge of casual spectators, die-hard hockey fans, and everything in between.

The smell of pizzas fresh from the wood-burning ovens, mixed with the sharp tang of draft beer, set the stage for tonight's fun. The South Dakota sports bar was a long way from Portland, Maine. Even though most of the patrons were Minnesota fans, there were two things they could all agree on — this was the first game of the first round of playoffs, and everyone had a collective dislike for the Florida team, especially their notorious pest, Chucky.

Sage, Jessica, Patty, and Luke snagged the girls' favorite spot. A table nestled in a corner, providing the best view of the largest television. The screen hummed with vibrant life, showing the Goshawks' pregame warm-up.

Jessica, with an anticipatory glint in her eyes, nudged Luke. "I bet you're glad to be out of the bartender trenches for this one, huh?"

Luke laughed, taking a quick glance toward Sage. "I wouldn't miss it for the world."

Jessica continued, "I'm surprised you're not hiding at home, avoiding the playoff madness."

Luke smiled. "Even though I'm not a hockey fan, it's nice to be on the other side of the bar for once."

Sage, her gaze flicking between the game and their group, asked, "How are your college courses coming along, Luke?"

Before he could answer, Patty staggered to their table, juggling a tray filled with four frosty glass mugs and a pitcher of the bar's best craft beer.

"Patty, why didn't you let me get that?" Luke reprimanded, as he lifted the pitcher and mugs onto the table, tucking the tray away by his feet next to the wall.

Patty filled each mug as she looked at Luke and her two friends. "You looked occupied."

Touching Luke's arm, Sage repeated her question.

Luke smiled, eager to discuss something other than hockey. "They're going well. Business Administration isn't thrilling, but it's all part of the plan."

"You. Have a plan?" Jessica teased, tilting her head to one side like a love-sick puppy. "I thought you might be turning into another pretty-boy career college student."

"Geez, Jessica, he's graduating next month." Patty came to Luke's defense. "So, Luke, tell us your plan."

Luke picked up his mug, wetting his tongue with the amber liquid. Looking at Sage, he answered, "This summer I'm taking over as foreman of my dad's quarter horse ranch."

Patty let out a low whistle. "That's a lot of responsibility being in charge of your father's billion-dollar business."

"I think that's wonderful, Luke." Jessica beamed as she leaned on his shoulder.

A chorus of "Snowman! Snowman!" emanating from the speakers, pulled their attention back to the television screen as the Goshawks' goalie skated onto the ice. The announcer introduced Olaf Svensson as the starting goalie, not Hunter. Sage's eyebrows narrowed as she took a long swig from her beer.

"Why isn't Hunter starting?" Patty asked, her forehead creased in confusion.

"Coach always has a game day strategy. He's notorious for mixing the lines up at the last minute," Sage murmured, although her disappointment was clear in the tone of her voice.

As the game progressed, Sage was their personal commentator, offering a blend of in-depth analysis and raw passion. They almost tipped the table over when the Goshawks captain scored the first goal.

The crowd in the bar also cheered when the Goshawks scored. They booed when Chucky did his dramatic fall, drawing a penalty.

"OMG, the ref needs glasses." Patty shouted, tossing a wadded paper napkin at the big screen, hitting Luke instead.

"You throw like a girl." Jessica laughed.

"Watch yourself, Patty. It's far too early in the game to cut you off," warned Luke as he switched into bartender mode, pulling the soggy napkin from his shirt.

Moments later, the Barracuda's young rookie scored on the power play.

"No Way!" the girls chimed in unison.

They in turn let out sighs of relief when the Goshawks regained the lead with two quick goals. The first period ended with the Goshawks ahead 3 to 1.

The second period was hard fought but uneventful. When the camera shifted to the bench, it focused on Hunter leaning on the side rail, dressed for the game. Yet it seemed odd to see him wearing his protective ball cap. A secret part of Sage loved looking at Hunter's strong facial features, normally covered by his goalie mask. Her gaze devoured him ... the close-trimmed beard, the deep dark hazel eyes, the way a lock of dusty brown hair escaped beneath his cap.

Moments before the end of the period the atmosphere in the bar shifted. Everyone's attention glued to the screens as Olaf crumpled to the ice.

"Dear Lord ..." Patty's voice vibrated through the bar.

Broadcasters replayed the incident ad nauseam: the brutal slap shot, the puck's violent impact, Olaf's fall a second after Chucky swept in to score. The blatant injustice of it hung heavy, the smell of outrage as thick as the hoppy scent of spilled beer. A silence fell in the bar as everyone held their breath, waiting for any sign that Olaf would be okay.

In the arena, both Goshawks and Barracudas fans applauded when the Snowman regained consciousness and was helped off the ice. An instant later, the whistle blew, ending the period ... then all hell broke loose.

The players on the ice became entangled in a mass of blue and red uniforms. Fists flew as everyone piled on each other; a mass of bodies shoved into the boards. The linesmen jumped into the mix, tugging and pulling at sweaters.

One camera zoomed into the Goshawks' bench, where the goaltending coach kept Hunter from joining the fight. The camera then panned back to the chaotic scene on the ice as the linesmen did their best to defuse the situation.

In South Dakota, the bar exploded with cheers, jeers, and defiant shouts. Chairs scraped against the floor, fists pounded on tables, the sharp clink of glasses added to the chaos.

"Don't let Hunter on the ice," Sage yelled, standing on her toes, eyes glinting in the dim light.

Luke stared at Sage. Turning to Jessica he asked, "Why does she care so much about a second-string goalie?"

"Hunter's their starting goalie. Plus, Sage has always had a thing for goalies."

Luke's jaw clinched. His eyebrows creased as he leaned back in the barstool nursing his ice water.

Jessica leaned towards Luke. "The Goshawks have to show the Barracudas who's in charge." She layered her explanations with a casual touch here, a light laugh there.

As the fight broke up, and both teams headed down their respective tunnels, the tension in the bar exploded into a round of cheers. The entire room now rooted for the Goshawks ... with exception of a big burly guy sitting at the counter wearing a Florida jersey.

When the second period started, Sage watched the screen as the five battered Goshawks' players returned to the ice. The camera close-ups showed a myriad of cuts, bruises, and grim determination etched on their faces. Now in the game, Hunter moved side-to-side, low in the net with a fluid grace that belied his hardened exterior.

Minutes into the game, Goshawks' defenseman, Liam Armstrong, collided with Poston. It was a hard, but legal, hit. Armstrong gained control of the puck. Cheers erupted from their table.

"Isn't Poston that Florida player who took out the Goshawks' goalie?" Luke was doing his best to appear invested in the game.

"Very good," Jessica cooed, batting her eyelashes.

Seconds later, Armstrong scored.

"Go Goshawks," Sage screamed. "They're not going down without a fight," She muttered, when Ryan and Finn sandwiched Chucky ... hard.

"Ouch. That had to hurt," Patty said, retrieving a slice of pizza. "But he deserved it," she added, picking off the mushrooms.

"I didn't know hockey was such a brutal sport," Luke said, now watching with true intent.

All three girls turned and stared at him, mouths agape.

"Luke," Jessica spoke first. "You've been bartending for the whole hockey season. How can you just have come to that conclusion?"

"Sports nights are busy. When I'm working, I don't have time to watch the game."

"What about when you're not working?" Patty sipped on her beer as she waited for his reply.

"On nights I'm not bartending, I'm studying, or working on my dad's ranch."

The girls just nodded with understanding.

—◆◦◆—

The third period began with lots of hard hits from both teams, most when the referees were looking the other way ... until late in the third.

"No Way!" Patty pointed to the TV, as a two-minute penalty was called on the Goshawks.

"NOW, the ref's paying attention?" Jessica grumbled.

With their team shorthanded, all four friends were riveted to the action.

"Wowser, our captain just made a shorty," Jessica cried out.

"And a hat-trick," Sage yelled. Grabbing Luke's ball cap off his head. She tossed it at the screen.

Everyone at their table stood and cheered. In a moment of excitement, Sage turned, wrapping her arms around Luke in a bear hug. Luke returned the affection, holding on just a little too long. To Sage, the hug felt warm, familiar, and just a bit too intimate. She pulled away, her eyes meeting Jessica's icy glare.

Moments later, Patty screamed, "Florida is letting out the Hounds-of-Hell!"

"I don't even want to know," Luke said. With his reclaimed cap back on his head, he took his seat, looking at Jessica. Instead of her usual snappy commentary, Jessica sat silently, drinking her beer.

Once more everyone focused on the flatscreen, as they watched Hunter along with the rest of the Goshawks defending the net, as if they were knights protecting their kingdom. It worked. When the buzzer rang ending the period, the Goshawks won with a final score of 5 to 2.

Cheers along with high-fives and clinking beer mugs echoed in the bar as the screen showed the triumphant Goshawks lining up to pay respects to their goalie.

Jessica pulled her phone out of her pocket. "Everyone together for a celebratory selfie," she said, as she motioned Luke to get closer to Sage. When he obliged, Jessica leaned in, smirking as she took the photo.

"Can you send me a copy?" Luke asked.

While Jessica and Luke were busy with the photo exchange, Sage scrolled through her phone, clicking on a number. She then turned her attention to Luke. "Thank you so much for driving us to the bar. Do you feel up to taking Patty and Jessica home?" She was confident Luke could drive, as he'd switched from beer to water after the first period.

Luke looked confused. "I drove you all here. I'll drive you all home."

Sage's phone pinged. "It looks like my Uber is outside. I had such a fun night, but I have to get going. You all stay and enjoy the rest of the evening." Sage gathered her things, gave Patty and Jessica a quick hug, and left.

"What was that all about?" Luke asked.

"Sometimes Hunter calls right after a game," Jessica said, her voice flat, with a tinge of spiteful anger.

"Sage is friends with the Goshawks pretty boy goalie?" Luke's eyebrows narrowed as reality hit hard.

"More than friends." Jessica continued to stab an absent Sage's back with verbal daggers. "She's been texting with him for weeks. You'll have to have her tell you all about it the next time you get together."

Luke tossed a handful of twenties on the table, fished out his keys, and growled, "Let's go."

Chapter 15

Missed Communications

April 17th [Game 1 of the First Round of Playoffs: Postgame]
The scent of the night air, heavy with a hint of sea salt from Portland's harbor, seeped through the partially opened window of Hunter's apartment. A muted hum of the city lingered in the background. Switching on his stereo before walking to the kitchen, he filled a glass with ice.

Reaching into the bar, he retrieved a dusty, coveted bottle of 25-year-old Macallan single malt scotch ... a gift from his captain on Hunter's twenty-first birthday. Reading the label, his lips twitched into a smile at the thought of the bottle's contents now aging him by three years.

Moving into the living room, Hunter eased into his favorite leather recliner, the glass of scotch in hand. He was still dressed in his post-game attire, a crisp white shirt tucked into tailored pants. The tie and suit jacket discarded on his bed earlier.

His fingers traced his phone's screen, hesitating before clicking Sage's number in his contacts. It was past midnight in Maine, but an hour earlier in South Dakota. He knew she liked to work at night and hoped he wasn't calling too late.

"Sage," he greeted. His voice roughened by the intensity of the game and subsequent celebrations.

"Hunter? You're up late, breaking playoff curfew already?" Sage's voice fluttered through the phone, a touch of surprise in her tone.

"Got back from the bar before midnight." He took a slow sip of his drink. The dark amber liquid warmth spread through his chest, loosening his tensed muscles. "Wanted to talk to you. That okay?"

"Of course. I was hoping you'd call."

"I'm not disturbing you, am I?"

"No, of course not. I was just editing today's photo shoot." Her voice lowered as she asked, "How is Olaf? The hit was sickening to watch. Of course, they had to replay it over and over in slow-motion."

Hunter's sigh was heavy. "He's concussed, but it's minor. He's got a thick head. The Goshawks' doctor said he could be out for a week. Right now, they have him listed as day-to-day."

"Wow, a week. Hope he doesn't miss all the first-round playoff games."

"The coach is confident Olaf will be cleared to travel with us when we play the Barracudas in Florida. If we sweep the first round, he should be good to sit on the bench for game four. I just hate the thought of winning our first playoff game on Florida ice."

"I agree. Their fans can be dangerous. I remember last year when they lost in the playoffs. The winning team had to run for cover from the fans tossing debris on the ice."

Hunter laughed. "Ya, I remember. That's why I never remove my mask until I get into the locker room when we play in the Barracudas' arena."

"So, who's going to be your backup goalie while Olaf is out?"

"They're bringing up the starting goalie from our farm team. He's no Snowman, but he's got a good record."

"And you?" Sage's question filled with concern. "I saw your goaltending coach holding you back from joining the fight."

Hunter let out a shallow laugh, tinged with weariness. "In all the years I've played hockey, I've never fought, nor wanted to."

Sage's response was immediate. "Then why the change now? Why are you allowing the Barracudas' players to provoke you?"

The clink of ice swirling in his glass gave evidence of his deep thoughts. "I don't know." More silence as he gathered his words. "Olaf, on the ice, flat on his face ... I just snapped."

"You've been doing a lot of that lately," Sage whispered.

Ever since I met you, Hunter thought, instead, he remained silent.

"The coach looked furious," Sage replied. "I've never seen him chomp his gum so hard, or his face turn so red. Was he mad at the Barracudas for what they did to Olaf, not to mention Chucky's sneaky goal? Or was he upset his players were fighting?"

Hunter paused, taking a sip of his scotch. "Both," he said, taking another sip, letting the liquid warm his throat and soften his words. "Before the game, Coach Harrison told us to play hard and smart, warning us not to get caught up in their drama of chirps and cheap shots. But you know how it is ... emotions run high in playoff hockey, especially against a team like the Barracudas."

The silence that followed was uncomfortable, filled only by the faint sound of music floating from Hunter's stereo. They had covered the game, but one question still lingered, one he wasn't sure he was ready to ask.

"Sage, did you watch the game alone?" Hunter's voice held a level of casualness that didn't quite meet his eyes as he took another sip from his drink. The strong liquid was the perfect antidote to the mixture of fatigue and restlessness brewing within him.

"No. I watched it at the bar with Jessica and Patty." Sage's voice filtered through the phone. "Hold on a minute. I need to turn off my computer so I can give you my full attention." After a brief pause, she said, "Sorry about that. I'm back."

Hunter gathered the courage to put forth the question he'd been yearning to ask all night. "And anyone else?" Hunter probed, an underlying intensity marking his words.

Unlike Hunter, Sage's response came quick and to the point. "Luke was with us too."

The mention of another man's name ignited a flame of jealousy in Hunter's chest. "Luke?"

"He's been our friend since grade school. He works at O'Sullivan's. Luke had the day off, so he joined us for a night of hockey at the bar ... as a spectator instead of a bartender," she clarified. Sage's light-hearted response made her seem oblivious to the tension coiling in Hunter's tone.

"A friend," Hunter echoed, the word leaving a bitter taste in his mouth. "Did he enjoy the game?"

"I guess so." Sage sounded taken aback. "He's not really into hockey, but he appeared to enjoy himself."

"I bet he did."

"What's that supposed to mean? Why the sudden interest in who I watch hockey with?"

"Just curious." His response came out clipped, the silence that followed resonating with unspoken accusations. "Jessica posted a photo on the Goshawks Facebook page tonight. All of you huddled together. Luke had his arm around you. He was looking at you as if he were that creepy vampire from that 'Twilight' movie."

"Now that is too funny. I would never have taken you as a Twilight fan."

"I'm not." Hunter replied ... without an ounce of humor.

"Hold on, let me check it out," Sage muttered.

Hunter waited, his fingers tracing the rim of his now almost empty glass. The ringing from the crystal danced around the living room. Seconds ticked away like hours.

Sage came back on, her voice heavy. "Hunter, that picture. I think she took it at the end of the game ... only because we were all smiling. I remember we were celebrating the Goshawks win." With hesitation and frustration in her voice, she continued, "I'm sure that's what Jessica is referring to in the caption, 'Everyone Scored.' That's just Jessica, being Jessica."

Hunter let out a doubting, muffled, "Harrumph."

Sage added, "Luke drove us all to the bar from my place. But the minute the game was over, and you left the ice, I left too ... alone." Her tone reflected her irritation. "I took an Uber home, so I wouldn't miss your call ... if you decided to call, that is."

The relief flooding Hunter was brief. Replaced by a strange restlessness. He remained silent.

"Are you okay?" Sage asked.

"Just tired," Hunter replied, his voice a tad gruff. He finished his drink, the sharp taste of scotch, a harsh contrast to the sweet concern in Sage's voice. "It's been a long night."

"You should get some rest."

"I will," he responded, but his mind was far from sleep. It was tangled in a web of thoughts; jealousy and longing tugging at him mingled with concerns about Olaf and his coach's ire.

"Oh, and please call whenever you want to talk."

"Not sure if I'll get time with our busy schedule and all."

"Okay. I just wanted you to know that I'm always here for you."

Disconnecting the call, Hunter sank further into the recliner. The silent apartment felt too big, too empty. Thoughts of Sage with another man clouded his mind, echoing louder in the quiet. The glass sat heavy in his hand, the remnants of the scotch an echo of the turbulence within him. He braced himself for a sleepless night.

Chapter 16
An Offer She Can't Refuse

April 23rd [Game 4 of the First Round of Playoffs]

The afternoon sun spilled through the windows of the farmhouse, casting long, dappled shadows across the wooden floor. Sage bustled about the kitchen with her mother. It was a little under an hour before the fourth game of the first round of playoffs. Although her parents were not hockey enthusiasts, they had agreed to indulge her for the day. Sage did her best to explain the importance of this game. The Goshawks had won the first two games in this round, but they had lost game three in a brutal overtime.

"I still don't understand why this one is so different from the others?" Lilly was busy shredding Cheddar in the cheese dip, the rich, tangy scent wafting through the room.

"Mom, how many times do I need to go over this with you?" Sage's tone had the sting of frustration."

"Humor me again. I remember you like the player who wears the extra padding. Has a prettier helmet. Oh, and he moves in front of the net with a bigger stick than his teammates."

"He's a goalie, Mom. He's called a goalie." Sage shook her head and laughed. "Anyway, right now, the Goshawks are only one game ahead. Each round of the playoffs comprises seven games. The first team that wins four games gets to advance to the next round." Sage stopped chopping veggies, waving her paring knife around to emphasize her point.

"Be careful with that knife, Missy."

Sage turned back to chopping the veggies. "The importance of this game is twofold ... if the Goshawks win today, they have home ice advantage for the next game. If they win that game, they win the first round of the playoffs. Every team wants to win a playoff round in an arena filled with their fans."

Sage's mom looked at the stove's clock. "I wonder what's keeping your father?"

"I hope he gets home soon, so he won't miss any of the game."

"Honey, I have to ask. Why aren't you watching the games with your friends anymore? It's not good for you to stay home alone all the time."

"I'm not alone all the time. I work."

"You know what I mean."

"I'm sorry. I don't mean to be so snarky. I just had a bit of a fallout with Jessica," Sage confessed, avoiding her mother's inquisitive gaze.

"Oh dear," Lilly murmured, a worried wrinkle appearing between her brows. She moved towards Sage, laying a comforting hand on her arm. "And what about your goalie friend?" She continued, "You haven't mentioned him all week. That's a record for you."

"It's ... complicated ... he's been busy with the playoffs and all." Sage ached at the mention of Hunter. The ghost of him haunted her. She sighed, brushing a stray lock of hair from her face. The last time they spoke, his voice had been deep and rough, his words accusing.

Sage could only imagine how down Hunter must be after the overtime defeat in game three. He always blamed himself when the Goshawks lost. The lack of communication from Hunter only added to her melancholy. "I was hoping he would call," Sage whispered.

The conversation fell into a comfortable silence, broken only by the sounds of their culinary efforts. Outside, the wind rustled the leaves of the big tree next to the house. Bringing with it the familiar scent of the farmland through the open windows—a mix of mowed grass, and damp soil from a recent hard rain.

Lilly was putting the cheese dip in the oven, as Sage covered the veggie tray, when the distinctive creak of the screen door echoed through the kitchen. Sage turned around, her heart skipping a beat at the sight of her dad walking in, trailed by two unexpected guests—Luke and Jessica.

"Luke stopped by to talk about purchasing one of our steers for his dad. I invited him and Jessica to watch the game with us." Jim hung his cowboy hat on the hook in the mudroom, oblivious to the tension radiating from the three friends.

Sage watched the scene unfold with a blend of surprise and disappointment. Jessica's grip on Luke's arm tightened as they crossed the threshold into the kitchen. Her friend's defiant show of possession left Sage feeling uneasy. She hadn't been in contact with either of them since watching the first game of the playoffs at the bar. Sage had held back from texting Jessica about why she posted the group photo to the Goshawks Facebook page, with the suggestive comment, knowing Hunter would see the post.

"Hi you two. Long time no see." Lilly wiped her hands on a kitchen towel, giving a worried sideways glance to Sage, before adding, "It's so nice to have you over."

Luke offered a weak smile in response to Sage's mom's warm welcome. "Your kitchen always smells so good, Lilly." As he spoke, he removed Jessica's hand from his arm.

The blush rising to Luke's cheeks didn't go unnoticed by Sage.

"I hope we're not intruding. Jim was very insistent that we join you." Jessica's words fell in short nervous clips.

"Don't be silly, dear. You know you're always welcome," Lilly said.

Jim Larson turned from washing his hands in the sink. Directing his attention to Sage. "Why don't you get everyone some lemonade and head out to the back porch? We'll call you when the game starts. I'll keep your mom company."

Sage poured three glasses with ice and lemonade, all the while wondering how her dad could not sense the tension in the room. Once out on the screened-in porch, Jessica and Luke sat on one side of the table. Sage placed the glasses of lemonade down. Pulling out a chair, taking a seat on the opposite side, a look of confusion etched her face.

Breaking the silence, Sage asked, "Luke, shouldn't you be working at the bar, being it's a Sunday afternoon playoff game?"

Luke grimaced. "I quit last week. Finals are coming up and I need to focus."

Before Sage could respond, Jessica cut in. "Geez, Sage. How could you forget Luke graduates in two weeks? Guess your invitation to his graduation party must have gotten lost in the mail." Jessica reached out, fingers turning into talons around Luke's hand.

Luke grumbled as he jerked his hand from Jessica's, wrapping his fingers around the icy glass in front of him. "There's no grad party. My dad doesn't believe in them." He took a sip of lemonade. "The second I receive my diploma, I'm heading to Montana to check out a prize stallion my dad's interested in purchasing."

Jessica's eyes widened, her hands falling to her lap. "Wait, what? You never told me that."

Luke shrugged, his steely gaze drifting to Sage, "Plans change."

Ignoring Jessica's hurt expression, Sage managed a smile. "Congratulations, Luke. Sorry your summer is going to be so busy, but working full time alongside your father is a big step."

Striking like a snake, Jessica launched her next attack. "So, Sage, are you planning to spend your summer with your online lover boy?"

Luke's eyes flicked to Sage, brows narrowing, temples throbbing.

Annoyance flared in Sage as she glared at Jessica. "What's your problem? You, of all people, know Hunter is a professional hockey player. I'm just a Goshawks' fan. Hunter contacts me only to thank me for my supportive comments. Our communications may be friendly, but I don't consider us even friends."

Jessica's smirk faded into a scowl. Before she could respond, Sage turned to Luke, a challenging smile playing on her lips. "So, Luke, when did you and Jessica become an item?"

Luke blinked in surprise before stuttering, "Wha...what? No, we're just friends. My dad recently hired Jessica to train his barrel racers."

As the silence settled on them again, they were saved by Sage's mother calling from the kitchen. "Time to get ready for the game. Come on in, everyone." She sounded cheerful, a stark contrast to the tense standoff on the porch.

The buzz of the game emanating from the television greeted the trio as they entered the family room. A plethora of snacks scattered across the coffee table, sending off a tempting aroma of spicy cheese. Jim was already nestled in his comfy chair, a low hum of a snore escaping his lips. Lilly was engaged in her knitting, the soft clicking of the needles providing a rhythmic backdrop to the pregame commentary.

Jessica, Luke, and Sage squeezed into the small couch, leaving Luke trapped in the middle. A surge of electricity ran up Sage's arm as it pressed against Luke's. The heat of his body permeated through her clothes. His scent, a comforting mix of hay and horse, calmed her nerves.

Sage observed how Luke evaded Jessica's grasp, instead extending his arms across the back of the couch, creating a loose barrier between them. The occasional gentle brush of his fingertips against Sage's neck made her body flutter. She breathed in the essence of lemonade still clinging to his fingers.

The first period of the game saw the Goshawks scoring two impressive goals: the first during a power play, the second a quick shorty. The girls cheered at the stellar performance, their shouts echoing around the room, jolting Sage's dad from his slumber.

By the second intermission, the scoreboard read 5 to 0 in favor of the Goshawks. The taste of impending victory was sweet. Jessica leaned towards Sage and shouted over the noise of the game, "Looks like Hunter is heading for a shutout!" The wide grin on Sage's face, coupled with the high-five across Luke's chest, was all the girls needed to start mending their friendship.

Near the end of the third period, Lilly woke her husband. "Come on, dear. Let's go for a walk and leave the kids to their game." The parental presence evaporated from the room. Luke slipped out to refill his glass of lemonade.

Alone on the couch, Jessica turned to Sage. "I'm sorry for being so bitchy." Her tone filled with sincerity.

"We all have moments we regret." Sage moved closer to Jessica, wrapping her arms around her.

Luke, standing in the doorway, watched them. Upon entering the room, he took the empty seat in Jim's chair.

The game ended on a triumphant note for the Goshawks, the final goal triggering an outpouring of joy. Olaf was the first to clear the bench. Skating hard towards Hunter, they embraced in a goalie bear hug. The rest of the Goshawks followed the Snowman, heaping physical and verbal affection on their starting goalie. As expected, the Barracudas' fans showed their disappointment by launching filled water bottles, popcorn boxes, and beer cups onto the ice directed at the Goshawks.

"That's just wrong," Luke muttered, shaking his head.

"I thought you didn't care about hockey?" Jessica jabbed playfully.

"I care about sportsmanship," Luke shot back, lifting his glass towards the girls. "Especially in defeat." The air was filled with the aftermath of the game, the muted cheers from the television, the sticky sweet smell of victory, and the undercurrents of something else, something more personal and complex.

The post-game celebration on the television faded into background noise as Sage's phone pinged. She opened it, hoping to see a message from Hunter. Instead, she was met with a text from the Goshawks Marketing Department. With caution, she began reading.

Jessica, drawn by her friend's sudden silence, wore a puzzled expression. What's going on?"

"I just got a job offer ... from the Goshawks."

"What? Read it to us," Jessica commanded.

"It's from the Goshawks Marketing Dept."

"OMG, what does it say?" Jessica reached for the phone. "If you won't read it out loud, I will." In a deep voice, Jessica began. "Hi Miss Larson. Our team photographer has been called away on a family emergency. He will be unavailable for the next game. Hunter Griffin showed us your photo gallery website. He assured us you were also an ardent hockey enthusiast. We are offering you an assignment to photograph the players arriving from Florida tonight as they depart the team plane.

We also need some casual photos of the team over the next couple of days, and of course, to cover game five of the playoffs."

Sage took the phone from Jessica, with a quiver to her voice, she continued reading where Jessica left off. "We realize this is a last-minute request and hope five-thousand dollars will be sufficient compensation. We will also cover all your expenses, including a place to stay, meals, and, of course, transportation."

"You've made the big time." Jessica hugged Sage.

"But wait, there's more," Sage said. "If you agree to our terms, please sign the attached contract and the NDA. As soon as we get both signed, we'll send a limo service within the hour. He will drive you to the Brookings airport. In anticipation of you accepting this assignment, we chartered a plane to take you to Portland. Time is of the essence. We are doing our best to coordinate your arrival, to get you here before the team's plane touches down. Sincerely, Margret VanAlen, Head of Goshawks Marketing."

Opening the attachments, with trembling fingers, Sage electronically signed both documents. Dropping her phone on the couch, the girls stood, squealing in excitement, hands clasped together as they bounced on the balls of their feet. Giddy with the sudden turn of events, they rushed outside to share the news with Sage's parents.

———◆———

Luke sat silent in the chair, left alone, forgotten. He felt the weight of being abandoned. The details of the contract ricocheted, as if they were bullets gone astray in his mind. He felt like a horse had kicked his stomach. A surge of jealousy coursed through his veins. He'd made peace with being in Sage's friend zone, but the thought of her being alone with a successful, handsome hockey player twisted a knot in his gut. Being a good sport was one thing, but the prospect of Sage spending time alone with her hero goalie was just too much.

Looking at the glass of lemonade, he wished it was a bottle of vodka. Sage was on the cusp of a thrilling adventure, an opportunity to combine her love for hockey and photography. The realization of what he was feeling was undeniable—it wasn't merely friendship he felt for Sage, but something deeper, something more intense. His gaze shifted to her phone on the couch. It too was abandoned. The screen was now dark, a silent witness to the abrupt change in Sage's life—and his own.

Chapter 17

A Familiar Face in the Crowd

April 23rd

The engines' thrum of the Goshawks' private jet was still in Hunter's ears as the plane touched down at Atlantic Aviation. Portland's private terminal tucked away far from the legitimate press and the prying paparazzi. Inside the cabin, the energy was a mix of exhaustion and relief, as players retrieved their bags from the overhead stowage compartments. The victory in Florida had been hard-fought, but now the weariness of the game had settled in.

Hunter was bone-tired, sore, and hungry, but a sense of satisfaction chased away his fatigue. The Goshawks were one step closer to the ultimate victory. Game five was riding on his shoulders. It was a heavy weight to carry. He could feel it in every fiber of his being.

The plane's passenger door opened with a hydraulic hiss. Hunter's seatmate, Ryan, clapped him on the back. "Come on, Hunter. Let's get home."

Hunter looked up in acknowledgment but stayed in his window seat. "I'm right on your heels. Just need to send off a quick text." Since leaving the Florida arena, he'd left several text and voice messages for Sage. Now that they had landed, he checked for a reply. Nothing. He couldn't blame her. The last time he'd contacted her was the disastrous late-night call, after the first game of the playoffs.

Leaning his head back, eyes closed, Hunter knew he had screwed things up royally. In his defense, he had to keep his head in the game. As a hockey fan, he hoped Sage would understand. Right now, the Goshawks and the playoffs had to have his undivided attention. Still, the thought of Sage in the arms of Luke caused him to doubt his decision to not fight harder for her. Shrugging, he stuffed the phone into his suit pocket.

The captain was the first off, followed by the rest of the Goshawks players. Olaf lingered at the front of the plane, his huge body blocking the exit door. "Come on Hunter, if you want me to drop you off at your apartment." He yawned. "It's been a long night and I need my beauty sleep."

"I'm just getting my bag. Go on, I promise I'm right behind you." Hunter stood, slinging the strap of his carry-on over his shoulder. A sudden breeze swirled around his face as he followed the Snowman through the door. The thick misty air left the taste of salt on his lips. It was good to be home.

Bringing his ball cap low on his head, nearly covering his eyes, he descended the ramp. The sudden chill of the night air contrasted sharply with his heated skin.

"Hunter?"

The sound stopped him dead in his tracks, a shock to his system, like sitting in an ice bath after a long practice. It was a voice he knew, a voice he thought he would never hear again ... certainly not here.

Looking up, for a moment he forgot how to breathe. There she was. Sage, standing on the tarmac a few yards from the plane's steps. Camera in hand. Even in the harsh runway lights, her eyes shone bright with delight.

"Sage?" he called. His voice filled with disbelief. When she nodded and waved, he dropped his carry-on, running straight for her.

Her laugh rang out, soft and warm, as her camera clicked away. "Hi, Hunter."

Upon reaching her, he lifted Sage off her feet, twirling her around, feeling a joy he hadn't known he'd been missing. "What are you doing here?" he exclaimed, setting her down but keeping her close.

"Working," she replied, holding up her camera, her smile teasing. "Surprised?"

"You have no idea."

A nearby chuckle made Hunter turn. Olaf was watching them, wearing a quizzical expression. "Hey Griffin, planning to introduce us to your lady friend?"

Hunter shot him a glare, but Sage's laughter defused the situation. "These are my teammates," he told her, motioning to Olaf, Ryan, and the two rookies who had gathered around. "Guys, this is Sage."

"Is this the infamous photographer?" Ryan asked, looking impressed. "Hunter's been singing your praises."

Sage blushed. "I'm flattered."

"You should be," Axel teased, nudging Hunter. "He never shuts up about you."

Hunter's eyes looked upward, but he couldn't suppress his smile. "Enough, guys. We're all tired."

"And hungry," Olaf added.

"We've had a long flight. Everyone needs to get home. Now!" Coach Harrison growled, as he appeared behind the group on catlike feet. Without a single goodbye, the four Goshawks rushed to their vehicles.

"Thanks coach, there went my ride," Hunter lamented.

The coach looked at Sage holding an expensive camera, standing next to Hunter. "Honey, I don't know how you got past security, especially with a camera, but this area is reserved for the Goshawks."

Before Hunter could intercede, Margret stepped forward, wearing her professional smile. "Stan. Let me introduce you to Sage Larson. The Goshawks just hired her to take over for our photographer." She walked next to Sage, draping a protective arm around her waist.

"What happened to Nikki?" Coach Harrison kept looking from Sage to Hunter. His frown deepening.

"His father died. The funeral is in Italy." Margret said, as the coach nodded in understanding.

"Sage is going to photograph the players during their practice, workout sessions, and some candid shots tomorrow. Most important, if Nikki's not back in time, she is going to photograph game five. We all know how important it is to have a competent photographer in our arena for that game."

"What's their connection?" Coach grumbled, waving his hand between Sage and Hunter.

"Thank goodness Hunter recommended Sage to us; otherwise we would be hard-pressed to find someone with her talent who also knows all the Goshawks players on such short notice." Margret squeezed Sage's waist, then took a step away.

Hunter frowned as he turned to Sage. "You're taking Nikki's place?"

Sage looked to Hunter with a questioning stare. "Wait a minute, I thought you recommended me?"

"I shared your gallery with Margret on one of our flights. I had no idea she hired you." Hunter's mind raced. Sage, here, with him, for the next few days? The possibilities were endless. If not for the coach's steely gaze, he'd be dancing around the tarmac.

Coach Harrison, a scowl plastered on his face, advanced towards Hunter, stopping mid-stride. Standing statuesque, he turned to Margret. "Please tell me this is not 'The Sage.' The Florida scoreboard Sage?"

Margret smiled, batting her eyelashes as she tilted her head slightly.

The coach rubbed hands over his face as if to wash away the memory of that night. Turning his attention to Hunter once more, he growled, "Griffin, this young lady is here on official Goshawks business. She is not here for your amusement. I expect you to keep your distance."

Hunter's body tensed as he moved closer to Sage. He was about to say something to the coach when Sage took two steps towards the burly man with her right arm extended.

"Coach Stan Harrison, it is such an honor to meet you." It seemed like a lifetime for the Goshawks' coach to reach out and reciprocate the handshake. "I've followed your career. You've done an amazing job of bringing an expansion team to the playoffs in just five seasons." The coach put his other hand on top of Sage's as she continued, "There would be no Goshawks without you." Her hard stare into his eyes assured the sincerity of her words.

"I promise you; I am more than a name on a piece of paper. As a professional photographer, I take my assignments seriously. As seriously as I take my deep love for hockey. I have a great respect for all the Goshawks' players and the organization."

Sage mirrored the coach by placing her left hand over his. She took another step forward. Just inside his personal blue crease, Sage appeared to stand taller than her five-foot-four inches.

"I would never do anything to prevent Hunter from winning the next game. Please, trust me when I say there is no one outside of the Goshawks organization that wants your players to kiss the cup more than I do." Sage made the coach an offer. "Let's make a deal. I will send you my daily shots. If at any time you are displeased with my work, I will return my paycheck and take the next commercial flight back to South Dakota."

"You're from South Dakota?" The coach quizzed.

"Oh, for goodness' sake, Stan," Margret piped in. "Go home to your family." Looking around, she noticed they were the only ones standing in the parking lot. "I'll make sure Hunter gets home, and Sage gets to the hotel." She pointed to his pretty young wife, arms crossed, tapping the toe of her Louboutin's as she leaned next to the coach's Land Rover.

"I look forward to viewing your work," Harrison said to Sage. To Hunter, he added, "You still have a curfew." With that, he turned and trotted to his car.

"Come on," Margret said. "Sage, I'll take you to your hotel."

"I want to get Sage settled into her room." Hunter shouted over his shoulder as he jogged back to the plane's steps to retrieve his bag.

"That boy is going to be the death of me." Margret laughed. When Hunter returned, she said, "Hunter, put your belongings in the trunk. I'll drop you and Sage at the Regency and have my driver come back to take you home at midnight sharp."

"Thanks Margret," Sage replied.

The soft leather backseat of Margret's vehicle held a quiet tension. Hunter sat next to Sage, their hands brushing, a contact that sent waves of anticipation coursing through his veins. The city lights of Portland streamed past them, creating a soft, moving painting behind Sage. He found himself entranced, not by the cityscape, but by the young woman beside him.

The drive to the hotel was short, filled with an anxious silence. Sage's presence beside him was overwhelming. Margret's driver, Lionel, took a corner sharp, causing Sage to lean into him, her delicate hand resting on his chest. The whiff of lavender from her hair sent his senses into overload. Even though Hunter's mind raced, he was at a loss for words.

"Sorry," she said, pulling away.

"Don't be." Hunter smiled.

Hunter watched as Sage pressed her face near the window as they arrived at the Regency. Twinkling lights adorned the trees around the majestic brick building. The grandeur of the hotel was a fitting home-away-from-home for Sage.

"Oh. My. This is magical." The words emerged from Sage in a whisper.

"Just like you." Hunter could not help but voice his thoughts aloud.

Margret took a quick glance at the time on her phone. Turning to Hunter, she said, "It's 10:30 on the dot. My driver has your number on speed-dial. I expect you to be in the lobby at midnight. Not a second later."

"Or what? I turn into a pumpkin?"

"Oh, worse, much worse. If you keep my driver waiting ... even one minute ... I promise I'll come up and drag you out. Don't test me." Digging around in her purse, she pulled out an envelope, handing it to Sage. "Here's your keycard. The room number and Internet password are written on the envelope. The room is on the top floor, with a beautiful view." She then looked at Hunter. "Yes. I have a duplicate keycard. I don't make veiled threats. Now get out, you two."

Lionel popped the trunk. Hunter and Sage retrieved her luggage, laptop, and photo equipment.

"My driver will take you to Hunter's tomorrow morning, Sage. We need you to get some candid shots on his day off. Have fun kids," Margret said. Lifting her phone and pointing to the time before driving away.

Entering Sage's suite, Hunter set the suitcases on the floor as Sage placed her laptop carrier and camera bag on top of the dresser. Hunter sat, bouncing on the edge of the king size bed. "You're going to sleep like a princess tonight." Hunter undid his tie. After a neat fold, he placed it into the inside pocket of his suit jacket.

"I feel like I've been given the royal treatment since I left South Dakota."
Sage sat next to Hunter. She nudged his shoulder and asked, "Something I've
always wondered about. Why do all hockey players dress up in suits and ties?"

"It's in our contracts. It's been a part of the collective bargaining agreement
since the mid-nineties. Dress codes are an important part of professional hockey. It sets us apart from other sports. Makes us special." His mischievous grin
extended to his eyes.

"I agree. Hockey players are very special ... especially the goalies." Her smile
matched his.

"I am so hungry." The rumble in Hunter's stomach punctuated his statement. He took out his phone, pulling up the room service menu. Before
entering an order, he turned to Sage. "You're not a vegan, are you? Not that
there's anything wrong with that."

"Hunter, my daddy owns a Black Angus cattle ranch. I can guarantee that
I'm a born and bred carnivore." Sage chomped her teeth at him.

"Any food allergies or dislikes?" He grinned as she shook her head, no. "So,
you don't mind if I order for us?"

"Just make it quick. As Margret says, time is ticking."

Hunter placed the online order with a note indicating a big tip if it arrived
ASAP. He watched as Sage opened her suitcase, filling the dresser drawers with
several black shirts and jeans. "Nice assortment of color." He couldn't resist
teasing.

"It's a photographer thing. I always wear black. That way, I can blend into
the background." She did her best to conceal a handful of underwear, which
she stuffed in the top drawer.

Hunter watched her every movement. He had only seen photos of her
online, and most of them had been cryptic portraits with half her face covered
with a camera. The closest he had seen her body was the picture Jessica had
posted to Facebook, in the clutches of Luke ... the other man.

His dark mood dissolving as he watched her leaning over, retrieving more
items. Feeling like a creeper, he took her in from head to toe. Her long hair
appeared to have been kissed by the sun, with its various shades of blonde. He
was surprised at her petite frame, but then he remembered how tall she looked
standing up to the coach. As a goalie, he couldn't help but notice how she
moved with ease and grace. Everything she did was done with a purpose.

Sage turned, leaning on the dresser, a blush coloring her cheeks. Calling Hunter
out, her words laced with a touch of humor. "You're looking at me with the same

expression my friend wears when he is examining a prize broodmare. Do you want to check my teeth?" She smiled a toothy grin.

"It's hard not to admire beauty." Sporting a smirk, he continued to devour her with his gaze.

Sage positioned herself in front of Hunter, putting her hands on his shoulders. In return, he placed his hands on her tiny waist. "Hunter," she began, her voice a soft melody that sent chills down his spine, "I hope you know how much this opportunity means to me. How much you mean to me?"

The sincerity in her voice made Hunter's heart skip a beat. He looked at her with a mixture of wonder and longing. "I should be the one thanking you, Sage. You are ... you are even more beautiful than I imagined," Hunter said, his voice thick with emotions. Their faces were so close he could smell her minty breath. More than anything, he yearned to taste her lips. Just as he leaned in, three sharp knocks on the door broke the magical moment.

"It can't be midnight already?" A frown etched on Sage's lips.

"Room Service," the loud voice preceded another three knocks.

With great reluctance, Hunter moved Sage to the side, adjusting his clothing as he opened the door.

A young man rolled a cart into the room, filled with beverages and covered trays.

"I'll take it from here." Hunter reached into his pocket, giving the server a generous tip. Showing the young man out, he hung the Do Not Disturb sign on the doorknob.

"What did you order?" Sage quizzed, "it smells delicious."

Hunter removed the metal dome from two of the larger dishes. "I wish it was more, but I like to eat light as it's so late."

"I'm sure it will be perfect." Sage sat down in the chair at the corner table.

After placing the food on the table, he sat on the chair next to her. "Hope Lobster Stew is okay. Plus, they bake their bread fresh." Hunter's hunger overtook his manners, tearing off a hunk of bread. Shoving it into his mouth, he realized his error in ordering, as the pungent garlic butter penetrated his taste buds. "Crap."

He watched Sage. With a knowing smile, in solidarity, she shoveled a piece of garlic bread into her mouth. Closing her eyes, she let out a low, pleasurable murmur. "This is so good." She then dove her spoon into the steaming Lobster Stew. Again, she closed her eyes and moaned. "Oh my gosh, I am having a party in my mouth."

"If you like this, I guarantee you'll enjoy dessert." Hunter teased, eyebrows wiggling.

"It's hard to imagine anything tasting better than this."

Hunter's smile widened watching her tongue flick over her lips in anticipation.

"What is this?" Sage asked, holding the tall, chilled glass filled with slices of green.

"Cucumber and mint water. Olaf introduced it to me. Now I can't get enough. It's my favorite late-night drink." *Next to Scotch*, he thought. Taking a sip again, he watched Sage mirror his actions. "So, what do you think?"

"I think I can't wait to get back home and make a huge pitcher of this for my mom and dad."

When Sage's bowl was empty, Hunter placed the last dish in front of her. "I remember you mentioned chocolate was top of your favorites list." He watched as her eyes grew large with disbelief as he lifted the dome cover, revealing a small decadent chocolate lava cake.

Without hesitating, she dug a fork into the middle, the dark, sticky lava flowing from within. "I think I died and went to heaven." After taking a bite, she concurred, "Yippers, I just visited heaven."

"That good?" Hunter was having too much fun, just watching her enjoy the meal.

"Where's yours?" Sage looked at the tray, realizing the last plate was in front of her.

"My trainer is going to kill me if he found out I was just watching you eat dessert." Hunter reached over, capturing a stray piece of chocolate from the corner of her lip. He then sucked its contents from his finger. "That is good."

For a long moment, the world seemed to slip away as they stared into each other's eyes. Hunter was getting lost, looking deep into her soul, as his phone began vibrating on the table in a steady stream of pings.

"I gotta go." He watched as Sage nodded in understanding. "I'll see you at my place in the morning."

"I hope I'm awake before Margret's driver comes to pick me up. I still have about an hour of editing tonight's photos before I can crawl into bed."

The phone pinged again. "I'll get out of here and let you work. Don't stay up too late." Hunter turned and walked to the door. Hoping she would follow. Hoping she would tell him to stay. Yet, all hope was dashed when he looked back to see the screen bright on her laptop.

Chapter 18
Unspoken Desires

April 24th

Hunter's apartment door opened wide, revealing the goalie wearing only his black spandex gym shorts. Sage stood frozen in the doorway, eyes tracing the lines of his defined abs. The vision of his athletic form, combined with his tousled hair, rendered him both irresistibly boyish and masculine.

Hunter blinked, rubbing the sleep from his eyes, a smirk curled his lips. "Enjoying the view?"

Sage feigned innocence, a playful smile dancing on her lips. "Just admiring the ... um, architecture of the place." Her eyes darted up to his, as he pulled on his Goshawks t-shirt.

"Well, come on in and get a better view." Hunter turned and padded barefoot into the kitchen. Pulling two cups from the cupboard. "You do drink coffee?"

"My mom says if I was cut, I'd bleed coffee." Sage stood in the foyer, taking in the view. The furnishings were sparse, what was there exuded masculinity. The scent of leather from the oversized couch and matching recliners reminded her of the tack-room on the farm. Sage kicked off her sketchers next to the door. Entering the front room, her stocking feet slid on the polished hardwood floor.

"Wow, that's massive. I've never seen one that size." Sage's eyes widened as she took in the gigantic flatscreen dominating one wall.

Hunter grinned as he walked to her with two mugs of steaming coffee. "Oh, the TV? Ya, the dealer said it was the largest they had. It makes it easier to critique my moves." He paused. "When I review my games ... hockey games."

"Ah, okay. I get it." Sage could feel her face grow warm. Taking the coffee cup, she took a sip. A hint of chocolate mixed with a dash of cinnamon lingered on her tongue. "This might be the best coffee I've ever had."

"It's my own blend from a local coffee shop. Hope you like it black. I don't stock sugar or cream ... way too tempting."

"It's perfect." *Just like you*, she wanted to add, instead she asked, "How'd you make it so quick? You look like you just crawled out of bed."

"Coffeemaker has an auto-setting. Plus, you came early." He ran a hand through his bedhead.

"I always come when I'm expected. Margret said you'd be up by six."

"Not always." He grinned again. "On a rest day, I take a little longer to get to full strength." He leaned closer, his voice a husky whisper, "You smell amazing. What is that?"

"It's called Early Morning," Sage replied with a sly grin, meeting his playful mood.

Hunter tilted his neck from side-to-side, the soft pops of his joints filled the silence. "If I knew early morning smelled so good, I'd get up before dawn every day."

Sage smiled, setting her coffee cup on the kitchen counter. She lifted her camera to snap a picture of him yawning.

"Hey. Now. That's not fair."

"Per my online meeting with Margret this morning ... my camera has an Ice Wall all-access pass for the next three days." She watched as an evil grin grew across Hunter's face reaching his hazel eyes ... eyes outlined by the thickest lashes she had ever seen.

For a hockey player, his face was surprisingly unmarred. No scars on his high cheekbones, nor his perfect nose. Patty would be impressed with his beautiful smile, especially his full set of pearly whites. Clearing her throat, she commented, "Pretend I'm not here. Just go about your morning routine."

"Margret's been after me for months to do this day-in-the-life shot. So, pretending you're not here would be hard to do ... since I only agreed to have my personal space invaded by you. So, welcome to my world, shadow." He flashed her another one of his killer smiles, before walking back into the kitchen, opening the refrigerator. Banging pans about.

Giving Hunter space, Sage explored his living area. She ran fingers across the loaded bar nestled in the room's corner, surprisingly dust free. She deduced he must have a cleaning service come in when he's playing away-games.

Moving to the picture windows, Sage lifted the camera, capturing the view of boats bobbing in the nearby bay. She imagined the photos she'd be taking tonight, when the city came to life with bright lights.

The smells and sounds coming from the kitchen drew her attention back to Hunter. Turning from the window, she stopped cold. A Goshawks banner hung over the couch, daunting her. She recognized it right away ... the backdrop of

Hunter's Instagram photo he took for her. *Shake it off,* she told herself. Grabbing the coffee mug in one hand and her camera in the other, she entered Hunter's other den.

Breakfast had always been her favorite meal. It reminded her of home and her mom. The aroma of raisin bread popping from the toaster, the sausage squealing in the pan, the sizzle of eggs and fried potatoes being flipped, made her stomach rumble ... a little too loud.

He chuckled. "Hungry, are we?"

"Always," she answered, taking a sip of coffee, the rich taste making her moan softly. "This is so good."

"Like everything in this apartment," Hunter shot back, winking at her.

Setting the mug on the counter, picking up her camera, she shot a quick succession of frames of Hunter cooking. He was making a mess, but it smelled delicious.

Shooting him from different angles, she spied three typed lists sticking to the refrigerator door with Goshawks magnets. Lowering her camera, she walked in for a closer view of the meticulously planned schedules, her fingers grazing over the words. "This is ... intensely thorough. You even scheduled times for naps?"

She heard Hunter turning off burners, removing pans, before moving behind her. He was so close, the warmth of his breath wafted over her neck. The fingers on his left hand tracing next to her fingers. "Naps are important. Plus, I like to be ... precise," Hunter said, as he tugged on her ponytail.

Hunter's actions caused shivers to run down her spine. Sage could feel his heart beating through her long-sleeved t-shirt. She turned around, their faces inches apart. "And what does your precise schedule say about distractions?" Her voice was a sultry challenge as she waited for him to respond. She couldn't ignore his lips had a slight upward slant, as though always on the verge of a confident smile.

His eyes darkened. "Depends on how tempting the distraction is."

Standing there, toe to toe, he leaned down, so they were eye-to-eye, nose-to-nose. His lips almost brushing against hers as he said, "Your breakfast is getting cold."

Sage was proud of herself for being able to force her wobbly legs to walk across the room to the table. In front of her, a country breakfast of two eggs, home fried potatoes, sausage, thick raisin toast slathered in butter, and a refilled coffee mug. Lifting her camera, she shot a quick photo of Hunter's plate, his piled double of hers. "Is this your normal breakfast?"

"Guess you need to study my daily routine list closer." He forked a section of sausage, sucking it into his mouth. Putting his fork down, wiping his lips. he stared at her. "You know so much about me, but I know so little about you."

"Like what?"

"Like everything. Like, do you know how to ride a bicycle?"

"Yes, I know how to ride a bike. Why do you ask?"

"After breakfast, I need to get some leg exercises. I thought we could ride through the neighborhood. I'll borrow a bike from Jill. She lives two doors down and works from home. I'm sure she won't mind." Hunter continued to eat.

"Oh. Okay." At the thought of a girl friend living two doors down from Hunter, Sage's appetite vanished.

⸺◦⸺

"Are you sure she'll be up this early?" Sage asked Hunter as they walked down the hall to his neighbor's apartment.

"Yeah, she's always up by first light." Hunter knocked twice hard on the door, followed by an additional three quick taps. Without waiting for a verbal invitation, he opened the door, shouting, "Hey Jill, it's only me."

"Come on in Hunter. I'm just finishing up."

Hunter entered. Sage lingered in the doorway. She noted the apartment had an identical floor plan to Hunter's; with one big exception. Jill had turned her front room into a massive office space. Strewn paper on the floor made it impossible to walk without stepping on documents.

A brunette, who appeared to be in her late twenties, sat at a large desk piled high with papers and folders. Three large computer screens flashed with graphics, numbers, and graphs. Jill's fingers raced over her keyboard, stopping with a dramatic downward stroke, as if she were ending a piano concerto at Carnegie Hall.

"Ah, finished," Jill swiveled her office chair around. "What can I do for you, Hunter?" Her wide smile and initial warm greeting vanished.

"I was hoping you'd lend us your bike."

"Hunter. Griffin. Manners. Please," Jill chided.

"What?" Hunter's expression was one of pure confusion.

"How about introducing me to your friend?" Jill looked from Hunter to Sage, then back to Hunter.

"Oh. Sorry. Jill, this is Sage. I wanted to take her for a bike ride. Show her around our neighborhood."

"No Way! Don't tell me this is Your Sage from the Internet?" Jill leaned back in her chair, rocking, arms folded across her chest as she looked Sage up and down.

Sage gave Jill a little wave of her fingers. "It's me."

"So, can we borrow your bike?" Hunter asked again.

"Sure Sweetie." Jill rummaged around in her desk drawer. Coming up with a set of keys, she tossed them to Hunter. "The small one's for the bike lock."

Hunter caught them in midair. "Thanks, Jill. I'll get the keys back to you in an hour." Hunter took Sage's hand, leading her to the door.

"Have fun," Jill shouted after them.

"Nice to have met you," Sage shouted back over her shoulder as Hunter ushered her into the hallway.

"That was kind of her." Sage was doing her best not to let jealousy show.

"She's a great neighbor."

"How long have you two known each other?" Sage followed Hunter to the elevator.

"We moved into this building the same day. So, I guess it would be a little over five years?" Hunter shrugged.

"Is she into hockey?"

"Nope. In fact, she's never seen a game." Hunter pushed the elevator button. The doors opened a second later. He gave Sage's hand a squeeze as they entered.

"Hmm, that's hard to believe. You've never invited her to one of your games?" Sage felt like her breakfast might come up, as the elevator was going down.

"Jill's a big tennis fan. She'd rather fly to England to watch matches at Wimbledon than have front row seats to a Goshawks game. I keep offering her tickets to our home games. She always turns me down. Jill can be a snob, insisting that contact sports are too barbaric," Hunter said, mimicking a high-pitched girly voice.

When the elevator doors opened on the basement floor, Hunter led Sage across the underground parking area to the storage rooms.

"Which car is yours?" Sage asked, looking over a slew of expensive vehicles.

"I don't drive."

"What twenty-two-year-old male, with an overabundance of money, doesn't drive?" Sage stopped in her tracks, looking at Hunter as if he'd grown two heads.

"Never found a need to." Reaching his storage unit, Hunter stooped, fumbling with the key.

Sage hurried to his side. "I thought every red-blooded American boy dreamed of the day he was old enough to legally get behind the wheel."

"Since I was a little boy, I've only had one dream ... to be part of a professional hockey team." With a sly look back at Sage, he opened the storage unit's door.

Shaking her head, Sage entered behind him. Her gaze latched onto a shelf over the bikes where two helmets sat, nestled together. "That is so like you."

"What?"

Sage walked closer to the shelf, running her fingers over the custom design of Hunter's helmet. "The paint job matches your goalie mask."

Hunter grinned. "I know, it's over the top ... a gift from my agent. He figured I'd wear a bike helmet if it mimicked the one I wear on the ice." Hunter retrieved his headgear, strapping it on. "I think he just wanted to keep his investment safe."

He then reached for the baby blue helmet. Motioning Sage over, he placed it on her head, strapping it tight. Hunter let out a soft laugh when Sage shivered as his thumb brushed across her jawline. Looking into her eyes, in a deep Smokey the Bear voice, he said, "Safety first."

With shaky hands, Sage balanced Jill's baby blue Schwinn ten speed, along with Hunter's white Tommaso racing bike, as he locked up. Unable to contain herself, she blurted out, "Why does Jill keep her bike in your storage unit?"

Hunter retrieved his bike, laughing as he answered. "If she didn't, I doubt she'd ever find it. I'm surprised she could locate the key to her bike's lock. Jill has a brilliant analytical mind, but in everyday matters, she is a real scatterbrain."

"Oh, I see," Sage said, even though she didn't see at all. This was a new twist to Hunter's life. One she didn't expect. A twist her mother had warned her about. As much as Sage wanted to ask Hunter more about his relationship with Jill, she didn't want to appear nosey. Instead, she brought her camera up, clicking off a few quick shots. Something she always did when she was caught in the crosshairs of indecision.

"Put your camera away and catch up." Hunter yelled over his shoulder as he rode his bike out of the garage.

Sage adjusted the camera strap across her body as she lifted a leg over the bike. She was used to riding horses ... not balancing precariously on two wheels.

Hunter rode back. He stopped short, leaning on the handlebars, watching as she wobbled to the garage entrance. "Are you sure you know how to ride?" Before Sage could answer, Hunter began riding circles around her.

"I'm sure. It's just been a while. You go ahead, I'll catch up." Finding her balance, Sage peddled down the road, shifting gears like she knew what she was doing.

Hunter rode his bike beside her, pointing ahead. "There's a little coffee shop in the next block. I'll meet you there. I just need to do some sprints." Hunter waited for Sage to nod before he took off.

She couldn't resist stopping her bike to take a few quick shots of Hunter's fine form, as he lowered his chest, lifted his derrière and raced away. Peddling after him, she looked forward to the end of the ride, and on to the next scheduled photo shoot with Hunter. Unlike this one, she knew she'd be better suited to it. This morning, she felt like she was constantly playing catch-up getting to know the off-ice Hunter Griffin.

Chapter 19
Players and Puppies

April 24th

The parking lot of Portland's largest animal shelter resonated with the excitement of something special, a fusion of altruism and camaraderie. Dressed as a team in Goshawks long-sleeve t-shirts and jeans, twelve Goshawks players were busy at work. Both goalies and the two top lines bustled about, unloading pet provisions from their vehicles. Laughter and conversation peppered the air, mingling with the distant barking of dogs awaiting forever homes.

"Hey Hunter, think we've got enough?" Chase asked, eyeing the mountain of pet supplies.

Hunter grinned, hefting a bag of dog food over his shoulder. "I think it's a start, Captain."

"Sage, be sure to get a photo of the Goshawks in front of the pile of pet supplies." Turning to the players, Margret barked, "Get together! We need some group shots for the cover of this year's shelter charity calendar."

At twenty-three, Margret VanAlen, with her stature of five foot eleven inches, stood at the heart of the action. Her attire, a tailored designer suit paired with sky-high heels, spoke of her refined taste. Her dark hair, swept into a tight bun, added to her stern demeanor. The Goshawks players, undisciplined off the ice, snapped to attention at her sharp commands, showing a level of adherence they reserved for their head coach.

Sage was in constant motion, her camera clicking nonstop, capturing each moment of unloading food and supplies. The sunny afternoon, coupled with a smattering of clouds, made for perfect shooting weather. After the requested group shot, Sage continued to take frame after frame of the team carrying the goods into the shelter.

Upon Sage entering the facility, the sharp scent of disinfectants mingled with the raw animal odors struck her, defining the shelter's atmosphere. She was at the forefront, her camera ready to document the heartwarming scenes. Through the viewfinder, she witnessed the Goshawks players' faces transition from stoicism to tenderness. Their gazes softening at the sight of wagging tails and earnest eyes welcoming them amidst the maze of kennels.

Sage leaned in a doorway, watching the players as they chatted and joked, picking out their canine partners for the day's shoot. The sight of these tough guys showing their tender sides was worth the trip to Portland. Sage zoomed in on Hunter, his face a canvas of emotion.

"Are you getting some great shots?" Hunter asked, looking up as he crouched by a cage, bribing a frightened dog with a treat.

"With subjects like these? How could I not?"

"Wait until you meet the puppies." Hunter's smile grew wide in anticipation as he made his way into the puppy enclosure. A Yellow Labrador puppy, who appeared to be eight weeks old, ran to greet him. Hunter scooped the chubby, wiggly boy up into his arms. The pup reciprocated Hunter's joy, lapping at his face with its small, wet tongue.

"That puppy looks like he knows you." Sage fired away, shot after shot, as she spoke.

"He was born here. The owner of a pregnant Labrador suffered a fatal heart attack. No relatives could be found, so she was surrendered to the shelter. Shortly after, she gave birth to these nine pups."

"Such a sad story." Sage placed the camera by her side, stroking the puppy behind his ear.

"Every time I'm home, I always stop by the shelter and visit him." Hunter's eyes misted. "I instantly bonded with this little fatty."

"Does he have a name?"

"I didn't dare. I'm already too attached."

"Come on team. Grab your four-legged partners. You all know where to go." Margret made a shooing motion with her hands. Turning to Sage, she said, "For a team that's so unified, it feels like I'm herding kittens when they're off the ice."

The Goshawks players proceeded to the outdoor meet-and-greet enclosure, a haven of greenery, surrounded by a stone sitting wall, with a smattering of shade trees. The players paired up with their chosen dogs, the connection between man and canine tangible.

Margret followed them. Her voice naturally amplified. "Okay, team, I want a group shot. Get control of your dogs. Gather. Pretend you've just won The Cup."

At the mention of the Holy Grail of hockey, Sage watched in amusement as the players jousted for a prime position, while paying special attention to protect their four-legged partners.

Looking for a nod from Sage, Margret continued to direct the shoot. "Great job guys, now scatter and wait your turn for the individual photos."

After switching from her wide-angle lens to a portrait lens, Sage showed Margret's limo driver, Lionel, the optimal way to angle the portable reflector. Turning to the players, she pointed to Chase. "Okay, Captain, you're up first."

Chase approached, leading a regal German Shepherd. The dog's nose quivered as the Goshawks captain kneeled by its side. His fingers scratched behind the dog's ears. "You and I," he murmured, "we're going to make some memories." Sage's shutter clicked at the exact moment the Shepherd responded with a gentle lick on Chase's cheek.

Next up, left winger, Finn O'Connell, with an Irish Setter, both sporting white chin hairs. Even with its advanced age, the red dog danced like a pup. "I think she's doing an Irish Jig," Finn's accent thickening with emotion. To settle her down, he put his face next to hers, their russet hair a perfect match.

"Beautiful," Sage said, as her shutter whirled.

"I'm right behind you." The young rookie, Etan, pushed to the front of the line. Reaching out his arms, a wiry Jack Russel Terrier mix jumped into them, their faces mirroring identical mischievous grins. "Look at us ... Quick Shot meets Quick Paws." Sage's swift reflexes caught every frame of the interaction.

Second-line winger, Daniel 'Bulldog' Murphy's soft cooing, caught her attention next. "You and me, buddy," he whispered to the English Bulldog, its stocky form leaning into Daniel's side. "Look at you, stout fella. Almost as handsome as me." Sage caught the moment both turned to the camera, sporting big toothless grins.

Ryan's Rottweiler mix mimicked the Goshawks' top-line defenseman's protective stance. In contrast, the high energy Axel surprised everyone as he gently interacted with a small mixed breed mutt.

The afternoon unfolded in a tapestry of connection, humor, and love. Sage switched to action mode, when the second-line forward, Steve 'Typhoon' Sturman speed-raced with a Greyhound. She switched back to portrait mode to capture the second-line center, Eddie Bennett's tender moment with a pregnant Weimaraner.

Sage's favorite candid photos were of second-line defenseman Matthew Preston cuddling with a Chihuahua ... both player and pup tongues out for the camera. Then there was Liam Armstrong's pick, a doppelganger for the big defenseman. A scruffy white dog with a black ring around his left eye, matching the shiner Liam sported from their last game with Florida.

Sage looked around for Hunter and found him sitting cross-legged under a shade tree. His powerful hands cradled a sleeping yellow ball of fur. Rocking the Labrador pup, while singing a soft lullaby. Hunter's protective demeanor echoed his role as the team's goalie.

Without looking up, Hunter asked Margret, "I think he would be a fantastic addition to the Goshawks. He could be our mascot."

"You guys win The Cup and I'll take it up with the Goshawks management."

"He'll be gone by then." Hunter's fingers stroked the puppy's belly, causing the Lab to twitch a back leg.

"Hunter, you do this every time we come to the shelter. You know, you are on the road too much to own a pet ... even a goldfish," Margret reprimanded.

"I know."

"Now, put the puppy back. You're going to be late for your physical therapy session."

"Don't forget about me." The Snowman tugged on Sage's shirt sleeve. When she turned around. Olaf was slowly guiding a huge Samoyed/Husky mix next to a stone bench. "She's the oldest dog at the shelter." Olaf's voice broke as he spoke.

A tear trickled down Sage's cheek as she looked through her lens into the senior dog's faded silver eyes ... a stark contrast to Olaf's steely blue gaze. At the same time Sage pressed the shutter button, the old girl rested her giant head on his lap. The juxtaposition of the imposing goalie and the gentle creature was pure magic.

The sudden clapping of Margret's hands shattered the silence. "Time to get going." Pivoting to Sage, she asked, "Did you get everyone?"

"Darn allergies." Sage wiped her cheek on the cuff of her sleeve. With her head still tilted down, fiddling with her lens, she mumbled, "Yes. I'm done."

Margret patted Sage on the back. "It happens to all of us. Next to visiting the children's cancer ward, this is the hardest assignment."

While the players returned their pooches. Sage rushed over to the shelter's main desk, whispering something to the director. The woman nodded as she pulled a form from the desk. After filling out the paperwork, Sage handed the director a credit card.

"Sage Larson ... what have you done?" Margret asked, her brows knitting together.

Sage turned to face Margret. "I trust you can keep this between us?" Her voice was a mixture of stern resolve with a hint of desperation.

"Lordy, and I thought the Goshawks were trouble." Margret slung an arm around Sage, leading her outside. "We'll discuss this in depth later."

Chapter 20
Surprises and Expectations

April 24th

Sage's fingers danced over the laptop's keys editing the last photo. Hunter's apartment was a quiet space, allowing her to concentrate; even so, her head ached. She was used to working under pressure, but nothing she had done before compared to her assignment with the Goshawks ... and this was only her first full day.

Creating a mock-up of the 'From the Crease to the Leash, Goshawks & Adoptable Pups' calendar, Sage sent the files off to Margret. Rubbing her temples, she leaned back, stretching, allowing herself a moment to take in the day's accomplishments.

Sage's rest didn't last long. Hunter would be back soon, and she wanted to surprise him. A quick exploration of his kitchen revealed a surprising treasure trove of culinary possibilities. The scent of marinating steak and cheese melting over baked potatoes soon filled the apartment, accompanied by the gentle crunch of fresh vegetables chopped for a salad.

Her phone pinged, lit up, followed by a text.

Hunter: Running late. Had to do extra icing on my knees. 5 minutes out.

Wiping her hands, she texted back.

Sage: Don't keep me waiting.

Panic struck as she once more fumbled through cabinets and drawers, gathering plates and silverware. "These will have to do," Sage muttered as she pulled sheets of paper towels off the roll to use as makeshift napkins. Setting the table for two, she went back into the kitchen.

The sizzle of the steaks hitting the large, hot frying pan filled the room, mingling with the savory aroma of melted herb butter. Basting the steaks, Sage inhaled the familiar aroma of home. Unsure of Hunter's preference for rare or well-done, she settled for a golden-brown sear on the steaks that hinted at the juiciness within.

Just as she was pulling the twice-baked potatoes from the oven, their crispy skins crackling under her touch, Sage heard the distinct creak of the front door opening. The sound of sneakers creating a soft thud as they hit the hardwood floor assured her it was Hunter, not a burglar coming to steal her carefully crafted dinner.

Sage's heart pounded as she plated the meat and potatoes, the warmth of the dishes seeping into her fingers. With a final glance at the table, she placed them beside the bowls of crisp salad and chilled glasses of cucumber water ... the pungent scent of added mint lingering in the air.

"Honey, I'm home," Hunter shouted as he walked from the foyer into the front room. He stopped short at the sight of the gourmet meal adorning the table. "What's all this?"

"Just a little thank you for letting me into your world," Sage replied. "I have no idea what kind of dressing you use on your salad, so I made a special vinaigrette." She watched him, hoping she had not over-stepped, crossed any invisible male boundaries. "Hope you don't mind."

"Mind?" Hunter walked closer to her. "If I could come home to this every night, I'd let Olaf play all the away games." Without asking for her permission, he engulfed her in a big bear hug, like the ones he often gave the Snowman after a winning game.

Sage breathed him in. He smelled of cedar soap, his hair still damp from a recent shower. Now it was her turn to play his morning game. "Hunter," she whispered, her lips brushing against his earlobe. "Your food is getting cold."

Hunter's laughter came deep and hardy. "Touché. I'm famished."

As Hunter sat down, Sage grabbed her camera. Before she could get off a shot, he said, "Please put that away for the rest of the night. I want to enjoy time alone with you. The camera always feels like a third wheel."

Sage nodded, packing her camera away, putting the bag near the front door. Returning to the table, smiling, she asked, "Better?"

"Much."

They ate the meal with little conversation, other than passing the salt or pepper. It was an easy quiet. The silence broke as Hunter began sucking on the bone of his Porter House steak.

"Was the steak to your liking?" Sage asked, doing her best to suppress a laugh.

Hunter dropped the bone onto his plate, wiping his lips, beard, and fingers with the paper towel. "Sorry, I'm used to eating with cavemen." Reaching across the table, he took her hand. "It was the best dinner anyone has ever made me."

"Ever?"

"Yep. Ever."

"What about your mom?" Sage asked, wanting to remove the dishes, but not wanting to release his hold on her.

"What about my mom?" Hunter let go of her hand, leaned back in his chair, crossing his arms. Eyebrows furrowed.

"I just assumed all moms cooked." Sage was taken aback. She had never seen this side of him.

"Not all moms." Hunter picked up his plates and headed to the kitchen.

Bewildered, Sage watched him leave. She racked her brain, trying to recall everything she had read about Hunter in the past five years ... every interview he had given. But she couldn't recall any mention of his parents or his home life. Other than he was a brilliant student, skipped a grade, and was drafted into the Goshawks out of his first year of college. But, no, nothing about his mother or father.

She cleared the rest of the table, handing Hunter the plates to rinse and fill the dishwasher. With the kitchen cleaned, she touched his shoulder. "Do you want to talk about it?"

Pursing his lips, Hunter turned facing her, placing his hands on her shoulders, squeezing lightly. Leaning, his forehead touching hers, he said, "Not tonight. We've better ways to spend the brief time we have together."

Taking her hand, he led her into the front room. He sat her down on the over-sized couch, sitting close to her, as he reached for the remote. "Tonight, I need to go over my past games with Florida. I need to find what they were doing right, and what I was doing wrong."

"Should I go?" Sage asked, still holding his hand. Unsure of her place in his world. She remembered the detailed list on his refrigerator. She worried she was intruding on his daily playoff schedule.

"Would you mind helping me? I know you've watched all our games. I could use another set of eyes, a different perspective." Hunter brought their inter-twined hands to his lips, kissing her knuckles, his eyes pleading for her to stay.

Sage shivered at his gentle touch, his lips pressing against her skin ... his soft, trimmed beard tickled. Her pride swelled at the thought he cared enough about her opinion to ask for advice. Lost for words, she nodded, as he clicked on the screen, bringing up a list of all his prerecorded games.

"Let's start with my last game and work backwards." Snapping his fingers, Hunter paused the TV as he hopped off the couch. Rummaging through his gear bag, he pulled out a tiny white box. "I almost forgot, here's a little something to remember me by." Flopping back onto the couch, he handed the box to Sage.

Puzzled, her fingers danced over the lid. "What's this?"

"Look inside." His smile grew.

With great care, Sage opened the box. "Oh, my gosh, it's beautiful," she said, lifting the silver chain with a small silver goshawk in flight. "When did you find the time to go shopping?"

Sporting a sheepish grin, Hunter replied, "I told Margret what I was looking for, and she worked her magic." He took the delicate chain from Sage, motioning for her to turn around. "Here, let me help you with that." Pulling her long ponytail aside, Hunter fastened the necklace. "I hope you like it."

His fingers sent a quiver through Sage's body. Touching the pendant, turning back to face him, she said, "I love it, Hunter. Thank you so much." Moved by the gesture, Sage leaned in, placing a gentle hand on his arm.

Hunter stared into her eyes. Without looking away, he un-paused the TV. "Ready to continue the game review?"

"Oh, yeah." Sage snuggled into the couch, with Hunter sitting even closer than before.

As they watched the game footage, Hunter intertwined his fingers in hers. Forcing her to lean forward with him whenever he paused on specific shots on goal, scrutinizing play-after-play. She felt a thrill at his touch, a connection that went beyond mere physicality.

Hunter let go of her hand to cover his mouth with a long yawn. "Sorry about that. There was no time for my nap today."

"Stretch out for a bit. I don't mind." Sage watched as Hunter stretched his six-foot-two-inch frame on the couch. Putting a Goshawks' throw pillow under his head, doing his best to scrunch up his legs. Still, the toes of his stocking feet wiggled against her thigh.

"I can move to the recliner. Give you more room." Sage started to get up, but Hunter blocked her by extending his legs, putting his feet on her lap.

"Stay," he said, then went back to scrolling through the games. His head turned to face her as he clicked the remote to pause.

Sage locked eyes with Hunters as she slipped her fingers inside his ankle socks, slowly removing one. Pausing, she watched his reaction. When all he did was raise an eyebrow and give her a sly smile, she removed the other sock. Her fingers massaged his right foot, paying special attention to the instep, until she heard him moan.

"Feel good?"

"You have no idea." With closed eyes, he sank deeper into the couch, his soft moaning morphing into a light snore.

Sage watched him slip into a deep slumber. Even the thud of the remote falling to the floor didn't startle him. Turning her attention to the left foot, she noticed the gentle rise and fall of his chest lulling him deeper and deeper into his world of dreams.

Was this connection real? It felt real to her, but she had no idea where it was leading.

With care, Sage eased herself from under the weight of his feet. She debated if she should wake him, so he could get a proper rest, or just let him stay on the couch. He looked so peaceful ... she decided on the latter. Taking the fluffy gray throw from a nearby recliner, Sage covered his long, muscular frame.

Before leaving, she reached for her phone, snapping a single shot. For her eyes only. Something to remember this time with him. Picking up the remote, she turned off the TV. The room now shrouded in darkness except for the neon lights seeping through his picture windows. Slipping on her sketchers, picking up her camera and computer bag, Sage tiptoed out of his apartment.

Once outside, she sent Lionel a text to pick her up. She was thankful for the benches and bright streetlights dotting the front of the apartment. With her phone still open, she sent messages to her mom, Jessica, and Patty. It was only 9:30pm ... early for most everyone but hockey players, apparently.

"Hi there." a soft voice broke the silence, causing a startled Sage to juggle her phone to keep it from landing on the sidewalk.

"Oh. Hi." Sage looked up, realizing who was standing next to her. "Jill? Right? Hunter's neighbor?"

"None other." Jill sat down next to her. "Are you coming or going?"

"Just finishing a long workday." Sage put on her best friendly smile. "How about you?"

"I'm just heading out. Going to meet some friends at the bar ... do you want to join us?"

"Thanks for the invite, but I'm looking forward to an early evening." Sage patted her camera and laptop bag to accentuate her words.

"It was so nice to finally put a face to your name." Jill fiddled in her oversized purse, retrieving a vape pen. "Hunter has told me so much about you. I thought he was making you up." Her laughter was light, drifting into the night.

Sage studied the attractive brunette sitting next to her. With her short bob and trendy clothes, Jill could be on a Wikipedia page as a prime example of East Coast

Preppy. "What has he been telling you?" Sage asked, a mixture of curiosity and suspicion creeping into her voice.

"Oh, you know. How he met this awesome photographer online. Who was not a puck bunny. Who really understands hockey, especially the Goshawks." Jill's eyes twinkled. Her smile widened. "He really admires you."

Sage felt a blush creep from her neck to her cheeks. "I didn't know he'd been talking about me."

"Well, Hunter's always been a private person, but he likes to share positive things when they come his way." Jill took a long draw from her vape pen, exhaling a thin cloud of vapor. "I've never seen him quite like this before. You must be pretty special."

Sage was unsure of what to say in response. *Was Jill insinuating she was having something more than a professional relationship with Hunter?*

"Anyway, my ride's here. Gotta scoot. Fun talking with you. Take good care of our boy." Jill sprang to her feet, heading towards the approaching car.

"Our boy?" Sage snarled under her breath as she watched Jill's car drive away.

Sage sat dazed, with a head full of thoughts and questions. She didn't notice Lionel arriving until he yelled out, "Need a ride?"

Startled, She grabbed for her camera bag, once more avoiding a tragedy. Gathering her things, she climbed in Margret's limo, the conversation with Jill replaying in her mind. *Was Hunter sharing his thoughts about her with others, or only with Jill?*

Back in her hotel room, Sage found herself unable to sleep. The images of the evening ran on a constant loop. The touch of Hunter's hands, the warmth of his smile, the casual intimacy they'd shared on his couch. It all lingered, tangible yet elusive. Jill's words added an extra layer of complexity to the situation.

Sage pulled out her phone, looking at the photo she'd taken of Hunter asleep on the couch. It was a personal, private moment, and yet she couldn't help but feel it symbolized something more.

With a sigh, she turned off the lights, slipping under the covers. But sleep was a distant promise, her mind buzzing with possibilities, uncertainties, and a growing sense that her connection with Hunter was becoming more complex every day.

Chapter 21
All I Want is More

April 25th

Hunter sat on the bench outside the practice facility dressed in jeans, sneakers, and a threadbare team t-shirt from his college hockey days. Like always, his Goshawks ball cap set low on his forehead. Leaning his head back, he enjoyed the warmth of the late afternoon sunrays bathing his face. The cool breeze carried the faint scent of the rink and the distant sounds of the city.

"Hey there, do you need a ride?" Olaf asked.

Hunter opened his eyes, looking around the players' parking lot he noticed only one car remained. "Thanks, but I'm good. Sage is running a little late."

"Okay. I'll see you in the morning."

As Olaf drove off, Margret's sleek limo pulled up. He watched Sage rush out, dressed in her all-black work attire: jeans, t-shirt, and sneakers ... her blonde hair in a ponytail.

"Sorry to keep you waiting."

"No worries. You look like I feel." Hunter jumped up, retrieving the camera bags hanging heavy on her shoulders. "Dare I ask how your day went?"

"It was a long one. I didn't know there was so much technical stuff involved in shooting a professional hockey game." Sage exhaled, rubbing her arms. "I was thankful the arena staff and Nikki's intern were there to show me the ropes. I'm nervous about messing up."

Hunter nudged her with his elbow. "You'll be fine. You've got the talent for this. If Margret didn't think you could handle it, trust me, she'd let you know." Hunter set Sage's bags down, engulfing her in a hug. "For what it's worth ... I believe in you."

"Thanks, Hunter. It's worth a lot." She melted into his arms. "How was your day?" She asked into his chest, her words muffled.

"Same old, same old," he replied with a shrug. "Practice drills, strategy meetings, a little weight training, physical therapy. Just getting ready for the big game." Releasing her from his hold, looking into her eyes, he asked, "Have you eaten?"

"I had a late lunch with Margret," Sage replied. "You?"

"Had a big lunch with the team," Hunter said. "I was thinking ... how about we explore the Old Port District?"

"I'd love that."

He waved his hand toward Sage's camera equipment. "Are you sure you need all this stuff?"

"I'd like to at least take my camera."

"Can you get by with your cell phone?" When she nodded, Hunter turned to Margret's driver. "Lionel, can you drop us off at the Old Port District?" With a sheepish grin, he added, "Would it be too much trouble to take Sage's equipment back to her hotel and my gear bag to my apartment?"

"No trouble at all, Hunter. Will you need me later?" Lionel asked as he stowed their bags in the trunk.

"Nay. It's too nice. We'll just walk back."

It was a short drive. Hunter and Sage sat in the back seat. Their fingers intertwined. Hunter felt a twinge of pride as Sage sat next to him, eyes wide with wonder as she viewed his hometown.

Exiting the car, the scent of fish and salt air enveloped them. The sounds of the city were both a stark difference and a comforting similarity to the inside of a game night arena. The street music was softer, the voices less boisterous, the atmosphere heavy with a different anticipation.

Sage lost her balance crossing the cobblestone street. Hunter caught her before she could fall ... doing what goalies did best ... protecting his home ... and Sage felt like home to him.

"Portland's streets are enchanting, but dangerous," Sage said, followed by a giggle.

"I'll always be here to keep you safe," Hunter reassured her without laughter as he moved closer, wrapping his arm around her waist.

He stopped at the next store front. With a sly grin, he watched Sage ogling the sign above their heads. A wooden cutout in the shape of a large acoustic guitar swayed on two heavy iron chains. The lettering read: Strings and Vinyl.

Hunter opened the door, allowing Sage to enter first. Larger than it appeared from outside, the room was filled with rows of records, organized by artists in long wooden bins ... beckoning music lovers to explore their contents. On the walls hung a myriad of acoustic guitars of all shapes and sizes. In the spaces between them were framed autographed photos of guitarists in every musical genre. The store smelled of old wood and aged album covers ... and something else ... it was infused with captured memories.

Sage stood, her mouth open, eyes blinking as she took it all in.

"Hey, Hunter! I was hoping you'd drop by," the owner called out from behind the counter, a friendly smile spreading across his face. He was a handsome middle-aged man with graying hair and a genuine, welcoming smile.

"Hey, Tobias," Hunter replied, walking to the counter. "This is my ..." He paused, unsure what label to attach to her, muttering only, "... Sage."

"Nice to meet you, Hunter's Sage," Sam said with a wink and a nod. He arched an eyebrow to Hunter. "This is a first."

Hunter looked at him with a quizzical stare. "First what?"

"The first time you've ever brought anyone in here with you." As he spoke, Sam reached behind him, pulling a guitar off the wall. "I know your heart belongs to your Martin, but I just got this in and thought you might want to take it for a spin."

"Is that ...?" Hunter was lost for words as Sam handed the instrument to him.

"Yeah. It's a Gibson Hummingbird Custom Koa Acoustic. Limited edition. This is an original, from 2002."

Hunter ran his fingers over the Koa wood on the back and sides before stroking the Sitka Spruce top. "I'm not even going to ask how this came into your shop." Hunter's words came out low, filled with deep admiration.

Sage reached out, her fingertips hovering over the mother-of-pearl hummingbird inlay. "This is a work of art."

Tobias held his hands up as Hunter attempted to give the guitar back. "Like I said, try it out. Your favorite booth is open."

Hunter stood frozen for a moment until Sage nudged him. "I didn't know you played guitar."

"I wouldn't trust my guitars to anyone but Hunter ... he has soft hands ... even if he's a stinking hockey player." Tobias' laughter filled the room.

Hunter shook his head as he led Sage to a small booth in the corner. Inside, the lighting was soft. The walls padded. Both created an inviting, intimate atmosphere. Shutting the door, he motioned for Sage to take a seat in an overstuffed chair across from where he sat on a stool.

Turning each tuning key with practiced precision, Hunter plucked the strings. When he was satisfied, he strummed a few cords ... the sound echoed with sweetness. He looked at Sage, giving her a wicked smile.

Sage's eyes filled with anticipation. "I can't wait to hear you play."

"Promise not to laugh." He felt the heat rushing from his chest to his neck.

"I promise." She paused a moment before asking, "Can I record you playing?"

Hunter's first response was to say no. This was a private moment he wanted to share with Sage. "This is only for you."

Her response was swift, honest. "I promise it's just for me. I want to have a memory of today." When he nodded his approval, she pulled out her phone, setting it to record.

"I've been working on this. It's nowhere near polished," he said as he strummed a few cords. His fingers moved deftly over the strings, the melody both soothing and stirring. The rich tones filled the booth, wrapping around them like a comforting embrace. Hunter stared into Sage's eyes as he began to sing.

In the net, under pressure,
I hold the line.
Win or lose, You're in my mind.
I need you here! I need you near! I need you!

You're the calm in my rage,
The eye in my storm.
When we're apart,
My focus is torn.
I need you! I need you!

You've set a fire in my soul,
Even in the heat of the play,
You're my entire desire.
I need you here! I need you near! I need you!

As Hunter played and sang, he looked for Sage's reaction, for her approval. Smiling as her eyes shimmered with emotion, knowing he'd hit the mark. He repeated the last lines of the chorus with yearning. "I need you! I need you!" The final notes filled the booth, followed by a lingering resonant silence.

He'd written the song from his heart. It was raw and honest, reflecting not just his feelings for her, but also the intense world he lived in. He wanted the music to weave a connection between them, stronger than his words could convey.

Sage's misty eyes filled with appreciation and a deep, unspoken understanding. "That was beautiful, Hunter," she whispered, her voice a hair above a breath.

Hunter placed the guitar on the stand. "I'm glad you liked it. I wrote it for you."

Sage stood, wrapping her arms around him. "I've never had anyone write a song for me. It means more than you know."

They separated at the sound of a light tapping on the glass. Tobias opened the door, sticking his head in the room. "So, Hunter, what do you think?"

"Whatever you paid, it was worth the price." Hunter smiled as he handed the guitar back to Tobias.

"Ready to continue our adventure?" Hunter asked, draping his arm around Sage. After saying goodbye to Tobias, they headed back into the streets. The cool air was a stark contrast from the warmth of the music store.

Walking hand-in-hand, Hunter adjusted his stride to keep their steps in sync. They spent the rest of the afternoon window shopping and talking to street vendors. Throughout their day, Hunter took time for a selfie or autograph request, thanking the fans for supporting the Goshawks.

"I love Portland," Sage said. "It has such an old-world feel ... like we've stepped back in time."

"A little different from back home?"

"South Dakota has its own unique beauty." She squeezed his hand. "I can't believe how many shops and restaurants are on each block. I bet you could eat out every night for a year and never go to the same place."

"You'd win that bet. Olaf is a foodie. He's always bragging that Portland has over five hundred restaurants." Hunter let out a low guffaw. "I'm sure over the past five seasons he's tried them all at least once."

Near the end of the street, Hunter steered Sage to a shop, its façade a row of picture windows. "I think you're going to like this."

Sage read the overhead sign aloud, "Gelato Fiasco." She let out a little squeal as she clapped her hands. "I've always wanted to try a gelato."

"You're in for a treat," Hunter said as they entered the shop.

"It smells so good." The scent of homemade waffle cones invited them in.

Hunter loved how Sage turned childlike; face near the counter, eyes filled with desire. He watched as she explored the flavors in the freezer section below the glass.

"There are too many options. I feel like a kid in a candy shop."

"Do you trust me to order for you?"

"Oh, please."

"I know just what you need." He motioned for Sage to turn her back to the counter. He then pointed to a specific tray in the display case. "Large, on a waffle cone, please."

He delighted in watching Sage's eyes open wide as he passed the cone to her, piled high with layers of gelato. "I know how fond you are of chocolate. I think this will fill your fix for a couple of days."

"Where's yours?" Sage asked, closing her eyes as she took a lick.

"My trainer would kill me if he knew I even walked in here," Hunter replied, grabbing a handful of napkins.

"Sounds like your trainer is a paid assassin."

"Sometimes it feels like he is."

"This is so good. Are these chocolate covered pretzel pieces?" she asked, inspecting the creamy goodness.

"You have a distinctive palate, Ms. Larson. It also has a brownie batter base, chocolate truffle, and brownie batter bites." He leaned close to her. It's called, 'All I Want is More,' he whispered, giving her ponytail a gentle tug. Moving away, his expression turned serious. "When I saw the name, I couldn't resist." *Just like I want more of you*, he thought.

Sage blushed, her breath hitched as she replied, "I knew I could trust you to get the perfect flavor."

Holding hands, they walked the short distance to the waterfront. The bustling sounds of the shops morphed into squawks of seagulls mixed with the gentle lapping of waves against moored vessels. They settled on a bench near the pier. It offered a perfect view of the boats bobbing in the harbor.

"I've never tasted anything like this. It's incredible." Sage took a bite of her gelato, a streak of the creamy chocolate running down her chin and fingers. "Napkins. Please!"

Hunter watched her, a mischievous smile playing on his lips. He leaned in. With a quick motion, he licked the drippings from her fingers. Taking a moment to gaze into her eyes, he removed the melting stream from her chin with his thumb.

"Your trainer is going to be so mad at you." She extended her arm to prevent the gelato from further spillage as Hunter leaned in again, his lips close to hers.

A greedy gull swooped down, grabbing the cone from her hand. The bird perched on a nearby pillar. Sage let out a sorrowful moan. Hunter let out a curse, waving his fist. "Great timing," he growled. Turning back to Sage, he said, "Sorry about that." Retrieving a napkin, he wiped the remaining gelato from the corners of her mouth.

"Thanks," she said, her voice soft. "You're pretty good at that."

"I forgot to warn you about our rats-with-wings."

"Eww." Sage's face scrunched.

Hunter chuckled, shaking his head, he leaned back on the bench. "I can get you another gelato."

"Not after that comment." She, too, laughed. "I will keep the memory of the taste with me forever."

"Me too," Hunter whispered.

He draped his arm around her shoulder, pulling her into him. "Sorry, I should have seen that coming. Protected you from the thief."

Sage snuggled into his chest. "I don't expect you to protect me, Hunter."

Without thinking, he placed a soft kiss on the top of her head. "That's good, because I would hate not living up to your expectations."

As late afternoon waned into early evening, they chatted about everything and nothing: their day, the upcoming game. A comfortable conversation flowed between them, as if they'd known each other for years instead of mere weeks.

Sage turned to Hunter. "I have a special request."

"I promise to fulfill all your wants and needs." Hunter's expression turned from playful to serious.

"You're too funny." Sage rolled her eyes upward. "Will you have breakfast with me tomorrow?"

"Of course."

"At the hotel's restaurant. My treat."

"Sure." Hunter regretted his answer the instant it escaped his mouth. "Wait, what?"

"I want to treat you to breakfast tomorrow. Margret said she considers the Eighteen95 a five-star restaurant."

Hunter sucked in his breath, biting his lower lip.

"What's the matter?"

He shrugged. "It's nothing ... you do remember I have a set game day schedule?"

"It's just breakfast, Hunter. You've done so much for me since I've been here." Her fingers touched the tiny goshawk hanging on the silver chain. "Let me buy you breakfast. Please."

"Okay. But I gotta be on the ice by 8:15 for practice." He pulled out his phone, noting the time. "It's getting late. We should head back." Standing, he reached for Sage's hand.

They strolled back in awkward silence. Hunter with his arm around her. Sage leaning into his body. The evening air was cool and crisp, filled with the faint hum of the city's nightlife revving up behind them. The cobblestones beneath their feet gave way to smoother pavement as they approached the Regency. They stopped outside the hotel entrance doors.

"Thanks for tonight," Sage said, her voice sincere. "I had a great time."

"Me too," Hunter replied, his gaze steady on her. "It's nice to show someone around my hometown. See it through fresh eyes."

"You want to come up for a bit?" she asked, her tone hopeful.

Hunter glanced at the time again. "I'd love to, but I have to get to bed."

"Hockey player hours?"

"Yeah, hockey player hours."

Sage nodded. "See you in the morning at 7:30?"

He hesitated, wanting to kiss her goodnight, but just as he leaned in Sage's phone buzzed with an incoming call.

She glanced at the screen and frowned. "It's my mom," she said, "I have to take this."

He nodded, stepping back. "No problem. I'll see you in the morning."

"You bet ya," Sage replied, a warm smile returning to her face. "Good night, Hunter."

"Good night, Sage."

Hunter called an Uber as he watched Sage disappear into the hotel. Regret of not kissing her washed over him. Yet, he was thankful for the time they'd spent together. Being with Sage had proven to be a welcome break from his strict routine.

The city lights blurred past the car's windows as it sped to his apartment. His mind replaying the day's events. By the time he reached his place, a sense of contentment settled over him. He had found something special with Sage. He looked forward to seeing where it would lead ... even if it meant disrupting his game day traditions.

Chapter 22
Best Laid Plans

April 26th

Hunter wasn't used to his game day routine being disrupted. But here he was, jogging on an empty stomach to meet Sage for breakfast at the Regency. He stretched near the outer doorway before making his way into the hotel's restaurant. For a moment, he wondered if the swanky joint, with its chandeliers and white carpeting, would allow him entrance; especially since he was wearing shorts, running shoes, and a well-worn Goshawks sweatshirt.

"Welcome to Eighteen95, Ice Wall," The young hostess cooed. "Just you this morning?"

"I'm meeting ... a colleague." Hunter flashed her a toothy grin. Being the Goshawks starting goalie had its perks.

Even at this hour, the dining room was a bustle of customers and waiters. The constant chatter made it impossible for him to gather his thoughts. If Sage had not waved him over to a table, he would have jogged back home.

Instead, Hunter looked at the hostess as he nodded to Sage. He hoped no one else recognized him as he walked to the table nestled in a secluded corner. Hunter had never been a fan of public displays of affection. Yet Sage's smile was so inviting he fought an urge to kiss her.

Unlike their easygoing first day together ... filled with laughter and puppies ... yesterday's pregame day had been a grueling whirlwind. A dangerous mixture of hockey with a dash of Sage. Not a good recipe for preparing for an important game. He ran a hand through his hair. He needed to get his head back into the game ... and only the game.

The waiter appeared with two cups of coffee, just as Sage stifled a yawn. "Sorry. I'm not used to having consecutive days filled with so little sleep and so much pressure." After taking a sip of coffee, she added, "How was your run?"

"Is there such a thing as a bad run?" Hunter's smile vanished as he looked over the menu. Slapping it on the table, he growled to the waiter, "No Oatmeal?"

His actions made Sage jump. Her fingers tapped her menu. Her shoulders tensed.

"Sorry Sir, but oatmeal is not one of our selections," the waiter responded, his tone laced with impatience. "I can come back if you need more time."

"No. I don't have time. I'll take the Greek yogurt with fruit."

"Make mine the same." Sage gathered the menus, handing them to the waiter. "Please keep the coffee coming." She mouthed a 'thank you.'

Turning to Sage, Hunter frowned. Leaning back, arms crossed, he grumbled, "I always have oatmeal on game day."

"Good Grief, Hunter. What's gotten into you? I thought you always had a big breakfast?" Sage cocked her head, letting out a huff as she waited for his response.

"Not on game day. On game day, I have a big bowl of oatmeal with nuts and berries."

"So, this morning you will have a big bowl of yogurt with berries." Sage sat back in her chair, inhaling the coffee's aroma before taking a sip. After a long pause, she conceded. "My bad. I didn't realize your game day breakfast was that important." Replacing her cup on the saucer, she absentmindedly rubbed her fingers over the linen tablecloth, picking on a stray thread.

"How often have I asked you to read my detailed routine lists on the refrigerator?" It was only 7:35 and Hunter's mood was turning darker by the minute.

"Do you want to go back to your apartment and eat there?" The words came out in a low growl. The scowl replacing Sage's usual sunny disposition was out of character.

Sage's sudden change in temperament took Hunter by surprise. He was used to her calming words of encouragement. He tapped the fitness tracker on his wrist to see the time. "I can't expect you to understand. Game day is not like a travel day, a rest day, or a pregame day. I have a specific schedule to follow. This is not just a job. This is my life." Hunter felt his heartbeat racing.

"You're right. I don't understand, but I'm trying my best." Sage's eyes glistened with the threat of tears.

Hunter waited to respond as a waiter placed their order on the table, and another topped off the coffee cups, both men vanishing as quickly as they appeared.

"I'm so sorry, Sage. My nerves are always frayed on game day morning." Hunter hated that he'd pushed Sage to the brink of tears. The last thing he wanted was to hurt her.

Sage's expression softened, shaking her head, a smile tugging at her lips. "Eat your yogurt."

Hunter did his best to change the subject. "Did Margret go over today's shooting schedule with you?" He took a moment to breathe in and out slowly, to lower his heart rate. Picking up the silver spoon, he scooped fruit into the bowl of yogurt.

"Yes. Margret filled me in last night." Sage patted her lips with the napkin. "I thought your schedule over the past three days was intense ... the late-night plane flight, the charity shoot, coupled with yesterday's marathon practice and workout sessions. Reviewing today's schedule, I can only imagine how brutal game day is going to be."

Sage reached across the table, touching Hunter's fingertips. "I don't know how you do it week after week. I never realized what a mental and physical toll playing hockey takes on its players." Sage leaned back once more. Her hands wrapped around the coffee cup.

Hunter watched with a strange longing to drink from Sage's cup, where her gloss left a perfect impression of her lips on the rim. "You're right, today is going to be brutal." Hunter searched for the right words. "There's always a lot of pressure on the whole team to get the job done. Tonight, even more so. We need this win. We have to win the first round of the playoffs on home ice." His stomach growled as his spoon scraped the last of the yogurt sticking to the bowl.

"So, will your parents be at the game tonight?" Sage asked, smashing berries into her yogurt, the creamy white turning blue with streaks of red.

Hunter's spoon dropped in his bowl, a rattle of metal and china resonating in the tension-filled silence. "No, they won't." His voice was flat as he picked up his napkin, wiping his lips and chin.

"Hmm. That's strange. I mean, if it were my mom and dad, nothing would keep them away from such a big moment." Sage leaned forward, curiosity in her eyes.

Hunter crushed the napkin in his clenched hand. "They've never been to a pro hockey game," he spat out. "We can't all be blessed with perfect parents like yours, Sage." He felt exposed, violated, as Sage kept pushing to open doors to this private part of his life he kept locked.

"Wow, that was uncalled for." Sage scooted her half-eaten bowl of yogurt away, eyes wide with surprise and hurt. "I get that you're on edge and have been since yesterday afternoon. What have I done this morning to deserve this animosity? Your mood swings are making me miss my crazy friends on the farm."

Hunter's heart beat faster, anger and regret warring within him. "Listen, I'm sorry. I just don't like being pushed about private matters," he stammered. His phone interrupted him with a beep, glancing at the message then up to Sage. "Look,

I care about you, but I can't do this now. I can't do this today." Pushing his chair back, he stood. "Finish your breakfast. Lionel's here. I'll send the car back for you."

For the briefest of moments, Hunter's gaze fixed on Sage. Her face, marked by confusion and hurt cut him deeper than he expected. A surge of regret welled up inside him. This was not how he wanted to start his day.

Doing his best to defuse the situation, Hunter managed a weak smile. "See you at morning practice," he said. Tossing a handful of twenties on the table, he turned and walked away, his chest heavy with the weight of their conflict.

"I'll be rooting for you and the Goshawks tonight ..." the hostess began as Hunter walked past her desk. Her interruption was a stark reminder of his celebrity status ... the intrusions it brought into his personal life.

"Can I get a quick selfie?" the hostess asked, her eyes wide with excitement.

Hunter calculated the time, always mindful of his fans. Relenting to the request, his eyes were drawn back to Sage, sitting alone at the table. Her glare met his, daggers in her eyes. Hunter felt the weight of his words at breakfast, realizing his actions might have crushed the fragile bridge that should have taken their relationship past friendship.

Chapter 23
Missed Goals

April 26th

Hunter entered the Goshawks' practice arena well before his teammates. The looming evening game, and his unresolved issues with Sage, gnawed at him, an incessant itch deep beneath his skin. The facility's early morning stillness echoed his craving for solitude, providing a much-needed respite for introspection and strategic focus. Here, within the silence, Hunter sought clarity and calm in the eye of the storm that was rapidly approaching with the night's crucial face-off.

Entering the locker room, Hunter began his game-day practice routine, dressing in silence, his mind on the ice. Lacing his skates, Olaf burst in, arms waving.

"Hunter, did you see the fans outside?" Olaf exclaimed, pulling out his phone.

Hunter's eyes remained fixed on his skates. "Not interested, Olaf. We have practice to focus on."

"But the signs, and the ..."

"I said, I'm not interested," Hunter interrupted, his tone as sharp as his blades.

Olaf shrugged. He tucked the phone in his locker. "Alright then. Let's hit the ice."

Entering the rink, Hunter pushed the row of pucks off the railing in a rhythmic, sweeping motion. He loved the early morning practice. It was a ritual, one that had served him well during his five seasons with the team. Before going to the net, he did a speed skate around half the rink, finishing off with some quick puck handling.

Olaf skated behind Hunter, bending over to catch his breath. He gulped out, "Hunter, I keep telling you, I became a goalie because I hate to skate."

Hunter tapped Olaf's shin pads with his stick. "You may be ten years my senior, but we both know you can still go the distance in the net."

Olaf rubbed his catcher glove on Hunter's Mask. "Well said, grasshopper."

Laughter echoed through the vacant rink as they parted ways, each gliding to opposite ends to join their respective goaltending coaches. Hunter cast an envious glance at Olaf and the Swedish assistant goaltending coach, Lars, sharing a light moment in their native tongue—a sharp contrast to the stern approach of his own Russian coach, Viktor Volkov.

"Laugh later. Practice now," Viktor reprimanded.

Hunter nodded to Viktor, doing his best to focus on the upcoming drills. In his peripheral vision, he spotted Sage in the stands, camera in hand, instantly shattering his concentration. He was relieved she was there, yet still frustrated over their breakfast fiasco. When Sage smiled and waved, Hunter waved his stick in response as he skated backwards. The impact with Viktor came with a sudden jolt, nearly knocking his coach's skates out from under him.

Regaining his footing, Viktor's fingers reached through the cage of Hunter's mask. Pulling him close, his coach growled. "Decide. Now. Do you want girl, or do you want Cup?"

Both, Hunter thought. Instead, he said, "The Cup, Coach."

"Good!"

Viktor skated to the boards. His eyes flashed with anger as he tossed a puck over the glass. Watching Sage catch it, he called out, "Go hop away, little bunny. Hunter has no need for shadow today. You do not belong here during game day practice."

Sage's reaction was instant. Her words hit Viktor like a slap shot. "Do not ever insinuate that I'm a puck bunny," she snapped, waving her camera at him. "I do not take orders from you. I've been hired to do a job. I suggest you do yours." Sage took a quick shot of Hunter, turned and walked towards Olaf's net.

Hunter's heart pounded. This was a side of Sage she seldom showed. It was fiery, unapologetic, just like she'd stood up to Coach Harrison on the tarmac. Right now, her defiance was a distraction he couldn't afford.

Viktor once more grabbed Hunter's cage, pulling downward until their eyes aligned. "Your head has not been in game since your first contact with girl." The tone in his voice reflected his ire. "Your parents brought me from Russia, all those years ago, to train you to be best goalie. Not to have you turn into a lovesick lapdog."

"My parents haven't paid your salary in years." Hunter dislodged Viktor's fingers. In the seventeen years Viktor had been his goaltending coach, he'd never talked back to the man.

"You're right," Viktor snapped back, "the Goshawks pay me now. I am Goshawks head goaltending coach." Viktor thumped a fist to his chest. "They pay me big monies to make sure you are best goalie." His Russian accent growing thicker as his annoyance grew. "Start thinking with your head." Viktor rapped on top of Hunter's mask with the butt of his stick. "Instead of ..." He moved the stick down, driving it between Hunter's legs, stopping just short of contact.

Hunter froze, speechless, eyes focused on the other end of the ice. Olaf, his goaltending coach, along with Sage, stood like statues. The silence in the arena was broken by a single defiant shutter click.

"Now, if you are ready ..." Viktor skated around Hunter's net, gathering pucks, "... get back to what matters. Warm up your body." When Hunter finished a series of dynamic and static stretches, Viktor commanded, "Shuffle Drill."

Hunter mentally and physically prepared himself for the drills to follow. His eyes never left the puck as he shuffled back and forth in the crease watching Viktor move the puck with skillful stick handling in front of the net.

The rest of practice went by drama free as Viktor put Hunter through more drills: T-pushes, up and downs, butterfly drops. Hunter's focus remained on the ice, the net, the puck. Viktor's voice became hypnotic, blocking out distractions.

"Good. Good." Viktor poked his gloved fingers into Hunter's chest. "Never forget, you are Ice Wall. Nothing gets through you."

A half-hour later, the rest of the Goshawks arrived, exploding onto the rink. Hunter's concentration was broken by the sounds of multiple skates slicing through the ice, the players loud verbal jousting, and the vibration of pucks bouncing off the boards.

Hunter took a break, sitting on the bench, taking note of his teammates as they went through their warm-up routines. He knew it wouldn't be long before he'd be protecting his net from driving pucks as their drills merged with his.

On the ice again, the Goshawks hard hitting winger, Steve Sturman, was the first to test Hunter's metal. He hit a high slap shot into the net's upper right corner. Stopping in front of Hunter, Steve raised an eyebrow. "Hey Griffin, what's with the fans outside?" His mouthpiece wiggling in and out of his mouth.

Before Hunter could react, the second-line defenseman, Matthew Preston, skated next to Steve. "Hey kid, looks like your girlfriend's gonna be as famous as you." A grin splitting his face.

Hunter was used to the team's good-natured prodding during this part of the practice. It helped him prepare for the upcoming battle with Florida, especially the constant chatter from his nemesis, Chucky.

From an early age, Viktor instilled in Hunter the ice rink was a domain of unwavering concentration ... taught to tune out any distractions once stationed between the pipes. Hunter had refined this skill over the years, sharpening his focus exclusively on the game and his critical role of guarding his net. However, this steadfast attention found its match—Sage's entrance into his life marked the first time something resonated deeply enough to penetrate his concentrated state.

The intensity of practice escalated, and with it, the taunting from his teammates became relentless. "Enough already! Goalies are off-limits for chirps," Chase barked, asserting his authority as captain. Gliding across the ice, he approached Hunter's net, offering a supportive tap on his shin pads with his stick.

The closing moments of practice found Hunter increasingly unsettled, grappling with the unexpected chatter about Sage among his teammates. Their casual banter, laced with her name, piqued his curiosity, pulling his focus away from the relentless barrage of pucks. Compelled, he scanned the stands for a glimpse of her, a momentary distraction that allowed two sharp shots to slip past him.

"Enough!" Viktor's voice cut through the air. "This again? Focus!" He pounded his stick on the ice, causing the Goshawks' shooters to scatter to Olaf's net.

Hunter's face flushed. "Sorry, coach. I just ..."

"You are here to work, to be the best. I warned you once. Did you grow two sets of ears this morning?"

"No. Coach, but ..."

"But? The only butts in hockey are the butt-ends of your sticks." Viktor's face turned red. His breathing labored. "I give up. You don't want to listen. I have better ways to spend my time." Viktor skated off the ice as another puck flew past Hunter.

Relief washed over him as the whistle blew, signaling the end of practice. Today's session had left him feeling exposed, humiliated. Striking his stick against the pipes in frustration, Hunter grabbed his water bottle to join his teammates off the ice. As he picked up a towel from the bench, snippets of the assistant coach's conversation floated his way, revealing Nikki would be back in time to photograph tonight's game. Initially, meeting Sage in person and having her document his daily routine had been a dream come true. Today, her presence was becoming his worst nightmare.

Chapter 24

Frozen Focus

April 26th

A whirlwind of masculine vigor unfurled in the post-practice locker room. The atmosphere thick with the scent of sweat and the metallic bite of sharpened skates. Conversations collided, reverberating against the walls while Goshawks players bantered and bickered. The clatter of equipment being shed and discarded resonated throughout the space.

Head Coach Harrison entered, his face a storm, eyes blazing as he marched straight to Hunter. "You call that focus, Griffin? Fans outside with signs ... you letting in soft goals? What the hell has gotten into you?"

Hunter's throat constricted. The room was stifling. He could feel the stare of his teammates, some faces filled with anger, others sported looks of confusion. Viktor stood nearby, his muscular frame leaning in the doorway, arms folded, head down.

"Speak up, damn it!" Coach Harrison snapped. "You're not playing on a farm team. But. By. God. I'll send you there in a heartbeat. How many ways can I tell you? Get. Your. Head. In. The. Game." With a final glare, he stormed out, followed by Viktor, leaving a tense silence in their wake.

Olaf sat down with a thud next to Hunter. The big Swede thrust his phone's screen inches from Hunter's face. Hitting play, a short video appeared of fans brandishing signs outside the front entrance of the Goshawks practice facility.

Hunter grabbed the phone, scrolling through and enlarging still images. Some signs displayed the infamous 'Hi Sage' screen grab. A grainy blowup of Sage from her website donned others. A smattering more wore the words 'Mystery Solved' scrawled on cardboard in sloppy red paintbrush strokes.

Olaf looked at Hunter. His expression filled with concern. "Better to know now. Get it out of your system before you hit the ice tonight."

"What the ..." Hunter groaned, tossing the phone back to Olaf. "Could this day get any worse?"

Chase's voice cut through the quiet, as hard and unyielding as the ice they'd just left. "Alright, Hunter, spill it. What's got you all tangled up?"

"Guess you didn't catch the scene outside?" Olaf looked from Chase to Hunter.

"I have no idea what you are talking about, Snowman. I arrived at the back entrance the same time Sage did. There was nothing unusual outside the arena."

"They must have only been at the front entrance. Some of us go through that door to grab coffee from the new café before morning practice." Olaf walked to the captain, showing Chase the video, along with the still images on his phone.

Hunter's heart pounded, the taste of the disastrous practice still bitter in his mouth, now coupled with the fans' chaos. He tried to speak, but Ryan beat him to it.

"No More Sage," Ryan said, his tone flat. "You were both hired to do a job. Do your job, Hunter, so she can do hers." Ryan stared at Hunter from across the room while removing his shoulder pads. "We need you, kid. You can't lose focus now."

Frustration boiled over in Hunter. "You think I don't know that?" His hands raked his hair, resting on the back of his neck. His voice became ragged. "I need to sort this out quick, or I'll be no good to anyone, including myself."

"Well, we're all in agreement on that." Ryan smiled as he unlaced his skates.

The room once more erupted in raised voices with hands gesturing. Finn struck his stick against the bench of his stall. The sudden outburst silenced the group. "Enough!" Turning to Hunter, he snarled, "What's the matter, Griffin? We need you locked-in on the puck, not looking at the stands with googly eyes. Get serious or stay off our ice."

Chase put his hand on Finn's shoulder. "Why don't you hit the showers?"

"Quit coddling him," Finn grumbled as he pushed the captain's hand away. "He's not a rookie. He's supposed to be our starting goalie. Our Ice Wall. What a joke!" he spat out the words. Going back to his stall, he stripped off the rest of his gear, grabbed a towel, and headed to the showers.

Hunter sat silent, knowing he deserved the verbal abuse. A part of him welcomed it. His hands balled into fists. For the second time in his life, he felt like hitting something.

Ryan looked at the rest of the group. "Give us some privacy." With a quick nod to Chase and Olaf, he added, "We've got this."

"Not us?" Axel and Etan asked at the same time.

"Especially not you two," Ryan growled.

The clamor of falling equipment, doors slamming, and bare feet padding followed, until only Ryan, Chase, and Olaf remained with Hunter.

Ryan's tone softened. "Hunter, over the past five seasons, you've earned your place as the Goshawks starting goalie." Turning to Olaf, he added, "No offense."

"None taken." Olaf's lips morphed into a silly grin.

Ryan paced around the locker room. "Hunter, we all know that you didn't get here by slacking off. I've never seen you like this." He stopped in front of the young goalie, clicking his fingers in Hunter's face. "Snap out of it!"

As Ryan began pacing again, Chase chimed in, "Hunter, you know we've all got your back. Now we need to know you've got ours. Prove it on the ice tonight. We need our Ice Wall back, not a slab of Swiss cheese guarding the net."

"Listen kid," Ryan piped in, "We know how much you care about Sage. We all like her."

"Except for Viktor," Olaf broke in. "But then, Viktor doesn't like anyone."

"True," both Ryan and Chase said in unison.

Olaf joined the intervention, "Hey, kompis. We've all got stuff going on off the ice ... but we leave it off the ice. We all know, you know, what's at stake tonight. The Goshawks need you. If you cannot keep your mind off Sage, let me know now. This is going to be a hard question, but ... do you need me to take your place tonight?"

Hunter shook his head. "Thanks, Olaf. I've worked too hard for this. Tonight, the net is my home. I protect my home from all intruders. That includes pucks and Chuck." He smirked. "No one is going to take this game away from us. I'm starving for this win."

"I'm hungry too," Olaf moaned. His stomach growled as if to emphasize his point.

"Hit the showers Olaf. You too Ryan. The sooner you two are dressed, the sooner we can all hit the dining hall.

"I can smell the lasagna and garlic bread from here." Olaf said, stripping off the last of his gear.

Chase took a seat next to Hunter. "This is what I propose. When we finish lunch, I'll drive you to your apartment. Gather what you need for tonight. Then come home with me. Emily will take care of you."

"Thanks Chase, but I don't want to be a burden on your wife. I can manage on my own."

"Emily won't mind. If you could manage on your own, we wouldn't still be sitting here in our wet, stinky gear." Chase laughed, slapping Hunter on the back. "One more thing. Sage is off limits until after the game tonight. Agreed?"

With great reluctance, Hunter nodded.

"I'll contact Margret. Have her explain everything to Sage." Chase reached for his phone, fingers dashing off a quick text.

A half-hour later, the Goshawks left the locker room as a group, a team united again. Fierce. Determined. They moved as a hungry pack of wolves, salivating for a meal ... desperate to sink their teeth into victory. Walking past Sage in the hallway, Hunter's gaze met hers for a fleeting second. His teammates surrounding him, a barrier against everything but the game.

———◆———

Standing in the hallway, Sage was about to leave when the locker room doors burst open. She watched the players emerge, fresh from the showers; dressed alike in gym shorts and Goshawks t-shirts. Their confident chatter felt like a universe away from her troubled thoughts.

She searched for Hunter, yearning for a connection, a sign that things were okay between them. Hunter's eyes met hers. A glance filled with something unreadable. Then, he was gone, assimilated into the Goshawks collective, leaving her adrift in a sea of uncertainty.

Chase broke from the group, walking towards her. His kind eyes touched with an unaccustomed severity. "Sage, care to walk with me?"

A knot tightened in Sage's stomach, but she nodded. They moved away from the locker room, the distant sounds of the team's laughter growing fainter. The aroma of brewing coffee from the practice facility's café teased her senses, overpowered by something else ... an unspoken tension that hung in the air like a thick fog.

"You know Hunter's off his game," Chase began, his words measured. "It's not like him. It seems to be tied to you."

Sage's breath caught, her sneakers stumbling on the polished floor. "What do you mean? I'm just doing my job."

"So is Hunter," Chase said, his gaze intense. "But his focus is faltering, and we can't risk that now. That means ... no contact with you until after the game."

Icy fear swept through Sage. "I had no idea ..."

"I know you didn't," Chase interrupted, his voice softening. "It's not just you. There's also the matter of the fans with signs outside. They've really gotten to Hunter."

"Signs? I don't know what you mean."

Chase sighed, rubbing his neck. "Talk to Margret. Right now, the important thing is Hunter's mental state."

The heavy reality settled on Sage. "Again, I didn't know he was going through this."

Chase's eyes softened. "It's not about blame, Sage. It's about what's best for Hunter and the team."

Nearing the cafe's entrance, Chase's final words were gentle but firm. "Talk to Margret about the signs. She'll explain. We'll figure this out." Chase nodded to Margret sitting at a table. "I have to go. I'm sorry that I had to have this conversation with you. Thanks for understanding." He patted Sage on her back, then walked back to his team.

Inside the café, Margret and a young man were deep in conversation, but they broke off as Sage approached.

"Oh, good, I'm glad you made it." Margret stood, giving Sage a quick hug. "Nikki, this is Sage."

Nikki stood, extending his hand. "It's a pleasure to meet you. Thank you so much for filling in for me."

"I'm so sorry for your loss." Sage shook Nikki's hand.

"I'm just thankful I could make it back in time to shoot the game tonight." Nikki managed a weak smile. "On the bright side. I love the shelter's charity calendar. It takes a talented photographer to catch those magical moments. I'm very impressed with the body of work you've done for the Goshawks."

"Thanks, Nikki, that means a lot coming from you." Sage's smile didn't reach her eyes. "I'm glad you got back in time, too. It appears I've been banned from shooting the Goshawks until after tonight's game."

"What?" Margret's voice raised an octave.

"Wow, isn't that a violation of her contract?" Nikki frowned.

With her gaze still on Sage, Margret addressed Nikki, "Be a dear. Get Sage a cup of coffee. She likes it black." The moment he was out of earshot, Margret looked to Sage with questioning eyes.

Sage had a difficult time finding words. Her voice felt broken. "Apparently, I'm the reason Hunter did poorly in practice today." Tears welled. Sage did her best to keep the dam from overflowing. "I'm too much of a distraction." She dabbed the corners of her eyes with a napkin.

"Even worse, Chase mentioned fans with signs?" Sage said, confusion in her voice. "I arrived just after Hunter. Lionel dropped me off at the back entrance. There were no fans outside. No signs."

"Geez," said Nikki, arriving from his mission. "I was only gone for a couple of minutes. Did you miss me that much?" He sat the steaming mug of coffee in front of Sage.

Margret fixed Nikki with a stern glance before shifting her focus back to Sage, her demeanor growing somber. "Upon the calendar's presale release on the Goshawks' website, they listed you in the photo credits. Some of Hunter's fans pieced it together. The more fanatical fans think Hunter's been taken off the market. They're not happy."

Sage's fingers trembled. Her words came out in gulps. "But. That's. Not. True. I'm just here to do a job."

Margret reached her hand across the table to cover Sage's, a touch filled with understanding and resolve. "I know. And we'll handle it."

"I've ruined everything. Poor Hunter. No wonder he never wants to see me again."

Margret looked to Nikki, "Do you still have that herd of interns from the University?"

Nikki leaned forward. "Tonight's their last game. Graduation is coming up." In an instant, his smile turned wicked. "I see where you're going." He sized up Sage. "With a college hoodie and some fake glasses, I think it could work."

Margret picked up where Nikki left off. "I can print you a college press pass. If you keep the hoodie up, and your hair pulled back ... you'll blend into the group. No one takes notice of the interns when they're shooting."

Nikki couldn't contain himself. "I'll even get you one of my Goshawks camera bags. If you shoot with a telephoto lens, yeah ... I think we can pull this off without Hunter—or any of the other Goshawks—knowing you're at the game."

Sage sniffed. "I was counting on seeing my first hockey game in person. Yet, I suppose it will be even better looking through a lens."

"I couldn't agree more. Everything looks better when viewing it through a lens." Nikki reached over to high-five Sage.

Margret looked around to see if anyone was nearby. When she was assured they were safe, she whispered, "I can't stress how important it is to keep this between the three of us."

"I agree." Nikki looked at Sage. "You must keep your distance from Hunter's net. For this to work, you must become a ghost. Can you become a ghost, Sage?"

Sage nodded. *For Hunter, I will be whatever he needs me to be.*

It was a simple but effective plan. Sage felt a glimmer of hope amidst the confusion and hurt. The next hour was spent mapping out the details. Sage's thoughts kept drifting back to Hunter's glance. That fleeting connection. Was it a goodbye or a plea for understanding? The uncertainty was a gnawing ache, a question left unanswered.

Exiting the meeting, the bittersweet taste of coffee lingered on her tongue. Sage realized the stakes had risen. It was no longer about fulfilling a contract ... now, it involved safeguarding Hunter's focus and performance while dodging harmful rumors. Sage needed to master the art of being visible and invisible at the same time. Most important, she would find a way to keep her focus frozen on Hunter, even from the shadows.

Chapter 25
Call of the Wild

April 26th [Game 5 of the First Round of Playoffs]
Hunter's hands were rough, calloused from years between the pipes, yet they moved with a practiced, meticulous grace. The feel of the stick, the pull of the tape. Every motion was part of a ritual, grounding him, forcing him to focus on the battle to come. The locker room was a din of noise, but Hunter's world had narrowed, sharpened to a razor's edge.

Viktor's deep voice broke through ... a gravelly baritone that spoke of old wisdom and hard-won battles. "Positioning, Hunter. Anticipation. Your net. Your home. No one must penetrate it. Let in no goals."

Hunter's mind was already there, on the ice, in the net. The cold, sharp scent filled his nostrils, a smell that had become part of him, embedded in his very soul. He was a goalie. The last line of defense. The rock on which his team's hopes were built. A mixture of Viktor's voice and the rhythmic wrapping of tape sent his mind spiraling to the past.

He was back in the indoor rink his parents built for him, the echo of his skates on the ice, the slap of the puck against his pads. Hours, days, years. The love of the game had filled him, consumed him, shaped him. His parents' absence, their indifference, had been a cold, hard fact, but the ice had been his refuge, his joy.

Then the bulldozer came the day he'd quit his freshman year of college, signing with the Goshawks. His father's cold eyes, the uncompromising set of his jaw, the finality of that betrayal. The rink was gone, and with it, a piece of Hunter's soul.

Hunter's nails dug into his palm, bringing him back to the present. "Are you even here?" Viktor snapped, his eyes piercing, demanding. "This is war, Hunter. You need to be ready."

Hunter's eyes met the old Russian's, a fire igniting in his chest. "I'm ready," he growled. "This game is what we've been training for."

Viktor held Hunter's gaze for a moment longer, then nodded, a smile tugging at his lips. "Good. Let them come. Let them try. You are Ice Wall. Now go. Prove it."

Hunter's muscles tensed, a primal, fierce energy surging through him. He was more than ready. He was hungry. The game was in his blood, the ice in his veins. Tonight, he would be unbreakable, unyielding. He would be the wall his team needed.

He stood, the weight of the coming battle settling on his shoulders, a challenge he embraced with every fiber of his being. His love for the game had never wavered, not for a second, and now it was time to lay it all on the line.

The roar of the crowd reached him as he headed towards the ice, a siren's call pulling him to the fight.

The National Anthem ended, but a charged silence lingered, a collective breath held as the lights in the arena dimmed. A spotlight shined on Hunter. Donning his mask, he stood between the singer and his net, arm raised, catcher glove extended. Five of his Goshawks' teammates waited on their blue line, a mix of curiosity and expectation in their eyes. The crowd, too, felt something in the air, a tremor of excitement building.

Another spotlight shined on a VIP box high above the arena. A goshawk launched, its wings sharp, controlled, eyes fierce, locked on Hunter. The crowd's anticipation turned to silence. A deep hush fell over the arena as the powerful bird descended. It was the first time the Goshawks had used a hawk in this way, and the spectacle was mesmerizing.

The goshawk landed, its talons gripping Hunter's catcher glove with a controlled force that spoke of wild nature tamed. The connection between the bird and the Goshawks' star goalie exuded a symbol of the team's spirit, the embodiment of grace, power, and determination.

"This is our ice, our fight," Hunter spoke to the bird, his voice raw and unyielding. "They want to break through. They'll have to get past us first." The goshawk's eyes glinted, reflecting the steel in Hunter's words, an understanding passing between warrior and raptor.

The hawk side-stepped up Hunter's arm, its movements deliberate and regal. In a display of kinship, the goshawk and Hunter bumped heads, beak to mask, a communion of spirits. Then, with a swift movement, it danced back to Hunter's gloved hand ... took to the air, soaring back to its perch high above the fans.

The crowd's response was volcanic, a roar of approval and excitement that shook the very foundations of the arena. Hunter skated to his net, the grace of the goshawk mirrored in his movements, each glide strong and purposeful. The Goshawks' starting line followed. One by one, they tapped Hunter's knee pads, an unspoken vow of fidelity.

The Goshawks' captain circled back to Hunter. Mimicking the hawk he bumped his helmet on Hunter's mask. Chase gave a rugged command. "This is our night."

Hunter's response was equally fierce, "We Take It All."

The connection with the goshawk still lingered in Hunter's soul, its primal energy fueling him. He was more than a goalie; he was a protector, a fighter, a force of nature ... a bird of prey.

The referee's whistle signaled the start of what Hunter hoped would be their last match against Florida. Stakes were never higher; their moment had arrived. Hunter's body tensed, ready, unbreakable. He was the Ice Wall.

The puck dropped. Game On!

Chucky skated into the Goshawks' zone, his eyes scanning for an opportunity, but his true intent was clear. Trying his old tricks, he parked in front of Hunter, aiming to throw the Ice Wall off his game.

"Not today, you little—" Hunter muttered under his breath.

The referee's arm shot up. Whistle blew. Goalie interference. Chucky had once again crossed a line. This time the refs were taking none of it. Two minutes in the sin bin. The crowd erupted, a wave of vindication washing over the arena.

"Your cheap tricks won't work in our house." Ryan sneered as he skated past Chucky, who was about to take his seat of shame in the penalty box.

Only minutes in and it was a power play for the Goshawks. The atmosphere thick with anticipation. The puck zipped around, tape-to-tape, precise and calculated. The Goshawks' formation tightened like a noose. Ryan Mitchell took a D-to-D pass from their star rookie Axel Berger. Ryan steadied himself, letting the one-timer fly.

"Light the lamp, Ryan," Hunter shouted, his voice barely rising above the noise.

The puck screamed past Florida's goalie, hitting the back of the net with a satisfying snap. The horn blared, red light on. Goshawks 1, Barracudas 0. The crowd went ballistic, their cheers shaking the arena like an earthquake.

GOAL! Goshawks—Mitchell

"That's how you do it, team," Chase roared, as Ryan skated past the bench exchanging a rapid succession of glove bumps with his teammates, a shared celebration solidifying their gritty resolve.

Ryan circled around, skating towards Hunter's net. A nod, a clap of the stick against the pads. Unspoken respect, mutual understanding. This was life or death in terms of hockey, and they were all in it together.

As the clock clicked down to the end of the first period, Hunter felt an energy inside him, an unyielding fire. He glanced up at the scoreboard. They had the lead, but in a game like this, that was a fragile thing.

Skating off the ice, Hunter thought about the goshawk, about his teammates, about the promise of victory just within reach. They were fighting for their lives, for their honor, for the very soul of the team. Mere seconds could make the difference between winning and losing.

The Goshawks had struck the first blow, but Hunter knew this war was far from over. He was ready for whatever was coming his way.

The second and third periods remained scoreless. Hunter's body was a coiled spring, muscles tensed, eyes narrowed. Pucks had whizzed, zinged, and ricocheted ... none had gotten through, a testament that he was still the Goshawks impenetrable wall. He blocked thirty-nine shots on goal. Across the rink, Florida's goalie was equally immovable, turning away thirty-two attempts. Except for Ryan's goal, it was a deadlock ... a trench war on ice.

The clock hit one minute. The Barracudas' goalie bolted for the bench like a dog off leash. Another skater jumped on, an added Barracudas' warrior for their last-ditch assault.

This is it, Hunter thought. *Everything's on the line. No second chances.*

Jacobson, the Barracudas' captain, rushed to the red line, sending a hard dump into the Goshawks' zone—a vulcanized rubber grenade landing just in front and to the right of Hunter's net.

"Mine," Hunter growled, his gaze fixed on the puck. With the intensity of a seasoned predator, he sliced through the ice. The heel of his stick's blade scooped beneath the puck, his movements a blend of instinct and skill honed over countless hours of practice. Dropping to one knee, his line of sight blocked by a surge of opponents, yet his determination remained undiminished.

Time slowed. "Aim high and let it rip," Hunter muttered to himself, his actions mirroring his words, sending the puck airborne over the heads of both teams' players. The disk soared above the ice like a missile cleared for launch. It landed between the enemy's faceoff circles, sliding with stealth into the gaping maw of the empty net.

GOALIE GOAL! Goshawks—Griffin

Hunter's hands shot up. "YES!" His roar drowned in the blare of jubilant screams and applause. The first line swarmed him, clattering against his pads and mask.

"To the bench, hero," Ryan yelled, his voice edged with pride.

Hunter froze, confused. He was a goalie. Goalies didn't celebrate goals.

"Go on, Hunter, you've earned this," Chase chimed in, pushing Hunter toward his waving teammates.

Hunter grinned, skating to the bench for glove bumps and congratulations. Touching the last player glove-to-glove, he felt it—an electric charge, a disturbance in the air. Sage. He froze, his gaze searching the stands to no avail ... but her presence crawled over his skin, making the tiny hairs on the back of his neck stand.

The referee jolted him back to reality. "Get to your net, Griffin. There's still time on the clock."

"Right. Right," Hunter mumbled, as he glided back to his net. The remaining twenty-seven seconds weren't just ticks on a clock; they were twenty-seven heart-pounding, breath-stealing, soul-testing mini-eternities.

When the final horn blared, the Goshawks bench emptied. Hunter was engulfed by his teammates—his brothers-in-arms. The scoreboard blazoned the hard-earned truth: Goshawks 2, Barracudas 0. They had done it. The first round of playoffs was theirs.

"Line up, Goshawks, it ain't over till it's over," barked Chase, as he led the team to the age-old ritual that was as much about honor as it was about sportsmanship—the playoff handshake line.

Hunter's mask sat high on his head, revealing his face. Shed of his gloves, palms calloused and red—battle scars he wore with pride, were pressed against like-hands on the opposing team. His teammates went down the line, a few gruff "Good games" and hard nods exchanged with their rivals. Something was amiss, though.

"Where's Chucky?" muttered Ryan, eyes scanning the line ... there was no trace of the player who had been the biggest thorn in their sides.

"Guess he didn't have the guts to face us. We'll remember that," Chase growled, his eyes narrowing—a detail that spoke volumes, a slight that would not be forgotten.

Hunter moved down the line, his massive frame a fortress that had stood unbreached. "Hell of a fight," one Florida player gritted out, reluctant admiration in his eyes.

"Good game Ice Wall," another added, his tone laced with frustration, but also with respect.

At the end of the line, Hunter lifted his gaze. His heart raced when he saw her. Sage, camera aimed at him, capturing all his raw, victorious intensity.

Skating to her, he took Sage into his arms. Like a hawk's talons, his grip was both fierce and gentle. Bending her back, he sealed his lips over hers. It wasn't just a kiss; it was a conquest, a claiming. The crowd's roar intensified.

Chase skated next to them, a wolfish grin on his face. "Alright, lovebirds ... no PDA on the ice. Hunter, we owe our fans a victory lap."

With one last smoldering look at Sage, Hunter spoke, his voice filled with desire, "Have Margret get you to the Frosty Nest. I'll catch up with you after I've faced the firing squad of reporters."

Sage's gaze locked onto his, her nod an unspoken promise of the evening to come. As she stepped on gripped shoes towards the tunnel, Hunter felt a calm settle deep within him. Rejoining his team, he raised his stick in a final salute, leaning his head back, he let out a loud guttural, "Ka-Ka-Ka." The action echoed back to him by the Goshawks' fans. Each hawk screech, each banner waved, stoking the fire within Hunter for the battles that lay ahead.

Tonight, they'd won the first round. But the war was far from over. Hunter was more than ready for what was coming. With every fiber of his being pulsating in a rhythm of readiness, he knew one thing for certain—the Goshawks were just getting started.

Skating off the ice, his gaze locked upward to the empty VIP box where the goshawk had perched. He felt the spirit of the raptor, fierce and free. Tonight, they had both soared. Tonight, they had both conquered.

Chapter 26
Life in a Fishbowl

April 26th

Deep within the media tunnel's seclusion, Sage rested against its cool, unyielding walls, easing the grips from her sneakers. Above her, the celebration's echoes cascaded down, a subdued but ever-present testament to the game's outcome. From a distance, the distinct clicking of stilettos announced Margret's arrival.

"Can you give me a ride to the Frosty Nest?" Sage's words came out rushed, reflecting the whirlwind moment.

Margret threw a quick, measured glance at Sage. "I have to officiate the press conference. Keep the reporters in line."

"But Hunter is expecting me at the bar." Sage's eyes grew wide with confusion.

"Come with me. When the press has had its fill of questions, I promise I'll get you to the Frosty Nest before Hunter ties the laces to his dress shoes." Margret draped an arm around Sage, guiding her further down the tunnel.

Following Margret into the Goshawks' press conference room, Sage's gaze swept across the unfamiliar territory, a space normally veiled from public view now laid bare before her curious eyes.

Margret's presence cut through the room's charged atmosphere, a prelude to the storm of questions soon to be unleashed. Although the press corps had yet to enter, the room buzzed with the orchestrated chaos of TV and sound crews preparing their equipment, ensuring every microphone, camera, and lighting rig was primed to capture the post-game narratives.

Amidst this hive of activity, Sage retreated to a shadowed corner in the back of the room. Her hoodie drawn tight as a cloak of anonymity. Sage stood like a silent sentinel. She was observing, learning, and waiting, all the while minimizing her presence. Her fingers played with her camera's strap, as it hung heavy around her neck, a silent testament to her role in this arena—not as a spectator but as a discreet chronicler of moments yet to unfold.

Sage took a deep breath, bracing herself as the main doors opened. Within the charged stillness of the Goshawks' conference room, a noticeable shift occurred as the hockey press corps settled into their designated chairs. The veterans, clad in suits and ties, positioned themselves in the forefront, filling the first three rows. They prepared their instruments of trade with practiced ease. Their murmurs filled the space with an undercurrent of anticipation.

The room's dynamic altered again when Margret introduced a new element into the established setting. "Ladies and gentlemen," she began, "today, we're joined by some fresh faces." Margret then motioned six youthful reporters into the room. Their casual attire of sneakers, jeans, and t-shirts contrasted with the room's prevailing formality.

"These enthusiastic individuals," Margret continued, gesturing towards the group, "are pioneering our trial program. They bring the pulse of social media platforms to our conference today."

A ripple of discontent stirred among the seasoned reporters as they sported furrowed brows, along with disapproving head shakes.

"What the hell, Margret?" Sam, one of the old-timers, spoke up. "There's never enough time for us to ask questions. Now you're parading a group of wet-behind-the-ears reporter wannabees to take our precious minutes?" An agreeing murmur from the first three rows followed Sam's statement.

Margret offered, "Now Sam, I know this is going to be a stretch, but do you remember when you attended your first post-game conference?"

"That was a different era," Sam muttered. Raising his voice, he added, "Kids nowadays have no respect for tradition." Again, a murmur of agreement rumbled among those seated in the first three rows.

"I hear you, Sam. All I'm asking is for everyone to give these young people a chance. The Goshawks organization believes in this innovative program. We are confident it will merge the rich heritage of hockey journalism with the dynamic energy of social media storytelling."

"I just want to go on the record that I don't approve." Sam crossed his arms, sporting a sour expression.

"Duly noted." Margret's smile turned deadly as she added, "And if it bothers you too much, you are welcome to leave."

Sam let out a loud grunt, but he remained seated.

Preceding the players' appearance, the tension in the room grew. Sage sensed the press corps' eager anticipation, akin to wolves at the hunt, each journalist primed for a fresh slant or revealing soundbite. A blanket of quiet fell as the door opened once more as the game's star players entered.

The room buzzed with excitement, the echoes of the recent victory resonating in the packed space. Margret ushered Chase, Hunter, and Ryan to the long table at the front of the room. Hunter sat stoic. The brim of his Goshawks ball cap cast a slight shadow over his intense hazel eyes. Sage brought her camera up, her hands shaking as she watched the press prepare to fire their questions akin to loaded ammunition.

Hunter, the figure at the center of this growing maelstrom, looked both the hero and the vulnerable man, his features softened yet stubborn. The banter began, a mix of technical questions and personal anecdotes, laughter echoing through the room like tinkling ice in a crystal glass of Scotch.

Sage stayed tucked in the corner, the camera an extension of herself, capturing raw unscripted moments that spoke to her skill.

A reporter in the front row shouted, cutting through the chatter. "Ryan, that first goal set the pace. How did it feel slamming that one past the Barracudas' star goalie?"

Ryan sported a cocky grin, a lock of damp hair clinging to his forehead. "It felt really good. The energy from the crowd, the teamwork ... it all came together. It was electric, man."

As the press scribbled down Ryan's response, another voice pierced the room. "Chase, clinching this round on home ice has to feel special, right?"

Chase nodded. The captain's demeanor was evident in his posture. He took a long swig from his water bottle before answering. "Absolutely. It's always a privilege to deliver for our home crowd. The fans are as much a part of the Goshawks as we are. Their energy fuels us. We wanted this win not just for ourselves but for them too." Chase flashed a toothy grin for the camera.

The energy in the room was high key, with each answer amplifying the room's fervor. A more curious question came next. "Who can give us the backstory on the goshawk? How long have the Goshawks been working on that?"

Chase leaned over, giving Hunter a nod. "I think Hunter can answer that one. It was as much of a surprise to us as it was for the fans."

Hunter laughed. "It was a secret mission. The falconer has been working with me over the season. We were waiting for the right game. I had a gut feeling tonight was going to be special." Pausing, he looked at Chase, adding, "I think the goshawk was as excited about the game as we were. It sure added a nice touch to the victory, didn't it?"

The room rippled with agreement, a momentary respite before the press shifted their focus on Hunter. A seasoned reporter in the second row fired, "Hunter, that goal ... it's not something we see every day. Only a handful of goalies have achieved what you did tonight. Have you been practicing that move?"

Hunter leaned forward. "You could say it's been a lifetime in the making. I've been working on that since I was a kid. It's every goalie's dream to score."

Sage was in awe, as she watched the press eating out of Hunter's hand, hanging on to every word. Another reporter pitched in, "What about the shutout, Hunter? Over thirty-nine saves on goal. Physically, how are you holding up?"

Hunter's smile faded, a hint of fatigue seeping through his armor. "I think you should be asking that question to Florida's goalie. But, yeah, I know I'll be feeling it in the morning. It's all part of playoff hockey, isn't it?"

Just as the conference seemed to wind down, one of the junior reporters from the media group stood. She veered off-track, touching upon the topic everyone had side-stepped. "Hunter, everyone is dying to know—the kiss on the ice. Was that the elusive Sage?"

Sage's heartbeat became the loudest sound in the room, drowning the inquisitive voices around her. Through her lens, she alone saw it—the tiniest twitch of Hunter's jaw, the sudden stillness that overcame him as the line was crossed. Sage could see the tempest in him, restrained but evident, his silence a loud testament to the personal boundaries being breached.

Hunter's eyes narrowed, his previous happy demeanor replaced by a steely reserve, as he leaned in again ... his lips close to the mic. The room seemed to shrink, the air thickening with tension. His jaw ticking.

"I will answer all questions you have pertaining to hockey," Hunter's voice was firm, leaving no room for negotiation. He paused, his gaze sweeping across the room, he asserted, "My private life is just that ... private."

In the pulsating silence, the word 'private' rang loud, an unyielding wall separating the man from the myth. Sage could feel the undercurrents in the room shift, an uneasy realization settling in. They had ventured too far.

The same young cheeky reporter, unswayed by Hunter's stern stance, pressed further, her fingers forming quote marks to emphasize her words. "I think it's a 'fair question,' considering you allowed us into your 'private life' when you kissed the mystery girl on the ice tonight."

Before Hunter could respond, Margret emerged from the shadows. Hands on hips, she stood before the press, her expression stern and unwavering. "That's it for tonight. Thank you everyone."

Through her lens, Sage saw the moment Hunter noticed her presence ... an invisible thread connecting them. Their eyes meeting, his gaze conveyed a whirlwind of emotions: anger, concern, and, most poignant a silent plea for understanding.

In that brief connection, Sage saw the man, the celebrity, the vulnerability that came with being thrust into a glaring spotlight. Hunter's world was a place where lines between personal and public became a dangerous blur. She saw the silent question in his eyes, a plea for discretion, for sanity in a world that thrived on sensationalism.

As the trio rose, the room erupted in a rumble of voices, and chairs moving. The conference coming to an abrupt end as Margret escorted the players out of the room.

The frenzy of activity subsided as the veteran reporters packed up, readying to leave. Sage let out a sigh, believing she'd remained unseen by everyone except for Hunter. Then, a perceptive young reporter caught sight of her. Recognition ignited in his gaze as he raced to Sage, his smart phone on record.

"You're the girl Griffin kissed on the ice, aren't you?" Barking his question, he thrust the mic attached to his phone, inches from Sage's face. His words tinged with a near-feral excitement. Sage attempted to back away, to shrink, to conceal herself in her hoodie.

Gasps from the seasoned reporters filled the room as the young rogue reporter became reckless. He stepped closer to Sage, attempting to pull back the hoodie ... to expose her face.

Sage's voice trembled but held an edge of steel. "Do Not Touch Me," she growled. Feeling a visceral need to protect herself, She began snapping photos. Her camera became both shield and weapon, documenting the predatory face before her.

The atmosphere shifted. The professional press vacated the room. Like sharks sensing bloodied prey, the smattering of youthful media novices remained. They zeroed in on Sage. Their expressions distorted with anticipation, eager to uncover a story that would skyrocket their online presence.

Sage found herself engulfed in a whirlwind of technology and relentless inquiry, surrounded by a sea of microphones, cameras, and smartphones, all wielded by individuals hungry for their breakthrough moment.

"Are you sleeping with Ice Wall?" someone shouted.

Not waiting for an answer as another chimed in with, "Did Griffin secure this gig for his new flavor of the month?"

Yet another accused. "Why are you trying to keep your relationship with Hunter from his fans?"

Sage felt her chest tighten. Each beat of her heart was accompanied by a crescendo of noise that threatened to engulf her. She could feel the prickle of sweat along her forehead. Her skin felt like it was stretched too tight over her bones.

"I'm getting Margret and security," Sam, the veteran reporter shouted as he ran from the room.

Sage tried to respond, to deflect, but her voice was swallowed in the rush of voices. Her breathing became erratic, the oxygen seeming too thin as the group closed in, trapping her. Sage's vision blurred, tears mingling with the stinging sweat as fear clawed at her throat, threatening to steal her breath.

Amid the chaos, a figure cut through the group, her presence commanding, her aura a fortress against the storm of greed and insensitivity. Margret emerged like a wrathful deity, her voice booming across the room, slicing through the din with the sharpness of a blade. "Enough!" she thundered. Her eyes blazing with a fire that promised retribution. "I want this room cleared now! I have all your names. I'm personally ensuring none of you will ever step foot in a Goshawks event again!" She threatened, her eyes narrowed, holding a venomous promise of her words.

Not far behind, Sam returned, followed by two security guards. Within moments, the group was escorted out. Silence descended as Margret moved to Sage, her features softening, her hands reaching out.

"Sage, breathe, darlin'," Margret urged, her voice drifting into a soothing Southern drawl.

Sage's panicked gaze found Margret, a beacon of safety within her turmoil. Yet, her breaths came in ragged gasps, tears flowing unchecked as the full weight of the verbal attack settled in.

Margret wrapped her arms around Sage with a firm yet comforting grip, doing her best to ground Sage to the present, away from the whirlpool of panic that threatened to suck her back in. "You are safe. You are safe with me," Margret reassured, her eyes holding a world of understanding and empathy.

Sage could barely form words, her voice choked with sobs, "I ... I can't ... Hunter ... his life ... my life." The fragmented sentences spoke volumes of her fears—for Hunter, for her vanishing privacy, for a potential relationship that was still in a delicate bud, now under the threat of being crushed.

Margret held Sage tighter, her resolve steeling. "We will sort this out. You are not alone," she vowed.

Gathering a package of tissues from her purse, Margret handed them to Sage. "Dry your eyes. Take your time to compose yourself."

"But ... what about Hunter?" Sage wiped her eyes, then blew her nose.

"You come first. Once we get you out of here, I'll see to Hunter."

With strong, guiding hands, Margret walked Sage through a back passage, away from any lingering reporters and ardent fans, into the cool, quiet night. The fresh air a welcome embrace.

"Let's get you home, Sage. My home, for now." Margret's voice was resolute. "Lionel," she called out, motioning to her driver. "We'll need to make a stop at the Regency to retrieve Sage's belongings."

As they drove from the arena, the limo passed chanting fans waving signs. "I think I know how Alice must have felt when she tumbled down the rabbit hole," Sage's words came with the realization that she had ventured too deep, too fast, into a world that relentlessly consumed the unprepared.

"You're safe now," Margret repeated.

Sage felt herself unravel, her fear giving way to a crushing exhaustion. "I just want to go home, to be with my mom," she whispered, her voice holding a world of weariness.

"We can make that happen whenever you want." Margret assured her.

"How late is the animal shelter open?" Sage sniffed.

"I'll send them a text. After all the money donated from the calendar pre-sales, I'm sure they will accommodate us at any hour."

"Even tonight?"

Margret pulled out her cell phone, her fingers dancing over the screen. "The hotel manager will make sure all your possessions are packed and in the lobby by the time we get there."

Two pings rang out from Margret's phone.

"Good news." Margret smiled. "Lionel, after we stop by the Regency, we need to make a detour, to the animal shelter."

"Margret, you are a miracle worker." Sage managed a weak smile.

"Oh, better yet. I contacted the pilot of the Goshawks charter plane. He can be ready to take you home in two hours."

"What about Hunter? Did you let him know what happened? Did you tell him why I won't be meeting him tonight?"

"Right now, let's concentrate on getting you home. I promise Hunter will understand."

Leaning against the cool glass of the plane's window, Sage watched Portland's city lights stream past. The eight-week-old Yellow Labrador puppy sitting on her lap, yawned, reached his head up, licking her chin.

She felt like a coward having Margret contact Hunter. Sage knew she was being selfish, but right now, she felt an overwhelming need to protect herself. She needed time to resolve her feelings for Hunter. Until tonight, their relationship had been platonic ... and then the kiss.

Her fingers went to her lips, recalling the passion, the yearning. Yet, she had to step back. It was beyond her comprehension how Hunter could live his life in a fishbowl, no matter how much he loved playing hockey. Sage's body ached with the thought of never being with Hunter again. She missed his laughter, his voice, his touch ... she missed him.

Chapter 27

Burning Going Down

April 26th

The air was thick with the anticipation of celebration as Chase, Hunter, and Ryan stood outside the pulsing heart of the night—The Frosty Nest. The familiar clamor of voices, laughter, and clinking glasses reverberated faintly through the oversized glass entrance door, a promise of the revelry awaiting them inside.

"The downside of meeting with the press after a game ... being the last ones to join the celebration." Ryan laughed.

"I didn't think there was any upside dealing with the press," Hunter grumbled. He ran fingers around the back of his neck, separating his damp hair from his dress shirt collar. He hated being late, especially now, with the prospect of being with Sage.

"If it wasn't for the press, there would be no fans. Without fans there would be no Goshawks," Chase said, as he started to open the door.

Before they could step inside, a whirlwind of youthful exuberance engulfed them: an eager gaggle of underage fans adorned in Goshawks jerseys. The girls' faces, flushed with excitement, were illuminated under the Frosty Nest's neon sign—a large nest composed of hockey sticks, with pucks instead of eggs. Sharpie markers in hand, the girls waved the backs of jerseys, programs, even sleeveless arms ... seeking the signatures of their idols.

"Please, Hunter! You were amazing tonight!" One brunette swooned, her eyes shimmering with unrestrained admiration.

Hunter exchanged a glance with Ryan, both sharing grins that bore a mix of humility and pride. Without a word, they began signing; the sharp scent of the marker ink mingling with the crisp night air.

Chase, ever the vigilant captain, signed one jersey but kept a watchful eye on the growing crowd. His glance swept over the eager faces before them, his posture signaling a readiness to proceed, urging his teammates to follow his lead. "C'mon, guys, the team's waiting for us," Chase's voice cut through the rising chatter, bearing the rugged undertones of a leader accustomed to being heard, especially amidst chaos.

Raptor, the mountainous bouncer, stood just inside the door. The moment he saw the trio, he signaled to his top security guy, Ron. The towering figure swiftly made his way over, his presence an unspoken authority that promised to keep the escalating excitement in check.

Ron guided the trio of Goshawks through the bustling bar. The place buzzed with activity, a dynamic blend of fans and regulars, all basking in the shared victory. The atmosphere was charged, a testament to the camaraderie and unity sports can inspire, drawing everyone together in a joint celebration.

"Yo! Griffin! No one saw that coming, not even Florida. You've got the Sunshine State weeping tonight," shouted a fan from the bar.

"Ice Wall, you're a legend. Seeing a goalie scoring a goal in person has been my lifelong dream," slurred the guy sitting next to him.

Still, another fan chimed in, "You're rewriting the history books, Griffin. Go! Goshawks!"

The chant of "Go! Goshawks!" reverberated through the bar as the trio passed.

"Griff! You're the friggin' man!" A patron sitting at a corner table hollered, his voice carrying the same rugged, hearty timbre echoed by the others.

The surrounding flatscreen TVs were playing the hymns of the Goshawks' victory, an altar where praises were sung by broadcasters, extolling Hunter for his monumental performance. Every replay of Hunter's goal brought forth a crescendo of cheers, the floor seeming to shake with excitement.

Hunter felt uncomfortable in the off-ice spotlight. He doubted if he would ever get used to hearing the rhythmic chant of his name becoming a living entity. Every replay of his goal, every enthusiastic pat on the back, the clinking of glasses filled with celebratory drinks ... it all wove into a tapestry of sensations that overwhelmed him.

"They love you, Hunter." Ryan nudged his friend's shoulder.

"I know how fast they can turn," Hunter mumbled, recalling the jeers after every loss.

"Enjoy it while you can." Chase nodded, his eyes scanning the room with pride and the weight of responsibility that came with leadership.

The VIP section, a sanctuary reserved for the warriors of the ice, awaited them, as the roars and cheers grew louder. The air was thick with the aromas of fried fish, craft beer, and the tangy bite of citrus-based cocktails.

Ron removed the velvet rope dividing the Goshawks and their guests from the general population of the bar. As Hunter entered the VIP area, his senses were on high alert, each sight and sound amplified to an unbearable degree. The joyous atmosphere in the Frosty Nest clashed with the emotions swirling within him. Hunter scanned the crowd, desperate to find Sage.

"Ice Wall, man, these lobster sliders are killer! You gotta try one." Axel thrust the bite-size mini sandwich near Hunter's lips.

"Come on Hunter, open your mouth." Etan encouraged.

Hunter's stomach grumbled as the rich aroma filled his nostrils. He obliged, opening his mouth wide. The savory taste of lobster, herb mayo, on the buttery brioche buns was only a temporary reprieve from his internal turmoil.

"Hey guys, have any of you seen Sage or Margret?" Hunter blurted, as he grabbed a napkin, wiping mayo from his lips and chin hair. His voice carried a layer of urgency. The image of Sage, standing alone in the back of the room during the press conference, fueled his rising anxiety.

Olaf, sitting at a long table, about to savor a hefty bite of Blueberry BBQ Wings, paused, a wing halfway to his mouth, sauce dripping down his fingers. He motioned for his teammates to join him.

After the group sat, Olaf looked at Hunter. "Haven't seen either. I was the first one here," his voice, always loud, cut through the surrounding celebration. "Hunter, buddy. You gotta think about the consequences, man. That kiss … it was all over the TV tonight." Olaf pointed to a flatscreen turned to a non-sports channel.

Hunter's jaw clenched as he watched his Instagram image flash, followed by a slow-motion version of him kissing Sage. He felt a hundred tiny needles pricking at his skin, a reminder of the scrutiny and pressure that came after the first fiasco in Florida. Waving to a nearby waitress, Hunter fished out a twenty-dollar bill. Flashing her a smile, he pointed to the offensive images. "Please, change that station."

Hunter's gaze locked across the table with Chase's, conveying a world of concern without a word being spoken.

"Ya, Ya, Hunter, that was one ballsy move on the ice tonight, wasn't it?" Etan stood behind Hunter, squeezing the goalie's shoulder. A mischievous grin flashed on the rookie's face.

Ryan glared at both the rookies. Looking to Hunter he said, "Listen, we all get the high of a win. Just don't lose sight of the big picture, man. Those kinds of antics can shift the whole team's focus."

"Remember, we're fighting for the Holy Grail, not negative headlines," Chase added.

"Keep your pretty lips reserved for kissing The Cup." Axel puckered his lips. Picking up a frosty beer mug, he placed a kiss on the glass.

"Hey, put that down," Olaf growled. "Leave my beer alone until you two turn twenty-one. I'm sure the barmaid will bring you boys a couple of Shirley Temples." Froth drizzled over Olaf's fingers as he grabbed the mug out of Axel's hand.

"Listen, Hunter," Chase said, his voice a deep rumble, commanding attention. "Your impulsive actions might have put Sage in a tight spot." His knuckles rapped on Hunter's head. "It's just not like you."

"Yeah, man. You've got to start thinking before you do stupid stuff, especially now," Ryan chimed in, his tone tinged with brotherly admonition. "We expect more of our star goalie." He paused to look at Olaf.

"No offense taken," Olaf said. Laughing, he licked the beer from his fingers.

"We can't afford any distractions," Axel and Etan sang as one.

Chase addressed the rookies, "Why don't you guys get us some pretzel bites and cheese dip from the buffet table?"

As the boys went on their quest, a waitress approached the table, carrying a tray over-filled with shots of Don Julio 1942. "These top-shelf tequila shots are courtesy of the boys at the bar ... for Ryan's top-shelf shot on the Barracudas' goalie."

Ryan downed one of the shots, lifting the empty glass high, nodding to the boys at the bar. In response, a half-dozen voices shouted back, "Great. Shot. Rock."

Hunter grabbed a shot glass, held his breath, tilted his head back, releasing the liquid ... warming his tongue and throat, soothing his nerves. He repeated the process a second time.

Chase looked as if he was about to give Hunter another lecture, but instead, he followed his teammates' actions.

Ryan looked at Olaf and Chase. "Where are your wives tonight? I thought for sure Sofia and Emily would be celebrating with us."

"Our ladies are having a PJ party at Chase's house with the little ones." Olaf said, as he too downed a shot. He then turned to Hunter. "Keep your focus, kid. I don't do well going into a game cold." He slammed his empty glass on the table.

"You think I don't know that?" Hunter snapped, the frustration in his voice raw. He took a moment, waiting for the tequila to do its magic.

No matter how he tried, the memory of the kiss grated on his nerves. He had no idea why he did it. Yet, he could still feel her soft lips on his, the electrifying current that buzzed between them, the sense of home he'd found in their embrace—it was all too potent to ignore, too sacred to cast aside for fear of scrutiny or adverse consequences.

"I don't get it?" Hunter blurted out.

"Don't get what?" asked Chase, a slight slur to his speech as he took another shot.

"I've never seen the press go after any of the other Goshawks' girlfriends or wives. Why Sage?"

Olaf raised his hand. "Oh! Oh! I got this one." He sported a wicked smile. "Most of the guys on the team were married, engaged, or otherwise entwined before they joined the Goshawks. Sofia's my high school sweetheart."

"So?" Hunter frowned, his index finger tracing the rim of a full shot glass.

"They are old news." Ryan leaned across the table, poking Hunter in the chest. "You, on the other hand, have never had a girlfriend since joining the Goshawks. You, my friend, have always kept your personal life private ... until Sage fell into your life, that is."

"When you posted the 'Hi Sage' image on your Instagram page ... and THEN kissed Sage on the ice ... you put chum in the waters." Olaf said, as he looked from Chase to Ryan, both nodding in agreement.

"Every time you do something only a rookie player would do; you're feeding the sharks. The sharks are a hungry bunch." Olaf shook his head, taking another shot. "If you keep doing stupid stuff, you and Sage are going to be eaten up by the press." Olaf chomped his teeth in Hunter's direction.

A silence fell over the group as Etan and Axel returned, placing two trays filled with a variety of succulent dishes on the table. "What's wrong?" Etan's smile morphed into a frown as he looked at the sour expressions in front of him. Turning to Axel, he grumbled, "I told you to put more lobster sliders on ... but nooo, you said they would like the Seafood Poutine."

"Who doesn't like the Frosty Nest's French fries smothered in seafood, cheese curds, and sauce?" Axel grabbed a dripping fry, sucking it into his mouth.

Ryan gave the rookies a stern 'shut up' glare.

"I didn't plan for this, you know," Hunter continued, his voice softer now, yet tinged with a determination that brooked no argument. "Something about her just ... draws me in. I can't explain it."

"Hunter, we're your team, your brothers. We only want what's best for you." Chase let out a loud belch. "But, man, I gotta agree with Ryan and Olaf. You have to start thinking before you keep doing this dumb shit."

Hunter met Chase's gaze, finding a depth of understanding and empathy in the eyes of his captain. He nodded, a new resolve solidifying within him.

Chase's phone buzzed. "I have to get this. It might be Emily." He clicked on the text. When he was done reading, he stared at Hunter.

"What?" Hunter's head pounded. Shots of tequila always did a number on him.

"It's a text from Margret." Chase grimaced. "Sorry bud, but Sage won't be meeting you at the bar tonight." He paused. Holding Hunter's gaze, he added, "She's on a plane back to South Dakota."

Hunter's body sagged as he reached over to take two more quick shots. He knew he'd screwed up royal. "I'm such a jerk."

"Hey, Griffin, Etan and I will find you a new girl."

"Shut. Up. Axel," Chase, Olaf, and Ryan shouted as one.

"Let's be logical, Hunter. What do you really know about this girl?" Chase leaned into Hunter's shoulder.

"I know how she makes me feel. Doesn't that count for something?"

"Feelings come and go." Olaf leaned forward. "But we, the Goshawks, have been here for you every day. You need us as much as we need you. This is going to be a hard lesson, Hunter, but we need you now, more than you need her."

Olaf was right. Hunter needed to be in the game without distractions. Yet, he couldn't stop feeling he'd lost something valuable. Something he would regret losing for a lifetime. He felt like a goalie who let the last puck in, losing The Cup for his team. His head told him to make a clean break of it ... but his heart was aching to hold her, to kiss her just one more time.

Hunter looked up at the flatscreen as it replayed his winning goal. He reached over taking the last shot ... this time it burned going down.

Chapter 28

Reunions and Revelations

April 27th

The first rays of morning filtered through the ancient oaks, casting elongated shadows dancing beside Sage as she made her way across the yard to the main farmhouse. The puppy pounced beside her on the dew-spattered grass.

The screen door's sudden bang signaled her father's approach. Seeing him on the porch stirred a comforting yet unsettling feeling within her, as though her recent trials had laid bare her emotions, making her feel transparent and vulnerable.

"Dad," she greeted, her voice shaky yet infused with a hint of joy at seeing him.

"Sage?" He squinted in the emerging daylight, his face breaking into a warm, welcoming smile. "Well, I'll be. Didn't expect to see you so soon, kiddo." His strong arms enveloped her in a hug.

"I ... I needed home," Sage mumbled into her father's shoulder. His familiar scent of hay and worn leather grounded her.

Jim stepped back, hands firmly gripping her shoulders as he studied his daughter. His eyes then flickered to the puppy, whose teeth were firmly attached to the leg of his jeans. "Who's this little fella?"

Sage managed a weak smile. She picked up the puppy, dislodging him from her father's leg. "Dad, this is Crease."

"I'd ask you how he came into your life, but I feel like it will be a long story, and I have to get my morning started."

"It is Dad. For only being gone a short time, I have lots of long stories to tell."

He nodded, his face turning serious, concern etching lines deeper into his sun-kissed face. "We have time, Sage. You know we always have time for you."

"Thanks Dad."

With a final squeeze, he left her on the porch, the promise of deeper conversations hanging in the cool morning air.

The scents of pancakes, maple syrup, and fresh brewed coffee seeped through the screen door, beckoning her in. Sage loved mornings on the farm. It always felt like a sanctuary of warmth and love.

"Hi Mom." Sage entered the kitchen, setting the wiggling puppy down.

"Sage? My word," her mom exclaimed, her face transforming with a beaming smile that held a hint of concern. Jumping from her chair at the kitchen table, she nearly spilled her coffee. Engulfing Sage in a tight hug, she said, "We weren't expecting you so soon, honey. Is everything alright?"

Sage hesitated, her gaze dropping to the puppy sitting at her feet. The innocence in his eyes reflected back at her, offering a solace she desperately needed.

Lilly followed her daughter's gaze. "Oh My. What a cute ball of fur." She picked up the puppy, returning to her chair. "He looks like trouble in the making."

"His name is Crease. Yeah, I suspect he's going to be more trouble than he's worth." *Not unlike Hunter* she thought. "It's temporary. I'm just keeping him for a friend." Sage knew if she kept telling herself that, it might come true.

"Oh, well, in that case, don't get too attached." Lilly paused while the puppy licked her chin. Looking the pup in the eyes, she cooed, "You are going to be a little heart breaker, aren't you?" Crease's tail thumped against the table.

"You have no idea," Sage moaned.

"Are you hungry?" Before Sage could answer, her mom put the puppy down and made her way into the kitchen. After giving Sage a cup of coffee, she poured pancake batter on the still hot griddle.

"Mom, you don't have to do that. I can just have coffee." Sage watched as her mom flipped the pancakes. Crease sitting at her feet, his nose twitching.

"Nonsense. Now, how many pancakes do you want?"

Sage was about to answer, when she noticed her mom was talking to the puppy, not her. "I think you have a new friend."

"One can never have enough friends." Her mom put a small pancake on a saucer, putting it on the floor for Crease. Then she placed a plate piled high with pancakes smothered with butter and maple syrup in front of Sage.

"I've missed you so much," Sage mumbled through a mouthful of syrupy goodness.

Reclaiming her chair, Lilly gave her daughter a long, hard gaze, filled with a depth of understanding only a mother could hold. Tapping her fingers on the table, she voiced her concerns. "We saw the game last night, Sage, and that … kiss."

Sage's fork paused midway to her mouth, the weight of her mom's words settling heavy within her. "I didn't expect our first kiss to be in front of hundreds of fans or televised to thousands of strangers." Her voice was a mere whisper, a reflection of the vulnerability that threatened to spill over. "Everything's so overwhelming, the spotlight, the crazed fans, the aggressive reporters ... I feel like I'm losing myself."

Her mom reached over, her warm hand covering Sage's, a rock in the swirling storm that threatened to consume her. "It's disheartening to see how fast things spiraled. You were always our quiet, introspective girl, more at home with nature's canvas than in a glaring spotlight."

Sage could feel the heat rise from her chest to her face, as her mother's words hit home.

"Do you have feelings for that boy?"

"His name is Hunter, Mom. Honestly, I don't know," Sage admitted, her voice cracking with emotion. "My feelings for Hunter ... they're even more complicated now that I've met him in person. We went from a budding friendship to ... a media frenzy. I don't know if I'm ready for all that comes with being ... with being in a relationship with someone like him."

Lilly squeezed Sage's hand, her eyes reflecting a swirling vortex of love and worry. "Sage, sometimes life throws us into the deep end, not to see us drown, but to help us discover we can swim, that we can navigate the choppy waters."

"I know. I just wish there was a class in how to swim in a tidal wave of emotions."

"Sweetie, some lessons you have to learn on your own." Lilly paused, her gaze holding a wisdom born of years. "But you don't have to do it alone. Remember, you have roots, deep and unyielding. No matter where life takes you, this will always be your sanctuary, your place to find clarity and peace."

Sage refused to release the tears pooling in her eyes. She had cried more in the past days with Hunter than she had in her whole life. Picking up the puppy, Sage smiled as Crease licked a drop of syrup off her finger. "Thanks Mom, I needed to hear your words of wisdom this morning."

After breakfast, Sage returned to her apartment, ready to dive back into work. Margret was waiting for the candid shots from the previous evening's game, prompting Sage to boot up her laptop. That's when she spotted the postcard on the wall over her desk.

'We Are Excited to Showcase Your One Woman Show on May 25th.'

Sage glanced at the calendar next to the postcard, realizing it was already April 27th. "Crap," Sage exclaimed so loud Crease jumped off her lap, scrambling under her feet.

Chapter 29

On Thin Ice

April 27th

Standing in the shower, Hunter hoped the piercing needles of cold water would cut through last night's lingering haze of alcohol ... that the frigid spray would somehow stop the relentless pounding in his head.

As the water rushed over him, Hunter's mind circled back to Sage. The kiss that lingered on his lips still tasted of sweet surprise. He never intended their first kiss to be a public display of affection. Hunter knew his actions were too impulsive, stepping beyond the boundaries of their growing intimacy. What was he thinking of, thrusting her into the glaring spotlight by his rash actions?

Hunter grappled with his conflicting emotions for Sage. He feared he'd crushed their potential for a real relationship before it had a chance to grow. As much as he loved hockey, he hated being in the public eye. Every fiber in him screamed for redemption, a chance to salvage the dream that seemed to be crumbling to ashes.

Stepping out of the shower, the mirror reflected a gritty vision, all sinewy muscles, and scars that mapped the landscape of Hunter's hockey career. The floor tiles were a cold shock under his bare feet, grounding him to the harsh morning that lay ahead.

Dragging a towel across his body, he barely registered the abrasive feel. His mind swirling with images of Sage—her warm smile, the softness of her skin, and the scent of lavender that clung to him long after she had gone.

He had just pulled on his running shorts, the fabric clinging to his damp skin, when the shrill buzz of his cell phone pierced through the silent house. His heart vaulted in his chest, his pulse pounding, thinking it might be Sage.

In his desperate haste to get to the phone, get to Sage, he barreled into the living room, his wet feet slipping on the hardwood floor. Before he could regain his balance, his toe collided with a thud on the massive wooden leg of the coffee table.

"Son of a—!" He roared, his voice echoing against the apartment walls. Hunter was used to pain. It was the price of playing hockey. Yet, the pain he felt now was fiercer than any he'd been dealt with on the ice. A flash of white-hot agony shot up his leg. He could feel his toe pulsating, a grotesque dance of swelling flesh and flaming nerves. His breath came out in harsh pants.

He stumbled to grab the still buzzing phone, his jaw clenched tight, fury and panic mingling in his eyes. "Sage?" he barked into the phone. His voice was harsh, unrecognizable to himself.

"No man, it's Ryan ... What's going on with ya? Sounds like you've been run over by a Zamboni," Ryan's words came through, tinged with confused concern.

In contrast, Hunter's voice was a blade, sharp and dangerous. He snapped, "I smashed my damn toe, feels like it's shattered into a million pieces."

There was a beat of silence before Ryan responded, "Damn, bud, just hold yer horses. I just pulled in front of your apartment. Keep yer stick on the ice ... don't go off half-cocked, alright?"

"A little too late for that," Hunter growled, as he threw himself on the couch, his foot elevated, throbbing in time with his racing heart. His living room had transformed into a battlefield, the sharp tang of adrenaline mingled with the undertones of fear.

The taste of bitterness of his current predicament was a cruel cocktail of pain and regret, the harsh reality seeping into his pores. Yesterday's game and its glorious triumph seemed like a distant dream now, fragments of joy replaced by harsh, biting reality.

His doorbell's abrupt sound snapped him back to the present, signaling Ryan's arrival, pulling Hunter back from the brink of despair. It was then he remembered locking his door the night before. Something he rarely did. With a heavy sigh, he pushed himself up from the couch. Limping to the door, he was ready to face the consequences of his actions, hoping his toe was not injured as bad as it felt.

The world of hockey was ruthless. There was no room for weakness, no space for faltering. Lately, his career path felt more like riding a roller coaster. One game the fans were tossing insults at him, the next game they were buying him drinks and heaping on praises. It was never ending.

His mind was a swirl of conflicting emotions—angry at himself for being reckless, mired with frustration for the careless injury. Above all, he felt a looming dread about the repercussions this could have on his career ... his team's chances in the playoffs. Yesterday, in the game's frenzy, the unexpected win, the euphoria had felt so pure. Now, in the harsh light of day, everything seemed disjointed, a mishmash of moments that led to his current predicament. He felt like a supernova, ready to explode, vaporize into nothingness.

When Hunter opened the door, Ryan's face mirrored his own. A look of concern and disgust.

"Damn! Hunter!"

"Yeah, I know. You can't say anything I haven't already said to myself." Hunter opened the door wider. Just as his neighbor, Jill, walked down the hall.

"Hi Ryan. Hi, Hunt …" She stopped short, scrutinizing Hunter. "Oh, my gosh, Hunter, what happened? You look as white as a vampire."

"He just stubbed his toe," Ryan answered.

"Looks more than just stubbed to me." Jill pushed past Ryan, helping Hunter back to the couch. Looking at Ryan, she barked, "Get him a bunch of pillows off his bed. His leg needs to be elevated." She then addressed Hunter, "Do you have ice packs in your freezer?"

"Always."

Jill hurried to the kitchen, rushing back with two big ice packs, as Ryan returned with three feather pillows. Jill lifted Hunter's leg, motioning for Ryan to put the pillows under Hunter's foot. She then wrapped each ice pack in a dish towel, placing one under and one over Hunter's toes. "Where's your shirt?" she scolded.

"I'll get him one," Ryan chirped.

With Ryan gone, Jill bent over Hunter and asked, "So, how bad is it really?"

Hunter's arm covered his eyes. Not wanting to answer any questions, especially from Jill. "It's not worth all this fuss. People stub their toes all the time. He tried to sit up, as Jill placed her hand on his bare chest, preventing him from rising.

"Geez, work out much," she teased. Her hand lingered on his abs. "I grew up with five older brothers. Your toe is more than stubbed. I hope it's a bruise, not a break, but you'll need to get an x-ray."

As Ryan came back, he tossed Hunter a Goshawks t-shirt. Looking to Jill, he added, "Hey, thanks for your help, but we got this."

Hunter reached for Jill's hand. "Do me a huge favor. Please do not mention this to anyone."

Jill squeezed Hunter's hand, her expression turning sour. "Do you even need to ask?"

"Yeah, He does." Ryan stood near the still opened door. "Like, I said, we got this."

"Fine." Jill glared at Ryan, then turned to Hunter. "I have a pair of crutches if you think you'll need them."

"That is the last thing he needs." Ryan scowled. "Do you want Hunter's picture plastered on the front page of the Portland Press Harold?"

"OK, I get it." Pursing her lips, she turned again to Hunter. "You need to get it looked at. Worst-case scenario, it's broken ... best case, it's a severe bruise. Either way, an injury to your foot can be catastrophic ... especially now."

"Bye, Jill." Ryan made a sweeping movement toward the door.

"I'm out of here. But, Hunter, if you need anything, anything at all, call." Jill brushed by Ryan, gifting him her best evil-eyed glare.

Shutting the door. Ryan walked to Hunter's wall of windows. "I didn't see any press outside your apartment building when I came in. Doesn't look like anyone is out there now." He turned to Hunter. "Can ya get your foot into a shoe?"

Hunter attempted to wiggle his toe. "I don't think so, man."

"I spotted some sandals when I was rifling through your closet for a shirt. I'll grab 'em along with a pair of socks." Ryan let out a chortling laugh. "Might not be the fancy duds you usually wear, but at least no one will photo your ballooned toe, buddy."

Hunter reached under his leg, pulled out a pillow, aimed, hitting Ryan in the face.

It took the two of them a half hour to get Hunter dressed, out of the apartment building, and into Ryan's car. Hunter wore his best goalie face, putting his full weight on his foot, collapsing as soon as he climbed into Ryan's SUV.

On their way to the Goshawks' training facility, Ryan turned to Hunter. "Can we trust Jill not to go to the press?"

"Yeah. I've known her for over five years. She's as loyal as they get." Hunter winced as he adjusted the ice packs over his toes. "Can you drive a little faster?"

The SUV screeched to a halt at the player's entrance of the practice facility. "Stay here and wait for me on the bench," Ryan instructed, his voice tinged with concern. His low growl reverberated with the urgency of the situation.

Hunter grimaced, hauling himself out of the vehicle. Each step a battle, a nasty reminder of the sharp pain shooting up his leg. He made his way to the bench, his toe throbbing with a relentless intensity. Raindrops dripped down his cheeks, a replacement for the tears he could not shed. Waiting for Ryan to park, Hunter couldn't suppress a cry of frustration. "God, not again. Why now?" Closing his eyes, Hunter's face contorted, a grim sculpture of frustration and agony under the darkening sky.

His voice echoed in the stillness, fragments of the past resurfacing unbidden, enveloping him like a suffocating fog. A memory flooded his mind in fragments. Age twelve. Star goalie on the high school team. Being late. Falling over untied shoelaces. Broken fingers. Sidelined for the season. His team fell from first place. He was to blame.

Now, a decade later, the cruel cycle threatened to repeat itself. He wouldn't—couldn't—let it happen once more. "Never again." Hunter moaned, a fist slamming the wooden surface he sat on.

"Are you okay?"

Hunter jerked as Ryan touched his shoulder. "Yeah, just reliving an old nightmare." Together, they ventured into the heart of the building, a sense of foreboding filling the icy air.

Entering the medical room ... three men stood waiting, arms crossed, faces etched with scowls. Hunter felt their piercing gazes as he hobbled to the nearest chair. The atmosphere was thick with tension. Hunter took a deep breath, his nostrils filling with the acrid stench of antiseptic.

Coach Harrison, the embodiment of raw, unrestrained emotion, bellowed, "Have you completely lost your mind again, Griffin?"

"It's just a stubbed toe, Coach," Ryan snapped, his voice strained yet firm, an anchor in the brewing storm.

"I'll determine how 'nothing major' this is," the doctor grumbled as he wheeled in the portable x-ray machine.

A hush fell over the room as the doctor removed Hunter's sandal and sock. The silence broken by the reveal of his swollen, discolored toe. The air filling with murmured concern coupled with disapproving head shakes. Hunter could feel their disdain. It prickled at his skin like a physical entity.

The doctor instructed everyone to leave the room while he took several shots of Hunter's foot.

"You can come back in," he called out a short time later, as he rolled the machine into an adjacent room to examine the x-rays in private.

The scene erupted into chaos when Viktor approached Hunter. His face inches from his prodigy's, his breath hot and heavy, the stench of anger mixed with disappointment. "How you manage this?" he snarled, his Russian accent thickening with every word. Poking a finger into Hunter's chest, he continued his verbal assault, "You are no longer small boy. Elite goalies ... they do not just fall when they step off ice!"

Hunter's face reddened. His jaw clenched so tight the grind of his teeth echoed inside his head. His silence was not submission. It was a fierce promise, a raging storm held at bay. Before he could unleash it, Viktor grabbed Hunter's t-shirt, his grip vice-like, his voice a volcanic eruption of frustrated fear, as he pulled Hunter out of the chair.

"It is because of girl." Viktor's spittle landed hot on Hunter's face. With a forceful shove, he sent Hunter back into the chair. A wild energy emanated from Viktor as he turned to Coach Harrison. "As long as girl remains in his life, he cannot be trusted to guard net." Without giving Hunter another glance, Viktor turned, storming from the room.

Hunter watched his longtime coach, his mentor, his father figure, walk away. The words echoing, singing, slicing through the tension-filled room like a blade. Hunter's flesh burned under the harsh accusation, a vivid reminder of the stakes they all faced.

The return of the doctor broke the uneasy silence. "You've got a hairline fracture on your index toe. It's a small crack, but it's why you're feeling that sharp pain."

"Just a hairline fracture is great news, right?" Hunter looked at the doctor for support.

Before the doctor could respond to Hunter, Coach Harrison ran his fingers across his bald head and asked, "So, you're clearing him to play?"

"I hate to be the bearer of bad news, but even a hairline fracture can be tricky to heal." The doctor kneeled, lifting Hunter's foot, uncapping a syringe. Hunter flinched as the needle jabbed into the base of his swollen toe.

"That will numb the pain, but you're still going to have to elevate, ice and stay off your foot as much as possible." The doctor then bandaged Hunter's injured index toe to the adjacent toes.

"So, are you going to clear him to play or not?" Coach Harrison pushed ... an urgency in his voice.

Standing, the doctor crossed his arms, shaking his head. "It's going to be a hard call to make. Right now, I have doubts Hunter can even get his foot into a skate, let alone defend his net."

The weight of the decision loomed. The doctor's cautious advice was a counterpoint to Hunter's fierce determination, now visible in every tense muscle and tightened jawline. Hunter rose and headed out the door.

"Where in the hell do you think you're going?" Coach Harrison shouted after Hunter. When he didn't answer, the doctor, the coach, and Ryan followed Hunter down the tunnel to the Goshawks' locker room. There, they found him maneuvering his bandaged toes into a skate.

Hunter was thankful the numbing agent was taking hold, and that he wore goalie skates. The wider, squarer toe of the skate made it easier to slide his foot into the protected area. He hoped the special material that absorbs high-impact shots from pucks would act like a brace for his injured toe. Once his foot was secure in the skate, he wiggled his toes the best he could before lacing the skate tight.

"Are ya outta your tree?" Ryan leaned his shoulder on Hunter's stall, hands in his pockets, a look of disbelief on his face.

Hunter ignored Ryan's comment as he laced up his other skate. Sweat trickled down his forehead as he strapped on his leg pads. Pulling on his workout sweater, and then his mask, and gloves, Hunter commanded, "Get your skates on. Find a bucket of pucks. Meet me on the ice." Hunter ignored the doctor but gave a nod to Coach Harrison as he headed for the rink.

The freshly groomed ice was Hunter's playground. His workplace. His home. He allowed the frigid air to fill his lungs before he put a skate on the ice. On shaky legs, he skated a few easy laps. When he spotted Ryan dumping the bucket of pucks, Hunter skated to the blue crease where his net normally stood.

He got into a butterfly stance. Inside the protective mask, his expression was one of raw determination. Every tightened muscle, every grimace a silent testament to his unwillingness to back down. The sound of his stick blocking shot after shot echoed in the empty rink.

Coach Harrison, witnessing the display of courage, was torn between the doctor's advice and the need to bring The Cup home. He watched as Hunter skated to the bench, with Ryan at his heels.

The coach addressed his goalie in a voice displaying a gravelly mix of compassion with firm resolve. "Listen, Griffin, I know how much you want this." The Coach's hand rubbed the back of his neck. He nodded to the doctor standing by his side. "After talking with the doc, I've made a decision."

"And?" Hunter asked, as he tapped his stick hard against the boards.

"Olaf will be the starting goalie for the next three to four games."

Before Hunter could object, the doctor raised his hand, palm facing outward. "We need you strong for the long haul." He walked closer to Hunter, arms folded across his chest. "We still have two more rounds of the playoffs. You need time to heal.

"But ..." Coach Harrison added, "...with you at 100 percent, we are confident your skills will take us all the way to The Cup."

The determination in Hunter's voice clashed with the coach's and doctor's caution. "Coach, I can do this," his words slipped into a misty vapor. Under the rink's lights, Hunter's breath appeared ethereal, like an ice dragon. This was becoming a battle of wills echoing in the freezing air. With desperate pleading in his eyes, Hunter's voice cracked as he added, "Please, don't sideline me, Coach."

"My mind's made up."

Ryan chimed in, his voice carrying a stern warning, "Coach, ya gotta consider the media hoopla, eh? They're all banking on Hunter stealing the spotlight, especially after that last game."

Coach Harrison steeled himself, laying out his strategy. "Here's the deal. Like I said, we play Olaf for the next three to four games. Hunter, you'll dress, but you will only be backup." Giving Ryan a sideward glare, he added, "You both need to keep your mouths shut about the injury. We'll have another goalie on standby for the Canadian games. If anyone asks, this was our strategy all along. Understood?"

Hunter nodded, a tight knot forming in his chest. "I'll do it for the team, but mark my words, I'm not sitting out all the games of this upcoming round." Flashing a sneer to both Coach Harrison and the doctor, Hunter skated off the ice.

The group dispersed, the heavy weight of secrets and strategies resting on their shoulders, a bond of trust and grit tying them together in the face of adversity.

Ryan, skating after Hunter mumbling, his words a dark anticipation of the upcoming game, "This is a friggin' powder keg just begging to blow, bud."

Chapter 30
Here They Come Again

April 27

It was mid-morning when Sage poured a second cup of coffee. She surveyed her workspace, looking for Crease, who was chewing on the edge of a crumpled piece of paper littering the floor. "How can I make such a mess when I haven't even printed a photo yet?" Sage took the time out of editing the Goshawks photos to pick up her strewn papers and find Crease a stuffed toy to play with.

From the open window, a gentle symphony of whispering leaves and distant nickers from the horses below her apartment weaved into the room. She breathed in the spring air, a soothing harmony that cradled her as she embarked on her intimate journey through the pixels of captured moments.

Sitting at her laptop, Sage once more mustered the nerve to click through the more intimate Goshawks images ... a digital gallery unfurling the tapestry of Hunter's world. It was like peeling back layers of an enigmatic yet familiar soul. Each photograph was a vivid testament to the depth of the man, whose essence, in such a short time, had intertwined with hers.

Her smile softened at the first image, a picture of Hunter disembarking the plane from Florida. His posture echoing a raw, vibrant energy. His collar up, his gaze downward. The next shot capturing the surprise in Hunter's eyes when he realized that it was her behind the lens.

Sage's fingers hovered over the keyboard, hesitating before categorizing the image into the 'print file.' "Crease, this is going to be hard to pick the best photos ... apparently, it's impossible to take a bad picture of Hunter." With the mention of Hunter's name, Crease put his tiny puppy paws on Sage's leg, trying to get a look at his favorite human on Sage's monitor. The Yellow Lab's tail thumped when he gazed on Hunter's face.

Reaching out, Sage's fingers found solace in the soft fur, a tactile anchor in the storm of emotions brewing within her. "Oh, baby, I forgot how close you two were." She bent down, placing a soft kiss on his head. "I miss him too," she said without thinking. The absence of Hunter hit her hard, more than she wanted to admit.

Picking up Crease, the puppy licked at a single salty tear rolling down her cheek. Holding him on her lap, she continued to sort through the images. Each photo unraveling a new layer of Hunter, allowing her to explore facets that were both public and personal. A picture of him riding a bicycle though the vibrant streets of Portland brought a flood of sensory memories—the feel of the wind, the laughter ringing in her ears, the taste of salt in the air, the sight of his tight backside as she tried to catch up and photograph him at the same time.

With one hand clicking the mouse, Sage stroked Crease behind the ears with the other. The puppy settled into a ball on her lap. It only took a few moments before Crease began whimpering in his sleep. Sage inhaled, the mingled aromas of fresh coffee and the puppy's scent enveloped her in a comforting embrace.

She found herself lingering on each photo, exploring Hunter's features as if she was seeing him for the first time. His face was a striking blend of rugged masculinity and refined symmetry. His short tousled brown hair, and close-cropped facial hair, blended perfectly with his sun-kissed tan, achieved from hours outside exercising. For a hockey player, Hunter had a beautiful smile. Something her friend Patty had admired often. And oh, his full yet masculine lips, with their slight upward tilt ... as though always on the verge of a confident smile.

In several images, his high cheekbones and well-proportioned features caught the light in a way that gave his face a sculptural quality. Yet it was Hunter's intense eyes that always took her breath away. They seemed to hold the depth of the universe within them. His gaze always warm and penetrating. The eyelashes, too thick and long to be sported by his manly features, shielded eyes which spoke volumes without uttering a word.

She had to remind herself that at twenty-two, Hunter was only a year older than her. Despite his youth, an undeniable wisdom shown in Hunter's eyes, a certain gravitas rare for someone his age. This, coupled with his impressive stature gave him an imposing, captivating presence, even in photographs. Sage ran the pointer over his perfect nose. "Who in the world of hockey has such an unmarred face?"

The puppy stirring on her lap brought her back to her task at hand. Sage scrolled to the next image. Once more, pausing. She had not seen this one since she shot it. The moment the goshawk landed on Hunter's outstretched glove. Then, the hawk dancing up his arm, mask meeting beak ... it was mesmerizing.

Yet, it was the next image that made her breath catch. Hunter skating towards her, mask slung back on his head, the look of victory on his lips, and hunger in his eyes ... his gaze locked on her. The image taken moments before he grabbed her in his arms, planting the infamous kiss ... the photo transcended the barriers of the screen, a magnetic force pulling at her very core.

Sage held her breath, the room pulsating with the vibrant energy captured in that frame, a silent beckoning to explore the depths of a connection that was both ethereal and tangible. She could feel the heat of the spotlight, the cool touch of the ice under her gripped shoes. More important, she recalled the electrifying charge that vibrated from Hunter to her in that frozen moment.

A sudden pop-up notification appeared on the monitor, a ringtone signaling an incoming Skype call. Margret's face appeared on the screen, her expression of both concern and business shrewdness.

"Sage, dear, I just wanted to check in on you. Last night was quite intense," Margret began, her eyes holding a touch of maternal concern. "How are you holding up? And how's the puppy doing?"

Sage offered a reassuring smile, tucking a loose strand of hair behind her ear. "I'm doing okay, Margret. Still a bit overwhelmed, I guess." Sage's gaze drifted to the puppy asleep on her lap. "Crease is settling in like he owns the place. He's already won the hearts of my mom and dad."

Margret nodded and smiled before switching gears. "Glad you are both home, safe, and happy. Now, about those photos from last night, could you send them over? The press is eager to see what you shot ... and, well, so am I."

"Absolutely. They're ready to go. I'll send them right now," Sage affirmed, her fingers swiftly navigating through the folders on her laptop before sending the batch of originals to Margret.

As the files transferred, Sage hesitated before asking, "Margret, I was just reminded that I have a solo gallery show in a month. I was wondering if I could showcase photos of Hunter in my show?" She bit her lip, anticipating Margret's response, quickly adding, "Tentatively titled: The Man Behind the Mask."

Margret froze for a moment, her face a canvas of conflicting emotions. "Sage, do you really think that's wise?" Margret asked, her voice revealing the weight of her reservations.

Sage inhaled, gathering her courage. "I know it has the potential of being a media frenzy, but the photos ... they tell a story, Margret. A beautiful one." Sage paused, looking out the window, gathering strength from the peaceful setting of blue skies, and nickering horses. "Besides, it's just a small sleepy town in South Dakota. I only expect locals to view it. It would mean a great deal to me if the Goshawks' organization would give me permission to use Hunter's images."

Margret went into stealth mode as her gaze drifted off-screen. The flipping pages of her desktop Rolodex planner breaking the silence. "You know, the timing might work for us. If all goes well, the Goshawks will be finishing the last round of playoffs and headed to The Cup round. The buzz could really bolster the team's profile, especially Hunter's."

Sage felt a flicker of hope ignite within her, yet a knot of concern remained. This time it was Sage's turn to pause the conversation. "Maybe I shouldn't ask this of you, Margret. We both know how Hunter covets his privacy." Bringing her thumb to her lips, Sage chewed on her fingernail. "The last thing I remember Hunter saying at the post-game conference, was how the press could ask him anything about hockey, but his personal life was off limits. I don't want to cross any boundaries."

Margret leaned back in her chair, steepling her fingers, the hint of a cunning smile gracing her lips. "Sage, technically, since the Goshawks commissioned these photos, we own them. But I promise you, I'll get Hunter's blessings."

"Okay, but only if Hunter is advised of the show in advance." Sage nodded, feeling a semblance of reassurance.

Turning to her assistant, Margret smiled. "I know you've been listening in on the conversation. How long will it take you to write up the contract allowing Sage to use photos of Hunter for her gallery show?"

Almost in a whisper, an invisible voice replied, "It's already done and ready to send. Do you want to read it over first?"

Margret, still looking to her left, asked, "Is it our usual binding contract?" She paused, and when her assistant indicated it was, Margret said, "Send away, along with the usual NDA."

The chiming notification of the received documents caused Sage to jump. Which in turn caused Crease to tumble off her lap onto the carpet. Sage reached down, comforting the puppy. "Sorry about that little guy. I'll be done soon and take you outside."

Sage returned to the computer, heart pounding fiercely in her chest as she opened the PDF email attachment. Briefly scanning the documents, she electronically signed both. As she hit the send button, returning the signed copies to Margret, Sage heard tires crunching on the gravel driveway.

"Hold on a moment, Margret." Sage walked to the window, moving the curtains to get a better look. She was startled to see several vehicles pulling up to her parents' house. One van had a huge sign with 'NEWS' embossed on its side. The clamor of voices and footsteps reached her, growing louder and more insistent.

"What's wrong?" Margret leaned forward, her face close to her monitor.

"Probably nothing." Sage's mind raced with confusion. She could not comprehend why her parents' driveway was filling up with cars and vans. Worse yet, why people were swarming towards her parents' house with microphones, cameras, and cell phones in hand? From her perch near the window, Sage shouted to Margret, "Do you have everything you need?"

"Yes. Both documents came through. Call me back when you get a chance."

"I promise." As Sage turned her attention back to the computer monitor, she saw Margret's face fade, replaced with the new computer screen saver; a closeup of Hunter, decked out in his goalie gear, staring back at her.

Lifting the puppy, Sage held him close to her chest. "Crease, what in the world is going on down there?"

Crease responded with a quizzical stare, then licked her chin, which seemed to be his answer to all human questions.

Peering out the window, Sage's heart thrummed in her chest, a steady beat mirroring the chaos erupting outside. The sun stood high in the sky, indifferent to the turmoil below, casting sharp, contrasting shadows.

A myriad of trucks and vans were transforming her parents' once peaceful driveway into a bustling hub of frantic activity. From her perch, Sage's gaze flitted from one alarming scene to another, her breath caught in a whirlwind of curiosity and angst.

She looked at the wall clock. The hands moved one tick away from high noon. Her father would be there. Unless he was out of town, he'd made it a point to always be at the kitchen table at lunchtime, eating a home-cooked meal. A fleeting sense of relief washed over her, knowing her mother was not home alone.

Logos from the Hockey Network and one of a Sioux Falls television station painted the sides of two more vans. The reporters emerging from them carried themselves with an air of professionalism. Attired in uniforms, adorned with their respective company's logos. Their sleek cameras and streamlined microphones glistened under the sun, capturing every movement with predatory precision.

Contrasting, a raucous group of younger individuals surged forward, their voices a disruptive crescendo of excitement ... each vying to catch a scandalous snippet with their cell phones. Their presence becoming more intrusive, more volatile.

Sage's phone buzzed as she was about to rush downstairs and enter the fray, stopping cold when she saw who the incoming call was from ... her mom.

"Stay where you are, Sage. Don't even think about coming close to that window," her mother admonished in a hurried whisper, tinged with a note of fear.

Click. The call ended, leaving Sage even more bewildered than before. Reluctantly, she heeded her mother's words. Grabbing her camera, she attached a telephoto lens. Using the instrument as a spyglass, she returned to the window. Standing further than before, the lens gave her a closeup view.

Outside, her father stood resilient even under siege, the flush of his face now visible through the lens. His voice rose and fell, a distant roar lost within the sea of clamors. Sage tried to decipher his words. Although she could read his body language, she yearned to read his lips. To better understand the storm that had descended.

"Damned right, you vultures have no business here!" Jim's shouts drifted upward. Followed by a creepy quiet, which only lasted a moment.

Sage picked up Crease, tucking the puppy under her arm. Rushing down the stairs to the horse barn below, the harsh texture of the wooden banister scraping her palm. Every fiber of her being trembled, fear morphed into adrenaline. Her heartbeat thumping, a frenetic drum-roll accompanying her descent.

Crease whimpered as Sage put the puppy in one of the empty horse stalls for safe keeping. She kissed his nose, waiting for him to settle into a hay-filled corner before closing him in. Like a child playing hide-and-seek, Sage melted into the shadows of the barn's open doorway, her breath coming in short gasps. Again, she turned her camera lens to the front porch of her parent's home, just as a familiar vehicle entered the scene.

The sheriff's car rolled in, kicking up a cloud of dust that caught in Sage's throat, making her eyes water. Sheriff Thor Engle, a close family friend, was a welcome sight.

Emerging from the vehicle, Sheriff Engle posed a stern figure of a seasoned warrior. Yet it was Hammer, the Belgian Malinois, snugged to his side that cinched their air of authority. The dog's presence was a silent threat, a living weapon with bared teeth and a low, guttural growl that reverberated with a primal warning. Sage could almost feel its fierce energy, a vibrating undercurrent of menace permeating the air, a clear message of impending danger.

Striding onto the porch, the Sheriff stood beside Sage's father ... the trio created a formidable barrier, a living wall protecting their territory. The image invoked a sudden flashback of Hunter, guarding his net ... safeguarding his home with fierce determination from the opposing team's intrusion.

After speaking with her father, Sheriff Engle turned his attention to the crowd. He stood, one hand on the dog's leash, one hand on his holstered gun. Once again, a sudden silence fell upon the crowd as the sheriff's voice cut through the noise, ringing with authority and finality.

"Everyone, off this property now or face arrest for trespassing!" he barked, Hammer echoing his words with a deep growl that seemed to shake the ground, sending a ripple of unease through the crowd.

Sage felt lightheaded. The world outside shone too bright, too loud. Surely, she must be daydreaming. Things like this never happened in her neck of the woods. She'd known Sheriff Thor Engle for years, yet today, she caught a glimpse of him she'd never seen before and hoped to never see again.

Logic beckoned her to retreat, to go back to the safety of her apartment. Instead, she found herself edging closer to the chaos. The crunch of straw beneath her feet was a stark contrast to the seething tension around her. Her senses were aflame, each sound amplified, each sight sharpened.

Relief rushed through Sage's body as she watched the once defiant press and social media gurus retreating in haste, fear replacing the greed in their eyes. When the last vehicle disappeared, Sage emerged from her hiding place, her legs carrying her with a speed born of desperation towards the house. Her mom opened the screen door, joining her husband, just as Sage walked up the steps onto the porch.

Sage's voice trembled with confusion as she asked, "What was that all about?"

The sheriff met her question with a knowing look that affirmed her worst fears. "Seems you are in the media spotlight." Hammer sniffed Sage's hand, offering a moment of canine comfort to offset the chaos.

"How ... How did they find me?" Sage stuttered ... her eyes wide with fear.

Her father's expression softened just a fraction as he glanced down at her, the anger in his eyes replaced by a glimmer of concern. "They tracked you through your photography business website, Sage."

His voice carried a note of disappointment that stung Sage more than she could express.

"Oh, Mom. I didn't think ... I didn't ..." Sage's voice trailed off, tears welling, threatening to overflow. She felt her mother's arms around her, a rock of comfort in a suddenly hostile world.

"That's right. You didn't think ... you haven't been thinking since that hockey player came into your life. Now ... look at the turmoil your 'Not Thinking' has caused." Her father's pent-up rage flowed with each accusation.

"Now, Jim," her mother interjected before the impending storm could break loose again, "this isn't Sage's fault."

The sheriff, now standing with them in a circle of solidarity, put a hand on Sage's shoulder. "It's a moot point now. The damage is done. I have no idea when they will return. But I'm certain they'll be back ... most likely sooner than later."

The weight of his words hung in the air, a somber note in the unsettling silence that set upon the property. It was a grim reminder of the impending threat engulfing their tranquil existence. Sage buried her face in her mother's embrace. Right now, all she needed was her mom ... a tether of sanity in a world that kept spinning out of control.

Stepping back, Sage froze. Her mind raced. She turned, jumping down the stairs, running to the horse barn.

"Where are you going now, young lady? We are not done talking about this," Jim shouted after her.

"I have to call Margret. I have to cancel my show."

Rushing into the barn, Sage checked on Crease. Finding him snoring in puppy bliss, she tiptoed up the stairs. Reaching her office, her heart pounded, not from the physical exertion but from the chaos that had just upturned her world. She raced to her computer, clicking the Skype icon. Within moments, Margret's face materialized on her screen.

"Sage. I'm glad you got back to me." Margret's eyes flicked from Sage to papers strewn across her desk, her fingers sifting through them.

"I need to cancel the show, Margret. The press just stormed my parents' farm." The words tumbling out as if she had sprinted through a minefield.

Margret leaned forward, her eyes squinting, shifting her full focus to Sage. "Hold on. Slow down. What happened?"

Sage's breath came in shallow gasps. "It was a circus out there. News trucks, and God only knows how many online reporters. They only left when the sheriff arrived. I can't go on with the show under these circumstances."

Margret removed her reading glasses, pinching the bridge of her nose as if warding off an impending headache. "Sage, you can't cancel now. The contract and NDA have already been forwarded to the Goshawks' top management."

"But I've just signed it." Sage's voice wavered between disbelief and desperation.

"Sage, you're not an amateur. You know how iron clad our contracts are. Welcome to the big leagues. Walking away isn't an option," she snapped. "Today you might be fresh meat for the media, but tomorrow, they'll move on to another carcass."

"I thought you, of all people, would understand. You saw how they attacked me in Portland."

Sitting taller in her chair, Margret's voice gained an edge. "You came to us, remember? You asked me for permission to use Hunter's images." Her facial features softened as she added, "Trust me, in a month, when the show opens, the press will have forgotten all about you."

Stunned, Sage stared at the screen, the cursor blinking in the emptiness like a solitary star in a dark sky. She'd expected empathy from Margret, a kindred spirit who understood the merciless glare of media scrutiny. Sage could taste the bile rising in the back of her throat.

The silence became uncomfortably heavy when, on the screen, Margret's assistant handed her a note. "I have to go, Sage. Something's come up. You'll be fine; just weather the storm."

As Sage sat frozen, staring at the void where Margret's face had been, a sudden aura filled the room. Her skin prickled, the hair on the back of her neck stood on end. His presence felt even before she saw him.

Luke's towering figure occupied her open doorway. He pushed his Stetson back, revealing his steel-blue eyes. "Your dad called. Figured you could use a friend."

Sage leaped from her chair, hurling herself into Luke's welcoming arms. She buried her face in his chest, inhaling deeply. He smelled of horses, hay, and hope.

Luke's chin rested on Sage's head. After a few moments, he broke the embrace. Looking into her eyes, he said, "Pack what you'll need for the week. We're heading to the ranch."

Chapter 31

Let the Games Begin

May 2nd [Game 1 of the Second Round of Playoffs]
"Ladies and gentlemen, it's a brisk night here in Portland, Maine, but inside the arena, the air is electric with playoff fervor. This is Tom Hughes, alongside goalie legend John 'The Gatekeeper' Hamilton, bringing you the first game of the second-round playoff clash between the Portland Maine Goshawks and the Toronto Shadows. John, as we dive into tonight's crucial game, what's your take on the atmosphere here?"

"The energy is explosive. You can feel the history and rivalry that defines this match-up. The arena has a lot of fans down from Canada to support their Shadows. You can bet the players on both teams are fueled with equal measures of intensity, ready to leave it all on the ice tonight."

Tom interjected, "Playoff games in Portland are always a spectacle, but with the Shadows in town, the intensity is dialed up several notches."

John nodded to Tom. "Keep your eyes on Goshawks' star forward Chase Rutherford and the Shadows' ace forward, René Béliveau .... It's gonna be a duel of the captains for sure. Their confrontation could very well steer the game's direction and outcome. But there's a burning question tonight—why isn't Hunter 'Ice Wall' Griffin guarding the net? He's been the backbone of the Goshawks this season. His absence is bound to raise some eyebrows and speculations."

"Brilliant observation. That question's on everyone's mind, especially after Griffin's remarkable showcase against the Florida Barracudas. A goalie netting a goal and securing a shutout in the same game? That's a feat for the history books. The Goshawks' fans must be wondering why their linchpin isn't guarding the net."

"And folks, the intrigue around Coach Harrison's lineup choice is undeniable. Griffin has been a fortress for the Goshawks all season, with a knack for game-changing saves. With such a pivotal match ahead, his absence from the starting lineup is baffling." As he spoke, John lifted his hands in the air in a questioning gesture.

First Period

On the bench, Hunter maintained an outward calm. Internally, he was all too aware of the mounting speculation around him. The murmurs and puzzled glances from the crowd didn't elude him; the underlying question lingered like a shadow—*why was he not in the net tonight?*

"Get ready, folks!" John announced with vigor. "And there's the face-off. The Goshawks' starting lineup hitting the ice—Etan Eklund, Chase Rutherford, and Finn O'Connell upfront with Ryan Mitchell and Axel Berger holding down the fort on defense."

"On the opposing side," Tom added, "the Toronto Shadows aren't holding back either. They've rolled out their top-tier lineup, an imposing presence with Vincent Storm and Jean-Luc Dupont leading the charge, flanked by René Béliveau on the wing, while Digger Baker and Leonid Kozlovsky are the defensive backbone."

Etan bolted down the ice, the puck glued to his stick as if magnetized. "Dish it! Dish it!" Chase bellowed from the center, demanding the puck.

Shaking off his captain's call, Etan executed a precision saucer pass to Finn, the left wing, and team's enforcer. Finn unleashed a blistering slapshot toward the goal, but the puck clanged off the post, the sound reverberating to the nosebleed seats.

"Ah, just inches away. That was an excellent setup by Goshawks' rookie Etan Eklund. A smart play indeed, but O'Connell finds metal instead of mesh," John moaned.

"Keep letting 'em rip, Finn! Good hustle!" Ryan shouted. His cheeks flushed from the heat of the game as he skated next to the Goshawks' winger.

Then the momentum shifted. The opposing team seized the puck. Hunter felt helpless as Jean-Luc Dupont executed the breakout.

"Dupont threads the needle to Béliveau," Tom shouted, as the Shadow's captain sent a perfect tape-to-tape pass to his line-mate.

Before anyone could blink, René Béliveau snapped the puck with laser precision, finding the back of the net ... kissing the toe of Olaf's left skate.

GOAL! Shadows—Béliveau

"And that's a sniper, ladies and gentlemen! The Shadows draw first blood!" Tom's voice rose above the din.

"Fan Också," Olaf shouted, reverting to his native tongue in frustration. His stick smacked against one post and then the other.

"Shake it off, Snowman," Ryan yelled, skating past Olaf, giving the goalie a tap on the pads. "Plenty of ticks left on the clock, bud."

As the game proceeded, Hunter clenched his fists. He could feel it—the sharp scent of the ice, the acrid smell of sweat in the air, and most of all, the tension winding itself around every player, every spectator, like a coiled spring.

"Ten seconds left in the period, folks," John announced.

Ryan sent the puck deep into Toronto's zone. Etan battled against the boards with Dupont for possession as the clock ticked down.

"And that's it for the first period!" Tom's voice echoed. "The Shadows lead by one, but the question remains ... why is Griffin not playing?"

The resounding blare of the horn marking the period's end echoed in the arena as the Goshawks vacated their bench. Amidst the sea of unvoiced questions, Hunter wrestled with his own solitary query, echoing louder than any fan's speculation ... *could I have kept Toronto from scoring?*

"Interesting start," John concluded. "The Shadows have set the pace, but I have a feeling the real story tonight is still unfolding. The Goshawks have more up their sleeves, or should I say, under their pads."

"Yeah, the night is young, and in hockey, especially playoff hockey, anything can happen."

Hunter quickened his pace down the tunnel, head lowered, dodging the press as they thrust microphones in his direction. Even worse, Hunter sensed the weight of numerous gazes—not only from the fans but also from his teammates, coaches, and even the arena staff—each one fixated on him, adding pressure to an already tense retreat to the sanctuary of the locker room.

Hunter's eyes met Ryan's, a wordless conversation in a single glance. Ryan was the only player that knew the truth about his condition, but in that moment, it didn't matter. What mattered was the team, the game, the war they were all enlisted in.

Second Period

"Welcome back to what's shaping up to be a nail-biter of a game! I'm Tom Hughes, alongside John 'The Gatekeeper' Hamilton. If you're just joining us, the score is 0-1 in favor of the Shadows. I bet the Goshawks are also questioning their choice of starting goalie. What do you make of it, John?"

"It's puzzling. Svensson is doing a solid job, but Griffin is the cornerstone of this team. He's been lights out all season. Why he's on the bench, we still don't know."

Hunter maneuvered into the far corner of the Goshawks' bench, his cap covering his face so the media couldn't read his expressions. The throbbing in his toe was easing thanks to the doctor's injection of the numbing agent. He thumped his gloved hand on the boards, a nervous habit he had when not an acting participator. He looked to Olaf, giving him a sharp nod of confidence, both goalies knowing the onslaught was about to begin anew.

"Alright, boys, let's even this up," Chase shouted, anchoring his stance for the puck drop.

"Time to dominate our zone, no mercy!" Ryan barked, setting an aggressive tone from his post on defense.

The opening moments unfolded with relentless speed and ferocity. Finn leveled one of the Shadows' enforcers with a thunderous hit, drawing jeers from the opposition's supporters and igniting the Goshawks' crowd into a frenzy. The hit was textbook perfect—no penalty called.

"Make 'em think twice, Finn! Show 'em what we're made of!" Etan cheered, his stick clattering on the ice in solidarity.

"Puck's deep! Cycle! Cycle!" Chase commanded as Axel drove it into Toronto's zone.

The Goshawks swarmed the net like a hive of angry bees. The pressure was mounting.

"Crash the net, boys! Look for the garbage!" Eddie Bennett yelled from the bench. And then it happened. Axel let a one-timer fly from the point.

"And it's in! The young rookie, Axel Berger, with a laser shot!" Tom erupted in the broadcast booth.

GOAL! Goshawks—Berger

"Precision is key, and Berger nailed it," John added.

"Way to go, rookie." Finn lifted Axel off the ice in a triumphant hug.

"Keep pushing, boys. Momentum's ours," Chase shouted, eyes locked on the game. The noise from the crowd was deafening, a mixture of boos and cheers, so loud it rattled the arena.

The clock counted down as goalies on both teams made numerous saves. Both Shadows and Goshawks were playing full throttle. Toronto's first line center, Digger Baker, broke away, a one-on-one situation that could tilt the game.

"And Baker shoots," shouted Tom.

Just as the puck appeared to be destined to slide past Olaf, Ryan dove across the crease, knocking the puck clear with a desperate swing of his stick.

"Denied by Mitchell! That's a game-saver right there!" John yelled.

"You can't teach that; that's just pure instinct and guts," Tom chimed in.

The clock was winding down, tension filling every inch of the rink.

"Ten seconds, hold the line," yelled the Goshawks second line D-man, Liam Armstrong, his voice tinged with urgency.

The Goshawks did just that. As the horn blared, signaling the end of the second period, they skated back to the bench.

"That's how you battle, boys!" Chase's voice cut through the exhaustion.

"And as we wrap up the second period, it's all tied up at 1-1," Tom announced. "The Goshawks have clawed their way back, but the spotlight's on Svensson now."

John chimed in, "Olaf stepped up tonight, showing he can hold his own under playoff pressure."

"Absolutely!" Tom agreed. "When we head into the third, it's going to be down to which team wants it more. With the score even, every shift, every shot could tip the scales. It's going to be a game of the goalies ... which one is hungrier for the win."

In the tunnel, Hunter was about to greet Olaf when reporters rushed in. Olaf waved Hunter on. Taking one for the team, The Snowman raised his mask before answering a myriad of questions.

When Olaf entered the locker room, the door closed behind him. "Sorry, man," Hunter said.

"No worries." Olaf put his beefy hand on Hunter's back. "All part of the game."

Hunter felt the adrenaline coursing through his veins, veiling the pain of his toe as the numbness wore off. Whatever happens in the third period, one thing was certain: the Goshawks were a force to be reckoned with, and they weren't going down without a fight.

Third Period

"We're back for the decisive third period in what's been a showdown for the ages," Tom declared as the camera swept across the charged stadium. "Joining me again is John 'The Gatekeeper' Hamilton, and folks, this is edge-of-your-seat territory—if you're just tuning in, brace yourself."

"That's right, Tom. Playoff hockey doesn't get more intense than this—every play, every decision is magnified. It's all about resilience, determination, and seizing those critical moments."

As the puck hit the ice, a surge of energy swept through the arena. It was a moment of truth for both teams. With the score even, the Goshawks, reinvigorated and relentless, were not just playing—they were battling, laying it all on the line with their sights set on victory.

Hunter clinched his gloved fist on the bench, his eyes darting across the ice as if willing the puck into the opponent's net.

"Pick up the man. No free rides!" yelled Ryan, his voice a gravelly command as he thwarted a Shadows' attack.

"Here comes Rutherford, flying up the center," Tom narrated, eyes widening as Chase maneuvered the puck masterfully through a pack of Toronto players.

"And he dishes it to Eklund ... Eklund shoots ..."

GOAL! Goshawks—Eklund

"Top shelf, where Mama hides the cookies!" John erupted as the puck flew past the Shadow's goalie, nestling in the top of the net.

"The Goshawks take the lead! Looks like the Goshawks' rookies are ruling the Shadows' net."

"Way to light the lamp, kid!" Finn spearheaded the on-ice celebration, with the other three players joining in.

"Back on D! Back on D!" yelled Goshawks' Matthew Preston, resetting the formation as play resumed.

Toronto came back with a vengeance. The Shadow's trash talker, right winger, Vincent Storm, found an opening and released a wrist shot that flew past Olaf's left shoulder.

GOAL! Shadows—Storm

"And just like that, it's 2-2. Storm with a rocket!" Tom shouted.

"The air just got sucked out of the Goshawks bench," John added. "The next goal could very well decide this game."

"Backcheck! Backcheck!" screamed Chase, making a quick line change ... the clock ticking down to the last five minutes.

There was a scramble near the Shadows' net, bodies colliding, sticks clashing—then a loose puck.

"Goshawks' winger, Steve Sturman picks it up, he's got a chance." Tom announced.

GOAL! Goshawks—Sturman

"And Sturman scores his first goal of the playoffs, and possibly just sealed this game for the Goshawks!" John screamed.

"Unbelievable! He's the hero no one saw coming!"

The Goshawks bench erupted, players hugging and shouting. But the game was not over.

"Lock it down, boys! Forty seconds!" yelled Goshawks' D-man Liam Armstrong.

Olaf appeared almost serene amid the mounting tension, executing a last-second glove save that sent the crowd into a suspended moment of silence. Then, the arena erupted. Groans and boos from the Shadows' supporters mixed with exuberant cheers from the Goshawks' fans.

"And that's it, folks! The Goshawks win 3-2!"

"As we wrap up here, one question remains," John added. "As a former goalie, I have to wonder, will Griffin be between the pipes next game? Especially since the Goshawks will be playing that game on home ice. I know the fans want to know. One thing's for sure, the Goshawks got the job done without him."

Hunter absorbed the announcer's final words, a heavy burden that stirred doubts about his necessity to the team. Struggling to hide his limp, he edged onto the ice to partake in the post-game celebrations. His gaze locked with Olaf's across the rink; in that silent exchange, a profound understanding passed between them. Yes, the team had triumphed, yet the victory underscored a vital truth: Olaf needed Hunter's support ... he couldn't be left to shoulder all the upcoming battles alone.

The euphoria in the Goshawks' locker room was intoxicating. Players exchanged manly hugs, fist bumps, all of them basking in the thrill of a hard-fought win. The noise fell to a murmur as Coach Stan Harrison walked in.

"Great win, gentlemen. But remember, it's just one game. We've got a long road ahead," the coach's voice carried the authority that had guided teams to championships. "I know you all want to celebrate tonight, but I want everyone in bed by eleven. No press, no sneaking off to the bar. We rest, we regroup, and we come back even stronger for game two. Clear?"

"Yes! Coach!" resonated through the room.

Coach Harrison nodded, pleased but not smiling. "Alright, let's pack it up."

As the coach made his way through the labyrinthine tunnels of the arena, a voice called out from behind him.

"Coach Harrison, a moment?"

Stan turned to see Lisa Morgan, a persistent reporter for Goshawks' media. Her microphone poised. Her eyes inquisitive.

"Lisa," Stan greeted, checking his watch. "What can I do for you?"

"Coach, a lot of fans, and frankly, sports analysts, are puzzled. Hunter Griffin has been the backbone of this team. Why bench him tonight?"

Stan leaned back against the cool concrete of the tunnel wall. "Lisa, you've been covering hockey long enough to know that it's a team sport. We operate with rotating goaltenders. Olaf started tonight, and he'll most likely be starting the next two games as well. It's been the plan all along."

Lisa's eyebrows lowered. "With all due respect, Coach, that's hard to buy. Hunter's been on fire. It's not like you to change goalies in the middle of a winning streak."

Stan stared at her for a moment, his facial expression giving nothing away. "There are times a coach has to make decisions that aren't popular with the fans ... or the press ... but they're always in the best interest of the team. My decision to start Olaf wasn't made lightly. He's a great goalie. He proved that tonight."

"So, you're saying Hunter's benching had nothing to do with his previous performance or ... perhaps an injury?"

Stan's eyes sharpened. "I've said what I have to say, Lisa. Now, if you'll excuse me, my team has a strict curfew tonight, as do I."

Lisa did not look convinced. Lowering her mic, then her voice, she asked, "Off the record coach. Is everything okay?"

"Everything's fine," Stan lied, but his expression remained sincere. With a nod and a wink, he added, "Everything has to be."

He then turned and walked away, leaving Lisa with unanswered questions, along with a skeptical expression.

Chapter 32
Dangerous Liaisons

May 10th [Game 4 of the Second Round of Playoffs]
Sage leaned over the large slab table, sorting through the printed photos strewn about. Her hands moving from one to another, doing her best to get organized. On her laptop, an equal number of images awaited, also in need of sorting and printing.

Stretching, she smiled, gazing at her temporary home. The guesthouse was one of a half-dozen small log cabins nestled around Luke's father's estate. Two weeks ago, taking her first steps inside her cozy hideaway, Sage was greeted by an intimate atmosphere of equestrian-chic. Although the décor was more elegant than she was used to, the scent of wood and leather made her feel right at home.

The walls were adorned with an array of black and white photos in elegant wooden frames. They were all photographs of Quarter Horses, that Sage had taken on assignment for Luke's father. Her fingers touched one of the pictures. Memories flooded ... it was an action photo of Jessica riding one of the championship quarter horses, dirt spraying, racing at a dangerous speed around a barrel.

Returning to her workstation, Sage traced the lines of the Goshawks photographs, capturing moments that seemed frozen in time—each image a puzzle piece of Hunter's life on and off the ice, each story a piece of her soul. Hunter's frantic save with ice flying was reminiscent of the photo she took of Jessica ... both rang of impending disaster.

An insistent banging jerked Sage out of her reverie. Rushing to the door, she nearly tripped over Crease, who was jumping around at her feet. Picking up the puppy, opening the door, she was surprised to find Luke standing with his arms full of firewood; wearing a smile that could melt the coldest South Dakota night.

"Hey there. Mind if I come in?" Luke asked, balancing the firewood precariously.

"Of course, come on in." Sage stepped to the side, putting Crease down. "It's only the beginning of May ... you look like you're preparing for a snowy winter."

Luke dropped the logs and kindling in the front room, next to the hearth of the stone fireplace. The earthy sweet scent of chopped wood filled the room. "I checked the Weather Channel. The temps are dropping tonight, plus the winds are supposed to pick up."

Kneeling, he gave the puppy a piece of kindling. It did the trick, keeping Crease occupied while he grabbed newspaper from a nearby stack, crumbling the sheets and placing them into the firebox. With expert hands, he arranged the kindling, stacking pieces of the split wood on top.

Turning his head to Sage, Luke smiled. "I know you'll be up late tonight working ... and watching the Goshawks. Didn't want you to catch a chill."

While Luke's back was turned, Sage paused to admire his tight-fitting wranglers as he brushed his hands on his hips. The cabin's decor framed him perfectly: stone, wood, and Luke—a triad as natural as earth, fire, and a breath of fresh air.

"So," Luke said, as he scratched Crease behind the ears. "I was wondering if you wanted to invite Jessica and Patty over to watch the game. It starts soon, doesn't it?"

Sage glanced at the big wagon wheel wall clock. "Yeah, it starts at six, but I don't feel like having the girls over tonight."

"No problem," Luke said, pulling a book of matches from his pocket. He lit the paper and kindling. "I'll get the fire going and get out of your hair."

"Do you have to rush off?"

Flames flickered in the firebox as Luke stood. Picking Crease up, he walked over to Sage, leaning a hip on the counter next to her. His eyebrows knitted as he asked, "I thought you wanted to watch the game alone."

Sage felt a sudden warmth rush to her cheeks. "I said, I didn't feel like having Jessica and Patty over. I know you're not into hockey, but I wouldn't mind your company."

"Isn't this the fourth game of the second round of playoffs?" Luke asked.

"Wow, I'm impressed."

"And ... they're playing in Toronto."

"Okay, now you are scaring me. Who are you, and what have you done to my friend Luke?" Sage stood with hands on her hips, head cocked to one side, eyes squinting.

Luke's smile widened. "For you, I can stand a couple hours of watching guys wearing knives on their boots, brandishing lethal weapons, and bloodying the ice as they bitch-slap each other."

Sage rolled her eyes. "Have you eaten yet?"

"Nope."

"Good, I have some chili that Mom brought over yesterday, and beer, lots of bottles of beer."

"You know I can never turn down your mom's cooking." Luke rubbed Crease's head. "What about you buddy, do you like your grandma's chili?"

Crease looked up with wide eyes, giving Luke a high-pitched bark.

"No people food for the pup. Unless you plan on staying the night and taking him out every hour." A long, tense quiet filled the room. Sage cleared her throat, breaking the silence. "The game's about to start. The remote's on the side table. I've already set it on the correct channel. Someone should make chasing hockey games on TV a sport. I'd win every time." From the kitchenette she called out, "I'll get us a couple of beers."

Returning to the front room, Sage breathed the scent of burning wood, its warmth spreading as the flames flickered. "There is something about a roaring fire that soothes my soul." Sage handed a beer to Luke. She watched as he plopped into the double recliner, its soft saddle-brown leather complementing the room, positioned perfectly in front of the flatscreen hanging over the fireplace. Crease snuggling on Luke's lap.

Placing her beer on a side table, Sage went back into the kitchenette. Taking a container out of the refrigerator, she put it in the microwave. Waiting for the chili to heat, Sage leaned over to smell the Sterling Silver roses mixed with sprigs of lavender. No one had ever bought her flowers ... until Luke had two days ago.

"Hey," Luke called out as the microwave dinged. "You're missing the big guy singing in French. Oh, and your beer is getting warm."

Sage quickly filled two bowls with the chili. The rich, spicy aroma made her eyes water. Bringing the food into the front room, she said, "I hope you have a cast iron stomach. This batch has extra hot peppers."

"Smells delicious." Luke reached for the bowl with one hand, while moving Crease off his lap with the other.

"So, how was your day on the ranch?"

"Oh, the usual." Luke stirred the chili, puffs of steam filling the air. "Up before dawn, checking on the horses, talking to suppliers. How about you? How's the photo selection coming along?"

"It's more difficult than I thought," Sage admitted. "I'm having a hard time narrowing them down. At the rate I'm going, I'll need a warehouse instead of a small gallery to show my work." Sage sat next to Luke, squeezing in beside him and Crease.

Luke nodded, taking a sip of his beer. "You'll figure it out. You have a good eye for capturing moments; it's part of what makes you special."

Their gaze met. For a moment, the air was sucked out of the room. Then the speakers roared to life, the horn blew, signaling the start of game four of the second round of the playoffs. Sage's attention snapped to the screen, her eyes lighting up with excitement.

Luke leaned back, once more stirring the steaming chili. His eyes were on Sage instead of the TV.

It was a fast played period with both teams racing from one end to the other. As the game-clock clicked to zero, marking the end of the first period, the score was tied 3-3. Sage felt the tension on the ice through the screen. Getting up from the double recliner she gathered their empty bowls.

"I'll be right back, just going to grab us another round of beers. Can you let Crease out to do his business?" Sage announced, her words layered with a subtle undertone of concern.

Picking up the pup, Luke headed out the door. "You better not dawdle. We don't want your mama to have to come looking for us." As he was closing the door, Luke flashed Sage a smile, which she didn't return.

Sage moved to the dishwasher. The clinking of bowls, and the opening of the fridge, provided a rhythmic backdrop to the broadcasters' speculation on why Hunter wasn't starting again. She felt a lump form in her throat. Something was wrong. She could feel it in her bones. Sage had already returned to the front room with two beers when Luke and Crease stormed through the door.

"For a little guy, he sure can run fast." Luke reclaimed his seat next to Sage, his wide shoulder leaned into her. "Are you okay?"

Sage handed him an open bottle of beer. Before she could answer his question, the broadcasters replayed an earlier image of Hunter on the bench. One leg elevated. Wearing a Goshawks' ball cap instead of his iconic goalie mask. The camera zooming in on eyes filled with anger. The broadcasters chirping growing increasingly passionate in their confusion about the 'Ice Wall' once more not in the net.

"I'm worried about Hunter. This is the fourth game he hasn't played," Sage blurted out.

Luke's thumb pressed the mute button on the remote, silencing the talking-heads. He turned to Sage, his eyes probing. "Do you have feelings for that goalie guy?"

The question caught Sage off guard. "What do you mean?"

"I didn't want to bring it up before, but I saw the kiss on the ice." Luke's words carried a complex mix of emotions—curiosity, evident jealousy, and beneath it all, undeniable concern.

Sage frowned. "I didn't think you followed hockey."

"I don't," Luke admitted, taking another sip of beer. "But the local newspaper had a story about a hometown photographer getting cozy with a famous hockey player. That kiss was all over the news."

Mortified, Sage looked down, sinking her fingers into Crease's fur. "Oh."

"So, what are your feelings towards Hunter?" Luke pressed.

Sage took a moment, wrestling with a sudden storm of emotions. "I don't really know, Luke. It's all so confusing."

"That doesn't answer my question." Luke shifted his body slightly to face Sage. "How close did you get with him in Portland? Was that the first time he kissed you?"

A flash of irritation shone in Sage's eyes. "That's really none of your business, but since you're so intent on knowing—no, it wasn't planned. Hunter kissed me ... for the first time. I was as surprised as everyone else. And for your information, Hunter was a perfect gentleman during my stay in Portland. He was doing his job, and I was doing mine."

Before Luke could respond, Sage picked up the remote, reversing the mute, just as the puck dropped for the faceoff.

Through the second period, Sage sat back in the recliner, arms crossed, wearing a deep divot between her brows. The sound of skates cutting ice and sticks hitting pucks filled the room, but the silence between them grew thicker as the game clock clicked down. Unanswered questions and unspoken thoughts hung in the air, as hot and heavy as the flickering flames in the fireplace.

The second period dragged on, with both teams spending an unusual amount of time in the penalty box. Sage sighed when the buzzer rang out. The camera cut away from the game to show the intermission report. The broadcasters were buzzing with speculation. The tension on the screen mirrored the tension in the room.

Gathering her courage, Sage turned to address Luke, only to find him and Crease softly snoring. She watched him slumber, wondering if she should wake him. Lowering the volume, she reached for a throw blanket and covered Luke's body.

Sage watched the third period without announcer commentary. It felt odd not to yell as a Shadow's slap shot soared over Olaf's left shoulder. She had to cover her mouth to stifle a scream, when the Toronto players emptied the bench in celebration as the digital game clock flashed zeros. To make it worse, the camera zoomed in to show a tight face shot of Hunter. His expression frozen with disbelief, anger, and disappointment. Final score: Goshawks losing 3 to 4.

She tended the fire, poking at the ashes, turning down the flue, banking it for the night. She eased Crease off the recliner, taking him outside one last time. Coming back into the house, Sage checked on Luke once more. He looked so comfy ... she didn't have the heart to wake him. Instead, she covered him with a heavier comforter, shut off the lights, and headed to bed.

Putting Crease in the portable crib next to her bed, Sage crawled between the sheets, doing her best to calm her monkey-brain. Her cell phone on the nightstand taunted her. Beckoning her to call Hunter, or at least send him a text. Her hand reached for it, then drew back. If he wanted to hear from her, he knew her number. She wasn't a lovesick puck-bunny. She had to give him space ... give her heart time to mend.

Tossing and turning her thoughts then went to the man sleeping in the front room. Luke had been a true savior since her return from Portland. He'd given her and Crease a safe place to stay. He'd bought her flowers. He'd held her when she was frightened. He'd wiped away her fearful tears. Perhaps it was time to bring Luke out of the friendship zone. She knew it would please her parents, especially her father. He loved Luke. But one question itched at her ... could she feel more than friendship for him?

⸻◦⸻

Crease's whimpering woke Sage with a start. Dressed in only an old T-shirt and baggy sweatpants a barefoot Sage picked up the puppy, rushing to get him outside. The aroma of freshly brewed coffee made her nostrils flare as she passed the kitchen. Flinging the door open, she was greeted by Jessica, who was about to knock. Pushing past her friend, Sage ran outside, putting Crease on the grass just in time.

Walking back into the house, Sage was met by her best friend, standing just inside the door, arms crossed, wearing a scowl. Looking to the kitchen, she saw Luke, wearing bedhead and a cocky smile, drinking a cup of coffee. "Ah, Crap!"

Chapter 33
Losses Pile Up

May 12th [Game 5 of the Second Round of Playoffs: Pregame]
The rain drizzled on the windshield of Ryan's SUV. Reaching for the wiper control, he looked to Hunter sulking in the passenger seat. "Cheer up, eh? Should be me who's all grumpy, don't ya think? I was in the middle of a beauty snooze when ya rang." Ryan guided the SUV into the Portland animal shelter's parking lot, classic rock jamming from the radio.

"Ah, 'Stairway to Heaven,' timeless." Ryan left the engine running after parking to air-guitar the last notes of the song.

Hunter looked out the window, ignoring the music, doing his best to ignore his D-man's mock instrumental. His thoughts were preoccupied with the game tonight, and his potential to return to the ice. He'd come here today to calm his nerves with the Labrador puppy who'd won his heart.

"Big game tonight. Wonder if coach will put you back in the net. How's the toe?" Ryan ventured, looking at Hunter with concern.

"To be honest, man, all I want to do right now is visit with the little guy. That pup's the only thing keeping me sane since I met ..." Hunter tried, but it was too painful to say her name aloud.

Ryan nodded, placing a hand on Hunter's shoulder. "Understood, bud. Life's been throwing ya some wicked slap shots of late."

The two men ran into the shelter as the drizzle turned into a downpour. Opening the door, they were hit by the usual chorus of barking dogs. The front desk staff gathered to greet the Goshawks players.

"Good to see you today, Hunter." The youngest volunteer ignored Ryan, saving her eyelash batting, lip licking, and exaggerated grin for the Ice Wall. Leaning forward on her elbows, she cooed, "We didn't expect you to be here on a game day."

"I just needed some puppy kisses to get me through the day." Hunter regretted his choice of words as he watched the receptionist's elbows buckle under her.

Ryan pointed to the door leading into the kennels. "Come on, Hunter, we don't have a lot of time."

Cages rattled as they walked down the long aisles of kennels filled with dogs of all shapes and sizes, each doing their best to get attention. Hunter quickened his pace as Ryan stopped to pet a raggedy mutt who insisted on licking his hand. Ryan pulled away from his new furry friend when he saw Hunter stop short at the end of the row.

"What's up?" Ryan asked as he approached Hunter.

"Not sure." Hunter ran a hand through his hair. "The kennel's empty."

"Ah, no worries. I bet they moved them to another spot."

Hunter flagged down a nearby volunteer. "Excuse me, there was a Yellow Lab pup in this kennel. Any idea where he is?"

The young man looked confused, speechless as he gazed opened-mouthed at Hunter. He wore a Goshawks ball cap and a tee-shirt with Ice Wall printed in bold letters. "I...I...I just started a couple days ago. I haven't seen any puppies. Let me get the shelter manager."

Moments later, Jennie appeared. "Hunter, I was hoping we'd get to tell you in person. All the puppies were adopted. You know how long the waiting list was for purebred Labs. The best part, the mama Lab was adopted too." She looked at Hunter with a gentle smile that didn't reach her eyes.

"All the pups?" Hunter's voice cracked. The air felt like it had been knocked out of him.

"I'm afraid so." Jennie rubbed her hand on Hunter's arm. "Sweetie, you've known all along this day would come."

"Yeah, but ... I didn't ... get to ... say goodbye," Hunter's words came out shaky, in uneven gulps.

"Man, that's harsh," Ryan whispered, his eyes filled with genuine worry. "You alright, bud?"

Jennie interjected, "I know how attached you were to him. I promise you ... he went to a loving home ... on a farm."

"How about you give me their name? That way, I can keep in touch."

"Hunter. You know I'd love to, but it's against the shelter's policy to give out personal information."

Hunter paced about in a tight circle. His hands balled into fists. Turning to Jennie, he said, "Can you at least give them my name and number ... you know ... just in case the adoption doesn't work out?"

"Stop and think, man." Ryan nudged Hunter on the shoulder. "It's not a wise move to give out your number to strangers." Hunter glared at him, but Ryan stood his ground.

"I tell you what I'll do," Jennie said. "I'll contact the new owners and let them know you would like to come for a visit." She paused. "If they agree, I'll have them contact me at the shelter, and I can make the arrangements. How does that sound?"

Hunter felt a weight lift. "Yeah, sure, thanks," he mumbled. "Let's go, Ryan."

As they headed back to the SUV, Hunter's shoes splashed in the puddles. He could taste defeat and hoped it wasn't a precursor to tonight's game. Focus only on the game, had to be his new mantra. Yet, his divided inner voice screamed ... first Sage, then my injury, now the pup, he thought. "Life! Sucks!" he shouted, looking skyward. The rain drenched his face and hair, soaking through his clothes to his skin.

"Yeah, and now there's a chance you might be defending our net tonight," Ryan grumbled under his breath.

⸻⸻⸻◇⸻⸻⸻

Coach Harrison walked into the locker room, followed by Hunter, who was doing his best not to limp. It always took a few minutes for the doctor's injection of the numbing agent to take effect.

The room was a hive of energy, drenched in the mingling scents of sweat, leather, and the stinging scent of menthol rub. Hunter moved past the players who were donning their hockey armor, taping sticks, and muttering last minute incantations under their breaths. To Hunter, the place smelled like victory.

Sitting in his stall, he reached into his gear bag, grabbing a protein bar. Tossing the wrapper in the bin, he took a huge bite, enjoying the sweet and salty taste of chocolate and nuts. It was the first thing he'd eaten since his breakfast of oatmeal, and his stomach was growling.

"Bout damn time, you got here Hunter," Finn slapped Hunter on the back so hard, he choked.

Coughing, Hunter found his voice. "Not. Late," was all he could muster.

Ryan chuckled. "Way to go Finn, kill our best goalie before he gets a chance to return to his net." Looking over to Olaf, he said, "No offense, Snowman."

Olaf looked up from tying his skates. "None taken."

Coach Harrison made his way to the front of the room. His voice echoed off the walls, "Listen up! There's a lot at stake tonight." He paused, taking his time to look each of his players in the eyes. "But we're used to fighting hard. Don't forget what got us here. Teamwork. No single player can win or lose a game. I want to see lots of shots on goal, smart passes, and most of all ... protect your goalie." He turned to his assistant coach. "Tonight, Coach Scott is going to read the starting lineup." He handed the younger man a single piece of paper.

Scott stood at the front of the room as he addressed the team. "Stay out of the penalty box guys. Leave the desperate, reckless plays to the Toronto Shadows. Play Hard. Play Sharp. Most important, play as a team.

He waited for the sound of stomping skates to stop. Clearing his throat, he began reading the starting lineup. "Tonight, on Left Wing, we have Finn O'Connell. On Center, your captain, Chase 'The General' Rutherford." After each name was read, he waited for the clapping to cease before announcing the next player's name.

"On right wing. One of our favorite rookies, Etan Eklund." The assistant coach then pointed to the player in the stall next to Etan. "And, our other favorite rookie, our big D-man, Axel Berger."

Axel gave Etan a sly grin and was about to jump up to take a bow. Something his fellow rookie usually did.

"Sit down Booger," yelled Liam, holding Axel back by his sweater.

"That's Mr. Booger to you, old man." Axel quipped, dodging several wet towels thrown in his direction.

"Settle down. Settle down." Scott waited for quiet. "Our other D, wearing the big A, Ryan 'The Rock' Mitchell."

Looking first to Olaf, then to Hunter, Scott took a deep breath and bellowed, "Tonight, for the first time since scoring the winning goal at the end of our first round of playoffs, back between the pipes, the one, the only, the fortress, our very own ... Hunter the Ice Wall Griffin."

Hunter's head shot up from adjusting his shin pads, eyes wide. His face wore an expression of relief.

The players looked at Hunter in unison, then a round of cheers erupted.

"Finally decided to earn your keep, huh?" Liam growled.

"Planning to actually step on the ice instead of warming your butt on the bench?" Finn wiped his arm pits with a towel, then chucked it at Hunter's face. The enforcer's smirk morphed into a full-fledged grin.

Second-line right winger, Daniel Murphy, piped in, "Yeah, let's hope you're a wall tonight, not a sieve, like the melting Snowman's last game." Turning to Olaf, he added, "Offense Meant!"

Olaf shrugged the words off, his Swedish calm unshaken. "I agree."

Chase clapped his hand on Hunter's shoulder. "It'll be good to have you back in the net."

Hunter nodded to Chase but looked at Olaf. His thoughts briefly drifted to his own losses, lingering on the off-ice ones: his parents, Sage, the puppy. *Shake it off,* he told himself. This was not the time for reminiscing.

The moment Coach Scott left the room, Viktor maneuvered his enormous body over Hunter, his expression as cold as a Russian winter.

"Your head. It needs to be in game. Not lost in clouds. This is playoffs!"

"I'm all in, Coach," Hunter snapped, feeling his own anger rise.

"This is not child's game! Must fight to win!"

The locker room's air turned thick. Eyes darted from player-to-player. Viktor held Hunter's gaze for a heavy moment before walking away. The Russian's rebuke hovered like a dark cloud over everyone.

Olaf gave Hunter a quick nod. Leaning close to his co-goalie, he whispered, "Ignore him. You've got this."

Chase tapped his stick against his bench to get everyone's attention. "Alright, boys. That's enough chit-chatting. Let's go show Toronto why they should never set foot on our ice."

Hunter pulled down his goalie mask, its weight a welcomed replacement from the Goshawks ball cap he'd been wearing for the past four games. The words of his teammates, the sting from Viktor, the emotional whirlwind—Hunter locked it all away. His focus became myopic. Winning this battle was all that mattered tonight.

Chapter 34
Redemption

May 12th [Game 5 of the Second Round of Playoffs]
"Good evening, folks! Welcome to a rocking big game here in Portland, Maine. I'm Tom Hughes, and with me is John 'The Gatekeeper' Hamilton. We're excited to bring you game five of the second-round playoffs between the Portland Goshawks and the Toronto Shadows. The Goshawks have a 3 to 1 game lead over the Shadows. All the oddsmakers are putting their bets on the Goshawks to win this round tonight."

"That's right, Tom. And the home crowd is buzzing. There's a change in the net for the Goshawks—Griffin is in, and fans are wondering why now, and not four games back?"

"Could be strategy. The Snowman did an outstanding job in the first three games, but with the loss at Toronto in game four, maybe they're looking to shake things up. What's your take?"

"Well, Griffin did help them clinch the first round of the playoffs against Florida, scoring that winning goal ... but, facts are facts, he's been cooling his skates on the bench for a while now. It's a gamble, for sure."

First Period

"Ice Wall! Ice Wall!" The arena shook with the crowd's chants as Hunter led the Goshawks onto their frozen fortress. Skates carved the ice as players locked into their positions, every man radiating a steely determination. The air charged with the anticipation of battle.

Chase took the draw against the Shadows' center Jean-Luc Dupont. Right winger, Digger Baker, tapped his stick on the ice. The puck dropped. Shadows won the face-off. Baker passed the puck to Béliveau.

"Look at Béliveau go," John commented, "slick as ever, maneuvering through the Goshawks' blue line."

"But here comes Mitchell! Oh, that had to hurt. Béliveau gets a slobberknocker into the boards!" shouted Tom.

The crowd roared, but Béliveau managed to make a saucer pass to Storm, who raced down the ice.

Hunter eyed Storm as he barreled toward him. "This is our ice, my net," he growled through a clenched jaw. "No one gets past this wall."

Storm unleashed a blistering wrist shot, aimed for the top corner. In an explosive movement, Hunter's catching glove shot up like a bear trap, snatching the puck out of the air.

"Gotcha!" he snarled, glaring at Storm as he tossed the puck to the ref. "This is OUR house!"

The arena erupted into cheers. The message was clear: Hunter was back in his element, a defensive structure between the pipes.

"What a mitt! Griffin starts strong!" Tom shouted.

The crowd's continued chants were deafening. "Ice Wall! Ice Wall!"

The game commenced, as Hunter denied fifteen more shots on goal. The Goshawks defense was playing hard, but the Shadows appeared to be possessed, winning every faceoff.

As the first period progressed, the tension on the ice heated up. Hunter, a veritable wall between the pipes, his focus unwavering amidst the relentless assault. Meanwhile, the Goshawks' defense dug in, battling to stave off the Shadows' onslaught. Despite their tenacity, the Shadows displayed an almost supernatural coordination, dominating faceoff after faceoff, maintaining an ominous pressure that seemed to foreshadow a looming climax as the period drew to its close.

Not to be denied again. After the next face-off, the Shadows cycled the puck in the Goshawks' zone, their passing sharp and crisp. Dupont took possession at the point, feigning a slapshot. Instead, he dished it to Béliveau, who was hugging the boards.

"Watch Béliveau," Jack cautioned. "He's looking for a shooting lane."

Béliveau cut to the slot, pivoting to create space.

GOAL! Shadows—Béliveau

"You called that one. Béliveau let that shot go top shelf." Tom shouted.

"Just like that ... the Shadows draw first blood!" John let out a low whistle.

Stay calm, keep focused. Hunter's thoughts remained internal as he slid back and forth with smooth precision in the crease. He did his best to ignore the angry fans now hurling insults in the seats behind the net.

"Hey Griffin, my grandma could've stopped that one!"

"Four games sitting on the bench, and now that's the best you got?"

"Bring back the Snowman."

"Looks like Griffin is getting a mixed reaction. The Goshawks' fans aren't sure what to make of the goalie switch tonight," John commented.

"It's a rough crowd out there, that's for sure. Griffin has two more periods to prove himself."

"Well folks, that's the end of the first period, with the Shadows leading 0-1 against the Goshawks. A tense game. This is going to be a night where Griffin's mettle will be tested," John concluded.

"It's going to be an explosive second period for sure," Tom added. "We'll be back after this break. Don't go anywhere!"

Second Period

The rink was a cauldron of tension as the players skated out. The raucous crowd waved their Goshawks towels with renewed intensity. Hunter pulled down his mask, feeling its weight align with his own resolve as he skated to his net. Time to shut them down. No more getting through me.

"Fans, we're back for what promises to be an exciting second period," John announced. "Goshawks looking to even the score."

"Absolutely. They need a quick answer," Tom responded.

Hunter skated into the crease, tapping the posts with his stick before settling in. His eyes narrowed as he locked into game mode. *Alright, wipe the slate clean. Show them why you're the wall they can't climb.*

Goshawks second line center, Daniel Murphy, squared off against Baker in the Toronto end. The ref's hand opened. The puck hit the ice. Daniel won it back to Goshawks' D-man, Matthew Preston, who unleashed a howitzer to the Shadows' net.

"Preston winds up. Big slapshot!" John was on the edge of his seat.

"Misses by a hair!" Tom added. "The Goshawks are turning up the heat."

Hunter dialed in, tracked every pass, every shot, as he muttered, "You won't get another one past me. Not tonight."

Fresh off a line change, Ryan intercepted a careless pass from Béliveau, snapping it to Chase.

"Mitchell intercepts! Finds Rutherford," John roared.

With a quick deke, Chase dodged Dupont's poke check, firing a low-flying missile from the hash marks, grazing the goalie's skate, slipping into the net.

GOAL! Goshawks—Rutherford

"The captain ties it up for the Goshawks. What a rip!!" Tom shouted.

Hunter clenched his gloved fist. "That's right, boys. Now it's my turn to lock it down."

His resolve was put to the test. Shadows' Storm picked up a slick feed from Baker and broke away.

Hunter's thoughts zeroed in ... *he's going five-hole.*

At the last millisecond, Storm flicked the puck up instead.

GOAL! Shadows—Storm

"Storm with the sleight of hand!" Tom bellowed.

Hunter hit the pipes with his stick, letting out a primal growl.

Daniel Murphy skated by the net, the tip of his stick tapping Hunter's pads. "Keep that up and we'll be needing a third backup goalie," he snarled as he skated off.

The period unfolded with a relentless pace, the intensity on the ice escalating as every second ticked by. The Goshawks, although a man down due to a penalty, showcased their resilience. Tempers flared, fists flew, and the crowd roared in response to the players' skirmishes.

Amidst the chaos, Hunter stood like a fortress in the net. Despite the Shadows' aggressive plays and their advantage in numbers, they were locked out of the Goshawks net. Both teams fought hard for dominance, but Hunter's unwavering focus kept the Shadows at bay as they braced for the horn's signal to end the period.

Hunter clenched his stick tighter, his gaze steely as the seconds ticked down. He couldn't afford another slip-up, not with the Shadows leading by one. He couldn't let that shot from Storm mess with his head. He knew the Shadows had a knack for making the best goalies look like amateurs.

The crowd roared as the Goshawks regained possession, Etan deftly maneuvering around the Shadow's defense. He passed to Chase, who took a hard slapshot—only to be denied by the Shadow's goalie.

"Wowzer! A phenomenal save from Toronto's netminder! Rutherford's gotta be frustrated," John announced.

"You can see it on his face, but there's no time for that. The clock's winding down," Tom inputted.

Hunter watched as the puck bounced, landing in the Shadows' possession. He set his jaw. No more goals.

The clock zeroed out as the horn blared.

"And that's the end of the second period, folks. Goshawks 1, Shadows 2. It's anybody's game," John summed up.

"Griffin has his work cut out for him, but don't count Goshawks out. We've got lots of hockey on the way," Tom's voice filled with hope.

Third Period

Hunter's eyes scanned the ice as the last period got underway. It was do-or-die time. His mind was a fortress, impenetrable, focused only on the game.

"And here we go, folks. The final period of what's shaping up to be an instant classic," Tom bellowed.

"You said it, John. I would have loved to have been a fly on the wall in the Goshawks' locker room during last intermission."

"You say that every game. But this time I wish I could've been there too."

The puck dropped.

Hunter watched as Chase and Axel managed to pin the Shadows in their zone. The Goshawks were relentless, a symphony of power and skill. Nevertheless, the tying goal eluded them.

Then, a breakaway. Shadows' Storm got his tape on the puck, charging down the ice like a man possessed.

"Uh-oh, this is dangerous. Storm is quick, and he's got a wicked shot," Tom shouted.

Hunter tightened his gloves. This was the moment. His moment. He glided to cut down the angle, eyes locked on Storm. Toronto's forward released a snapshot.

With cat-like reflexes, Hunter's glove snapped upwards, catching the puck out of the air. The arena erupted.

"What a save by Griffin! That could be the game-saver," John yelled.

"I agree ... that was one incredible save. Storm must be wondering what happened!"

Hunter tossed the puck to the ref, then tapped his stick on the ice. It was a good save, but it had to be. No more room for error. No room for doubt.

Dialed in, Hunter felt each click of the clock amplifying the tension in the arena. He felt the vibration of the ice beneath him, the heat of the crowd's focus behind him. He was in the zone. Blocking shot after shot. Yet the third period was ticking away, and the Goshawks were still one goal down.

"Less than seven minutes left in the period, folks. If the Goshawks are going to make their move, it has to be now," Tom's voice held an edge of urgency.

"You're right. The tension is unbearable. Toronto has put up a fantastic fight, but can they hold off Portland's offensive juggernaut?"

The Goshawks gained possession in the Shadows' zone. Etan and Chase executed a perfect give-and-go, pulling the Shadows defenders out of position. The captain fired the puck toward Finn, who deflected it in mid-air.

GOAL! Goshawks—O'Connell

"What a tip by O'Connell!" Tom raised his hands in the air.

"And just like that, we've got a tie game. The crowd's going crazy!"

Hunter pumped his fist, breaking his stoic game-face. His team was back in it. Now it was his job to make sure they stayed in it.

"Okay, less than five minutes on the clock. Do you think we'll be going into overtime?" Tom wiped the sweat trickling from his brow.

"Your guess is as good as mine, and the way this night's going, it's anybody's guess."

The Shadows won the next faceoff, quickly moving the puck to their offensive zone. Hunter readied himself as Dupont skated in with Béliveau. They were setting up for a one-timer. He could feel it.

Dupont passed. Béliveau shot.

With a surge of adrenaline, Hunter slid across the crease, his pad meeting the puck just in time to divert it from the net.

"Another spectacular save by Griffin! How did he get across the crease that fast?" Tom asked.

"That's why he's been this year's top goalie in the league."

The crowd roared chants of "Ice Wall! Ice Wall!" filling the arena. Hunter tried to shut it out, focusing only on the game. The clock was ticking down. He couldn't afford a lapse in concentration now.

Portland regained possession, storming towards Toronto's net. With just seconds left, Chase took one final shot—a laser to the top corner.

GOAL! Goshawks—Rutherford

"HE SCORES! Rutherford puts it away with less than 15 seconds to go," Tom screamed.

"This place has just erupted! What a comeback. They've clinched this round. The Goshawks are on their way to the Conference Final," John bellowed.

The buzzer sounded, signaling the end of the game. Goshawks 3, Shadows 2.

The locker room door burst open. The Goshawks flooded in, exuding a wave of sweat, adrenaline, and triumph. Cheers and hand claps filled the air.

Chase tapped the top of Hunter's mask. "Way to make a comeback, kid. Good to have you in the net where you belong."

Ryan chimed in, wearing a huge grin, "Told you. You've still got it!"

Finn, in his usual enforcer role, even off the ice, growled, "Who said Hunter was rusty? Huh? I'll fight 'em!" He tossed off his gloves to back up his statement.

Etan danced around with Axel, joining in the celebration. "We're going to the Conference Round." They sang. "We're gonna shut them down too!"

Chase spoke up, "Alright, gather round. That was some prime hockey out there, boys. But it's not over. One more round to get us to The Cup rounds ... Are We All In?"

A unified shout of agreement filled the room, "All. In. Captain!"

Even Viktor cracked a smile. "Hunter, maybe you are not lost cause after all?"

"Thanks, Coach." Hunter smiled back, savoring the rare compliment.

Coach Harrison stepped up. "Alright, we've got a few days off before we face the next team. I know you want to celebrate, but remember, you still have a curfew." He waited for the moaning to cease. "Get some rest. We've still got a conference round to win!" The room rattled with exuberant celebration.

One-by-one, the players showered and dressed, heading out for a brief celebration at the Frosty Nest.

Ryan approached Hunter. They were the lone players in the room. "You Okay bud? You gonna join us for a couple of drinks before heading home? I'll drive."

"I'm fine Ryan. Gonna take a raincheck on celebrating. It's been a long day. I'll catch an Uber home." Hunter looked up. "Give me a ride to the gym tomorrow?"

"Always."

Hunter sat in the locker room, still wearing his pads. His gloves and mask sitting beside him. The room felt as empty as his soul. Despite the earlier buzzing victorious euphoria from his teammates, Hunter felt a nagging dissatisfaction. Sure, he'd made some great saves, but the two goals he let in still irked him.

He thought about calling Sage. He wanted to share the moment, to feel connected. But he questioned whether he deserved to celebrate at all.

Reaching for his cell, he scrolled through the short contact list. His finger resting on Sage's name. Pausing, he wondered if she would even take his call. After all, it had been over two weeks since they last saw each other. Since they last spoke. He had not contacted her since her sudden departure after the Florida win. After the PDA kiss.

His finger hovered over his phone, over her name. He'd been such a fool, putting Sage in the media spotlight ... only thinking of himself ... not really thinking at all ... so unlike him. But then he'd been doing a lot of unlike-him things since Sage stumbled into his life.

Yet, he had to know how she was doing. He felt an inner pull to just hear her voice. Hunter's finger pressed the call button. After several rings, he was about to hang up when an AI voice came through his phone.

"The number you have dialed has been disconnected. If you think you have dialed in error, please hang up and try again."

Hunter stared at the phone. The words felt like a body check he didn't see coming. He felt as cold and empty as the locker room. The weight of the day crashed in on him. Logically, he knew tonight's win put the Goshawks, put him, one step closer to his biggest dream ... playing for The Cup.

Yet, right here, right now, he felt lost, once more abandoned. Without thinking, he heaved his phone with the force of a lifetime of pent-up anger. He watched with dispassion as it hit the wall, shattering to the ground.

Staring at his cell, dead and in pieces, just like he felt inside. A sudden wave of regret flooded him but passed just as quickly. With muscle memory of a thousand games played, he removed his gear and headed for the warmth of the showers. One more game, one win at a time ... the Goshawks were his family, his friends, all he needed.

Chapter 35
Framing Choices

May 15th

Sage sat at her worktable, surrounded by a vibrant medley of emotions captured in ink and canvas. Each image told a story, each pixel represented a heartbeat in time. Yet, as a collection, they felt like a maze she couldn't navigate. The images had consumed every inch of the open concept living room in the guest cabin: leaning against sofas, sitting on coffee tables, even occupying the dining area. Chaotic as it appeared, Sage felt as if she were inside her gallery show.

Pushing her chair back to take in the whole of her work. Large canvas prints depicting intimate moments with Hunter were scattered about—36x48 inches of raw emotion and skill, all waiting to be placed in her first solo show.

Her laptop sat open. A digital replica of the gallery's layout displayed on the screen. With a simple drag and drop, she placed each virtual image, saving her hours of physical labor. Sitting back, she took a long sip of her just brewed coffee. The aroma of chocolate, cinnamon and fresh ground coffee beans lingered in the air. She could almost feel Hunter's presence.

"Goodness, Sage, it's like walking into an art store that exploded," Jessica announced as she entered the guesthouse, Patty trailing behind her.

"It feels more like the art decided to have a party, and no one knows who's hosting," Patty added with a giggle, amused by the disorder.

Sage laughed too. "Well, consider this the pre-party chaos. Any suggestions where I should start hanging these on the virtual walls?" She gestured towards her laptop.

Jessica walked over to Sage's workstation, squinting at the screen. "It is so obvious. The goshawk picture should be the centerpiece. That's the showstopper right there. I mean, who gets a hawk to pose with them?"

Sage nodded, clicking and dragging the 60x36 canvas image of Hunter and the goshawk to the freestanding entrance wall. "It's an emotional focal point for sure."

A tiny bark sounded from the corner. All eyes turned to Crease, who was wagging his tail at a casual photo of Hunter. It was one of the 16x20 prints Sage had considered placing on one of the interior freestanding walls. The photograph captured Hunter at the animal shelter holding a yellow ball of fur. That was back when Crease was just another nameless puppy in the shelter.

"I think Crease just decided for you. That photo is making the cut," Jessica declared.

Sage looked at Crease, then back at the photo. For a moment, her uncertainties faded. Crease knew nothing about complicated relationships, or career-defining gallery shows. All he knew was the man in the photograph was someone worth wagging his tail for.

"Alright, little one," Sage said, clicking and dragging the photo of Hunter and Crease into the lineup on one of her digital gallery walls. "You've got the eye of an art critic. Let's make this show as unforgettable as the moments I've captured."

Jessica stopped, setting down a framed photograph of Hunter. She turned to Sage. "Look, I need to apologize ... again."

Sage looked puzzled. "For?"

"For what happened last week. I saw Luke in your kitchen and jumped to conclusions. I was out of line." Jessica's voice wavered. "And if I'm being totally honest, I was also insanely jealous. Which is silly, given how Luke only has eyes for you."

Sage blinked, stunned. "Jealous? Why? Jess, Luke and I are just ..."

"Just what? Friends? Yeah, and if you believe that, I've got some oceanfront property in South Dakota to sell you."

Sage's mouth opened and closed. "You think Luke has deep feelings for me?"

Jessica rolled her eyes. "Sage, you're the only one who doesn't see it."

Patty, seizing the moment, chimed in. "Seriously Sage, if you were any more oblivious, you'd be a rock."

Jessica's expression softened. "All joking aside, I'm sorry, Sage. I let my feelings for Luke interfere with our friendship ... again. And that's on me."

Sage took a step closer to Jessica. "I forgive you, Jess. And for what it's worth, your feelings do matter. To all of us."

Jessica nodded. Her eyes glistening. They hugged, a genuine embrace mending the frayed threads of their friendship.

Patty broke the silence. "Group hug?"

"Come on over here," said Sage, as they included Patty in their embrace.

Sage stepped back, looking at her friends and then at Crease, now snoring in his sleep. "With a support system like this, how could anything go wrong?"

"Talking about a support system. Sage, why didn't you let us know you changed your phone number?" Patty scolded. "I've been trying to call you. I thought your phone was on the fritz. You know, like it was last summer."

"Yeah, that's what I thought, too. Except I kept getting a disconnected message," Jessica added.

"Oh, and another thing." Patty leaned on the table. "Did you take down your business website? What's going on?"

Sage exhaled, her eyes darting to the ceiling for a moment. "You remember the media frenzy outside my house, right? Apparently, some so-called 'Social Media Guru' got my phone number off my website and posted it on his Facebook page."

Jessica's eyes widened. "You're kidding!"

"I wish I was kidding. But I'm not." Sage sighed. "He encouraged all his followers to call me, day and night, to get the 'inside scoop' on Hunter and our relationship. He even tried to blackmail me, saying he could make the calls stop if I gave him an exclusive interview."

"That's ... that's manic!" Patty's words came out like a fire-breathing dragon.

Sage nodded. "It was terrifying, especially when he said he was at my parent's house during the media circus. I've been bombarded with calls and messages since. Changing my number last week was the only way I could get some peace."

Jessica clenched her fists. "That's not just invasive, it's criminal!"

Patty growled, "You can't trust people these days. It's a good thing you changed your number. Removing your website until this blows over was the right thing to do."

Sage stomached ached thinking about what she'd been through. "Yeah, it's been a tough couple of weeks."

The room fell quiet, the weight of what Sage had been dealing with sinking in.

Patty broke the silence. "Well, whatever this guy thinks he's doing, he's not going to break you, Sage. You have us, and we've got your back ... always!"

Jessica nodded, her eyes locking onto Sage's. "You're not going through this alone."

Patty glanced at Sage, her eyes narrowing. "Speaking of phone numbers, did you give Hunter your new one?"

Sage fidgeted with a photograph on the table, her fingers tracing the edge of the frame. "I tried. I called him after his first game back on the ice since being benched. He didn't pick up."

"Maybe he didn't recognize the number," Patty suggested.

Jessica also chimed in, her eyes reflecting concern and a spark of curiosity. "Did you leave a voicemail or a text?"

"Both. Neither went through." Sage replied, her voice tinged with frustration. She clicked the mouse to close the gallery mock-up on her laptop, the screen going dark. Crease whimpered in his sleep. The noise punctuated the tension in the room.

Patty arched an eyebrow. "What about Margret? Have you thought about asking her to pass your new number on to Hunter?"

Sage looked up, her eyes meeting Patty's. She reached over, moving a nearby photo of Hunter. "I did," she admitted, "but no call or text from him."

The room fell into a contemplative silence, each lost in her own thoughts. The smell of coffee had faded, replaced by the bittersweet sense of unresolved matters.

Patty leaned into Sage. "For what it's worth, it sounds like you've done all you can for now."

Jessica walked over, placing a reassuring hand on Sage's shoulder. "And remember, you have us. No matter what happens."

The three friends exchanged glances, their eyes locking for a meaningful moment. The unspoken thoughts and feelings lingered in the air, but for now, they had the tactile comfort of each other's presence.

The afternoon light filtering through the sheer curtains cast shadows on the hardwood floor. Sage waved to Jessica and Patty as they drove away, feeling a weight lift from her shoulders. The tensions were resolved, friendships mended, and now, she had work to do. Just as she was about to turn back to the cabin, her phone buzzed. Luke's name flashed on the screen.

"Hey, how would you feel about going out to dinner tonight? And wear something nice, let's make it special," Luke suggested.

"Sure, Luke, I'd like that." After her emotional roller-coaster of the day, dinner with Luke sounded like the perfect reprieve.

Pulling to a stop in front of the restaurant, Sage watched as Luke hurried around his truck to open her door. She smoothed the cotton material of her baby blue sundress. She couldn't help but feel grateful for the normalcy Luke offered.

Upon entering, the hostess escorted Sage and Luke past a series of candlelit tables, each set with rustic elegance. They were led to a snug corner of the restaurant, where the décor paid homage to the local heritage—walls adorned with Terry Redlin artwork, depicting the rolling South Dakota plains and the majestic grace of pheasants in flight. The subdued lighting emanating from antler chandeliers cast a soft, inviting glow across the room.

The atmosphere laced with gentle strains of acoustic music blended with the ambient sounds of congenial conversation, and the occasional clink of crystal glassware. Luxurious aromas wafted from the kitchen, hinting at the culinary wizardry at play. Their table, set with simple yet elegant earthenware, was flanked by chairs upholstered in supple leather, offering comfort and a hint of luxury.

"This place is amazing," Sage murmured, her voice tinged with awe as she took in the surroundings that married rustic charm with understated sophistication. Here, in this cozy nook, the world outside seemed to fall away, leaving only the warmth and beauty of South Dakota's distinctive elegance.

"It's rather new. It's fast becoming one of my father's special places to wine and dine his clientele." Luke stood behind Sage as he pulled out her chair. "I thought tonight called for something special."

Her eyes caught the shimmering glow of the candles on their secluded table, casting a warm, golden light. She felt grateful for the momentary escape it offered.

"Thank you, Luke, it's beautiful."

As the first course arrived, the conversation remained light; they chatted about Luke's work, their mutual friends, and the one-woman art show Sage was preparing for. But as the night wore on, and the wine flowed, Luke's mood changed.

He gazed at her ... eyes filled with intent. "Sage, how are you really feeling? About everything ... about Hunter?"

Sage's mouth went dry, and for a moment, she felt caught. How did she feel? A sudden surge of confusion washed over her. She paused, measuring the contrasting calm she felt with Luke, against the swirling vortex of unresolved emotions she had for Hunter.

Before she could answer, Luke reached across the table, placing his hand over hers. "I care about you, Sage ... more than as a friend. It's okay if you're not ready to think of me like that, but I need you to know how I feel."

Sage stared into Luke's steel-blue eyes. She felt like a tightrope walker, teetering between the past and the future, between Luke and Hunter.

"Luke, I'm so confused right now," she admitted. "About Hunter, about me, about you. I can't give you what you deserve, what you want. It's just not fair to you."

At first, Luke's facial features tightened, his hand pulling away from hers. Leaning back in the chair, he relaxed. "I understand, Sage. Whenever you're ready to sort it out, I'll be here. I can wait."

Her heart fluttered when Luke said he could wait for her. A part of her wanted to lean across the table and recapture his hand. Another part held her back—a part that wondered why she was wishing it was Hunter sitting across from her.

She felt a pang of annoyance at herself. Why was she thinking of Hunter, who hadn't reached out for weeks, instead of cherishing this moment with Luke? Luke had been there for her. From protecting her at the sports bar filled with rowdy Minnesota hockey fans, to giving her a sanctuary to work on her art show, Luke had been a steadfast presence. He had even brought her flowers, a first for her. Plus, he was a gentleman ... he was also funny, rich, and handsome. Most of all, he cared about her and her feelings.

Studying Luke, Sage couldn't deny the uncomfortable question nagging at her: why couldn't she view Luke beyond the boundaries of friendship? Why was she still lingering on the mere possibility of what may be, what could be, with Hunter?

Chapter 36
Choices in Focus

May 20th [Game 2 of the Eastern Conference Final]

Sage held Crease in a firm embrace, preventing him from placing his puppy paws on the rich mahogany stairs leading to Luke's father's man cave. She knew Sterling Wheatfield was well off, but until now, she had no idea how rich he was. It was like entering another world as she stepped into the room below. She was surrounded by masculine luxury, married to perfection with a love for equestrian elegance.

"Holy Crap." Patty let out a low whistle. "This room is so big it needs its own zip code."

"Wait until you see the custom bar, the multiple flatscreens, and the massive leather sofas." Jessica piped in.

"There's more than one?" Patty stopped short, gawking, causing Jessica to bump into her.

"There's only three," Luke said, as if everyone had that many sofas in one room.

"Well, that's good to know," Patty quipped. "Any more than three would be ostentatious."

Ignoring Patty, Luke walked to the stocked bar ... the crown jewel of the room. The grand scale of it taking up half the wall, hand-carved from cherry wood, accented in polished leather. "What would you girls like to drink?"

"What kind of craft beer do you have on tap tonight?" Jessica pulled out a stool, taking a seat at the bar.

"So, this is how you became so proficient in making drinks?" Sage asked, as she watched Luke slip into his old role of bartender.

"Years of serving my dad and his friends was a great learning experience." Luke laughed as he opened the mini freezer, pulling out four frosty mugs, filling each with frothy ale.

Sage wandered deeper into the man cave, with a pool table on one side and a poker table on the other. Her gaze landed on the framed prints lining the walls. Like the ones in her guest cabin, these were all images she had taken. Yet, these were more than mere photographs; they were a testament to her skill, a bridge connecting her to Luke's life in ways she had never appreciated. Amidst the shared history and current revelations, Sage felt an unexpected sense of integration into Luke's world, a realization that both comforted and unnerved her in its intimacy.

"Do you have a favorite?" Luke asked, handing Sage her drink.

"It would be hard to pick just one. Each horse has its unique qualities." Sage took the mug of beer, taking a sip.

"Hey guys," Jessica shouted from the viewing area. "I thought we came here to watch the game."

"I'm coming." Luke walked over to the pit of leather sofas. Finding the remote, he clicked on the game. "Which round are they playing now?"

"The Goshawks are playing the Carolina Riptides. It's the second game of the Eastern Conference Final." Sage walked into the room, her body sinking into the soft leather of one of the couches. Across from her, was a huge flatscreen that put Hunter's TV to shame.

The game was about to start when Sterling Wheatfield made a brief appearance. "Enjoy the game, girls."

"Thanks, for allowing us to invade your home, Mr. Wheatfield," Sage said, smiling at Luke's father.

"My pleasure." His good humor fading as he noticed Crease on the couch. He looked like he was about to say something. Instead, he tipped his cowboy hat, exiting as quickly as he entered.

"Boy, it was nice of your dad to have us over." Patty said as soon as Luke's father left.

"He has his moments." Luke sat next to Sage. Putting Crease on his lap, he took a long swig of beer.

The puck was about to drop when Anita, the live-in housekeeper, wheeled in a cart loaded with pizzas and wings. "I hope this is to your liking, Luke," she said, placing the trays on the coffee table, along with plates and napkins.

"Wow, you went all out for us," Jessica said as she swooped in for a slice.

"I've never entertained on my own. Hope it's okay. I tried to emulate what you girls ate and drank at O'Sullivan's on hockey night."

"At least you don't have to keep drunks from tossing insults at us about the Goshawks," Patty added as she, too, took a slice of pizza.

The room went quiet as the game started. Each Goshawks' shot brought cheers. Each missed pass groans. Luke refilled the girl's mugs when the Goshawks scored their first goal. The room erupting in high-fives and celebration.

Although Sage's gaze was glued to the screen, she was not concentrating on the puck or the score. Her attention was solely on Hunter in the net. She watched his focus on the puck, the swift, confident way he moved.

As the game intensified, Jessica, Patty, and even Luke became engrossed in the play, shouting and celebrating each Goshawks' victory.

During the second intermission, Luke brought the girls new frosty mugs filled with a dark brown porter. He then poured kernels into a popcorn machine at the end of the bar, filling the room with a buttery aroma. The clatter of the vintage machine added to the festive atmosphere.

While Luke was away playing super-host, Sage's eyes never left the TV screen. She listened to the broadcasters, hoping to hear something, anything, about Hunter. Throughout the game, every save he made tightened a knot in her stomach, a knot she didn't understand. Was it pride? Anxiety? Longing?

With their bellies full of ale and food, the group sat on the edge of their seats as the seconds on the clock ticked down. The tension rose as the Riptides' goalie dashed to the bench.

"Nothing good happens when a team pulls their goalie," Jessica sang out. "The Goshawks are going to score on the Riptides open net. Mark my words."

This time Jessica was wrong. The last-ditch desperate attempt paid off for the Riptides ... tying the game.

"A little premature celebration, Jessica?" Patty tossed a handful of buttery popcorn at her friend. Laughing, she looked to Luke, whose expression grew dark. With the speed of a slapshot, Patty rushed to pick up the popcorn, aiming to beat Crease to it. "Sorry. Sorry."

Luke just let out a low grumble.

Two minutes into overtime, the Goshawks fought back, Etan scoring the winning goal. The room erupted with more spilled popcorn as Patty and Jessica hugged. Even Luke let out a victorious whoop, sloshing beer on the pristine white carpet as he jumped up, lifting his mug in the air.

"Two wins down. Two more to go." Jessica hugged Patty.

Sage loved the post-game tradition after a win; each player acknowledging their goalie's contribution with a respectful tap and or hug. When Hunter glided away from the net, he raised his mask. The camera zoomed in as he gazed upward, as if searching for her through the screen. In that instant, Sage felt an intense bond with Hunter, as if no distance separated them.

When the post-game interviews began, the room's atmosphere shifted from tense excitement to relaxed small talk. Sitting amidst the laughter and the chatter, Sage's mind was miles away, tangled in a web of emotions she couldn't quite decipher. It was a bind that not even the joy of victory could untangle.

"Thanks for letting us stay overnight in one of the guest cabins." Patty stifled a yawn.

"Yeah, Luke, I appreciate it too." Jessica turned to Patty. "I'm ready to go if you are."

Alone with Luke, Sage looked around at the mess they'd left. "Let me help you clean up before I go," she said, stopping Crease from upending another bowl of popcorn.

"Best not. Anita gets cranky when I try to do her job."

"Okay then. I guess I should be going too."

"I'll walk you to your cabin."

Before she could reply, Luke scooped up Crease, preceding Sage up the staircase.

Outside, the air was fresh with a bit of a bite, carrying with it the scent of late spring. Crease trotted beside them, his tiny paws padding along the gravel walkway.

Reaching her cabin, Luke turned to Sage. "Tonight was fun."

"Yeah, Luke. It was fun," Sage replied.

At the door of her cabin, Luke picked up Crease, handing him to Sage.

"Thanks again, Luke." Sage cradled Crease in her arms. Her eyes met Luke's, and in that instant, a universe of unsaid words hung between them.

Seizing the moment, Luke leaned in, perhaps to kiss her, to cross that boundary they'd both been tiptoeing around for weeks. Just as their lips were about to meet, Crease raised his puppy head, licking Luke's lips with gusto.

They both burst into laughter, the mood broken. Luke brushed a stray lock of hair from Sage's face, his touch gentle, lingering. He placed a soft kiss on her forehead. "Good night, Sage," he whispered, then turned, walking back to the main house.

Sage closed the door behind her, still holding Crease. Her gaze fell on the framed photos of Hunter still scattered about. His captivating smile and piercing eyes haunted her. Not wanting to deal with her conflicting emotions, she turned the portrait to face the wall.

Crease bounced behind Sage as she turned off the lights, making her way to the bedroom. Her thoughts drifted between Luke, the man she'd known for a lifetime but was just beginning to see anew; and Hunter, the man who had captured her imagination but seemed to be slipping further away each day.

Chapter 37
Spotlights and Shadows

May 24th [Game 4 of the Eastern Conference Final]

"Friends, we're on the edge of our seats here, in Raleigh, North Carolina, with only five minutes remaining in game four of the Eastern Conference Final. The roar from the Riptides' home crowd is matched by an abundance of Goshawks fans ... and it's thunderous. I might lose my hearing to their enthusiasm," John remarked, covering his ear free of the headset.

"A one-goal lead is as thin as rice paper. There's still time on the clock for the Carolina Riptides to make a comeback. One wrong move, and the Goshawks could see their lead slip away," Tom added.

"Rutherford finding that gap in the Riptides goalie's five-hole last period was a clutch moment," John's voice boomed, cutting through the charged atmosphere. "Without that critical play, we wouldn't be on the edge of witnessing a clean sweep tonight," he added, capturing the raw energy and anticipation pulsing from the stands.

"Don't count the Riptides out. They're playing hard and seem hungrier," Tom countered.

"I gotta disagree with you. If the Goshawks keep playing like this, they could go all the way."

"I know we both agree on one thing at this point ... it's anyone's game," Tom responded, his voice breaking. "But in a battle of the goalies, I have to admit Griffin is coming out on top. The kid's been standing on his head all night."

In the crease, Hunter's hold on his stick intensified, his fingers wrapping tighter. Through the bars of his mask, his gaze sharpened, fixating on the puck. He took a deep breath, drawing in the cool, crisp scent of the rink mingled with the lingering aromas of popcorn and beer drifting from the stands.

The atmosphere in the arena engulfed him. It was a powder keg of anticipation and raw emotions. The Goshawks needed this win. Most of all, *he needed* this win. Just this game to be the conference champions.

The fans of both teams exuded a pressure cooker of raw, unfiltered anticipation. This wasn't just another game for the Goshawks fans. It was the decider, the one that could stamp their team's ticket to the Cup Final.

For Hunter, it was even more personal. After the stunner of a win last week, he was geared up, more than ready. This game was theirs to seize. It all came down to grit, to battling for every inch on the ice, every check, every save a declaration of their sheer determination to clinch the win.

"Heads up, boys! No slacken," Ryan barked, his voice amplified by adrenaline and the fan's screams echoing across the rink.

Chase won the faceoff, sending the puck straight to Etan. With a skillful move, Etan corralled it, keeping the puck glued to his tape as he skated to the Riptides' net.

"Here comes Eklund! Look at that speed!" John shouted.

"The kid's a rocket, no doubt!" Tom interjected.

Etan, skates carving arcs in the ice, dodged past the Riptides' defenseman as if he were a statue. With a snap of his wrist, the puck flew from his stick like a missile. It sailed past the Riptides' goalie, ringing off the post before nesting in the back of the net.

GOAL! Goshawks—Eklund

"For a rookie, that kid's got hands of gold," John announced.

Etan's face erupted into a maniacal grin. Dropping to one knee, he rocketed across the ice. Fist punching the air, he roared, "Jaaa! Take that."

"You're a beast, rookie." Finn was the first in for the on-ice celebration, soon to be joined by the other three players. They mobbed Etan, their brotherhood evident in the rough, joyful melee.

"What a play," Hunter yelled from his net, using his gloved hands as a megaphone.

"Twenty seconds on the clock! Can Griffin shut them out?" Tom asked.

The Riptides' forward, Jacob Jackson, retaliated, barreling down the ice, muscles tensed, skates eating up the distance. Winding up, he let a slapshot go—the puck a blur, screaming toward the net like a bullet.

Hunter lunged as time seemed to slow. His glove outstretched; he caught the puck before it could escape into the net ... invade his home.

"He's done it! Griffin slams the door!" John shouted.

"Looks like my prediction of a shutout may be coming true for this young goalie," Tom added, unable to contain his awe.

Hunter hoisted his glove in triumph, the captured puck a treasure. "That's how we do it, boys! Shut 'em down!"

"You're a legend, Griffin! Stone-cold legend!" Ryan poked Hunter in the chest, hard enough to make his friend stagger into the net.

The moment the puck hit the ice for the last faceoff, the buzzer shrieked signaling the end of the third, and the beginning of the Goshawks's celebration. With a burst of energy, the Goshawks' bench cleared. Players piled over the boards, their skates cutting the ice, converging into a swirling mass around Hunter and Etan. Gloves, sticks, and helmets launched into the air, twirling and spiraling down onto the ice.

"And there it is, the yard sale of victory!" Tom shouted, pointing at the debris-covered rink.

"What a sight. Pure chaos! Pure joy!" John shouted back.

"Unreal, Hunter! We're going all the way!" Chase roared, rapping Hunter on the top of his mask.

"To The Cup, boys! To the damn Cup!" Finn shouted. His voice sandpaper rough.

The team erupted into a mass of tightly knit bodies, a wild clump of jubilation on ice, with Hunter anchoring the core.

From the chaotic joy of victory, the atmosphere shifted as if on cue to the solemn tradition that marks the sport's honor. The raucous celebration tapered into a procession of athletes, transitioning from the euphoria of triumph to the dignified ritual that hockey holds sacred.

In a ceremonial moment, the teams lined up for the customary post-series handshake, the air thick with the scent of sweat and underlined by respect. Bare hands clasped in firm grips, eyes meeting in a mutual acknowledgment of each other's efforts and valor.

"It was an honor to compete against you," Chase said, shaking hands with the Riptides' captain.

"You too, man."

"You played one hell of a series. Your saves were something else. Till we meet on the ice again." Hunter leaned into the Riptides' goalie as he spoke.

"Great series, my friend. You were a wall tonight. I look forward to next season," the Riptide's goalie replied, his eyes filled with sincerity.

The Goshawks players then gathered near the boards, anticipation in the air, as Ted, the equipment manager, hurried over with a box tucked under his arm. He popped it open to reveal a collection of sleek, blue ball caps, each embroidered in silver threads with the words Eastern Conference Champions.

"Time for the crowning ceremony, boys." Ted grinned like a proud father.

"Sweet lids, Ted!" Axel said as he grabbed a cap, placing it on his head.

Hunter handed over his goalie mask to Ted, who handled it like a sacred artifact.

"Here's yours, Hunter." Ted handed Hunter the last cap.

Hunter took the time to absorb the win. He rubbed the cap's fabric between his fingers, taking a moment to appreciate the embroidery ... Eastern Conference Champions. Placing it on his head, he snugged it tight.

"Feels like victory." Hunter smiled at Ted; his voice tinged with gratitude.

Even though the presentation was on the Riptides' home arena, fans from both teams quieted in a show of respect as a carpet runner was rolled onto the ice. Then two men wheeled the Eastern Conference Championship trophy to the end of the carpet, placing it on a small table. The Conference Cup shimmered under the arena's lights. The league's Deputy Commissioner stood ready to present the trophy to the Goshawks.

"Ladies and gentlemen. I present to you, your Eastern Conference Champions, the Portland Goshawks!" The announcement reverberated throughout the stadium.

Chase, Ryan, and Daniel skated up, forming a tight line in front of the table. The captain and his alternate captains positioned themselves with a shared resolve; a silent agreement to keep a respectful distance from the trophy—a nod to the superstition that touching it could curse their chances of winning The Cup.

"Come on over guys," Ryan shouted when the official presentation was over.

The players lined up in a charged procession behind their captains, who served as the trophy's staunch guardians. Arrayed against the backdrop of a plush royal blue cloth draping the table, the players clasped their hands behind their backs in a gesture of respect. All except for Etan, who glided closer, his hand stretched in a brazen attempt to touch the trophy.

"Easy, rookie!" Finn barreled in, slamming Etan's hand away with a sharp swat. "Rule number one—Eyes Only. Nobody on this team lays a finger on it."

Etan blinked, retracting his hand as if he'd almost touched a hot burner. "I forgot. Sorry."

"Only one trophy you lift, kid ... and it ain't this one," Finn grunted, his voice gruff as he led Etan to the back of the pack of players.

Wearing slip-resistant grips on his designer shoes, Nikki ventured onto the ice. "Everyone gather around. Smile like you just won the Eastern Conference—oh wait, You Did!"

The team converged around the table, forming a solid, unbreakable formation with the trophy taking pride of place at the forefront. Each player's stance reflected their strength and unity, embodying the collective skill and triumph that led them to this victory. As the camera shutter clicked, it immortalized not just their conference win, but the indomitable spirit and tight-knit bond that propelled them to this pinnacle of success.

"What a sight, Tom. These Goshawks look ready to take on the world!" John declared from the announcer's booth.

<hr />

The players regrouped, heading towards the Goshawks' Boeing 737, the arena's energy trailing far behind. Gear bags in hand, their steps echoed through the airport's corridors, mixing with bursts of laughter and excited chatter.

"Hustle guys, the celebration starts as soon as we board the plane. Our fans might not be with us in person, but they're with us in spirit," Chase announced, his voice echoing with authority and anticipation. His call to action sparked a renewed energy among the team, their pace quickening towards the awaiting jet.

Once in the air, the cabin of the plane vibrated with the raucous energy of victory, as the Portland Goshawks soared through the night sky to home. Their triumph over the Carolina Riptides was more than a win; it was a statement to the team they would play next. The Goshawks were in full celebration mode, the limited space of the plane barely containing their exuberant energy.

Hunter leaned back in his seat, a half-smile playing on his lips as he observed his teammates. Etan and Axel, both nineteen, embodied the recklessness of youth, darting among the seats with their laughter bouncing off the cabin walls. They headed straight for the mini-bar, their eyes locked on the prize—alcohol.

Finn, the team's enforcer on the ice … and tonight, apparently, off it … stepped into the rookies' path. Towering over them, his broad frame blocked access to the bar, his grin sharp, almost predatory. "Think you're slick, huh?" Finn's voice, deep and laced with amusement, still carried an undercurrent of no-nonsense authority. "This isn't your first team flight. Don't make it your last, boys."

Disappointment flickered across the rookies' faces. Finn's presence became a storm cloud dimming the sun of their jubilation. Axel, the more audacious of the two, puffed out his chest, a retort on his lips, but Finn's hand raised in a stop sign cut him short. "Not tonight, lads. Save the rule-breaking for the ice."

The rest of the team, well-versed in balancing celebration with restraint, joined in, poking fun at the rookies' expense. From his seat, Olaf lifted a can of non-alcoholic beer with a flourish. "Join me in the high life, rookies," he called out, his voice tinged with mock seriousness. "It's all the buzz, minus the hangover."

Laughter filled the plane, a brief reprieve from the undercurrent of tension that always accompanied the aftermath of intense games. Talk soon turned to the upcoming days off, the brief respite in their grueling schedule.

"Now that we have some free time before The Cup rounds, I'm dedicating it to family," Olaf declared. His attention wandered as a flight attendant placed a basket of Buffalo Wings in front of him. Grabbing one, sauce oozing into his beard, he resumed, "I've been away from my wife and girls too long."

"Well deserved Olaf. I know that will make your wife happy." Ryan raised his bottle of beer to the goalie.

"Ya. She can get some sleep while you watch the kiddos," Axel inserted. His comment followed by snorting laughter between him and Etan.

"We are going to train and watch video games." Etan piped in, then he turned to Axel. "That reminds me, where did you hide the controller?"

"No idea." Axel sported a cocky grin. "Maybe we bring your mama over from Sweden to pick up after you."

"Keep dreaming, Axel. I'll find it before you'll see me calling for backup ... and leave my mama out of this."

"Woooo! Snap!" Hunter interjected, an amused smirk playing on his lips. "Save some of that fire for the upcoming games, boys."

"Ah, to be young and foolish." Olaf laughed. "I remember those days." With a concerned expression, he wiped sauce off his Cup Ring, then continued devouring his wings.

A flight attendant, sporting a uniform with Hunter's number and 'Griffin' across the back, leaned in with a mischievous glance. "What about you two?" she inquired, nodding towards Hunter, then to Ryan across the aisle.

Ryan sported a flirtatious grin as he gestured towards Olaf, who was moaning as he sucked on a chicken wing. "We'll have what he's having."

"Coming right up." The flight attendant winked at Ryan before making her way back to the galley.

Hunter was going to bemoan about his non-plans when Margret appeared beside him, motioning for space. As he scooted towards the window, she took the now vacant seat, her presence distracting.

"Geez, Margret, way to inject some life into the party," Ryan quipped.

She pivoted to Ryan, her retort swift, "Oh, lighten up. You're all glowing brighter than a fresh Zamboni cleaned rink before a playoff match."

Hunter did his best to read her. Although Margret was only a year older than him, she'd always been an enigma dressed in business high fashion. "So, what brings you to our end of the plane?"

"I have a little something for you." Margret handed Hunter a postcard. Once he took it, she reclined her seat, cradling a glass of champagne.

Hunter cast a wary glance at her, taking in the postcard she handed him. Her presence was always marked by a distinct blend of professionalism and a subtle scent of Chanel No. 5, that seemed to linger in her wake.

Turning his attention back to the postcard, Hunter's fingers brushed against its glossy finish. He was transported back to the ice, under the spotlight, the moment frozen in time. The image before him—a powerful snapshot of the goshawk's beak touching his goalie mask, captured by Sage.

It wasn't just any photo; it was the photo from the night the Goshawks clinched the first round of the playoffs, a night filled with personal milestones. Flipping the card over, a frown formed as he scanned the invitation. The creases in his forehead deepened as he processed the public display of a moment that, while witnessed by thousands, felt like an intimate connection tied to Sage.

Axel, ever curious, leaned over Hunter, grabbing the postcard. "It's an invitation to Sage's one-woman photo gallery opening, titled: The Man Beyond the Mask. Featuring images of the Goshawks goalie, Hunter 'Ice Wall' Griffin." He read, putting on a strong German accent for emphasis. "Dude, that sounds awesome! I'm in!"

"Me too," Etan added, as he leaned over Axel, scanning the invitation.

Ryan piped in, "If the kids are going, count me in too. Someone's gotta be their sitter. Plus, I'm a lot more fun than Finn.".

Ignoring his teammates, Hunter turned to Margret, his eyes ablaze, his temples throbbing. "You gave Sage permission to use images of me in a gallery show?"

Margret glared back. "I shouldn't have to remind you, Hunter. Your images, especially the ones Sage took under contract with us, belong to the Goshawks' organization," she paused before adding, "as do you." Her words were sharp, a clear delineation of the business side of hockey that was often lost in the on-ice battles and off-ice friendships.

The interior of the plane fell into a brief silence, the weight of her statement settling over all of them. Seething, Hunter's gaze shifted from the postcard to

Margret, a silent acknowledgment of the complex ties that bound him to the team, to Sage, and to the sport itself.

"Besides, this is good publicity for you, the Goshawks ... even for Sage," Margret said, as she took a sip of her champagne.

Hunter's chest tightened. His breathing labored. He felt a sensation akin to a puck smacking against his chest ... without wearing his goalie pads. "And you're just now telling me about her show because ...?"

"Because I've arranged for the Goshawks' private charter plane to fly you to the gallery opening," Margret continued, giving him a look that dared Hunter to object.

Hunter once more checked out the dates on the postcard. "The opening is tomorrow night!"

"Remember, we're going too." The rookies chimed in as one, oblivious to the growing tension between Hunter and Margret.

Their excitement was a sharp contrast to Hunter's introspection. Etan and Axel's anticipation of attending the gallery opening, along with their admiration for the postcard photo—and by extension, for him—served as a reminder of the influence he wielded. This influence extended not just within the confines of the rink, but beyond its barriers as well.

Margret offered a strained smile. "I'll talk to Coach Harrison about letting you three join Hunter." Suppressing a yawn and rising to leave, she added, "Despite the fun you're having tonight, make sure you're not late tomorrow ... and remember your tuxes. Gather at Hunter's place; my driver will collect you at noon, sharp." Her gaze fixed on Hunter, her voice hardened as she said, "Missing tomorrow's flight isn't an option."

Hunter nodded, the postcard feeling as heavy as a puck in his hand. Margret's departure lightened the mood of his teammates, who resumed their celebrations. Yet, Hunter was somewhere else, his mind a battleground, caught between the glare of the spotlight and the anonymity of shadows, a goalie at the heart of the storm.

Chapter 38
Calm Before the Storm

May 26th

The interior of the gallery was church-quiet ... with every wall poised for the final touches of the installation. Sage stood alone. She savored the mingled scents of fresh ink and canvas, filling the air like a promise. Her gaze lingered on the exhibit's showstopper: Hunter and the goshawk locked in a silent, powerful exchange, illuminated from above by a spotlight, lending the scene an ethereal quality.

Sage jumped at a sudden rap at the door. Approaching the gallery's frosted glass entrance, she made out vague shapes behind the panes. Swinging the door open, Patty, Jessica, and Luke tumbled in, a bundle of energy and eagerness. They had all insisted on lending a hand with the last-minute details, and more important, on being there to quell the storm of nerves brewing within Sage, hours before the opening.

"Wow, Sage. Just Wow!" Patty broke the silence, her gaze falling on one of the standalone walls, featuring Hunter and Crease. "I don't remember seeing that one."

"It was a last-minute addition. It's from the Goshawks' charity calendar shoot." Sage stood next to Patty, admiring the image. "The animal shelter director gave me permission to use it, only if I promised to gift her the image after the show."

"Stop ogling the photos, Patty," Jessica said, ever the pragmatic one. "Everything looks great so far, Sage. What's left to do?"

"There are just a couple more large canvases to hang, and a few adjustments to make here and there with the smaller framed images," Sage responded, her voice tinged with both anticipation and vulnerability.

Luke, his eyes meeting Sage's, nodded. "Let's get to it."

The next hour, they hung and adjusted the remaining photos. Picking up the last image, Sage felt the physical and emotional weight of the photograph printed on an oversized canvas. Its tactile presence mirrored the heaviness in her heart when she thought of Hunter. With trembling fingers, Sage secured it to the wall. Stepping back to admire her work, she couldn't help but wonder if Hunter, so private off the ice, would appreciate this form of tribute, or whether he would see it as an invasion.

Luke sensed her unease. He was about to reach out when Jessica intervened. She handed him a hammer, directing him to adjust a crooked image on the wall. Grasping the wooden handle, Luke shifted his focus to the physical task at hand, providing a momentary distraction from the emotional weight filling the room.

Patty walked to Sage, leaning on her shoulder-to-shoulder. "You've done an amazing job. Tonight is going to be a huge hit."

Sage squeezed her hand. "Thanks, Patty, I needed that."

"Are we all fixed for drinks and munchies for tonight?" Jessica took her place on the other side of Sage, mirroring Patty's pose.

Patty looked at her watch. "I've arranged for the caterer to deliver the hors d'oeuvres a half-hour before the opening. The gallery director said there was a kitchen in the back we can use for the overflow."

"The portable bar's tiny, but I've got it covered." Luke leaned on one of the free-standing walls, nodding to the back corner of the room.

"Thanks for manning the bar tonight, Luke. Be sure to thank your father again for footing the bill for the booze." Sage broke away from her girlfriends to give Luke a quick hug.

"I can't believe he did that." Patty looked at Luke with wonder in her eyes.

"Dad's embracing his inner art aficionado." Luke said, creating air-quotes with his fingers. Flashing a mischievous grin, he added, "Boy, is he ever having a hard time figuring out how to write supporting an East Coast professional hockey player off as a business expense."

The girls exchanged glances, then laughter spilled out, a soothing balm to Sage's nerves. Their mirth seemed to seep into the gallery's very walls, infusing the space with a sense of anticipation for the evening ahead.

Once more, Sage stared at Hunter's photos, her eyes lingering on each frame as if it would reveal an insight into her complicated feelings. It was Jessica who snapped her out of her deep thoughts.

"Earth to Sage. You, okay?"

Sage nodded, pulling herself back to the moment. "Yeah, let's finish up."

The group walked around the gallery doing last minute straightening and moving images. At last, they stepped back to admire their work. The gallery now felt like a living entity—each canvas, each framed photograph, a heartbeat, each spotlight a glimmer into the soul of the image it shined upon.

"Looks amazing, Sage. Hunter would be proud." Jessica gave Sage a quick hug.

Patty agreed, "Totally! This is going to be one heck of an opening night!"

Preparing to leave, Luke helped Sage on with her jacket, holding it for a moment longer than necessary, he leaned in and whispered, "You have a rare gift," he said, his voice husky, imbued with sincerity. "You always capture the inner essence of your subjects."

She switched off the lights, the gallery plunging into an eloquent darkness. Turning the key to the door, the click of the lock echoed in the empty corridor.

Sitting in her SUV, Sage's thoughts were a whirl of emotions. In the enveloping quiet, she couldn't help but wonder how Hunter, a world away yet so present in that room, would feel about being immortalized on these walls.

Chapter 39
A Flight to Uncertainty

May 26th

The gentle hum of the Goshawks' charter plane's engine punctuated the contrasting worlds at each end of the cabin. Near the front, Margret was all business. Nikki settled into the plush leather seat next to her, going over the day's agenda.

"Remember, I want you and your crew to capture every moment of this trip, starting with Hunter departing the plane ... and especially his reunion with Sage." Margret adjusted her reading glasses.

Nikki jotted down rapid notes. "Got it, boss. Anything else?"

"I need an interview with Sage," Margret suggested. Her focus shifted from the flurry of keystrokes on her laptop to Nikki. "I'll press Sage on her decision to spotlight Hunter in her first solo gallery show."

Nikki froze. "Are you sure that's a good idea?"

Margret stopped typing, looking up from her screen. "Since when do you doubt my decisions?"

Nikki lowered his pad and pen. "Margret, you know how hard this is going to be on Hunter. Over the past five seasons with the Goshawks, he's made a point of keeping his hockey persona and his personal life separate. I have doubts he's going to appreciate his off-ice images plastered all over the walls of an art gallery."

"Hunter needs to grow up." Margret adjusted her glasses with a deliberate motion. "What's he going to risk? He's not about to throw away his shot at kissing The Cup over this."

"Have you talked to management about the show?"

Margret went back to typing. "Upper management approved the idea. This is a PR gold mine, so let's not mess it up."

"What about Sage?"

"Are you serious, Nikki?" Margret fixed him with a stern stare. "Sage is a professional photographer. This gallery opening, coupled with the publicity from the Goshawks, is going to catapult her career. Besides, everyone keeps forgetting, the show was Sage's idea." Margret waved Nikki off. "If there's nothing else, I have to get back to work."

— ◆◇◆ —

In the back of the plane, the atmosphere was less formal. The sharp scent of musky cologne clashed with polished dress shoes and a pair of new sneakers.

Ryan was doing his best to assist the rookies in a dance of wardrobe malfunction, as Etan held one end of his bow tie around his neck as if it were a grenade's pin.

"I swear, dis thing is out to get me," Etan bemoaned.

Ryan shook his head. "How can you two rookies put on your hockey gear quicker than any Goshawks' veteran ... yet, when it comes to getting into a tux, you're having problems buttoning your shirts."

"We've been dressing for hockey all our lives." Etan yanked the tie off, shaking it at Ryan. "Margret made us buy these when we signed our contracts with the Goshawks." He waved his other hand up and down his body. "This is the first time we have ever had to play dress-up. And we don't have fancy buttons on our hockey sweaters."

Axel sported a wicked grin as he added, "Plus, we place bets on who gets into their gear first. So far, I'm winning."

Ryan grabbed the tie from Etan. Placing the silk around the rookie's neck, with masterful ease, he tucked, looped, pulled and tightened the bow into a perfect knot. "It's all 'bout the wrist action, eh?"

"Kumpel, you be the James Bond of hockey." Axel grinned, doing his best to imitate his fellow D-man.

Ryan turned to him. "Do you need help too? Or are you gettin' the hang of it?"

"Ja, it's like tying skates, but for your neck." Axel's grin widened, his German accent coloring the edges of his words.

Ryan adjusted Axel's bow tie. "Get used to it, boys. If you stay with the Goshawks, you'll be wearing this formal gear a lot."

— ◆◇◆ —

Dressed in his tuxedo, Hunter had long removed himself from both worlds. Sitting next to the window, he held the gallery invitation like a fragile relic. Images of his moments with Sage in Portland flooded his memories. He traced the texture of the gallery invitation with his thumb, every fiber pulling him into his thoughts—lost between the hope and trepidation of the evening ahead.

Hunter couldn't shake his concern about which pictures Sage would use in the show. He worried about his intimate moments with her being exposed to the public; moments he considered not just private, but sacred.

He slipped the postcard into his jacket pocket as Margret eased into the seat beside him. "Hey, Margret."

"How are you holding up, Hunter?" Margret squeezed his shoulder.

"As good as can be expected."

"You have *but face*. What's up?" Margret turned her body, giving Hunter her full attention.

"I just don't understand any of this. We both know how much Sage despises the media. Why would she put herself in the spotlight again, by featuring images of me in her gallery show?"

"Frankly, I'm getting rather perturbed reminding everyone that this was Sage's idea. She contacted me for permission to use images of you in her show." Margret pulled papers from her briefcase, placing them on the tray in front of Hunter. Her index finger tapped the signature on the bottom of the contract. "Go ahead. Read it."

Hunter glanced at the words, then pushed the document back to Margret. "It just doesn't make any sense."

Margret refiled the contract. "Hunter, you are both dedicated to your chosen life paths. You are being selfish to deny Sage an opportunity to advance her career."

"Sage would never do that. She values her privacy as much as I do. I just don't understand why she chose to feature photos of me. You've seen her website. It's filled with amazing images of local landscapes, people, and their cultures."

"She's a smart businesswoman. She wants her show to stand out. To make a statement."

"But why photos of an East Coast goalie? Her Quarter Horse images would make a stronger statement. They showcase Sage's natural talent to capture a subject's power, grit and raw talent." Hunter pressed his fingers to his throbbing temples, fighting hard to keep a headache at bay.

Margret's sly smile moved from her lips to her eyes. "I think you just answered your own question."

Her words left Hunter speechless.

"Besides, Sage is a professional. I received an advance list of the images she'll be using in the show. Most of them are shots of you on the ice."

"And the ones off the ice?" Hunter sat up straight. His gaze burned into Margret.

"I only recall a handful of non-hockey moments. Sage captured you at your best in all the images. How can you object to that?"

Unable to find a hole in Margret's logic, Hunter took a new tack. "How do you know she'll be okay with us showing up unannounced?"

Margret reached into Hunter's jacket pocket, seizing the postcard. "We have an invitation."

"Hey! Give that back."

"I'll return it to you after the opening," she said, sliding the postcard into her open briefcase.

"I didn't read our names on the invitation."

"If Sage objects to you being there, then that's on me, not you," she countered, her voice firm. The airline captain's announcement of their imminent arrival into Brookings interrupted them. "This will be good for both of you." Margret stood, making her way to the front of the plane.

Ryan took the seat next to Hunter, vacated by Margret. Across from them, the rookies adjusted their seatbelts, readying themselves for landing.

Moments later, the plane touched down, quieting its peaceful hum. Disembarking, they were greeted by the faint scent of jet fuel and tarmac, mingling with the warm, strong South Dakota wind. Outside, Nikki and his crew busied themselves with cameras, capturing the moment. The rookies, caught in their usual banter, jostled and chirped at each other. Margret corralled them, along with Hunter and Ryan, into one of the two waiting limousines, orchestrating the move with practiced ease.

"Man, I can't wait to see this art stuff," Axel said, bouncing in his seat.

Ryan glanced at Hunter. "You good, bud?"

"I keep feeling like I've been facing slapshots without pads," Hunter offered, a hint of a weary smile playing at the corners of his mouth.

The first limo pulled in front of the gallery. Margret exited, followed by Nikki and the rest of the Goshawks' media team, who positioned themselves to capture the moment the Goshawks players emerged from the second limo.

Margret's heels clicked with authority on the pavement as she led the way to the entrance. Behind her, the players' laughter faded, giving way to an air of tension upon noticing the security detail stationed at the door.

At the top of the stairs, a sheriff straightened, his Malinois plastered to his side growled, muscles tensed. Beside them, a middle-aged man wearing a suit, cowboy hat and boots stood firm. With caution, they watched the approaching entourage.

The trio before them—the sheriff, his vigilant Malinois, and the cowboy—cast an imposing silhouette against the gallery's entrance. Each step Hunter took felt elongated, as if moving through a charged silence, an unspoken challenge hanging in the air as the group drew closer.

Margret hurried up the steps to the entrance landing. She extended her hand to the cowboy. "Mr. Larson, such a pleasure to meet you," she said, her voice smooth and assured, bridging the gap between them with a familiarity born from Sage's shared photographs.

Jim paused, eyeing Margret with suspicion before accepting her handshake. "I don't know who you are, missy. But this is a private event." His gaze sharpened as it swept over Nikki and his entourage, all decked out in black, laden with smartphones, tripods, high-end video equipment, DSLR cameras, and bulging gear bags.

Margret presented their invitation to Sage's father. "My apologies for the oversight. I'm Margret VanAlen, Media Manager for the Portland, Maine, Goshawks," she explained, gesturing towards Nikki and his three assistants. "These are my colleagues."

Mr. Larson scrutinized the invitation, then passed it to the sheriff for further examination while he checked a clipboard for Margret's name. "Not sure where you got this invitation, missy, but neither you nor your group are on here."

Sheriff Thor Engle, and his police dog Hammer, stepped forward as a unit, blocking the gallery entrance. "If your names aren't on the list, entry to the premises is prohibited." The Malinois gave a low warning growl.

"Wow! That was a long plane flight for nothing," Axel said. The rookies turned back to the limo.

"Jim, what's going on out here?" A petite woman darted through the entrance.

"These media vultures are trying to crash Sage's event." Jim Larson nodded toward Margret. His wife brushed past him, embracing the young woman who was standing her ground.

"Margret, it is so good to meet you in person," Lilly said as she released Margret from a gentle hug. "Sage will be so surprised to see you."

Margret snatched the invitation from the clipboard, handing it over to Lilly. "Sage invited us."

"Apologies for the mix-up. I handled the invites and never imagined you'd come," Lilly explained, offering a reassuring nod to her husband and the sheriff. She hesitated, then added, "After all, flying from Maine is quite the journey for an evening's event."

"No. Media." Jim grumbled, glaring at his wife.

"They are from the Goshawks organization, Jim." Lilly's smile was strained. "If not for Margret and her crew, Sage wouldn't have these images to hang in the gallery."

"Harrumph!" was the only sound from the sheriff, punctuated by another low growl from his Malinois.

"They can enter, but mark my words, I don't approve." Jim's attention then went to the giants dressed in tuxedos standing at the foot of the stairs. "Are they with you?"

Lilly's eyes lit up as she turned her attention to the group. "Oh, my goodness! Is that you Hunter? I didn't recognize you without your goalie gear," she exclaimed before hurrying down the steps to envelop Hunter in a warm embrace.

"Mrs. Larson?" Hunter froze, unaccustomed to warm embraces. Teammate bear hugs were one thing, but this felt foreign. Unsure how to respond, and with his upbringing leaving him unpracticed in such affections, he remained still, arms hanging awkwardly at his sides.

Lilly stepped back, but kept her hands on Hunter's arms, as if afraid to let him go. "I feel like I know you already. Sage has told us so much about you."

"Nice to meet you, Mrs. Larson." Hunter looked into Lilly's eyes. They were the same deep blue as Sage's.

"Lilly. Please call me Lilly. Now, introduce me to your friends."

"Lilly, this is Ryan. Over by the car are Etan and Axel."

"Welcome to South Dakota, boys." Lilly said as she interlocked her arm into Hunter's. "Now let's all go into the gallery. Sage will be so excited to see you."

Hunter allowed himself to be led by Lilly, even though he was unsure if Sage would be as excited as her mother was to see him. The trio of players followed, as Nikki and his crew hustled to get in front, to video their grand entrance.

Margret was the last to enter. Walking near the sheriff, she lowered her voice. "You might want to call in additional security. We're about to go live with our coverage." She then gave Jim Larson a dainty wave before joining her group.

Hunter stopped short at the end of the gallery's entrance hallway, coming face-to-face with the iconic image of his mask touching the beak of the goshawk. The postcard image had been impressive, but this ... this bigger than life version was breathtaking.

"I hope you like the show," Lilly leaned into Hunter. "Sage put her heart and soul into it."

"Look at that, under the photo." Etan pointed to the show's title.

Axel bent down, reading aloud the same words that adorned the postcard. Standing, he looked at Hunter. "Geez, what a way to take all the stars."

"Real funny," Ryan said, as he guided the rookies into the gallery. Looking back at Hunter, he asked, "Are you coming?"

"Yeah, yeah, I'm right behind you." Hunter stood mesmerized by the image.

"Come on inside. If you like this one, I know you'll love the rest of the show," Lilly coaxed.

Chapter 40
Puzzle Pieces

May 26th

Standing at the far side of the gallery, Sage noticed a commotion near the entrance. "Excuse me please," she said, as she walked towards several people dressed in black, all taking photos of someone hidden from her view behind the entrance wall. Nearing the group, she was about to ask what was going on when she saw three men dressed in tuxedos walking towards her.

"Sage," Etan and Axel sang out in unison as they swarmed her. Ryan followed close behind.

"Hi, guys," Sage managed, her voice laced with a mix of excitement and nerves. "It's so good to see you." Out of the corner of her eye, she noticed Margret, who seemed to materialize at her side with her usual impeccable timing.

"Sage, I hope you don't mind, but when the boys heard about your show, there was no stopping them from coming." Margret gave Sage a quick hug.

"Of course, I don't mind." Sage frowned as she motioned to Margret's entourage. "I just didn't know Nikki and his crew would be here."

"We already discussed this, Sage. It's even in your contract. We allowed you to use Hunter's Goshawks images. You get the recognition. We get the publicity. Quid pro quo."

Sage was about to respond when she looked past Margret and froze. She forgot how to talk, how to move. There, walking around the standing wall, looking like he stepped out of a fashion magazine, was Hunter ... on the arm of her mother.

"Hi, Sage."

She wanted to respond to him, yet words remained captive within her. Her heart, beating overtime, signaled an emotional turmoil deep inside. A month had passed without hearing from him, and now he stood before her at her gallery opening—unexpected, uninvited. A warmth surged in her chest, igniting a hope that her rising blush remained hidden.

"You clean up nice." *Oh, my gosh, did I just say that?*

Hunter flashed her one of his dangerous smiles. "You look beautiful."

Sage's hand went to the front of her little black dress, smoothing invisible wrinkles. She noticed Hunter's gaze fall to her neck when her fingers fidgeted with the silver goshawk necklace. Looking into his eyes, the unspoken words of '*I've missed you*' passed between them.

"Sage, why don't you take over the gallery tour?" Lilly said as she steered Hunter towards her daughter.

"Hold on, we need a few photos first." Margret motioned to Nikki and his team, who swarmed into position in front of Hunter and Sage.

"Do we need to do this now?" Hunter growled.

"Hey, man, I'm just doing my job," Nikki scolded, "just like you're doing yours."

Sage could feel the tension vibrate through Hunter's body as he pulled her closer. Looking up at Hunter, she whispered, "I'm sorry."

"Smile, you two," Margret chirped. "The sooner you cooperate, the sooner you'll be on your own."

Looking at Hunter, Sage was surprised to see he'd adopted his familiar pregame demeanor—a confident smile lighting up his eyes. She did her best to emulate his new mood, failing miserably. That changed, however, when she saw Axel and Etan goofing off behind Nikki, their antics bringing a genuine smile.

"Excellent!" Nikki said, clicking off a quick round of shots.

"Okay, kids, go enjoy the show." Margret turned to confer with Nikki and his crew, directing them to the other side of the gallery.

"How are you holding up?" Hunter asked, his arm still wrapped around her.

"Hunter. I didn't mean for any of this to happen."

"It's okay. It's not as if we can take any of this back now." Hunter emphasized his words with a quick sweep of his arm around the gallery. "You were brave enough to enter my world. Now, I'm ready to enter yours."

I'm not sure you are, Sage thought. Instead, she untangled herself from his embrace. Taking his hand, she led him to the first series of images. A 36x46 inch canvas print of Hunter emerging from the Goshawks' private plane at night. It was the first time they had met in person. Hunter dressed in a herringbone suit, his ice blue tie flapping in the wind. He looked both put together and disheveled. A quizzical expression adorned his face, as she had taken the shot the instant she'd called out his name, capturing a once-in-a-lifetime memory.

"I remember that moment." Hunter squeezed her hand. "I recognized your voice and thought I was having a sleep deprived hallucination."

"Nope. It was just me." Sage paused. "I hope you like the images."

"No one has ever captured the real me like you have," Hunter remarked, moving to the next canvas, a larger-than-life portrait of himself as he came face-to-face with Sage. "I remember this one too." He looked down, his eyes meeting hers. "The moment I saw you in person, I knew you'd be someone special in my life."

"I felt the same," Sage whispered.

"I've missed you."

"I've missed you more." Sage had the sudden urge to be alone with Hunter. To find a quiet place away from everyone where they could sit and talk. They had so much to catch up on. But she knew that was impossible, at least for now.

Hunter paced along the gallery walls, seeing himself through Sage's eyes—through the lens of her camera. Her work transcended mere photography; it was a vivid capture of his essence. Part of him recoiled at the thought of his private moments being exposed to public scrutiny. Since childhood, he thrived on the accolades of being part of a winning team; victory had become a familiar territory. Even so, he had always cherished his privacy. Away from the ice, he was still a celebrated goalie. Yet, he yearned to be just a man, seeking refuge in anonymity.

When Sage entered his life, the boundaries between his professional and personal worlds blurred. He recognized his own culpability, having been the initiator in their relationship. The first move was his, marked by the 'Hi Sage' image he shared on his Instagram. Logically, he understood Sage had every right to reciprocate his rashness, using his images, displaying him in her gallery show.

"Over here, Hunter," Etan called out. "You gotta see this."

Sage had been called away by one of her guests, so Hunter ventured over to see what the rookies were up to. When he viewed the standing wall, featuring never showcased scenes of the animal shelter calendar charity shoot, he stopped cold. In front of him were a half dozen images of him and the Labrador puppy. His throat tightened as he reached out to touch the image of the yellow bundle of fur licking his face.

"Great shots." Axel said, putting a hand on Hunter's back, leaning in for a better view. "I like the one where the pup is asleep in your arms. I only remember him bouncing around and chewing my shoelaces."

"Yeah, whatever happened to him?" Etan asked.

"Adopted," Hunter grumbled. "Hey, where's Ryan?"

"The last I saw; he was flirting with a sexy, dark-haired girl over at the food table."

Hunter's gaze drifted to the back wall, where he was captivated anew by a sequence of images. Sage had captured the moment the puck launched from his stick, followed by a series of shots showing the puck soaring over the heads of both Barracudas and Goshawks players. The subsequent image depicted the puck as it found its home on the blue ice, culminating in the final, triumphant shot of the red lamp lighting up inside the net. He had seen videos of his goal, but the still frames made his feat even more monumental.

"She sure captured that to perfection," Ryan remarked, offering Hunter a small plate heaped with various appetizers. "Figured you could use some fuel."

"Thanks for thinking of me."

"I always have your back." Ryan nodded to the opposite long wall with various photos of Hunter and the Goshawks in celebration. First Hunter skating to the bench to receive his celebratory glove bumps after his goal. The next image was a motion shot as the Goshawks bench emptied after their win against the Barracudas. One more in the series featured Hunter in the post-series handshake line. The last image captured Hunter skating toward Sage's camera, his mask pulled back, his expression filled with pure ecstasy.

Ryan patted Hunter on the head, reminiscent of a victory celebration, as if he were wearing his goalie mask. "That was one epic night."

"Yeah. I agree. In lots of ways." Hunter recalled the kiss he had planted on Sage just after she snapped that photo. The memories filling the gallery were overwhelming. "I think I need to get out of here." Hunter handed the plate back to Ryan as he looked around for a backdoor exit.

"Wait a minute while I gather the rookies and call the driver."

"No, you guys stay. I just need to get a breath of air."

"Hey, I think I saw a door near the food tables. Maybe it'll lead to a backdoor." Ryan nodded to the back of the gallery. "I'll keep Margret occupied while you make your escape."

Hunter scanned the gallery while Ryan headed towards the media manager. The place was packed with mingling strangers. He spotted Sage by the bar, laughing with a man Hunter recognized as Luke. That sight made him reconsider his plan for solitude, sparking a desire to pull her away. Jealousy was new to him, unsettling yet undeniable. Sage had a way of awakening his deepest emotions, for better or worse.

Instead of seeking an exit, Hunter walked to the bar, standing dangerously close behind Sage. Leaning over her, his lips brushed her earlobe. "I was wondering where you got off to." He sported a sly smile as she jumped at his touch.

Turning slightly, she looked up. "I didn't mean to leave you on your own."

With a steely dagger glare, he stared at Luke, who mirrored his expression. Hunter felt as if he was a gunslinger in an old western shootout.

"Hunter, this is my good friend Luke," Sage said, hoping to break the tension.

Still pressing against Sage, Hunter extended his hand. "Nice to meet one of Sage's friends." His gaze was intense. Softened by his practiced welcoming smile.

Luke reciprocated Hunter's handshake, one large muscular hand engulfing another. "Sage has told me a lot about you." Luke's words held a threatening edge.

Retracting his hand, Hunter put his arms around Sage's waist. Keeping his eyes on Luke, he replied, "Funny, Sage never mentioned you." His friendly smile turned into a smirk as he added, "Do you have any top-shelf scotch?"

Jessica scooted behind the counter, pushing Luke to the side. "Hi Hunter, you don't know me, but I'm Sage's best friend ..."

"Jessica. Right?" Once again, Hunter extended his hand but this time giving her hand a gentle shake.

"OMG, he knows my name." Jessica looked to Sage, letting out a gigglesnort.

"Of course I do. Why wouldn't I know all about Sage's best friends?"

Luke let out an inaudible murmur as he leaned against the wall, arms folded across his chest, staring intently at Hunter.

"We're serving a signature drink tonight. It's been one of Sage's favorites." Jessica looked to Luke, who nodded to her. But kept his stoic stance. "It's called The Goshawks' Elixir."

"Oh, ja, and it's fantastic." Etan plopped his empty glass on the bar just as Axel put his next to it. Looking at Luke, Etan asked, "Can you make us another?"

"You're not serving alcohol to minors are you, *Larry*?" Hunter snarled.

"No worries, Hunter," Ryan said as he sauntered over. "Luke's cool. He's making sure the rookies' drinks are virgins ... just like them."

"Tanks a lot, Ryan," Axel quipped, his German accent always thickening when annoyed.

"Hey, you two. When you're done over there, I just put out some fresh bison sliders and pheasant spring rolls," Patty shouted from behind the long table filled with hors d'oeuvres.

"We'll be right back for the drinks." Etan said as he and Axel headed to Patty's station.

"What about you, Hunter?" Jessica asked.

"I'll have a scotch if you have it ... over ice." Once again, Hunter put his lips next to Sage's ear. "What would you like?"

Sage shivered. Looking at Luke, she said, "I'd like an adult version of that."

"Anything for you, Sage," Luke drawled, picking up a shaker, placing a scoop of ice inside. He then poured in a generous amount of Tanqueray No. Ten and Blue Curaçao, adding lemon juice and simple syrup. Luke kept his gaze on Sage as he shook the drink with expert hands until it was chilled to perfection. With a slow sensual motion, he rubbed the rim of a martini glass with lemon juice before dipping it into a plate of silver sugar. Straining the mixture from the shaker into the glass, he topped it off with a splash of soda water. Smiling at Sage, he finished the drink with a dash of edible silver dust.

Hunter's body tensed as he watched Luke create the cocktail, especially when he reached across the bar, and noticed Luke's fingers brushing across Sage's when he handed her the drink.

"Hunter? I hope this will be okay. I poured you the good stuff," Jessica cooed.

"What? Oh yeah." Hunter looked at the proffered glass of scotch. "Would it be too much trouble to make it a double?" He watched as Jessica added a long pour of amber liquid into the Glencairn crystal.

"Thanks so much," Sage said to both Luke and Jessica. Wiggling out of Hunter's arms, she inquired, "There's an empty bench in the corner. Shall we go over there?"

Hunter maintained a gentle hand on Sage's waist, a grounding touch that kept his rising emotions in check. He knew any misplaced action towards Luke could land him in trouble, akin to a penalty call on the ice. Leading her to a dimly lit bench tucked away in a corner of the gallery, they settled. After a moment of quiet, both took a tentative sip of their drinks. "How is it?"

Sage looked at him, a bit puzzled. "How is what?"

"The drink." He nodded to the light blue, shimmering silver concoction in her hand.

"Oh yeah, it's great. You want a sip?" Sage held up her drink near his lips.

Hunter hesitated, doubting her drink would mix well with his scotch, but he couldn't resist placing his lips where hers had been. Keeping his eyes on Sage, Hunter took a slow sip. "Nice. It's not as 'frou frou' as I thought it would be."

"I was surprised too." Sage reclaimed her drink but kept her eyes locked on Hunter. "So, what was all that about back there?"

"I have no idea what you are talking about." A sly grin appeared on his lips, extending to his mischievous eyes. Hunter then sipped on his scotch, the smooth yet bitter tang blending with the icy blue liquid that still lingered on his tongue. It tasted like Sage, a mixture of sweet and tart.

"So, how long do you have between games?" Sage's eyes seem to plead for Hunter to give her a straight answer.

"We have seven days off." Hunter sighed. "Well, not seven full days off ... you know how hockey goes." He waited for her to nod in acknowledgement. "Coach gave us three free days, including today, before training starts up again."

"Oh." Sage's expression betrayed her concern. "Do you have to leave in the morning?"

Hunter reached over, taking Sage's hand in his. "We don't have to leave until the day after tomorrow. I'd like to spend a full day with you ... if it's all right?"

Sage scooted closer to Hunter until their bodies pressed against each other. Unable to conceal her grin. "Would you be willing to spend a day on the farm? I'd love for you to get to know my parents?"

Hunter touched his forehead to Sage's. "I'm not sure your father is my biggest fan."

"Dad will come around. Besides, my mom loves you already." Sage laughed.

"The only drawback, my entourage."

"They're all welcome." Sage hesitated for a moment before adding. "Does that include Nikki and his crew?"

"I've been informed that where I go, they go." Hunter closed his eyes, leaning back against the wall.

"That's okay. We can make it work. I'm sure we can get some alone time ... if that's what you want?"

As he opened his eyes, Hunter's smile emerged, slow and seductive. "I want."

"Sage, there you are." Margret approached the bench, followed by Nikki. "We need you two for an interview."

"Oh, I wasn't expecting that." Sage looked like a deer caught in the headlights of a truck on a dark country road.

"We can do it right where you're at," Nikki assured them, as he pulled out his video camera and set it on a gimbal stabilizer. Two of his assistants attached lavalier microphones to both Sage and Hunter.

The Interview

Margret: "Hi Folks, we are here in beautiful Brookings, South Dakota, for Sage Larson's photography gallery opening, featuring images of our very own Hunter, the Ice Wall, Griffin. If you've been with us earlier tonight, you've seen the stunning Goshawks' images. Now, we want to introduce you to the artist behind the photographs.

Margret: So, Sage, tell us your decision making in why you turned your first one-woman show into a one goalie show?

Sage: [after taking a long sip of her drink] Well, Margret, you know, last month, I was hired by the Goshawks' organization to fill-in for Nikki, the official Goshawks' photographer, to take photos of Hunt... of 'Ice Wall.' When I returned home, there was a reminder that I had a gallery show coming up. What better way to combine my three favorite loves, photography, hockey, and especially goalies.

[Sound of glass breaking near the bar area]

Margret: [unfazed continued] That seems a little odd, that you would follow professional hockey, living in a state that doesn't have a professional team. How long have you been a hockey fan ... more important, a Goshawks fan?

Sage: An old high school boyfriend, who had moved here from Portland, introduced me to hockey. I've been a Goshawks fan from day-one of their franchise.

Margret: With Minnesota so close, why fangirl the Goshawks?

Sage: First off, I'm not a fangirl, and I'm not a puck bunny. I fell in love with hockey as a sport. It's fast-moving. Precise. It holds an element of danger that other sports don't. I'm still intrigued on how players can interact with each other, as they chase a small disk with sticks while skating. I especially love the handshake line after a playoff round win. The respectful civil side of a raw barbaric game.

["Don't forget the bitch-slapping." A male voice shouted from the bar area]

Margret: [again unfazed continued] Okay, that answers the question of why you love hockey, but why the Goshawks?

Sage: I love their brotherhood. There are no egomaniacs on the team. Even though they've only been together for five seasons they're unified. Above all else ... they're the most exciting team to watch ... win or lose.

Margret: It wouldn't have anything to do with the Goshawks' goalie, would it?

Sage: It has everything to do with both the Goshawks' goalies ... plural. When it comes to netminding, the Goshawks have two of the best players between the pipes.

Margret: So, Hunter, what do you think of Sage's show? How does it feel to see yourself blown up bigger than life?

Hunter: [he cleared his throat] Margret, as you know, I'm used to seeing myself on the big screen, on the ice. I love my job as a goalie ... wouldn't want to play on any other team ... no matter what the media asks of me. [He took a deep swig of his scotch]

Margret: Hunter, you are even more evasive than Sage when it comes to getting a straight answer. Your fans want to know what do you really think of the show? Especially the off-ice photos. We're all aware of how you covet your off-the-ice privacy.

Hunter: [sporting his famous grin] Honestly? I think Ms. Larson is an amazing photographer. She's able to capture her subject's inner soul. I've never known anyone who can do that to the extent she does.

Margret: [her attention still on Hunter] Would you mind answering some questions from your fans?

Hunter: As long as they are hockey related. I'm always here for my fans.

Margret: [reading from an index card] After your big win against Florida, you were benched for a lot of games. Did that have anything to do with your relationship with Sage?

Hunter: [looking straight into the camera's lens] Olaf and I are both Goshawks' goalies. Other than that, Coach Harrison will have to answer those questions. As to Ms. Larson. We are not in a relationship. Over the past months, we have grown into good friends. We also both know our careers come first ... maybe that's *why* we're such good friends.

Margret: Well folks, that looks like all the time we have right now. Thank you for tuning in to 'Inside the Nest.' As always, we appreciate, and read, all your thoughts in the comment section. Oh, and if this budding friendship between Sage and Hunter blooms into something more than friends ... you'll hear it here ... and only here ... first. I almost forgot ... if you are out there viewing this broadcast in the Portland area, Sage's photographs will be featured in our arena for all the home games of The Cup Final. Stop by if you can. Tickets are limited.

CUT

As soon as Nikki put up his camera, Hunter ripped his mic from his tuxedo lapel, as he ripped into Margret. "What the hell was that all about?" Hunter growled in a tone so low it could barely be heard, a smile still plastered on his face. He knew to be cautious. He also knew that even though the Goshawks were the only official press at the gallery opening, everyone owned a cell phone ... and they were not afraid to post misleading videos.

"We'll talk about this later," Margret said through gritted teeth, while also sporting a veiled smile.

"Oh Margret, how could you?" Following Hunter and Margret's lead, Sage did her best to mimic the farce ... showing a calm façade ... checking her emotions.

"Sage, this does not concern you."

"What doesn't concern my daughter?" Lilly said in a sugar sweet voice, as she walked through the crowd, standing next to Sage.

"It's nothing, mom, just a little misunderstanding." Sage mirrored her mother's mild-mannered composure. Raising her almost empty glass, she raised her voice and said, "Hey, everyone, thank you so much for coming tonight. There's still food and drinks left. Please enjoy the rest of the evening."

The lingering guests, who had watched the interview, dispersed. Some went to the food and beverage area, others let Sage know how much they loved the show. Another group with pen in hand waited to get Hunter's autograph on their invitation postcards.

Over the next hour, the gallery emptied. Sage's father walked in, making a beeline to Sage. "How'd it go, kiddo?"

"Dad, I'm sorry you felt you had to stay outside the whole time."

"Your mom brought us plates of food, and some of those goofy blue girly-drinks. So, I don't think we missed much." Jim turned to Margret. "It was surprisingly quiet out there, other than a small swarm of dumb kids with smart phones, asking about an interview."

Sheriff Thor Engle stood beside Sage's father. "I told them the last time some punks wanted to get photos of my Goddaughter; I tossed their behinds in jail ... after I let Hammer chew on them for a while." On cue, the Malinois sat at attention, wagging his tail, as the sheriff slipped him a pheasant spring roll.

"Thanks again to all three of you," Sage said, hugging first her dad, then the sheriff. Hammer continued to wag his tail as Sage kissed the Malinois' nose.

Hunter extended his hand to Sage's father. "Thank you, Mr. Larson. The Goshawks appreciate all you and the sheriff have done to keep Sage's gallery opening night safe."

"Sorry, we got off to a rocky start. I'm not used to this much attention being dealt on my daughter, especially negative attention," he said reciprocating the handshake. "You can call me Jim."

"Dad, Hunter and I would like to talk to you and mom ... alone." Sage said, guiding her mom and dad to the other side of the gallery, far from Margret.

"Mr. Larson, er, Jim, Sage invited us to visit your ranch tomorrow. I wanted to make sure you were good with it too." Hunter rocked from one foot to the other, a goalie habit on and off the ice.

"Who is us?" Jim narrowed his brows, the lines between his eyes deepening. He glared from Sage to Hunter.

"Dad, the Goshawks have flown a long way to make my opening a huge success tonight. If not for Margret and the Goshawks organization, there would have been no opening. So, yes, I invited everyone over to the ranch."

"Sage, do you think that's wise? Remember what happened the last time you were home?" Lilly asked.

"Mom. That was over a month ago. Margret said she brought her own media crew to offset the others. She gave access to the interviews and the gallery photos to the local media. She also made it available to the online media. We ..." Sage pointed to herself and then to Hunter, "...we are no longer an exclusive. Margret assured me we are now old news."

"Can we trust her?" Jim turned his full attention to Hunter.

Not as far as you can toss her, Hunter wanted to say, but instead he answered with a half-truth, "Margret is a shrewd and savvy media manager. If she says there will be no more media frenzy at your farm, I will bet my goalie mask on her word."

Looking at Sage, Jim raised his hands. "What does a hockey mask have to do with your safety?"

Sage looked first to Hunter and then to her father. "It means everything, dad ... it means everything."

Chapter 41

Horsing Around

May 27th

Standing on the porch of the main house, Sage's hand shaded her eyes from the rising sun, as she watched the Goshawks crew—Hunter, along with Ryan, Etan, Axel, Margret, Nikki, and his three assistants—pull up in a caravan of dust.

She leaned against the porch railing, her gaze sweeping over the group of familiar faces as they stepped out, stretching and yawning. Everyone, even Margret, was dressed in jeans and Goshawks' t-shirts. Their eyes were wide at the expanse of her family's land stretching to the horizon, shimmering in the early light. The group appeared to stand as one, a world far removed from the rinks and arenas of their professional lives.

"I haven't smelled air like this since I left Sweden," Etan said, inhaling the sweet smell of the countryside—the musky scent of the soil and the crisp aroma of the dew laden grass.

"I agree with you, Etan. Portland always smells like salt and fish, this ... this reminds me of home too." Axel also took a deep breath, his smile widening at the sound of cattle mooing in a not-so-distant field.

In the nearby building, Jim, framed by the barn's wide doors, his silhouette strong against the backlit interior, raised a hand in welcome. "I sure hope you hockey folks are ready to trade ice for dirt today?" Jim's voice carried the gravelly timbre of the heartland. He strode towards them, his boots leaving firm impressions in the moist earth, a testament to his life rooted in the land.

Lilly emerged from the main house, her apron, a canvas of her morning's labor, dusted with flour as she carried a basket overflowing with hot out-of-the-oven muffins. The smell of baked goods mingled with the robust country air as she approached, her smile an inviting beacon.

"Good morning. You all must be famished. Come on up, help yourselves," Lilly offered, gesturing to a card table set up on the oversized front porch. Upon it sat a large stainless steel coffee machine on one side, next to it several frosty glasses filled with freshly squeezed orange juice.

"Thank you so much, Lilly," Hunter said as he approached the steps, only to be pushed aside by the two rookies.

"We never say no to pastries or coffee." Axel picked out a muffin for himself, tossing one to Etan.

The group gathered on the porch, an impromptu assembly of city souls syncing with the farm's rhythm. Hunter's gaze found Sage, her presence always a grounding force.

Sage handed Hunter a cup of coffee. "Sorry for getting you up so early."

"I'm glad you did. Since we only have this day, I wanted to spend as much time with you as possible."

As the group settled onto the wooden benches and rockers on the porch, laughter and conversation bloomed alongside the morning. Hunter sat, sipping on a steaming mug of coffee.

"I hope you like it. I told mom how you used cinnamon and cocoa powder to spice up your brew, and she's been using it ever since." Sage leaned on the railing next to Hunter, their fingertips touching.

"It's perfect."

The conversation steered to the day's activities as Jim asked, "How many of you know how to ride a horse?"

Etan raised his hand first. "I used to ride all the time on my parent's farm when I was little."

"That couldn't have been many times, Etan." Axel paused, taking a bite of his muffin. With a full mouth, he added, "Since you've never been little."

"You are such a funny man." Etan was about to toss his napkin at Axel, but he hesitated, remembering where he was. "How many times have you been on a horse?"

"More than you, I bet. Every summer, I would visit my cousins in the country. We rode from dawn to dusk."

"Sure. Sure you did," Etan said, as he grabbed another muffin.

Sage nodded to Ryan. "How about you?"

"I like to keep my feet on the ground, or on the ice. Being in control is the motto I live by."

"So, you've never been on a horse?" Axel asked.

"I've never been near a horse. I hope riding one involves less falling than hockey." Ryan turned to Hunter. "How about you?"

Hunter shrugged. "I'm a fast learner. I've mastered riding a bike, so how hard can it be to ride a horse?"

Ryan, nursing a glass of orange juice, quipped, "You're about one cowboy hat away from starting a line dance, Hunter."

Nikki spoke up next. "There is no way I'm getting on one of those beasts." He looked at his crew. All three nodded their heads in agreement. "We were born and bred in the city. Everything we ride has wheels."

"Not a problem." Jim put his hand on Nikki's shoulder. "I have two ATVs you can use."

"That will work out better anyway," Lilly said, as she emerged from the house with a refilled pitcher of juice. "I was wondering how the picnic basket I packed would fit on the horses."

"It will also give us a place to put our camera equipment. Thanks so much for the offer, Jim."

Margret sat in an Adirondack rocker, her eyes taking in the pastoral scene with a knowing glimmer. "Don't let the peace fool you boys," she teased, "I've seen enough country fairs to know it's all fun and games until someone ends up in the pig pen."

With those words, everyone's attention turned to Margret.

"What?" Margret scowled.

"Oh, I can't wait to hear this story." Sage's laughter, along with the others, echoed from the porch.

"In my wayward youth, I won a few ribbons in the show ring."

"Dressage?" Sage asked. This was a new and baffling side of Margret. She had to push for more.

"Some, but more show jumping. My parents owned a small thoroughbred ranch in Kentucky." Margret said in a nonchalant tone.

Ryan almost spit out his orange juice. "Holy Moly, Margret. Who knew?"

Before anyone could get another word out, two trucks approached, tossing dust and gravel. The small, beat up, red Chevy belonged to Patty. The big black Ford, pulling a long horse trailer, was Luke's. Sage frowned as she looked at her father with questioning eyes.

Jim shrugged. "You said you wanted to take the boys riding. Unless everyone wanted to ride double, you needed extra horses. So, I asked Luke if he could bring a few of his father's Quarter Horses over."

"And I invited Jessica and Patty," Lilly added. "I thought having the girls along would be fun for the boys."

Sage stared at her father with suspicion in her angry eyes. She knew her dad adored Luke. She had a gut feeling he was meddling in her life, trying to push them together.

As Luke and Jessica emerged from the Ford, Patty hopping out of her Chevy, the group on the porch descended to greet them. Luke, with a grace that spoke of his comfort both in the saddle and on the ranch, tipped his cowboy hat to Sage. His signature smile played across his lips.

Hunter took Sage's hand. An unspoken claim amidst the friendly chaos.

"Morning all," Luke announced, as he began unloading the horses. Each one was a testament to his family's legacy of excellent breeding standards. "Brought the best of the stable for today's ride."

The air crackled with an unspoken tension between Luke and Hunter, their mutual respect for Sage the only common ground in a landscape of rivalry.

Etan and Axel were already admiring the horses, giddy with enthusiasm. "Hope these beauties are ready for some Goshawks riders," Etan quipped, earning a chuckle from Axel.

"Just don't spook them with your goal cellies," Axel shot back.

Sage led Hunter, along with Patty, into the barn to tack up their mounts. "You'll be riding my palomino mare," Sage informed Hunter, a hint of pride in her voice. Patty and Sage saddled the bays, prepping them with the ease born of countless morning rides. The sounds of leather and metal filled the air alongside the scent of fresh hay and the warm musk of the animals.

Leading their horses from the barn, Sage was surprised to see the rest of the group mounted and waiting. Nikki and his crew were on the two ATVs, their cameras already documenting the gathering. Sage noticed her mom had gone overboard packing the back of an ATV with a picnic basket and a large cooler..

Hunter mounted the palomino with surprising grace. While Luke watched, his charm failing to mask the tightness in his jaw, as he leaned forward in his saddle.

The standoff between Luke and Hunter unfolded in a subtle choreography of dominance and deflection.

Sage, her foot in the stirrup, about to mount her mare, felt the silent vibrations of Luke and Hunter's rivalry. Her gaze flitted between the two men, causing a knot to tighten in her stomach. "You're a natural, Hunter," she called out.

"Yeah, maybe I'll add horseback riding to my off-season training," Hunter replied, his casual tone belying the effort he made to appear at ease.

Luke rode over, moving as one with his gelding. "There's a bit more to it than just sitting pretty. These animals can sense hesitation."

"Are you joining us on the ride today, or are you just here to give us tips on horse sense?" Hunter shot back.

Luke's smile morphed into a sneer. "I wouldn't miss the ride for anything." He then turned his attention to Sage, "I hear we have a couple of virgins ... virgin riders ... among us." Luke's gaze flicked to Hunter and then to Ryan, an unspoken challenge hanging in the air.

Ryan, ever the peacemaker, deflected the situation. "As long as I stay upright, I'll count it as a win." Turning to the camera crew, he added, "But hey, if I fall, make sure you get a great shot, Nikki."

"Let's get this day started," Luke announced as he led the group down a well-worn path.

Riding beside Hunter, Sage felt the weight of the day ahead. The ranch ... usually a place of solace ... now felt like an ice arena, with Luke and Hunter on opposing teams, hungry for a win.

The clatter of hooves and the muffled thuds of the earth reclaiming its impressions provided a rhythmic backdrop to their journey. Sage's lifelong familiarity with Luke was a stark contrast to the thin thread connecting her to Hunter. She had grown up with Luke's easy smiles ... the weight of his arm thrown over her shoulder in a brotherly embrace. With Hunter, every look, every word, every touch, felt charged with the excitement of discovery.

At the front of the pack, Luke was drawing everyone in with his charisma, the surrounding air alive with his passion for the land on which they rode. Margret, at his side, appeared captivated by his stories. Sage was thankful for her presence; a bridge between the two rivals.

"I've been a part of these horses' lives before they were foals," Luke bragged, a proud tilt to his chin as he leaned forward in the saddle, rubbing his horse's neck.

"How so?" Margret asked, her voice unusually coquettish.

"I selected their bloodlines. Every win in the show ring is a testament to their breeding."

Margret laughed, the sound light and free. "I admire a man who knows what he wants and goes all out to make it happen."

Hunter edged his horse closer to Sage, his posture reflecting an unspoken need to carve out a space for them amidst the group.

"So, this is your world." Hunter's voice flowed in a soft rumble, almost inaudible over the sound of the horses. "Feels like I'm getting a glimpse behind the curtain."

"Quite different from the ice rink, isn't it?"

Before Hunter could reply, Patty's voice rang out, her words woven with a playful lilt. "Hey, rookies," she shouted, "I meant to tell you last night. I'm impressed with your beautiful smiles."

The rookies flashed Patty wide grins, their excitement on display as their horses transitioned into trots. Despite their earlier boasts about riding prowess, it was clear by their bouncing bodies, they were more at home on the ice than on a saddle.

Jessica, with the practiced ease of a professional barrel racer, guided her horse, circling Ryan. "If you think handling a stick is tricky, try barrel racing."

Ryan nodded, sitting stone still on his mount, his knuckles white. One hand gripped the reins, the other glued to the saddle horn. "I can see why people get saddle sores," he bemoaned, bouncing in his saddle as his horse pranced about.

Hunter watched the exchanges, the muscles in his jaw working overtime. "Luke's quite the charmer," he mused. "Who'd of guessed those two would get along?"

"Luke's always been a people pleaser. It's just his nature." Sage regretted her words as soon as they left her mouth.

"Yeah, I can see. He's a real smooth talker," Hunter mocked.

Sage ignored Hunter's tone, turning her attention to the group in front of her. She'd ridden these trails countless times with Luke, Jessica, and Patty; their laughter was as much a part of the landscape as the whispering grass. But today, with the Goshawks intertwined with her childhood friends, the atmosphere became charged with a new energy.

She studied her friends riding ahead of her and their interactions with the Goshawks. Sage expected Patty's playful banter with the rookies, and Jessica's teasing flirtations with Ryan. What surprised her was the unexpected ease between Luke and Margret.

As they neared their destination, Sage slowed her horse to a walk, as did Hunter. They rode in silence for a while, as the conversations of the others fell away. It was just the two of them, surrounded by the expansive blue sky, and the rustling whispers of the wind through the trees. There was a promise in that quiet, a sense that even with the underlying tension and the competition for her attention, something real was unfolding between them.

Rounding a corner, the trail broke into a clearing of grass and wildflowers. Beyond that, a small lake. The early morning sunlight danced on the water, beckoning them to dive in. Sage pulled her horse to a stop next to Hunter. "Beautiful, isn't it?"

Hunter gazed into Sage's eyes. "Almost as beautiful as you."

Sage was saved from responding, as Nikki and his crew appeared, cameras and microphones in hand. He directed his team with a low-voiced authority, his presence an anchor in the shifting currents of the morning.

"Why don't you guys take the day off?" Hunter shouted, doing his best to steady the beast between his legs.

"Okay. You win," Nikki said as he clicked off a few shots. "Guess we'll help Margret set up the picnic." As his assistant turned the ATV around heading back to the lake, Nikki shouted, "Oh, and she said not to dawdle."

"We're right behind you," Sage yelled at Nikki's fading back.

"Looks like we've been paged by the commander." Hunter followed his words with a fake salute. Turning to Sage, he shouted, "Race, Ya!"

"No! Hunter!" Sage shouted back. But before she could get the words out, Hunter was four horse lengths ahead of her. *This is not going to end well*, Sage thought, as she watched the palomino gallop to the water's edge. The mare stopped abruptly near the shoreline, head down, front hoofs planted in the sand.

Sage's hands went to her mouth as she watched Hunter catapult out of the saddle, the lake swallowing him whole.

Galloping her horse to the shoreline. Sage dismounted in haste. Disastrous thoughts going through her head, the most prevalent ... she would never forgive herself if Hunter was injured.

The rest of the group followed, except for Luke, who continued to unload the ATV. As Nikki and his crew ran past him, Luke hollered out, "I hope you got a video of that."

Hunter stood, spitting. Submerged from the waist down, water dripped from his hair and his close-shaved beard.

"I think you're supposed to yell, Cannon Ball before you jump into the water," shouted Ryan from the shore, as he grabbed hold of the palomino's reins.

Hunter was about to let out some gritty hockey curses, but thought better when he noticed the crowd of people converging on him.

"Did you break anything?" Were the first words out of Margret's mouth.

"Nothing broken, just a badly bruised ego," Hunter admitted, as he wobbled to the shore. Pulling his phone out of his pocket, he sighed. "Glad I insured this one." His sly grin broke the tension, causing the group to break out in laughter.

"No one told us we were going swimming," Etan moaned. "I didn't bring my bathing trunks."

"I'm not letting that stop me." Axel shrugged off his t-shirt and sneakers. Then he started unzipping his jeans.

"Please tell me you're not going in commando?" Patty stood behind Axel, covering her eyes with her hands, peeking between her fingers.

"We always wear our hockey briefs," Etan said as he, too, dropped his jeans. Below his hard six-pack stomach, he wore thick black spandex briefs that stopped mid-thigh. With a nod to Axel, he ran to the dock, diving into the water.

"You should come in too." Axel winked at Patty and Jessica before following Etan's lead.

Jessica looked at Patty. "Are you wearing your bathing suit under your clothes?"

"I always do when we ride to the lake in late spring." Both girls giggled as they too removed their tops, jeans, and boots. Joining Etan and Axel.

Margret looked at Hunter with a stern expression. "You. Get out of your wet clothes. Let them dry before we ride home. If you catch a cold, upper management will have my job."

Hunter looked first at Margret, then at Sage as he removed his t-shirt, jeans and sneakers. Staring into Sage's eyes, Hunter smirked as he raised his voice loud enough for Luke to hear. "It's not as if you haven't seen me with my shirt and pants off."

Sage's mind raced to the morning Hunter had greeted her at his apartment door, wearing only his gym shorts. She could feel the heat rising from her chest up to her cheeks.

In a moment of defiance, Luke unbuttoned his shirt, kicked off his boots, and dropped his jeans. Like the girls, he always wore swim trunks under his jeans when he rode to the lake.

A soft moan emerged from Margret as she gazed at Luke's toned, tan physique. She let out a low long whistle. "And I thought hockey players worked out."

"Ranchers work out all day, unlike your hockey boys who have to go to the gym." With that said, Luke ran into the lake, swimming out to the rest.

"Geez, suddenly I'm feeling over-dressed," Ryan voiced as he sat on the blanket, opening the picnic basket.

"Why don't you join Etan and Axel," Hunter asked, as he wiped his body down with a towel Sage had tossed him.

"I don't swim," Ryan admitted with a shrug. "I never felt the need to. Plus, I grew up in Calgary. I prefer my lakes frozen."

"I can't argue with that." Hunter gathered his wet clothes. Walking to the lake, he draped them on the dock's railing.

"Lucky it's a warm, windy day. Your clothes will be dry in no time." Sage kept her distance from Hunter as they walked back to the picnic area. "I hate to bring this up, but that was rather a rude thing you said in front of Luke."

"I don't remember being rude."

"You implied that I'd seen you without your clothes on." Sage stopped walking, turned to Hunter, hands on hips.

"I'm sorry. It just slipped out. You should be having this conversation with Luke. He's the rude one."

"You two need to stop this right now, or I'm riding home alone." Sage stomped her booted foot.

"Has anyone ever told you how cute you are when you're mad?" Hunter took a step towards Sage, engulfing her in his arms.

"Think of me as a referee," Sage said. "If you misbehave again, I'll give you five minutes in the penalty box for unsportsmanlike conduct."

Hunter bent low enough to place his chin next to Sage's. He whispered, "You know goalies never sit in the penalty box ... but I'll gladly do my time in the Sin Bin if you'll join me there."

Sage pushed out of his arms, smacking him on the chest. "You are not funny."

Hunter pulled her back in, embracing her in another hungry hug. "I promise to be good."

I won't hold you to that promise, Sage thought as she melted into his arms.

Chapter 42
Food For Thought

May 27th

The early evening sun cast long shadows across the yard as Sage and Hunter returned to the farm, their horses' lazy gaits kicking up small clouds of dust. They dismounted in a comfortable silence, their ease with each other a testament to the bond formed over the day's adventures.

As they led their horses to the barn, Margret rode up. "I'm heading over to Luke's with Nikki and his crew," she announced. "We plan to take some candid photos at his ranch."

"Mom's going to be so disappointed. She's cooking a big dinner tonight." Sage sought Hunter's hand for comfort.

Hunter's gaze hardened at the thought of spending the evening away from Sage, especially at Luke's ranch for publicity photos. "I'm not going," he stated, meeting Margret's eyes with a steely resolve.

"You weren't invited, nor were any of your teammates," Margret replied, adjusting her horse's reins. "I mentioned to Luke how intrigued I was by his father's Quarter Horse operations. Exploring potential donors for future projects never hurts."

"That doesn't make any sense." Hunter's frustration found a new focus, returning to an earlier bone of contention. "On the flight here, you did your best to convince me that showcasing my goaltending images in Sage's gallery show was a smart move for Goshawks' visibility," he said, skepticism coloring his tone. "Now, you're courting ranch sponsorship ... in South Dakota ... from Luke's father? How's that going to promote hockey in Portland, Maine?"

"Funding knows no geographical boundaries, Hunter." Margret leaned on the saddle horn, her lips sporting a smug upturn. "Since when did you start moonlighting as a PR consultant?" She gave Hunter's cheek a pat. "You, focus on pucks not entering your net. Let me focus on the marketing intricacies of the Goshawks' operations."

Hunter resented Margret and her ability to make him feel like a commodity, a mere monetary asset. Before he could respond, the other riders rode in, filling the air with their loud and lively conversations. An organized chaos ensued as Luke and Jessica began loading the horses into the trailer.

"Hey Margret," Luke shouted, "bring your horse on over, we need to get going."

Margret waved to Luke. Turning her attention back to Hunter, she said, "I thought you'd appreciate a night off with your new friends." Margret dismounted. "I have no idea when we'll be finished shooting." With a final look from Luke to Hunter, she added, "Don't make it a late night. Our flight's scheduled for an early morning takeoff." Turning, she led her horse towards Luke.

"Wow, I didn't see that coming," Sage admitted, her gaze meeting Hunter's.

"Can't say I'm disappointed," Hunter replied with a cheeky grin. "Without the marketing team's prying eyes, I'm looking forward to some quality alone time with you tonight."

"Hey, guys. I didn't realize you'd left before everyone," Patty said as she rode to the barn. Dismounting, she joined Sage and Hunter. "What's up?"

"Yeah, we needed a little quiet time before Sage's dad decides to grill me during dinner."

"Better than grilling you *for dinner*." Patty responded.

Sage smiled, shaking her head as she led the way into the barn. Hunter followed her, leading the palomino. Patty brought up the rear with her horse. As they walked past the first empty stall, Crease began whimpering. Before Sage could detour Hunter, he peered over the boards. There, looking up at him, was a three-month-old pup, wagging its tail.

"You didn't tell me you owned a puppy." Hunter handed his horse's reins to Sage, opened the stall door, and walked inside. "Looks just like my puppy from the shelter." Hunter squatted in the straw, cuddling Crease in his arms, his face now wet with puppy kisses.

Sage sighed. Turning to Patty, she asked, "Do you mind taking care of the horses?" She handed over the reins to her friend's outstretched hand. Sage waited until Patty was on the far side of the barn before approaching Hunter.

Standing in the open stall's doorway, Sage watched Crease wiggle in excitement. It was obvious he remembered Hunter. Less obvious that Hunter would know for certain that Crease was the puppy he had practically raised from a newborn.

"He sure is a friendly little guy," Hunter looked to Sage. "Why didn't you mention him to me?"

"If you recall … until last night we hadn't spoken in over a month. Hard to communicate with someone who ghosts you."

Hunter held the puppy close, taken aback by Sage's sudden change of mood. "I tried to call you after one of our wins, but your number was disconnected."

"I was getting disturbing calls and texts all hours of the day and night from your avid admirers. I had to change my number. I didn't have a choice. I tried to text you my new number, but nothing went through."

"Did you think to contact Margret?"

"I did. I emailed Margret about everything. Are you telling me she never gave you my new number?"

"Maybe she never got your email?"

"Maybe." Sage's stomach was turning with the thought Margret might be conspiring to keep them apart. "So, what was wrong with your phone?"

"I smashed my phone the night I tried to call you and couldn't get through," Hunter admitted with a sheepish grin. "I thought you changed your number because of me. That you didn't want to hear from me after the media fiasco. After I kissed you … in front of everyone tuned into the game."

Sage sat in the straw next to Hunter. She scratched Crease behind the ears, but the puppy refused to leave Hunter's lap. "I was never embarrassed by the kiss, Hunter." Looking deep into his eyes, she continued, "I just couldn't handle the media pouncing on me. I don't know if Margret told you, but after you left the post-game interview, I had a full-blown panic attack. I couldn't breathe."

"Sage, I didn't know it was that bad." Hunter pulled her close, placing a tender kiss on her forehead. "You're safe now."

"Thank you, Hunter." Her fingers caressed his face, tracing the soft hairs of his beard.

"Hey, you guys," Patty said, leaning over the stall. "The horses are put up. I'm heading to the main house. When I rode in, your mom said dinner would be ready soon. I'd hate for her to send your dad looking for you." Patty winked at Sage, then scurried out of the barn.

"Hunter, I have something to confess."

"Go on." Hunter said, his joyous expression replaced with a cautious stare.

Sage swallowed hard, cleared her throat, and began. "You remember when I shot the photos for the Goshawks charity calendar at the Portland animal shelter?"

"How could I forget? It was the best day of your visit: spending it with you, my teammates, and, of course, my favorite puppy." He paused a beat. "I have sad news about the little guy. The last time I went in for a visit, he'd been adopted." He paused again. "I suppose it was for the best. The shelter's manager said he went to a loving home ... on a farm. Ironic isn't it. That you would have a pup that looks just like him?" Hunter held the bundle of fur close to his heart.

Sage grinned. "I know he went to a good and loving home."

A scowl formed on Hunter's face. "How can you, living here ... no contact with the shelter ... know for certain the pup is being well-cared for?" His cross tone caused Crease to jump and cower into Sage's arms.

"Hunter, let me introduce you to Crease." The puppy squirmed in Sage's outreached hands as she presented him to Hunter. "I adopted him from the shelter the night I left Portland."

Hunter's face bore a shocked expression. He grabbed the puppy from Sage, holding him tight to his chest, inhaling Crease's scent. "How could you do such a thing behind my back?" Hunter stood, backing into a corner of the stall, as if backing into the protective crease in front of his net.

"I thought you'd appreciate what I did. The shelter manager told me there was a long waiting list of approved adopters for him. I couldn't bear someone else taking him, with the possibility of you never seeing him again." Sage stood, wiping the hay off her jeans. Her eyes pooled with tears. "I did this for you."

"You took him without asking me first." Hunter's body shook. "You, of all people, know how much I've lost in my life, and you dare take something from me I loved without letting me know." Hunter closed his eyes as if willing himself to calm.

"What?" Sage's voice grew deep, guttural. "The only thing I know about you is hockey related, and that you can cook breakfast ... oh, and ride a bike. Every time our conversations went anywhere near your personal life, you shut down."

Hunter took another step back as if he'd been slapped.

"Hunter. Griffin. Shame. On. You." Jessica growled. "Do you ever think of anyone but yourself?" She stood in the stall's open doorway, hands on hips, legs wide apart with an 'I'm ready to kick butt' stance. "Sage has been worried sick about you. First, you and your teammates treat her like a pariah the last day she was in Portland. Then, out of nowhere, you kiss her in front of millions of your fans. Then you don't even bother to contact her for weeks. Adopting the puppy was a grave expense and inconvenience to Sage, but for some reason, she felt she needed to help you out."

Jessica raised her hand, palm toward Hunter when he attempted to speak. "That poor girl has been fighting stalkers ... your fans ... and moping about after you. I told her you were shitty boyfriend material, and here you are proving me right." Jessica appeared to have difficulty catching her breath, yet she squeaked out, "Oh, and Sage, your mom said to get to the house right now. Dinner is about to be served." With that, Jessica turned on her heels, stomping out of the barn.

Dazed, Hunter walked over to Sage. Still holding the puppy, he gave her a one-armed hug. "I'm so sorry, Sage." Crease reached up, nibbling on Sage's earlobe. "Jessica's right, I am shitty boyfriend material. I don't deserve a good friend like you." Pausing before he continued, "I know your world has been turned upside down since I came into your life. I have no business asking you this ... but can you ever forgive me?"

Through teary eyes, Sage's fingers caressed Hunter's cheek. Standing on her tiptoes, she placed a tender kiss on his lips.

Hunter put Crease down, taking Sage into his arms, his lips pressed hard against hers. Moving his lips from hers, he kissed away the tears trickling down her cheeks. "Let's agree to never fight like this again." Stepping back, he brushed a stray hair from her face.

Sage nodded. "We'd better get to the house before my dad comes looking for me with his shotgun."

<hr />

Hunter and Sage walked into the house just as everyone was taking their places at the long dining table. "Wash up you two," Lilly sang out as she put a bowl of water and food in a corner of the kitchen for Crease, next to his dog bed.

Sage and Hunter washed their hands in the mudroom sink before joining the rest of the crew. The only empty seats were next to Ryan and Jessica.

"Hunter, I saved you a place," Jim announced, sitting at one end of the table, smiling at his wife at the other end.

Before taking his seat, Hunter pulled out Sage's chair for her, as she took her place next to Ryan. Across from them sat Axel, Patty, and Etan.

The aroma of a Black Angus roast filled the room, its rich savory scent blended with the buttery smell of homemade biscuits, and the sweet tang of honey-glazed carrots; the food a symphony of flavors.

"About time you two got here. I'm starving." Axel was about to dig into a bowl of mashed potatoes when Jim cleared his throat.

"Not so fast, young man." Jim looked around the table, then reached out a hand to Axel and the other to Hunter. "Around here we say grace before we chow down."

The Goshawks joined hands with the South Dakotans as Jim led them in a blessing. When he said, "Amen," a wide-eyed Axel and Etan remained frozen, until Jim said, "Pass me the carrots."

Without hesitation, Hunter handed the steaming bowl of honey-glazed carrots to Jim, as Sage passed him the biscuits.

Axel shoveled a mound of mashed potatoes on his plate, passing the bowl to Patty.

"Don't forget the gravy," Lilly reminded the boys.

Axel and Etan looked a bit confused until Jim poured a thick brown liquid from the gravy bowl over Axel's mashed potatoes.

Axel leaned forward across Patty and said to Etan, "Ah, she means the sauce."

"Oh, ya, ya, da sås." Etan agreed, as Patty passed him first the potatoes and then the gravy bowl.

"Everything looks and smells so good." Ryan layered slices of roast beef on his plate as if he hadn't eaten in a week.

As the dinner progressed, the table came alive with the sound of clinking cutlery, the murmur of conversation, and the occasional burst of laughter.

Jim, looking every bit the head of the household, turned his attention to Hunter. "So, what's the shelf life of a hockey career these days?" he asked, waving a slice of beef on his fork in Hunter's direction.

Hunter coughed, then replied, "Well, sir, it varies. A lot depends on health and performance. I hope to be on the ice for a long time."

Jim raised an eyebrow, chewed for a bit. There was a hint of skepticism in his voice as he asked, "And after that? Got any plans for an actual career?"

Before Hunter could reply, Sage jumped in. "Dad, Hunter's one of the youngest and best goalies in the league. Being a professional hockey player is his chosen career."

Jim nodded. His expression unreadable. "What about injuries? Luke was telling me a friend of his went to a fight and a hockey game broke out." Jim looked to Hunter with a questioning expression. "I didn't get the joke, but Luke seemed to think it was funny."

"Luke would," Hunter mumbled, stuffing a buttered biscuit in his mouth.

"What's that?" Jim asked, but Hunter only shook his head.

Sage interjected, "Dad, please stop. Hunter's one of the toughest guys on the team."

"Plus, he wears the most padding," Axel piped in, reaching around Patty's back, he high-fived Etan.

The sound of a bottle being uncorked drew everyone's attention to the other end of the table. "Wine anyone?" Lilly offered.

With an impish grin, Etan moved his glass toward Lilly, just as Ryan's hand shot across the table, stopping Lilly before she could pour. "Not so fast, rookie."

Etan, leaning back in his chair, looked around the table. "In Sweden ... and in Germany ... it's normal for us to have wine with meals, especially when in the company of family."

Axel glanced first to Lilly and then to Jim, adding with all sincerity, "And this feels like family, doesn't it?"

Hunter side-eyed Jim, pondering his reaction. After a moment of consideration, Sage's dad stood and walked to Lilly's end of the table. Picking up the bottle of Cabernet Sauvignon, he poured wine into his wife's glass, and then those of Sage and her girlfriends.

Jim then opened a second bottle. The cork's pop echoed in the voiceless room. In a silent answer to the boys' request, Jim walked behind Axel, Etan, and Ryan's chairs, filling their glasses.

Standing next to Hunter, a challenging glint in his eye, Jim asked, "You old enough to drink?"

Hunter, being caught off guard by the question, managed a half-smile as he looked up to Jim. "Yes, sir, I've been legally drinking for a while now."

Jim placed a hand on Hunter's shoulder as he poured the dark ruby liquid into the glass. Taking his seat again, Jim filled his own glass.

"To good food, new friends, and making it through dinner without too many rookie mistakes," Ryan said, lifting his drink in a toast. Laughter rippled around the table, mixed with the clink of glassware.

Nodding to the Etan and Axel, Jessica whispered to Ryan, "Looks like you've got your hands full keeping those two in line."

"You have no idea." Ryan grinned, taking a long sip of his drink.

"So, Etan," Patty asked, "did Luke's horses live up to the Swedish steeds?"

Etan, with a mouthful of food, nodded. After a long pause, he swallowed, then answered, "They did. Although I don't remember horse riding being such a challenge."

Axel chimed in, "I think my horse knew I was a rookie. He kept trying to outmaneuver me."

Patty laughed. "Sounds like you met your match, Axel."

Jessica leaned into Ryan. "After today, are you ready to trade your skates for cowboy boots?"

Ryan looked pensive, as if pondering the idea. "I think my chances of falling off a horse far outweigh the chances of me being hit by a flying puck to the face."

Lilly, witnessing the interactions, beamed with maternal warmth. "I'm just glad everyone had fun. These city boys did well today, didn't they, Jim?"

Jim grunted, but the corners of his mouth twitched in what almost resembled a smile. "They all came back in one piece. So, I suppose they did, Lilly. Suppose they did."

The meal continued with the clatter of dishes and the easy flow of conversation. Hunter relaxed, the initial tension easing under the combined effect of good food and even better company. As the laughter and stories continued, the bonds at the table grew stronger, a mix of old friendships and new connections forming over shared experiences, and a mutual appreciation for Lilly's culinary skills.

Jim's gaze once more lingered on Hunter, a hard edge to his curiosity. "So, Hunter, you boys make decent money playing hockey?"

Hunter, sensing the scrutiny, replied with caution, "Yes, sir. We're compensated well for our performance on the ice."

"Young goalies with Hunter's talent are in big demand." Ryan leaned forward, making sure Sage's father heard him. "They easily bring in seven-figure salaries a year."

"Oh, and don't forget the bonuses," Etan added, before shoveling his last spoonful of potatoes and gravy into his mouth.

Hunter glared at Etan. He hated that the table talk had turned to his value instead of his worth.

"What?" Etan said, looking to Hunter who wore a sour expression. "Our salaries are posted on every hockey website, along with our age, height and weight."

"If we keep eating like we have today, Margret is going to have to make adjustments to our weight stats." Axel leaned back, rubbing his protruding stomach.

Jim looked at Hunter with a surprised expression. "You make that much money ice skating?"

"DAD!"

"Pie anyone?" Lilly gave her husband 'the look,' before going to the kitchen.

"I'll help." Hunter jumped up, following Lilly.

In the kitchen, Lilly rubbed her hand on Hunter's shoulder. "Oh, Hunter, I apologize for my husband's behavior. I don't know what's gotten into him tonight."

"He's just being a protective father." Hunter leaned his hip on the kitchen counter as he watched Lilly cut and plate the blueberry pie. "I can't fault him for caring about his daughter."

"Be a dear and get the ice cream out of the freezer."

Hunter enjoyed being in Lilly's company almost as much as he enjoyed being with Sage. He'd never experienced a family before. Even with Jim's interrogation, Hunter thought, *this is the kind of life I could get used to.*

"Place a scoop on top of each piece, and two on the ones for the growing boys," Lilly said, handing Hunter an ice cream scoop.

"Thank you so much for having us over, Lilly." Hunter felt an overwhelming urge to give her a hug. To once more feel Sage's mother's arms engulfing him with a loving embrace.

"Hey mom, I thought you could use more hands?" Sage came into the kitchen, followed by Patty and Jessica. Each of the girls carried empty dinner plates and serving dishes.

"Thanks girls. Just put everything on the counter for now. We'll deal with them after dessert."

"Let me guess, Lilly." Patty pointed to the plates with extra ice cream. "I'll take those into the rookies, along with mine." Patty expertly balanced the three plates.

"I've got Ryan's." Jessica picked up two of the plates, following Patty back to the table.

"I've got ours," Lilly said, leaving Hunter alone with Sage.

Sage nudged Hunter. "How are you holding up?"

"Better, now that you're here next to me," Hunter whispered to Sage, nibbling on her ear. "I really like your mom."

"Sorry about dad."

"Not a problem, I like him too ... not as much as your mom though ... she's a really, really good cook." Hunter took a glance into the dining room, when he was sure the coast was clear, he placed a quick kiss on Sage's lips.

"What's keeping you two?" Jim shouted. "My ice cream's melting."

Laughter continued to fill the room during dessert, the atmosphere around the table light and lively. The rookies exchanged glances and jokes, their exuberance adding a youthful energy to the gathering.

The meal wrapped up, with everyone leaning back in their chairs, sated and content. Sage stood, signaling the end of dinner. "Let's finish cleaning up," she suggested. Patty and Jessica jumped up too, their movements efficient and practiced.

Jim watched the group for a moment, then his face split into a broad grin. "You boys know how to play poker?"

Ryan's eyes lit up. "Poker? Count me in."

The rookies, too, nodded, their earlier banter replaced with a keen interest in the challenge ahead.

"Are you girls in?" Jim asked.

"Not us," Jessica replied, as she continued to clear the table. "I have to work early in the morning, and Patty's my ride home."

As Jim escorted the boys to the screened-in back porch, Hunter sat alone at the table. He'd only played poker a handful of times and always lost. Yet, looking at his friends, he felt a sense of fellowship building. The tension from earlier dissipated, replaced by a feeling of inclusion and acceptance. Hunter glanced into the kitchen, glimpsing Sage laughing with her mom and friends as they washed dishes, wiped counters, and filled the dishwasher. Within the walls of Sage's home for the first time in his life, Hunter felt a deep sense of contentment.

In the kitchen, Sage playfully swatted Lilly with a kitchen towel. "Mom, we can finish up here. You've done enough today. Besides, I don't want to spend the night playing poker with dad. There's some prints in my apartment I'd like to give to Hunter. Plus, Crease has been cooped up all day. He could use some outside playtime." Sage's words flew from her, as if she were spewing a tsunami worth of excuses at her mom.

"Sure, honey, you kids have fun. Just, well, you know, be careful." Lilly kissed her daughter on the cheek.

"Mom, it's nothing like that. Hunter and I just need a quiet space to talk. There's some things we need to sort out. You know," she stammered, "about the Goshawks photo shoot."

Lilly wiped her hands. She gave Sage a hug before calling out to her husband, "Deal me in, Jim."

When Lilly left, Jessica turned to Sage, "We've got this." As Patty began pushing Sage out of the kitchen.

"Thanks guys, I owe you one." Sage picked up Crease. Catching Hunter's attention, she hurried from the house, knowing he would not be far behind.

Chapter 43
Hanging Out

May 27th

Sage flipped the switch in her apartment. The lighting bathed her room in a soft glow. The small kitchenette, functional and neat, faced the long desk that held her tools of trade: a laptop, a drawing tablet, an additional large monitor, and a couple of printers. Sage stood in the doorway, holding Crease as she watched Hunter explore the room, inspecting the images adorning her walls, her life's work, her passions on display.

He stopped, leaning over her workstation to get a better view of a large bulletin board, a mosaic of her photographic journeys—landscapes that spoke of her love for the outdoors, random shots from a wedding, and numerous pictures of horses, including a dynamic one of Jessica during a barrel race.

"These are amazing. I love how you capture the inner souls of your subjects." Hunter turned to Sage. "Your website images don't do your photography justice."

"Website images would be great if everyone's monitors were calibrated correctly." Sage put Crease down, refilling his water bowl.

"I thought puppy slobber was sticky." Hunter wiped his hands on his jeans. "Horse slobber is twice as slimy."

"My bad. I shouldn't have let you feed the horses apples before we came up here."

"Is there somewhere I can wash up?"

"Sure, it's through my bedroom." Sage pointed to an open door just off the front room. "I always leave a light on in the bathroom."

As Hunter disappeared into the semi-dark room. Sage called out, "Do you want something to drink?"

"A water would be great, thanks," Hunter replied, his voice trailing off.

Sage moved toward the refrigerator but stopped abruptly, a sudden realization hitting her. With a sense of panic, she rushed to her bedroom, flipping on the light. Scrambling onto her dresser, she reached for a framed poster sized photo hanging on the wall. It was a personal shot of Hunter asleep, a moment captured in Portland, one she decreed too intimate for her gallery show.

Just as she tilted the frame, Hunter emerged from the bathroom. "Need a hand?" he asked, his brow furrowing in confusion at the sight of her perched on the dresser.

As Hunter approached, he looked at the photo, a soft laugh escaping. "Is that me?" he asked, taking the frame from her hands. He rehung it with care.

Sage climbed down from the dresser. Her cheeks flushed with embarrassment. "I ... I was never going to put it in my show. It was too private of a moment. It's from my second night in Portland."

Hunter, stepping back, bumping into the foot of Sage's bed, sat down with a thud. His laughter filled the room, a light, calm sound that eased the tension. "So, I'm the last thing you see at night and the first thing in the morning?"

Sage, despite her embarrassment, couldn't help but grin. "Guilty as charged." She could feel the blush rushing from her chest to her cheeks.

Hunter's smile turned mischievous. "I'm flattered. It's not every day you find out you're someone's ... bedroom décor."

Sage laughed, the sound was light and genuine. "Well, when you put it that way."

The moment hung between them, a shared understanding of its intimacy, the depth of their connection evident in their smiles and unspoken words. It was a candid glimpse into the private world they were building together, one filled with trust, laughter. Sage hoped it was the beginning of something special.

<hr />

Hunter took Sage's hand. "Now that you have inadvertently let me into your private moment. I feel it's the right time to share some of mine with you."

Sage squeezed Hunter's hand. A silent acknowledgement that she'd been waiting for him to say those words since she met him.

"You know, Sage," he began, his voice a soft, uneven murmur, "back when I was drafted into the Goshawks, it was like stepping into a dream. Everything I'd worked for was about to come true. But not everyone saw it that way ... not my college professors, and especially not my parents."

Sage's expression softened, her fingers intertwined with his, an unspoken offer of support.

"My parents wanted a different life for me. One of diplomas, degrees, taking over my father's business." Hunter continued, his words threading through the growing silence. "But I wanted the ice, the adrenaline, the roar of a crowd. I chose the rink over their expectations."

"I'm confused Hunter. Didn't your parents want you to play hockey? Didn't they encourage you to become not just a goalie, but one of the best?"

"That's where things get complicated. My parents always insisted I excel in everything I did. I was always the top in my class; to the point of skipping a grade. Whatever I wanted to do, they spared no expense in making sure I had every advantage."

"Why hockey? Why a goaltender?"

"I was only four when I showed an interest in playing hockey. My nanny at the time had a boyfriend who played goalie at the college level. When my parents were out of town, which was often, she'd take me to his games. She even bought me a toy hockey stick. I loved pretending I was the goalie. Six months later, my parents became tired of replacing lamps and objects of art from my imaginary indoor hockey games, and they fired my nanny."

Sage leaned her head on Hunter's shoulder as she listened intently to his story.

"I remember the day my father sat me down in his office. He presented me with an iron-clad contract, stating he'd build me a regulation indoor hockey rink, if I promised to practice every day until I graduated from high school. Plus, I had to keep a GPA of 4.0."

Hunter ran fingers through his hair. "Jeez, Sage, I wasn't even five years old, and my mom made me look up GPA on the computer. My dad told me the contract was legally binding and had me sign my name on the dotted line. It took another six months to design and build the rink in a corner of our estate. While it was under construction, my parents interviewed retired goalies for the position of my private goaltending coach."

"I was wondering when Viktor would come in."

"You remember, Viktor?" Hunter's eyebrows raised, as if he was surprised.

"Oh, I remember Viktor. He's a jerk."

"Yeah, kind of, but he's one hell of a coach."

"Viktor was from Russia. In fact, he was one of Russia's top young pro goalies, until one day when he jumped a horse over a ditch. The horse fell. Viktor's leg was crushed. His career ended. He was only twenty-six."

"Okay, I guess I should give the guy some slack," Sage said.

"He'd just finished extensive rehab in Russia, but his injury prevented him from returning to pro-level hockey. His wife left, draining his bank account." Hunter leaned his head so that it touched Sage's. "So, seventeen years ago, my parents hired Viktor to be my live-in goaltending coach."

"Wow, that's impressive. Your parents were over-the-top supportive."

"You'd think so. An indoor pro ice rink and a personal goaltending coach ... seemed like they cared, right?" A weary smile filtered across Hunter's lips. "In reality, they hired Viktor to be a glorified nanny. My parents didn't expect me to make a career out of being a goalie. It was just another way to keep me busy, to ensure I achieved in a sport, without them having to be involved."

"Didn't your parents go to your hockey practice, or to your games?" Sage put her hand on Hunter's chest.

"Neither of them ever went to a school practice. In high school, when I started getting outside recognition for my playing, my dad took an interest. He had no idea I was being fast-tracked and scouted by the pros ... even in high school. I was only thirteen the first time my name appeared in print; for being the youngest starting goalie on our high school hockey team." Hunter looked up to the ceiling, uncertain if he should continue.

"I tricked my mom into hiring an agent for me in my senior year of high school. I was offered a full-ride hockey scholarship to college. Dad made me turn it down. He said it was an embarrassment for the college to even offer it to me, as they knew he could afford to send his only child to college. Mom agreed, stating I was selfish to take away a scholarship opportunity from a deserving boy, from a low-income family."

"I can kind of understand their position." Sage shrugged.

"I guess so. But that didn't stop me from playing goalie on the college hockey team. My parents insisted I live at home rather than in the dorms, stating I needed to keep my grades up." Hunter paused a moment to help Crease on the bed. "Dad wrote a caveat into our original contract, agreeing to pay for Viktor's services, as long as I kept my 4.0 GPA in college."

"Wait, you lived at home while going to college?" Sage's face scrunched as she sat up straight, shaking her head as she looked at Hunter. "But you don't drive. How'd you get to classes?" She looked at him, waiting for an answer. When he rolled his eyes to the ceiling, she squeaked out, "No, you didn't?"

"Yeah, my parent's driver took me to school. By the time I started college, I was used to it."

"Good grief, Hunter, just how rich are your parents?"

"Very."

Sage shook her head in disbelief, whispering, "Wow, I'm glad the only *very* my parents are, is kind."

Hunter nodded in agreement, then continued, "It wasn't just hockey, Sage. When I was fourteen, I asked for a guitar for my birthday. Instead of gifting me one ... you know, all wrapped up with a bow. My parents flew me to the Martin guitar headquarters in Nazareth, Pennsylvania. I spent the day touring the facilities, ending with a consultation with the man in charge of designing me a custom-made Martin."

"Whose parents do that?"

"Don't know." Hunter shrugged. "But mine did."

"Did your mom or dad go with you?"

"They wanted to send Viktor, but he was against me playing guitar. He thought it would take away from goalie practice time. In protest, he took a well-deserved two-week vacation to visit friends back in Russia."

"Who took you to Pennsylvania?"

"My parent's driver."

"Of course he did. Do you still have the guitar?" Sage sat cross-legged on her bed. Crease snuggled between her legs.

"Yeah, even though it became a breach of contract deal with my dad. When hockey became all-consuming during my last year of high school, he threatened to take the guitar away. He said if I was no longer interested in guitar lessons, then I didn't need the guitar. I just couldn't let him destroy such a beautiful piece of art. I gave it to my agent for safekeeping. He stored it for me until I signed with the Goshawks."

"Did you get punished?" Sage asked, her eyes wide, waiting for the answer.

"What were they going to withhold from me, Sage?" Hunter put his arm around her, pulling Sage and Crease close. "They'd been withholding the one thing I craved more than anything ... their love and affection."

Crease stood on his back feet, putting his front puppy paws around Hunter, nuzzling his muzzle into Hunter's neck.

"The day I was drafted into the pro's," Hunter started, his voice a mere whisper, "it should've been the happiest day of my life." He looked away, his eyes glazing over with the sheen of unshed tears. "My parents invited me and their friends to a house party. I thought it was to celebrate my going pro. Instead, everyone stood on the back patio, sipping champagne as they cheered a bulldozer tearing through my ice rink—the one my parents built for me. I've never felt so depressed. It was like they were demolishing my childhood."

Sage let out a sigh, a visceral reaction to the pain lacing Hunter's words. "That's ... that's cruel," she said, her voice tinged with disbelief and anger.

"Yeah, it was their way of showing their disapproval. They couldn't stand me not following their blueprint for my life." Hunter's laugh was hollow, echoing the emptiness of that moment. "I used to skate there every day. Viktor, my coach since I was five, he ... he was more of a father to me than my own ever was."

Hunter exhaled as he met Sage's gaze. "That was the last time my parents spoke to me. No congratulations. No 'we're proud of you.' Nothing!" He paused, the hurt clear in his voice. "And that kiss, after the Florida playoff game ... I just wanted to share my triumph with someone who ... someone who cared for me."

Sage's fingers tightened around Hunter's, her spirit rallying in silent defiance against the injustice of his childhood. The air around them hummed with the gravity of his confession, carrying the weight of unspoken words and pent-up emotions that spanned years.

"I'm so sorry," Sage whispered, her hand now enveloping his, a tangible connection amidst the internal turmoil. "I wish I would have known your backstory before now. I would never have pushed you about your parents when I was in Portland."

Hunter shook his head, a weary smile touching his lips. "I should've been open with you. It's just ... not even my teammates know. You're the first person I've ever told any of this."

Sage placed a soft kiss on his lips, her presence a grounding force.

"As much as you dislike Viktor, he always believed in me, pushed me to be better, to do better. My parents weren't about support. It was all about... convenience. My mother's one of the top neurosurgeons in Maine. My father's a corporate lawyer, owns his firm, and dabbles in international mergers and acquisitions. They were always too caught up in their careers, too unavailable. I was an obligation, a project."

Crease slipped down Hunter's chest, falling asleep on his lap.

"The irony? Viktor is now my coach with the Goshawks. He's never stopped believing in me. Viktor and my teammates are now the only family I've got." Hunter's voice broke, revealing the depth of his bond with the man who had been his mentor, his coach, and ultimately his father figure.

Sage took Hunter's chin in her hand, moving his head to face her. "Never think you are alone in this world, Hunter. Viktor and the Goshawks may be your family in Portland. But never forget, you'll always have a family in South Dakota with us."

Searching her eyes, Hunter became overwhelmed with a sudden urge to consume all of her. He only stopped by the realization that this was not the place, nor the time. Sharing his childhood memories, a piece of his guarded past lay bare between them, a sacred revelation that he hoped would draw Sage closer into the circle of his inner world—a world filled with ambition, passion, and a poignant solitude.

Leaning into each other, their lips were about to meet when a phone chime disturbed their quiet interlude.

"Well, I know it's not mine. Your mom has my phone in your kitchen, sitting in a bag of rice."

Sage retrieved her phone from her back pocket. "It's a text from mom. Dad wants to know what's keeping us."

"Can you hide your dad's shotgun ammo when we get back to the house."

Chapter 44
Time Capsule

May 27th

Hunter and Sage, followed closely by Crease, made their way to the main house. The glow from the windows cut through the darkness, a beacon guiding them home. The night had wrapped Sage's family farm in a blanket of serene quiet, pierced only by a distant coyote cry, along with the occasional rustle of leaves from the South Dakota winds. It was late, especially by farm standards, and the air was filled with the anticipation of farewells, coupled with the unspoken dread of the early morning departure.

Walking through the house, Sage called out, "Where is everyone?"

"Out here, honey," Lilly answered, her voice trailing from the back porch where the last hands of the poker game were wrapping up.

"Are they still playing?" Hunter whispered to Sage.

"That only means one thing. Dad never stays up this late playing poker unless he's trying to recoup his losses."

When they entered the back porch, Jim sat grumbling at the table, gathering the playing cards. "Well, if it isn't the night owls." Turning his attention to the couple, Jim gave Hunter a pointed stare that lingered far too long.

Sage walked to Jim, kissing his cheek, "Hi daddy, looking at your lack of chips, I can only guess the Goshawks won in overtime."

"Humph," was the only sound escaping Jim's lips.

At the other side of the table, Etan and Axel were in the middle of dividing their winnings. "I kept telling you, Jim, you needed to watch Axel," Etan said, nudging Axel with his elbow. "He has the best hands of any defenseman on or off the ice."

"Etan's just sore because his 'strategic' bets turned out to be as effective as his passes." Axel held his hand in the air.

"Real funny, Axel," Etan said, as he reciprocated Axel's hanging high-five.

Lilly, opening a trash bag for the empty beer bottles, shook her head. "Well, Jim, at least you'll have some good stories to tell your friends."

"Don't feel bad, sir." Axel stopped stacking his chips. "We're a hard team to beat. But it's a sure bet that you're the only person in South Dakota who's played against the Goshawks' top line."

Ryan leaned back in his chair, stretching his arms above his head. "Thanks for the game, Jim and Lilly. Haven't had so much fun playing cards since ... well, since the last time I was back home in Calgary."

As if wishing to change the subject, Jim pulled out his pocket watch, the lines between his eyes deepening as he glanced from the timepiece to Hunter. "It's getting close to eleven, son. Don't you Goshawks turn into pumpkins at midnight?" The hint of a smile tugged at his lips, a begrudging admission of the night's enjoyment, despite his earlier reservations.

Hunter met Jim's gaze as he swallowed hard. "Just lost track of time, sir," he said. The evening with Sage had blurred the hours into moments.

"It was my fault, Dad. I was showing Hunter the outtakes from the shots I took of him and the Goshawks when I was in Portland." She waved a handful of prints.

"Just don't forget where you are, missy," Jim addressed Sage, but his gaze fixed on Hunter. "This farm might be far from Maine, but we have our own strict set of rules."

"Now, Jim, we were all having too much fun to watch the clock, but, oh my, I didn't realize it was so late." With a worried expression, Lilly looked at Sage. "Can the boys still call an Uber?"

"Dang it, I forgot about that. In the city, it's not too late, but I doubt we can get anyone to come out here at this hour."

"Well, that settles it. You boys will just have to stay the night." Lilly gave her husband *a don't even try to object* look.

"Are you sure you have enough room for all of us?" Hunter asked, reaching out, squeezing Sage's hand.

"We have more than enough guest rooms in the main house," Jim replied, his gaze homed in on Hunter's fingers entwined with his daughter's.

"Let me shoot Margret a quick text." Ryan retrieved his phone. After a few moments, he looked up. "We're all set. Margret is staying the night in one of Luke's father's guest cabins. She's going to send a driver over to the hotel to gather our things in the morning, then he'll pick us up."

"Sounds good," Lilly said. "Give me a few minutes to clean up, and I'll show you boys your rooms." Without being asked, Ryan and the rookies began helping her gather empty beer bottles and straightening chairs.

"Well, it's been fun, boys, but I've got to head to bed. Morning chores don't accept excuses from late nights." Jim made his way to the master bedroom on the first floor.

"I should get to bed too." After saying good night to everyone, Sage guided Hunter from the room.

On the front porch, Hunter went in for a quick kiss. Leaning on the porch railing, he watched as Sage and Crease crossed the yard to her apartment. Going back into the house, he followed Lilly as she ushered Ryan and the rookies upstairs.

At the end of the long hallway, Lilly turned on the light to one of the guest bedrooms. She looked at Etan and Axel. "I hope you boys don't mind bunk beds. The other guest room only has one bed."

"Thanks Mrs. Larson, we appreciate all you've done for us today." Axel said, as he went in for a hug. Followed by Etan, who mimicked Axel's moves. The rookies then pushed into the room, both vying for the top bunk.

"Oh, and the bathroom is across the hall. I'll put out extra towels. Thanks to Patty, we have lots of new toothbrushes and toothpaste. Sleep tight, boys," she said, shutting their door. She then led Hunter and Ryan down the hallway. "I think you two will be more comfortable in Sage's old room, instead of the other guest room ... her room has two full size beds." Lilly gave Ryan and Hunter both a hug before saying, "Good night, boys."

Once inside the room, Hunter felt like he stepped inside a time capsule of Sage's teenage years: untouched and filled with memories. Hunter and Ryan explored the space; noting the trophies topped with miniature metal horses or cameras, along with an array of blue ribbons.

"Wow, I didn't expect to see that," said Ryan, spotting a poster of Hunter taken in his rookie year with the Goshawks.

Hunter walked to the poster, noting the yellowing tape securing it to the wall, flashing a sly smile when he realized the poster was hung opposite the beds.

"Looks like Sage has been an Ice Wall fan for a long time." Ryan laughed, as he began undressing.

On a side wall, Hunter's gaze fell on a corkboard covered with photos. One image of a young Sage and Luke caught his attention. The intensity in Luke's expression, and the carefree laughter on Sage's face, caused Hunter's jaw to clench. Without thinking, he tore the photo from the board, crumbling it. He tossed the image in the trash. Looking to Ryan, Hunter silently dared him to say anything.

Overwhelmed, Hunter stalked out of the room, having the sudden urge to stand under a cold shower. The day had brought him closer to Sage's world, but it had also unveiled new layers to the complex tapestry of their relationship.

———————— ◆◇◆ ————————

It was pitch black when a disoriented Hunter woke up in a strange bed, something he was still trying to get used to from hockey travel days. A quick look at his tracker caused him to groan as he realized it was only 5am. Knowing he wouldn't be able to get back to sleep, he gathered his clothes. Exiting the bedroom, he headed for the bathroom. After dressing and doing his best to finger comb his hair, he stumbled in his stocking feet down the polished oak staircase.

Reaching the bottom of the stairs, a familiar aroma hit him. His special brew of coffee, with a hint of chocolate and cinnamon. As he approached the kitchen, he was surprised to see Sage, her mother and father, already starting their day. Crease jumped up from his dog bed, tail wagging, running to Hunter. When he picked him up, Hunter's face was covered with puppy kisses.

"Good morning," Jim said, as he gulped down his last bit of coffee. "I didn't expect a city boy to be up this early."

"It was a surprise to me too, sir," Hunter said as he stood near the kitchen table.

"I hope you slept well," Lilly asked, as she busied herself in the kitchen mixing the dough for homemade biscuits.

"I've always had a bad habit of getting up early when on the road."

Sage handed Hunter a cup of coffee. "Looks like you could use this."

Hunter raked his fingers through his unruly bedhead again. "Thanks," he said, accepting the cup. "I didn't realize you had to get up so early. If I'd known, we would have let everyone get to bed earlier. I apologize for the intrusion into your daily routines."

"Don't be silly." Lilly smiled as she rolled the dough onto the counter. "It was fun to have you young people in the house. Plus, Jim is always looking for fellow poker players." She looked at her husband. His chair scooted on the hardwood floor as he stood.

"I got to get to work." Jim first kissed Sage on the cheek, then kissed his wife. Turning to Hunter, he said, "It was nice to meet Sage's goalie crush in person."

"DAD!"

Ignoring his daughter, Jim continued. "I doubt I'll see you before you leave, so you all have a safe trip. Be sure to stop by again if you're ever in our neck of the woods." Jim reached out to shake Hunter's hand.

Hunter quickly placed his mug on the table and the puppy on the floor. Reaching his hand out to receive Jim's. "Thank you so much for your hospitality, sir. I promise when I return to South Dakota, your place will be the first one I visit."

"Have a good day, Dad." Sage walked her father to the door. She then motioned to Hunter. "Want to sit on the porch, drink coffee, and treat yourself to a South Dakota sunrise?"

"I wouldn't miss it for the world." Hunter picked up his coffee mug, joining Sage on the front porch, with Crease on his heels. Sitting in one of the Adirondack rocking chairs, he steadied the mug while settling the puppy on his lap.

Crease snuggled in, falling asleep. "Looks like someone in your family isn't an early riser." He stroked the puppy's head. "Oh, and I like his name."

"It seems to fit him." Sage's soft laughter filtered through the misty predawn air. A silence fell between them, only broken by the sound of horse hooves as Sage's father rode out, followed by a half-dozen ranch hands.

"How many people does your father have living on the property?"

"It depends on the season. Right now, we have a handful of cowboys staying in the bunkhouse. The number grows and declines. Spring and fall are the busiest times."

"Does Luke ever help out on your dad's farm?" Hunter could not keep the sting of jealousy out of his voice.

"No, never." Sage let out a hardy laugh. "Luke has his hands full just keeping his father's massive quarter horse ranch going. I'm surprised he was allowed to take time off yesterday, let alone for the years he took off to get his college degree."

"I saw old photos of you and your friends on the corkboard in your room last night. You and Luke grew up together?" He sipped his coffee, waiting for Sage's confession.

"Hmm, I thought I'd mentioned that to you before?" Sage cocked her head to one side, then shrugged her shoulders. "I've known Jessica, Patty, and Luke since … jeez, since I can remember. We all went to kindergarten together. Luke's dad sent him off to a private school for his freshman year of high school. Luke hated it. He insisted on going back to public school with his friends, and his father relented."

"So, did you and Luke ever date?" Hunter sat back in the chair, gently rocking the puppy.

"Oh. My. Gosh. No. Luke and I are just good friends. He's one of the girls ... in a very manly way, of course."

Hunter grumbled.

"Why so many questions about Luke, anyway?"

"Just curious."

"Somehow I feel there is more to this than mere curiosity." Sage stopped rocking, giving Hunter an intense stare.

Hunter finished his coffee, placing the mug on a small table between them. He then reached over, taking Sage's hand in his. "We've only known each other for a short while." Taking a deep breath, he continued, "I don't know quite how to say this ..." He gathered his thoughts to create the right words. "Even though we've spent most of our getting to know each other time online ... I still feel very close to you."

Sage squeezed Hunter's hand. "I have to confess. I feel the same."

"Well," Hunter sported one of his killer smiles, "You have had an advantage. I've only known you existed for a couple of months." His grin widened. "I thought seeing my photo across from your bed in your apartment was a onetime thing," he paused a beat before adding, "but last night, I discovered you've been waking up with me for the past five hockey seasons."

Hunter watched Sage's expression turn from puzzled to a sudden realization that he had slept in her old bedroom last night. The room with Hunter's rookie poster taped to her wall. He was especially amused when he noticed a hard blush on Sage's cheeks.

"How ... how embarrassing," Sage stammered. "Mom's going to get an earful when we go back inside."

"Nay, don't do that. I thought it was rather special. I like the thought of you thinking of me every night when you turn off the lights, and seeing my face every morning when the sun fills your room." He couldn't resist the urge to continue teasing her.

"Let me die now." Sage said, putting her coffee mug on the table next to Hunter's. She attempted to cover her face with her hands, but one hand was still captured in Hunter's hawk-like grip.

"Never say that, not even in jest. If anything would ever happen to you, I don't know what I'd do." Hunter raised Sage's hand to his lips, placing soft kisses on her fingers.

They sat there for what seemed a lifetime, holding hands and rocking as they watched the sky turn from dark, hazy gray to brilliant hues of pinks, reds, and purples. Once again, their silence was broken, but this time by a distant rooster's crow.

"So, circling back, why so interested in Luke?"

"I saw all the photos of you and Luke growing up tacked to your board."

"There were only a couple photos of Luke. Most were of the girls, and of course horses."

"The only ones that caught my attention were those of Luke looking as if he could devour you with his eyes." Again, Hunter watched as Sage wore a confused expression. "The way he looked at you made me feel ..." Once again, Hunter struggled for the words. He wanted to say that Luke's expression made him want to drop his gloves and knock Luke out, bloodied, onto the ice. Instead, he said, "It didn't give me a warm and fuzzy feeling about the two of you."

"It just came to my attention that Luke may have had feelings for me. I can assure you ... Luke is only a very good friend. Not a boyfriend. That would just be too weird, especially around Jessica. She's had a crush on him since grade school."

"I know we're in an awkward position. It can't be easy on you with me living states away." Hunter leaned his head back, closing his eyes. "I know it hasn't been easy on me."

"I feel responsible for getting between you and hockey." Sage once more tried to pull her hand from his grip, but he held her there.

"Don't." Hunter's response came out harsher than he intended. "What happens on the ice is on me. Most of the Goshawks' players are in relationships, either dating, or married, some with kids. Everyone has someone they care for off the ice." Hunter turned his body to stare into Sage's eyes. "Until you came into my life, I had no one special to root for me. No one waiting outside the locker room to greet me after a win, and especially after a loss."

He swallowed hard and continued, "Sage, you have no idea how much it means to me to know you were there for me, win or lose. You were never there as a fan, only as a friend. Other than the Goshawks' players and Viktor, I've had no one in my corner ... no one special."

"I'm so sorry, Hunter. It must be a lonely way to live. I can't believe you've never had a girlfriend. Not in high school or college?"

"From my first day with Viktor, he drilled into me that going pro was never easy for any hockey player. It was harder for goalies, as there's limited positions open for pro goaltenders. Every day he told me, if I wanted to go pro, I couldn't let anything, or anyone, come between me and hockey ... he was especially adamant about no girlfriends. To be honest, it never bothered me until you came into my life."

"Thanks, I think?" Sage frowned.

Hunter brought Sage's hand to his lips once more. This time, he opened her hand, placing a soft kiss on her palm. "I should have said I never knew what I was missing until you came into my life. You filled a void I never realized was there." He took a moment to pet Crease before turning his attention fully to Sage. "What I'm trying to say is, I need you in my life."

Sage's eyes softened, a shy smile on her lips. She paused before answering, "I need you in my life, too. But I don't want to be the reason you lose a game. Or regret you ever met me because I'm taking your concentration away from hockey."

"You are the best thing that ever happened to me. I don't know how to convince you of that, other than by my words."

"Your actions are more important. I was crushed when you ghosted me. I thought you were done with me. That I was too much trouble, not worthy of your time. That someone else would suit you better than me."

"I can't express how wrong I was to not get back to you on your last night in Portland. I can be such a jerk."

"Sometimes."

"I don't deserve to ask you to understand me. I don't even understand myself half the time. Right now, for the better part of next month, I know my world is going to be myopic."

"I understand." Sage's eyes held his gaze. "With The Cup so close, you can't afford to think of anything but hockey. You have to keep your head in the game."

"That seems to be the mantra of everyone of late. Yet, I can't fully concentrate on hockey if I'm worried about ..." he paused for too long.

"About what?"

Hunter was afraid to tell Sage the truth, but he knew if he didn't, it could ruin everything. Not only his budding relationship with Sage but also his hard-fought relationship with his teammates. "I'm worried about who you're with. Whose arms are holding you. Whose lips are touching yours."

"Hunter. I don't know what to say." Sage leaned forward. Her eyes glistened with tears.

"Yeah, I was afraid of that." Hunter gave her a crooked smile, letting go of her hand.

"No, no, no, Hunter. You don't understand. I've had feelings for you for a long time. I think from the first time I saw you in the Goshawks' net. No, even before. I remember my heart fluttering when I first saw you sitting on the bench five seasons ago, as the Goshawks' backup goalie."

Sage secured his hand in hers. "The Goshawks were the reason I became obsessed with hockey, but you are the reason I fell in love with hockey."

"Oh?" This time it was Hunter's turn to look confused.

"Your total dedication and respect for the game, for your teammates, for your fans ... it was inspiring. Once you got between the pipes, you had a special magic. Some of your saves were unbelievable, and your grace, your easy way of controlling your opponent, is a natural skill, not something that's taught. Oh, and don't even get me started on the first time the camera zoomed in on your face, and your killer smile."

"You think I have a killer smile?"

"Is that the only thing you heard me say?" Sage nudged his shoulder.

"Trust me, I always hear everything you say. Your words stay with me."

"Please know that I'm not in a relationship with anyone. I have not been in one for a long time. I have been too busy watching you and your career over the past five years."

"Can you tell that to Luke? Or do you want me to?"

"I've had that talk with Luke already. He wasn't happy with my choice, but he understands that my heart belongs to a pro goalie in Portland, and not a cowboy in South Dakota."

Hunter held up his free hand and raised two fingers. "Well, as far as I know, there are only two pro goalies in all of Maine, and one of them is already spoken for."

"I'm hoping you will allow me the honor for there to be two Maine pro goalies spoken for." Sage leaned her head on Hunter's shoulder.

"This is where the hard part comes in." Hunter felt Sage stiffen at his words. "You have to know how much I care about you. But our timing is always off. If we would have met during the summer break, things would have been easier."

"I know, life can suck. There are always complications. I'll step back, stay out of your life, if that's what you need until this year's quest for The Cup has ended ... or even after that, the last thing on earth I would ever want to do is to come between you and hockey."

"That's not what I'm saying. I want you in my life. In fact, I'm miserable to be around when you are not in my life."

"Then what are you saying?"

Again, Hunter ran his fingers through his already unruly hair. "I don't know Sage. It's so complicated. All I know is that my feelings for you run deep. Something that's new and confusing to me. Like I said, I've never been in a relationship. Yet I can't see myself without you in my life. I want us to work this out."

"Me too. You've just worked so hard to get where you are now. I can't let you sacrifice your career for me." Sage leaned forward in her rocker, staring into Hunter's eyes.

"Sage, I want you by my side. I want to hear your voice cheering for me in the stands ... every game I play. I want to have you waiting for me after each game. I want your arms around me when I come out of the locker room, win or lose. Sage ... what I'm saying is I want you to come back to Portland with me."

"Oh, Hunter, you need to think this through. Talk to Margret. Talk to your coaches. Talk to your teammates."

"I'm tired of letting other people make decisions for me. Everyone has been doing that since I was a small boy. No one seems to notice that I'm not a child anymore."

"I've noticed." Sage leaned toward Hunter, placing her hand on his cheek. Hunter turned his head, placing another kiss on her palm.

"I know I'm being selfish, and I haven't taken you into consideration. I need you in my life. If you can't fly back with us today, at least think about it, and let me know before we play our first Cup game. I'll pay for your flights and your hotel rooms. I just know I'll play like shit unless you're watching me in person ... then you really will be the reason the Goshawks don't bring home The Cup. Do you think you can bear that burden?"

Sage reached over punching Hunter's shoulder with her free hand. "Blackmail will get you nowhere. Today is out of the question, on so many levels. I promise to think your offer over. I just couldn't stand to be treated like the team treated me the last time I was in Portland." Sage sat back in her chair, her eyes searching the horizon.

"More important, I couldn't live with myself if you resented me being with you. I think we both need some time to think your proposal over." She paused, realizing what she said. "Ah, I didn't mean proposal, like proposal. I meant proposal like proposition."

Hunter didn't answer. He just nodded, shooting her one of his deadliest killer smiles.

"Hey, you two," Lilly shouted from behind the screen door. "Come and get breakfast with the rest of the crew. You have to get going soon."

Hunter put Crease on the porch as he stood with Sage, taking her into his arms. Holding her in a goalie bear hug, he then broke away just enough to bend down and kiss her with all the passion he could muster. If his words wouldn't persuade her to come to his games, his only other option was to hold her and never let go.

Chapter 45
Falls and Fallouts

June 3rd [Game 1 of The Cup Final]
Sage pulled her suitcase with one hand, juggling her pinging phone with the other. Margret scheduled a car to pick her up in half an hour. She hated being on a tight deadline, but she had a photoshoot this morning that couldn't be reschedule. With the three-hour flight from Brookings to Portland, she'd arrive at the Goshawks' game with an hour to spare.

"Hey, Hunter. Yes, I'm all packed. I'm just waiting for Lionel. I feel so bad about not being able to leave sooner. Sorry, i don't mean to babble ... so, how are you feeling about tonight?"

"I know it's just another game." The phone went quiet on his end.

"It's okay to be nervous. Please don't let the pressure get to you." When he didn't respond, Sage continued, "For what it's worth, I believe in you."

"That means everything to me, Sage. More than you can know." Another long pause. "You being at the game tonight will make all the difference in the world."

"Margret is meeting me at the Portland airport. Hopefully, I can sneak in the tunnel to give you a good luck hug before the game."

Hunter's doorbell buzzed in the background. "Ryan's here to take me to the arena. Looking forward to seeing you."

"Same here, Hunter." Sage said as the connection went dead.

Walking behind Sage, Lilly embraced her in a loving hug. "We're going to miss you."

"I'm going to miss you and dad too."

"You're packing light, especially for being away for over two weeks."

Sage shrugged off her backpack, sitting it next to the suitcase. "Mom, we've been over this already. There's no telling how long I'll be gone. With luck, I'll be back in two weeks." She put her phone on the table to hug her mom.

"I made a big batch of cookies. Make sure Hunter shares them with those sweet boys he plays with." Turning, Lilly walked to the kitchen, just as Crease woke up and ran between her legs.

A second later, the room was filled with a mixture of screams, yelps, and thumps. Lilly lay in an awkward position on the floor, blood seeping from her forehead as she held her arm close to her body.

"Mom!" Sage rushed to the kitchen, grabbing a clean dishtowel. She knelt next to her mom, pressing the cloth to her mom's head gash, while pushing a concerned Crease away.

"Good Lord, I think I broke my hand," Lilly moaned, as she showed Sage her swollen fingers.

"We need to get you to the ER." After helping her mom out of the house and into her SUV, Sage jotted a quick note to her dad. She then picked up a bewildered Crease, putting him in an empty horse stall with food and water. Rushing back to her mom, Sage raced to town.

<hr />

In the ER exam room, the nurse took charge. "Let's look at that cut," she said, guiding Lilly to sit. With swift, practiced movements, she checked Lilly's vital signs, nodding. "Everything looks good. Now, let's clean this wound up and see what we're dealing with."

The nurse dabbed at the gash with saline-soaked gauze, causing Lilly to wince. "Is it bad?"

"It's a pretty long cut. You'll need stitches," the nurse explained, pressing to stem the bleeding. "Don't worry, we'll take good care of you."

After injecting a numbing agent, the nurse stepped out to prepare for the doctor's arrival, Lilly grabbed her daughter's hand. "Sage, the medical team can take care of me now. You need to get back to the house, or you're going to miss your flight."

"Mom, there is no way I'm leaving until we find out how you're doing. I'll give Margret a call after the doctor sees you." Sage leaned in, giving her mom a light kiss on her cheek.

The curtain to the exam room pulled back as the doctor walked in reading Lilly's chart. "Hello Mrs. Larson. I'm Doctor Wilson. Looks like you've had a nasty fall." He approached Lilly with a calm demeanor, ready to address the gash on her forehead. "First, we're going to get you stitched up," he explained, preparing the suture kit. Lilly nodded her understanding.

Sage watched as the doctor cleaned the cut again, his hands steady despite the urgency of the situation. Dr. Wilson began stitching, his movements precise. "You're doing great, Lilly," he reassured her. The tension in Lilly's body eased with his calm voice.

With the stitching complete and the wound dressed, Dr. Wilson glanced up at Sage. "Now, we'll proceed with the CT scan to check for any internal injuries to her head. It's a precautionary measure, but it's important after such an impact."

He then turned his attention to Lilly's hand, examining the swollen area before confirming the need for an X-ray. "And we'll take care of that hand right after. The priority is to ensure there are no serious injuries we're overlooking."

As nurses prepared Lilly for the imaging tests, Sage felt a mix of relief and concern. The immediate care her mother received was reassuring, yet the potential findings from the scans loomed heavily on her mind. "Thank you, Dr. Wilson," Sage said, her voice laced with gratitude and worry.

"You're welcome. We'll do everything we can for her," he responded, offering a small, encouraging smile before proceeding with the next steps of Lilly's care.

It wasn't until they pushed Lilly out of the exam room for the CT scan and x-rays that Sage glanced at the clock on the wall. Her stomach went sour when she realized they'd been in the ER for over three hours. In a panic, she reached for her phone. It was then she realized she'd left it on the kitchen table.

"Crap, crap, crap." She knew the Goshawks would be entering the ice soon for their pre-game warmup. She could only imagine what Hunter would be thinking. Looking upward, she asked, "Why was the universe constantly conspiring against us?"

Rushing to the nurse's station, she inquired, "Can I please use your phone? I left mine at home. I need to call my dad to let him know what happened to my mom."

"It's against hospital policy to allow personal calls," the head nurse chided.

As Sage was about to plead with the nurse to break the rules, just this one time, she heard the familiar sound of boots rushing to her.

"Sage, how's your mom?" Jim asked as he hurried to Sage's side.

"They just took her in for x-rays," Sage gulped out, trying not to fall apart. "Mom, tripped over Crease. She hit her head on the edge of the counter, and we think she broke her hand in the fall."

Jim put his arm around his daughter. "When I got to the house, Thor was sitting on the porch with his Malinois. Apparently, Margret called the sheriff's office when her driver saw the front door open, and a puddle of blood on the floor. Thor read the note you left. He called the hospital, and waited to give me an update on your mom's condition."

"Thank goodness, that means Margret's driver read the note too."

Jim removed his cowboy hat, running fingers through his hair. "Well, that's debatable. Apparently when her driver saw the state of the kitchen he boot-scooted out of the house ... fast. I guess those east coast types get a little nervous when they see blood and no body."

"Thor called Margret back and explained everything ... right?"

Wearing a sheepish grin, he answered, "After their encounter at your gallery opening ... I can't say Thor and Margret are best friends. According to Thor, she called demanding he get to the bottom of what happened. You know Thor, he'll bend over backwards for you if you ask nicely ..."

"... But he dislikes pushy people," Sage finished.

"Pretty much."

"Oh, daddy, I've ruined everything again." Sage moaned after reading the note from the driver. She then collapsed into her dad's arms, weeping.

Jim held his daughter in a protective embrace, allowing her to get it all out.

"I left my phone on the kitchen table. I can't imagine what Hunter must be thinking right now."

Jim pulled out his phone. "I wish I would have noticed it on the counter, but I was in such a hurry to get to your mom." He pulled tissues from the box on the nurse's desk and wiped his daughter's tears. "You can use my phone to call him."

"Margret must be furious with me, too." She took the tissues from her dad, blowing her nose. "I don't know her number by heart, and Hunter will be on the ice. Oh daddy, why does this keep happening to us?"

"I'm here now. You go home and try to fix things," Jim assured her.

"No, it's too late, plus I want to stay with mom. She needs me more than Hunter." The last part she doubted was true. Sage could only hope Margret covered for her. That Hunter wouldn't realize she was not at the arena until after the game was over. The sound of Lilly being wheeled back into the exam room brought Sage's concerns back to her mom.

"Doctor Wilson will be in with the test results," the nurse said as she hooked Lilly up to various monitors. "We gave her something for the pain, so she may be a little groggy."

Sage held her mom's hand as they waited for the doctor. It was not long before he came into the room.

"I've just got the test results back. Mrs. Larson has a mild concussion. She also has what we call a Boxer's Fracture." He raised his own hand, showing where Lilly's hand was injured.

"Oh my gosh." Sage's knees felt weak.

"I want to keep her overnight for observation. We're going to ice her hand. When the swelling goes down, we'll wrap it with a soft cast. She'll have to keep her arm immobilized for up to six weeks." He looked at Sage and her dad. "Will someone be around to help her out when she gets home?"

Without hesitation, Sage answered, "I'll be there to take care of her."

"Good, good. She will need to rest." Looking at Sage's dad, the doctor said, "Mr. Larson, I presume?" When Sage's dad nodded, the doctor continued, "We'll take good care of your wife. You might as well go home. Barring no complications, she can go home in the morning."

After thanking the doctor and saying goodbye to her mom. Sage followed her dad to the farm. She was relieved to be home. Sage sat in the SUV doing her best to compose herself before interacting with her father.

Once in the house, Sage rushed to the front room, turning on the game. Her head ached when she noted it was well into the second period, and the score was 1 to 2 in favor of the Las Vegas Savages. The cameras panned to Hunter, as he appeared to be looking to the stands as one of the Savage's players rushed his net.

"It's a goal from Lane. That puts another point on the board for the Savages," the announcer blared out.

Sage ran into the kitchen, retrieving her phone. "Dad, I have to make some calls. Will you be okay?" Waiting for her father's reply, Sage noticed the pool of dried blood on the kitchen floor.

"You go ahead, honey. I'll be fine." Jim shouted from the front room.

Sage sighed, stashing her phone in her back pocket. She grabbed a bucket from under the sink, filling it with hot water. Then she gathered a roll of paper towels and a sponge. Kneeling on the kitchen floor. The day catching up with her, tears fell as she scrubbed the stains from the tiles. She kept reminding herself that her dad's peace of mind was more important than a hockey game. Plus, no one ever had their phones turned on during the game. Not even Margret.

After cleaning the floor, Sage made her dad soup and a sandwich. Adding a bottle of beer and a couple of cookies to the tray, she brought it to him in the front room. "Here dad, it's not much but you need to eat."

Jim looked up from reading a book, the television turned off. "Oh, you're back already?"

"I never left. What was the score when you turned the game off?" Sage looked at the blank TV screen, unsure if she wanted to know the answer to her question.

"Don't recall. I know the Goshawks were not winning. It was half-time. I didn't feel like listening to everybody chit-chatting."

"Dad. It was the second intermission, not half-time. Plus, I'm sure the announcers had some insight why the Goshawks were down." She watched her father take a bite of his sandwich, followed by a long swig of beer.

"Sage, you know I'm not into hockey. Just a lot of boys with sticks running around with short pants and long stockings." He winked at his daughter.

"If I can't get you anything else, I'm heading home. I want to go with you to pick up mom in the morning, so be sure to let me know before you leave." Sage leaned over and kissed her dad on the forehead,

"Do you need any help with your suitcase?"

"No, I'll take care of it in the morning. I have to let Crease out and try to contact Hunter."

"Don't stay up all night pondering the fate of your goalie being a sieve tonight."

"OMG. Dad. You can't remember how many periods the team plays, but you know all about goalies and sieves?"

"I've been on The Google." Again, he sported a quirky smile.

"Night, Dad," Sage said, not waiting for a reply. She rushed out the door, running across the yard to the horse barn. Opening the horse stall door, Crease gave out several sharp barks. After letting him out for a quick romp in the grass, Sage picked up the puppy, racing to her apartment.

After fumbling for the light switch, instead of turning on the TV, she made her way to the tiny kitchen, starting up the Keurig. She knew it must be close to the start of the third period. She needed some caffeine running through her veins before confronting Margret or Hunter. Taking her coffee cup into the front room, she plopped on the couch. Crease snuggled at her feet as Sage retrieved her phone.

There were three messages from Margret: two texts and a voice message. She read the texts first.

3pm—Margret: What happened? Lionel just called. He was there to pick you up. the screen door was shut, but the front door was open. He looked inside and saw your baggage in the hallway. He said he walked into the house calling your name. When no one answered, he walked into the kitchen. Why's blood all over your kitchen floor?

3:30pm—Margret: I contacted your local sheriff, the one we talked to at your gallery opening. He's going out to do a wellness check. I haven't let Hunter know what's going on. Only that your flight was delayed. CALL ME!!!!

With shaky fingers, Sage clicked on Margret's voice message.

6:30pm: Sage. What in the world is going on? No one has gotten back to me. The charter plane arrived with my driver, but no you. No word from you. No word from the sheriff. Do you know how worried I am? Let alone, do you know how much time I put into getting you to the game, and how much this is costing Hunter? Not just the price of the charter, but I'm sure it will cost him his concentration on the ice tonight. The game is about to start, and I can't take any calls until it's over. I better hear from you by the end of the third period.

Sage clicked on the television. It was halfway through the last period. The score was now 2 to 5 ... again, in the Savages' favor. With shaky fingers, she clicked on Margret's name from her phone's contact list, leaving a hasty voice message.

Sage: Hey Margret. I'm so sorry to have worried you. My mom fell, hit her head and broke her hand. There was a lot of blood. In my rush to take her to the hospital, I left my phone at the house. It took forever in the ER. They are keeping my mom overnight. Please let Hunter know I'm so sorry I couldn't make the game. Please have him call me when he can. I'll find a way to reimburse Hunter for the cost of the charter plane.

"GOAL!" The announcer's voice vibrated through her tiny apartment. Sage was afraid to look at the screen, not knowing which team scored.

"That puts the Goshawks closer to a comeback," the announcer screamed.

"Yeah, but if Griffin doesn't wake up soon, will the Goshawks be able to score three more goals before Vegas scores another?" the second announcer asked.

Sage watched the rest of the game sitting on the edge of the couch. The good thing, Hunter kept the Savages to 5 points. The bad news, as hard as the Goshawks tried, as the buzzer closed out the period, the score remained the same: 3 to 5 in favor of the Savages.

"This is all my fault." Sage sobbed, as Crease jumped on her lap, licking her tears.

Chapter 46
Not Standing Down

June 3rd [Game 1 of The Cup Final: Postgame]
Hunter sat in his stall watching his teammates file out. He was thankful Ryan and Chase volunteered to face the press. The thought of recounting the game's failures to a room of reporters was unbearable. Yet, the loss weighed on him like a leaden cloak, every misstep replaying in his head.

The locker room had transformed into a mausoleum of silence after the game. Disappointment saturated the air, underscored by intermittent muttered curses and the slamming of equipment. Typically, a loss of this magnitude would provoke a storm of reprimands from the coaches, but tonight they remained uncharacteristically quiet. Their energy, too, had been dampened by the heavy blanket of desolation.

Before the game, Assistant Coach Scott collected their cell phones, a ritualistic severance from the outside world during The Cup Final games. "Focus," Head Coach Harrison had demanded. "Dig deep. Play hard but play smart. Give everything you have." But Hunter's everything had been lacking, his thoughts ensnared by Sage's absence.

"Hey Hunter, are you decent?" Margret covered her eyes as she stepped into the locker room. Her expression was somber, a stark contrast to her usual vivacity.

"What's going on, Margret?" He was about to stand, but she motioned for him to stay seated as she sat in the stall next to him.

"Has something happened to Sage?" Hunter's mind raced to dark places he didn't want to go right now.

Margret put her hand on Hunter's shoulder. "Sage is fine."

"If she's fine, why wasn't she at the game?" Hunter looked into Margret's eyes. Something disastrous must have happened, because Margret had never stepped her designer shoes into the Goshawks' locker room.

"As I was trying to say, Sage is fine, but her mother fell. She's in the hospital."

"I don't understand. Did Sage have to fly back to South Dakota?" Hunter did his best to calm his racing heartbeat.

"Lilly was injured before Sage left."

Hunter stared at Margret, waiting for her to elaborate.

"I really don't know any more than that. The only communication I've had from Sage was a quick voice message."

Hunter leaned his head back into the stall. Closing his eyes, he rubbed palms over his face. "How serious was Lilly injured?"

"Honestly, that's all I know," Margret repeated, as she reached in her purse, pulling out Hunter's cell phone, which she held at a distance. "You can call her after you listen to what I have to say."

Hunter sat up straight, his eyes narrowing. "Give me the damn phone, Margret!" He grabbed for the phone, but Margret put it back in her purse.

"I'll give it to you in a minute. I have something important to discuss with you first."

"After the shitty game I just played, I'm in no mood for your games. I'll give you five minutes. Then I'm taking my phone back." Hunter glared into her eyes.

"Your shitty game is exactly what I'm here to talk to you about." Margret glared back. "Normally, your coaches would have this conversation with you. Since they're not getting through, they asked me to intervene."

Hunter grit his teeth, looking at Margret, with a *time is ticking* expression.

"The Goshawks' management and coaches have agreed, it would be best if you put your relationship with Sage on hold until the end of the season. This is not a mere request. I know you want Sage to be a part of your life, but now is not the time."

Hunter did his best to remain outwardly calm ... inside, he was seething.

"Tonight was a prime example," Margret continued. "You allowed your need for Sage to come before your desire to win The Cup. You let your teammates down. I'll be honest with you. After tonight's disastrous display of goaltending, Coach Harrison is being asked to bench you for the rest of The Cup games. There's even talk about bringing in a backup goalie."

"It was One Game, Margret. One Loss." Hunter's body shook with anger. "I can count the number of my regulation losses on one hand ... and I played the majority of regulation games."

"That was before Sage fell into your life."

"Are you trying to tell me the Goshawks have such little faith in me, they'd replace me after the first loss in The Cup Final?"

"I'm only forewarning you of what could happen if you don't get it together and put your full concentration in the game. I know you've heard this all from Coach Harrison, as well as your goaltending coach. I offered to deliver their message, thinking you might listen to me."

Margret's words only fanned the flames of his internal struggle. The idea of putting his relationship with Sage on hold felt like an amputation of part of his soul. Yet, the logic in her words was irrefutable, the harsh reality of his profession cutting through the fog of his emotions.

"If you're so wise, Margret, maybe you can answer this question. No one else has been able to. How do the other players do it? How do they switch off their personal lives?"

"It's never easy. Sometimes, sacrifices are necessary for the greater good of the team."

"But at what cost? Why does it have to be an either-or situation? Why can't I have my career and Sage?" Even to his own ears, Hunter knew his words came out as a pathetic whine.

Margret's expression softened, a hint of sympathy in her eyes. "Sometimes, we have to make tough choices for the things we care about most."

Hunter's frustration spilled over. "But who gets to decide what's too much for me to handle?" His fist hit his chest protector. "Why can't I make that call?"

"It's not just about you. It's about the team's overall dynamics. New relationships, especially during high-stakes times like these, can complicate things." Margret reached out to take his hand, but Hunter pulled away.

He shook his head, disbelief and anger intermingling. "But that's just it, Margret. They're my complications to manage. Not the team's, not management."

Margret nodded, understanding yet firm. "I get where you're coming from, Hunter. But this is how the industry works. The management ... they're looking at the big picture."

"The big picture," Hunter echoed, a bitter edge to his words. "And where do I fit in that picture, Margret? Just a piece to be moved around? Bought or sold on a whim?"

Margret met his gaze, her voice earnest. "You're a key player, Hunter. But sometimes, we need to look beyond ourselves."

Hunter balled his fists tighter, his resolve crystallizing. "No, Margret. It's time for the Goshawks' management to see my full picture. It's time they see me as more than a body in the net, with the threat of being traded when I no longer meet their expectations." Hunter smiled, nodding his head. "I'm going to talk to them."

"Be careful, Hunter. This is a dangerous game you're playing. I shouldn't have to remind you that you'll be a restricted free agent at the end of this season."

Standing, Hunter squared his shoulders, his determination unwavering. "I appreciate your concern. But I can't let others control my life anymore. Sage means more to me than anyone will ever understand." He reached out his hand. "You can tell your bosses that their message was delivered. Now give me my phone, and leave. I still have to shower and get dressed."

Sage paced the floor of her tiny apartment, waiting for the perfect time to call Hunter. There was a lot to take into consideration. His time zone was an hour ahead of hers. She knew the game had been over for a while, but she was unsure how long it would take Hunter to leave the arena.

Would he have to spend time with reporters? Would he get reprimanded by his coaches for his poor performance? When would he get to his apartment? She knew from talking to him after games, it always took Hunter at least two hours post-game to unwind. *How late could she call him before he went to bed?*

She checked the time again. It was near midnight in Portland. She was about to send him a text to see if he was available to take her call when her phone lit up with his name.

"Hunter?" There was a long pause at the other end.

"Hey Sage. How's your mom?"

She sighed in relief. His question could only mean Margret had spoken to him, yet Sage was unsure how much she'd told him. "They are keeping her overnight in the hospital. Just as a precaution."

"What happened? Margret only told me she had an accident."

"Mom tripped over Crease. Fell. She hit her head hard. Lots of blood. She also fractured her hand." Sage felt the weight of the day catch up to her, but she knew she had to be strong for him. After seeing how poorly he played. After tonight's loss ... Hunter had to be devastated.

"I'm so sorry Sage. I feel responsible for Lilly's accident."

"Oh, Hunter, how can you possibly be responsible?"

"If I hadn't insisted you come to Portland, none of this would have happened."

Sitting on the couch, Crease jumped on her lap, licking her face as if to beg for her forgiveness too. "It was a freak accident. It could have happened anytime. No one's to blame, especially you." Sage paused, waiting for Crease to settle on her lap. "I'm the one who should apologize to you."

"For what?"

Sage could hear Hunter pacing. Hear ice being plopped in a glass. She knew the sound of liquid pouring over it was scotch. "I should have contacted the airport, or the limo driver, or texted you or Margret. But in the chaos of getting my mom to the ER, I left my phone on the kitchen table." She did her best not to cry. Sage kept reminding herself that she needed to be strong for him. "Can you ever forgive me for not letting you know why I missed your game?"

She could hear Hunter taking a long drink of his scotch. "Sage, this time it's my turn to say it wasn't your fault." He paused, the ice rattling in the glass. "It seems the universe is doing its best to keep us apart."

"I was thinking the same thing today." Sage let out a soft laugh. "How are you?"

"Did you have time to see the game tonight?" His words were followed by a low growl.

"I caught the last period."

"Then you know how I am. I can't keep letting my team down, like I did tonight." The sounds of Hunter refilling his glass could be heard in the background.

"I'm so sorry. I keep telling you, I never intended to come between you and hockey." Sage put her head into Crease's fur to muffle her sobs.

"It's not your fault, Sage. What happened tonight was all on me. When on the ice, a goalie must be focused only on the game ... at all times. Tonight, I failed miserably at that."

"Perhaps it's a good thing that I'm not at your games." Sage felt the heavy weight of the burden her relationship with Hunter was causing him.

"Perhaps." There was another long pause on Hunter's end of the phone. "I don't know what to do. I've never felt the way I do about anyone ... before you. One thing I do know for certain ... I'm still not ready to give up on us. I need to figure this whole thing out, and I need to figure it out fast."

"I understand. My feelings haven't changed about you either." Once again, she gulped out her words. "We can work through this."

"Hope so," Hunter's voice broke as he spoke.

"This is such a crucial time for you. Playing in The Cup Final is your biggest dream come true," Sage assured him.

"I used to think it was. Now I know that my biggest dream come true is you."

Hunter's words took Sage's breath away. No one had ever said anything like that to her. "You know that I feel the same way about you. Yet we can't let our feelings get in the way of you winning The Cup. We just can't."

"I know... you're right. I've got to get myself together. Hockey has been my whole life ... until I met you. I'm not willing to sacrifice one for the other. I need you."

"You need hockey in your life too." Sage refused to be the reason for him to give up on his dreams. To give up on his first love, being a pro goalie for the Goshawks. For a chance to kiss The Cup.

Without thinking, she blurted out, "We need to take a break from each other. You need to concentrate on the game. On the Goshawks. On winning," she paused, "and I need to concentrate on my photography career and helping my mom until she's able to help herself."

"Forgive me, Sage, for being so selfish. I'm always thinking of me, and not what you must be going through. But I can't let you go."

"I know, Hunter, but I think it's for the best if we both step back for a while. Our timing is off. I don't want us to stay apart forever, just until we can get our lives back on track."

She could hear Hunter take another long sip of his drink, rattling the ice cubes in the glass.

"I ... I just don't understand why I can't make this work. All the other players that are in relationships have no problem juggling their personal lives with their dedication to hockey. What is wrong with me that I can't do that too?"

"Nothing is wrong with you. Like I said, our timing is off." Sage held the phone away, in hopes he wouldn't hear her sobs. "I care about you. I can't imagine my world without you in it. But for now, I think it is best we put our relationship on hold. At least until the Goshawks season is over."

"I know you're right. Yet, there's one thing that no one is taking into consideration." Hunter's voice became low, barely understandable.

"What's that?"

"I love you, Sage." This time, Hunter's words came out strong, with a hunger.

Sage was taken aback. She didn't know how to respond. She yearned to say the same words back to him ... yet something caused her to hesitate.

Hunter waited for a beat, before saying, "I don't expect you to feel the same way. Hey, it's getting late, I have early practice. I'll call when I get some free time."

The phone went dead.

Sage called Hunter back, but he didn't answer. *Why didn't he wait for my response?* She thought of sending him a text but stating 'I love you' for the first time that way seemed far too impersonal.

Chapter 47
Games People Play

June 16th [Game 6 of The Cup Final]
Sage maneuvered around the confines of her tiny living room, placing chips and dips on the front room tables, while Jessica made sure everyone had a beer. The atmosphere was ripe with anticipation as they readied themselves for game six.

Jessica and Patty claimed the couch, while Sage eased herself into one of the overstuffed chairs. Luke leaned against the wall, his attention on Sage rather than on the TV.

"I hate games that start at 9," Jessica whined as she took a long swig of her beer.

Patty clutched a beer bottle in one hand as she grabbed a handful of chips with the other. She nodded in agreement. "I don't care what time the game starts. I can't wait to watch the Goshawks beat the hockey pants off the Savages."

"It's so good to see Hunter back on his game," Sage added, coaxing Crease onto her lap.

"He's sure the comeback kid, winning the last two games." Patty snuggled into the couch, pulling her legs under her.

Luke continued to check the time on his phone. "Hope he doesn't choke like he did in the first game." He pushed off the wall, sitting in a chair across from Sage.

Sage stared at Luke. "I'm not sure why you came tonight, Luke? But, since you're here, you have to root for the Goshawks ... or go home."

"He's got to stay," Jessica said, staring at the TV. "He's my designated emotional support cowboy."

"Well, in that case, you best behave yourself, mister." Sage tossed a throw pillow at Luke. The other two girls mimicked her actions.

"Game's starting," Patty announced, pointing to the flatscreen as the players took to the ice. The anticipation in the room culminating in a shared moment of silence, before the storm of emotions the game was certain to bring.

The tension in the living room mirrored the intensity on the ice as the game between the Goshawks and Savages unraveled with fierce competition. The Las

Vegas Savages lived up to their name, with aggressive plays that had everyone on the edge of their seats. Sage's front room soon filled with a roller-coaster of cheers and moans, as the teams clashed.

"Oh. My. Gosh. Did you see that hit?" Jessica shouted as another scuffle broke out along the boards. The linesmen struggled to separate the players. "The Savages are playing so dirty tonight."

Patty leaned forward. Her eyes narrowed. "There's been more fighting and blood-shedding than playing hockey. I hope our boys are keeping their mouth guards in place tonight."

"What is wrong with the ref? I can't believe he only called penalties on Finn and Axel." Jessica screamed at the TV, as one of the linesmen guided the two Goshawks into the penalty box. "That's so not right."

"Looks like the Savages have the refs in their pockets," Luke quipped, bringing the beer bottle to his lips, concealing a smile.

Moments later the Savages surrounded Hunter's net, scoring on a five on three power play. Bringing the score 0-1 in favor of the Savages.

On the play after both penalties were served, Finn and Axel rushed the Savages' net with clean, short, on the tape passes. In front of the Savages' blue crease, Finn faked a pass to Axel. Finn drove the puck into an open net, tying the score 1-1.

"This game is going to cause me to go bald," Jessica said, her fingers entangled in her long dark hair.

As the clock ticked down, the Goshawks were called back to their defensive zone for icing. The Savages won the faceoff, racing to the Goshawks' net. In a clash of bodies and sticks, the puck bounced over Hunter's pad, coming to rest inside the net. Once more the Savages took the lead ... the score now 1-2.

The red light was still flashing when one of the Savages' enforcers landed a heavy check to the back of Goshawks' third-liner, Jake Carter's neck. The force sending the D-man face-planting on the ice like a fallen oak, knocking his brain bucket off. He lay motionless for a full, heart-stopping minute.

The front room was suddenly bathed in a creepy quiet as they watched and waited for Jake to move. The silence, evoked by the seriousness of the play, dampened their festive mood.

A stretcher was called onto the ice as Jake regained consciousness. The young Goshawks' player waved it away as he attempted to stand. Two Goshawks' players supported a hunched over Jake off the ice, where he was then assisted to the locker room.

"Looks like the ref found his glasses," Jessica yelled at the screen as a linesmen escorted the Savages' enforcer off the ice, pointing to the tunnel.

After a brief review of the play, the referee skated to center ice, turning on his mic. "Match Penalty, Savages, number 22."

Luke looked at the girls. "What does that mean?"

All heads turned to Patty, as she casually spewed, "If a player purposefully delivers a hit severe enough to knock out an opponent ... especially with a hit like that to the back of the neck ... that player will get ejected from not just this game, but most likely he'll be out for game seven as well. That is, of course, if the Goshawks get to game seven."

Patty, took a quick sip of her beer then continued, "Plus, and this is the good part, the Savages will have to select one of their other players to serve the five-minute penalty in place of the dufus who attacked poor Jake ... oh, and, that Savages' player has to serve the full penalty in the box, even if the Goshawks score."

"What the hell, Patty?" Jessica said, staring at her friend as if she'd turned into an alien.

"What? It's all covered under Rule 48.5 in the 'Official Hockey Rules' book ... you can google it." Patty sat back, frowning at the TV. "Jake has such a pretty smile. I sure hope he didn't knock any teeth out when his face hit the ice."

The room broke into a fit of laughter, along with beer bottles clinking from one person to another.

After a commercial break, the game resumed, with the Goshawks on a five-on-four player advantage. Even outnumbered, the Savages got control of the puck. Ryan and Axel worked together defending their zone. In a moment of chaos near the crease, Axel kicked the puck into his own net ... the score 1-3 in favor of the Savages.

The mishap had Sage covering her face with her hands. "Oh, Axel," she groaned. "I know he's going to beat himself up over that one."

"Only if the Goshawks lose their chance to play game seven by one goal." Luke leaned back in the chair, stretching out his long legs.

The Goshawks weren't down for long. Chase, seizing an opportunity during the last few seconds of the Savages' penalty, broke away, outmaneuvering the Savages' goaltender. The buzzer ended the first period with the score 2-3. The room erupted in cheers. Their hopes renewed with the display of resilience.

Sage leaned back, trying to calm her racing heart. "This is going to be a long night," she said, catching Luke's gaze.

He nodded, tipping his beer bottle in her direction, a smile breaking through his stoic demeanor; looking as if he too was caught up in the game's excitement despite his earlier reservations not to.

Patty lifted her beer in a toast. "To the Goshawks! Let's bring this home!" The group clinked their bottles together, their spirits lifted by the team's comeback, ready for whatever the next periods would bring.

Inwardly, Sage was not celebrating. She watched as the Goshawks shuffled down the tunnel to the visitor's locker room, hoping to see Hunter's face, to read his mood, but the camera only caught the back of his masked head.

———◆———

The second period belonged to the Goshawks. They stayed out of the Sin Bin, even though the Savages incurred three more minor penalties: two for tripping, and one for delay of game when a Savages' player shot the puck over the glass in their defensive zone. The Goshawks scored on every penalty. By the end of the second period, the Goshawks led the Savages 5-3.

The night ended with a 6-3 Goshawks victory, with Hunter shutting out another period, as the Goshawks scored another goal.

"On to game seven!" Jessica shouted, as she danced around the front room with Patty and Crease.

"Oh, I love this part." Patty stopped celebrating long enough to watch the Goshawks form a line in front of Hunter.

"Me too," said Sage, waiting for the camera to zoom in on the Goshawks' goalie. When it did, Hunter raised his mask, looking intensely into the camera. Sage felt his hazel eyes looking straight into hers.

Sage reached for the remote, knowing there was never a Goshawks press conference after away games. Her fingers hovered over the 'off' button as the TV camera captured a reporter in front of Hunter as he walked down the tunnel.

"What an amazing game Hunter, what lit the fire under you in the second and third periods."

Once again, Hunter stared into the camera. "It wasn't a what, it was a who." He then mouthed, "Hi Sage." Without another word, he turned, following his teammates to the locker room.

"Did you see that?" Patty squealed, her voice so high Crease ran into the bedroom, scurrying under the bed.

"I need another beer," Luke side-eyed Sage before walking to the kitchen.

"Hey Luke," Jessica called after him, "Are you sure you want to do that? You still have to drive home."

Luke grumbled as he opened the refrigerator, walking back into the front room with a bottle of water in his hand. "There, happy now?"

—◆◇◆—

Sage walked between her front room and the kitchen, picking up the leftover mess from the Goshawks' win. Jessica and Patty left right after the game, spending the night in Sage's parent's house.

Luke lingered to help with the cleanup. Sage froze when their hands touched as they placed empty beer bottles into the recycle bin. Their eyes met before Sage pulled away, letting out an uncomfortable laugh.

"That was some game," Luke said, as he picked up the filled garbage bag, tying it before placing it by the front door. "Hunter's teammates and fans treat him like a hero when the Goshawks win."

"Yeah, they do," Sage said over her shoulder as she walked to the front room, gathering empty chip bowls. Returning to the kitchen, Sage placed the bowls in the sink. When she turned, Luke's presence was dangerously close, nearly causing her to stumble into him. Regaining her balance, she met his gaze, the proximity catching her off guard.

Luke's expression softened, his fingers brushing a stray lock of hair from her face. "So, are you going to call him?" he asked, his voice deep and harsh.

Sage ducked under his arms. "Yeah, I think I should."

"Come on Sage," Luke turned around, leaning his back on the counter, crossing his arms. "You've got to see that he's playing you. He only wants you when he's on a goalie high."

The glare in Sage's eyes burned into Luke like a laser. "I appreciate you helping me clean up, but I think it's time for you to go. I ... I've got to get up early to fix dad's breakfast." Crease moved to her side, plastering his body to her leg. Sage walked to the front room, opening the door.

Luke pushed off the counter, ambling towards the open door. He stopped in front of her. Bending down until their noses touched, he whispered, "When you finally tire of his games, remember I've always been here for you." He kissed her forehead before retrieving his cowboy hat from the nearby rack. Picking up the garbage bag, he left her standing.

Crease let out a low growl as Sage slammed the door. Looking at the protective puppy, she patted him on the head. "My sentiments exactly." Turning off the kitchen and front room lights, she made her way to the bedroom.

Retrieving her cell phone, Sage scrolled through her contact list. Checking the time, she hovered a finger over Hunter's name. She knew the Goshawks would be flying home right after the game and wouldn't land in Portland for hours. After making her calculations, Sage left him a text, even though she really wanted to hear his voice.

Sage: Great game. I'm so proud of you. Call me when you get home. I don't care what time it is. I need to hear your voice.

After sending the text, she blew a kiss to Hunter's picture hanging across from her bed. Turning the bedroom light out, she fell into a restless sleep, only to be woken with a start at the sound of sharp pings. Still half asleep, she reached for the phone. "Hello," she mumbled.

"I'm sorry to wake you, Sage. Go back to sleep. I'll try to reach you later." Hunter said in a weary voice.

"No. No. Don't hang up." Sage panicked. "What time is it?"

There was a long pause, as if Hunter was unsure of the answer. "Oh, gosh. I didn't think about the time difference. Looks like it's around 3:30 your time."

"Where are you?" Sage sat up in bed, reaching over to turn on the light. Crease snuggled into her legs, tail thumping.

"I just walked into my apartment."

"My gosh, Hunter. You must be exhausted."

"I think I'm still on a high from last night's game, plus a little tipsy from the champagne we had on the plane." His words punctuated with a hiccup.

"I'm surprised your coach let the players drink." Hunter had mentioned the Goshawks' coaches had a strict no partying policy after games during The Cup Final.

"Under normal conditions, it would be a dry flight home, but considering our win put us back in contention for The Cup, the coaches turned a blind eye this one time. Did you watch the game?"

"I never miss any of your games." Now wide awake, Sage fluffed the pillow behind her, sitting up straighter. "You were brilliant last night." Even through the phone, Sage knew he was smiling.

"It was a team effort. If not for a great defense, I couldn't have done my part for the win." A clang of metal on wood could be heard as Hunter put his keys on the counter.

"You are being way too modest. You only let in three out of forty-three shots on goal from Vegas ... I was happy to see you awarded the first star of the game."

"The only game that counts is the one we're playing Monday." Hunter let out a stifled yawn.

"Sounds like it's you who needs to get some sleep," Sage's voice was edged with concern. "Do you get today off?"

"Yeah, today's a free day, but back to practice tomorrow."

"What are your plans?" *Talk to you all day*, Sage hoped he would say.

"I wish I could sleep for the next twenty-four hours, but my agent sent me a text. He set up a meeting with Goshawks' management this afternoon." Hunter let out another yawn.

Sage sat up in bed tossing the bedcovers off, her heart pounding. "Is something wrong?" She knew players didn't have meetings with management on a whim, plus it was unusual to have one so close to game seven.

"It's just a quick sit down, nothing major." Hunter's tone was not as convincing as his words.

"I hope it goes well." Sage got out of bed. Walking to the front room, she let Crease out the door to do his morning business. Sitting on the top of the steps leading to the barn below, she pulled her nightgown around her legs. "I don't want to let you go, but you should get some sleep."

"I know, and you need to get your morning started." Hunter paused. "I miss you, Sage. It's been far too long without hearing your voice. It's killing me. Tonight, I had an overwhelming need to have you near me. To get a celebration hug from you after the game."

"I miss you too." As she was talking, Crease came bounding up the steps, jumping into her arms, causing her to almost drop her phone.

"Hey, how is your mom doing?"

"She's doing great on her own. Her soft cast is not slowing her down."

"That's excellent news." There was a long pause before Hunter said, "I talked to Margret, Ryan and the rookies on our flight home. We're all chipping in to charter a plane from Brookings to bring you and your friends to Portland on Monday. I know it's short notice, but do you think everyone can get the day off? The hotels around here are booked solid. But Margret has a big house with lots of guest rooms.

Please say you'll come. There's no way I'm playing game seven without you in the stands. I'll need you there after the game … win or lose."

Sage held the phone as far as her arm would reach, to muffle her screams of delight.

"Sage? Are you still there?"

"Are you sure you want me there? I would never forgive myself if I distracted you."

"Stop. I wouldn't be asking if I wasn't sure. Oh, and don't forget Jessica, Patty, and yeah, even Luke's invited … everything will be paid for. We'll fly everyone home Tuesday afternoon. I know it's a lot to ask, and I know I'm being selfish, but Sage, I need you to be here for me." Hunter's tone turned urgent, pleading.

"Yes! Yes! I'll make it happen even if I have to camp outside the airport on Sunday night." Sage stood, jumping up and down with Crease. "I'm sure Jessica and Patty can get away, not so sure about Luke. I'm surprised he was invited."

"That was all on Margret. Luke was her idea. Since she's the only one with enough pull to get you all into a sold-out game, I didn't have a choice but to agree." Hunter could be heard taking off his shoes, as one, then the other thumped to the hardwood floor. "Apparently, she has a thing for your South Dakota cowboy … go figure."

"Good luck with your meeting today. Try to get some rest. See you Monday."

"I think I'm more excited about seeing you than I am about playing game seven."

Chapter 48

Negotiations

June 17th

In the quiet corner of the bustling coffee shop near to the Goshawks' training center, Hunter and his longtime agent, Erik Donovan, found a semblance of seclusion amidst the gentle murmur of late-morning patrons. The air was rich with the aroma of ground coffee and fresh baked goods, a symphony of scents that mingled with the soft clink of cups. Any other day, this environment was a refuge, a place to unwind. Today, it couldn't ease the storm brewing within Hunter.

Erik, who always navigated the treacherous waters of sports management with a blend of cunning intellect and razor-sharp wit, regarded Hunter with intensity. "Keep your cool, Hunter. Remember, this is about being strategic. You've moved beyond the rookie tag; you're now a cornerstone for the Goshawks," he advised, his words a blend of mentorship and partnership.

Hunter's response was a series of rhythmic taps on the tabletop. "I understand, Erik, but it's as if they want to micromanage my whole life, not just the hockey parts. It's suffocating."

Erik's hands wrapped around his coffee mug. His eyes, steadfast, met Hunter's. "Concentrate on the elements within your grasp. Articulate your concerns with clarity but remain receptive to their viewpoint. This meeting is a dialogue, an opportunity for negotiation, not an arena for dispute."

With a deep, steadying breath, Hunter rose, the future of his career perched upon his shoulders. They exited, stepping into the damp embrace of Portland's salty sea air. The chill sharpened Hunter's focus as they made their way to confront his future, both on and off the ice.

───◆◆◆───

The Goshawks' offices, nestled high above the bustling streets below, stood in stark contrast to the vibrant energy of the coffee shop. As they stepped inside, the spacious room welcomed them with its sleek, modern furnishings. The air was tinged with the understated scent of polished wood, with a whisper of high-quality leather from the chairs. The distant, rhythmic hum of printers offered a soft counterpoint to their steady footsteps on the plush carpet, a subtle reminder of the business at the heart of the sport of hockey.

George Stonebridge, the Goshawks' General Manager, rose from behind his expansive desk, his silhouette framed by the panoramic window overlooking the city. He offered each man a firm handshake. The warmth of his grip contrasted with the cool, calculated demeanor he carried like a mantle.

"Good to see you, Hunter." Stonebridge's smile was brief but genuine. "And Erik, always a pleasure."

"Thank you for meeting with us on such short notice, George." Erik's voice was smooth, practiced.

As they settled into the chairs, Stonebridge began speaking, "First off, Hunter, I want to commend you on your performance in Vegas."

"Thank you, sir," Hunter said, his tone civil, betraying none of the storm brewing beneath his calm exterior. "My performance last night is not the only reason we're here today," Hunter leaned forward, his gaze locked with Stonebridge's. The air became thick with anticipation, the tension building as the conversation shifted from professional accolades to personal grievances.

"I'm here because I'm concerned about the organization interfering with my personal life, especially regarding my relationship with Sage Larson." Hunter's voice was steady, a controlled edge to his words, the undercurrent of frustration idling beneath the surface.

Stonebridge's expression remained impassive, his eyes narrowing as if readying for a debate. "Hunter, we value you as a player, but you must understand the team's success is our top priority."

Hunter's jaw tightened, the muscles flexing with tension. "I get that. But I'm more than a body in the net. For the past five seasons, I've dedicated every moment of my life, personal and professional, to the Goshawks."

Erik interjected, his voice calm, diplomatic. "We're not here to create conflict. We want to find a middle ground that respects Hunter's personal life and ensures his continued commitment to the team."

Stonebridge leaned back, his fingers steepling. "Let's discuss this further. I'm interested to hear your perspective, Hunter."

The room was charged with the same tension preceding a big game, a silent battle of wills unfolding. "I understand the need for focus," Hunter continued, his voice low, firm. "However, if you think I'm going to sit back and let management dictate my personal life, then maybe it's time I consider my options."

Stonebridge's expression hardened, a flicker of challenge in his eyes. "Hunter, be reasonable. You're a key player, but this isn't just about you. There's the team to think about, the franchise."

"Gentlemen let's keep this productive," Erik's voice cut through the rising tension, smooth but firm. Addressing Stonebridge, he said, "Throughout this season Hunter's performances, despite distractions, have been pivotal in getting the Goshawks to the playoffs. Without Hunter's goaltending, the Goshawks would be golfing instead of preparing for game seven."

Hunter leaned in, his gaze unwavering. "Let's not skirt around the fact that my private life only became an issue when I started seeing Sage. My commitment to the Goshawks has never wavered, not once in five seasons with the team."

"That's not entirely true, now is it, Hunter?" Stonebridge opened a folder on his desk. "There was the incident in Florida involving a player's destroyed mouth guard. The Goshawks' organization considers goaltending to be a coveted position. We do not condone our goalies getting unsportsmanlike conduct penalties." Stonebridge looked to Hunter as he flipped to another page. "Then there's Viktor Volkov."

"What does my goaltending coach have to do with this discussion?" Hunter asked, his forehead creasing, eyes narrowing, lips tightening.

"Our reports from Viktor confirm our concerns." Stonebridge began reading the page, "Your goaltending coach, states that your game has been off ever since a Miss Larson came into your life. He further states, when you are on the ice, your mind is no longer completely in the game ... on protecting your net."

Erik put his hand on Hunter's arm, doing his best to stop him from storming out of the meeting. "George, we all know how controlling Viktor can be. He's an outstanding goaltending coach, but sometimes he's unwavering regarding Hunter and his need to be committed to hockey, on and off the ice."

Stonebridge looked from Erik to Hunter. "Do I need to remind you both? Viktor is only on the Goshawks' team because he was written into Hunter's contract ... which is up for renewal at the end of this season."

"We're well aware of that," Erik's voice held a restrained calm.

"Then you understand that we cannot guarantee a spot for Viktor on the Goshawks' team next season."

"Are you using Viktor as a bargaining chip?" Hunter spat out the words.

Stonebridge didn't respond. Instead, he flipped to another page in the folder. "How about your careless off-ice injury before playing our first game with Toronto?

The multi-games you missed could have cost us a chance to advance in the playoffs." Shutting the folder, he tapped the cover with his index finger. "The folder's contents proves my point ... and yes, we can pinpoint your lack of commitment beginning with your interactions with Miss Larson."

Hunter's breath became labored. "How can one incident, one injury, in one season define my career? I've been standing on my head for this team since day one. You want commitment? I've shown it every time I step on the ice."

"Do you realize how many games the Goshawks have lost since you met Sage?"

"If everyone thought Sage was ruining my game, why did the Goshawks' management insist that I attend her gallery opening in South Dakota?" Hunter leaned forward, his legs shaking.

"That was entirely Margret's initiative. She believed your visit would generate good publicity, attracting more attention to the Goshawks, filling more seats at our games," Stonebridge explained, his tone implying the decision was strategic. "Margret is a shrewd businesswoman, and we respect her judgment on media matters." He paused, staring at Hunter with a challenging gaze. "Your appearance was not only beneficial in terms of publicity—it also turned out to be financially profitable, thanks to a sizable donation from a South Dakota rancher."

"I'm confused," Hunter exclaimed, slumping back into his chair. "One minute, the Goshawks' management demands I stay away from Sage; the next, they're orchestrating ways to bring us together. It's incredibly frustrating." His tone was resolute. "This inconsistency only reinforces my point ... I need the Goshawks to stop meddling in my personal life."

Erik glanced at Hunter, then back to Stonebridge. "What we're proposing here is a balance. Hunter gets the autonomy he deserves off the ice, and in return, he continues to be committed to the Goshawks on it."

Stonebridge paused, his gaze softening as he considered their words. "Hunter, we're not blind to what you've contributed. But it's a two-way street. I repeat, we need to see you focus on the game."

Hunter answered, clear and unwavering, "I'm willing to prove my worth when I'm on the ice. But off ice, I need to know I'm more than just a number on a sweater. I need respect, or I'll find it with a team that's willing to give it to me."

The room fell into a heavy silence, Stonebridge appeared to contemplate the weight of Hunter's ultimatum. He finally nodded ... a silent reluctant agreement. "Alright, Hunter. I can't promise anything, but we'll work on a compromise. But remember, the team's success should be a top priority with you as well."

As the meeting concluded, Hunter felt a sense of hard-won achievement mixed with uncertainty for the future. Exiting the GM's office, the corridor greeted them with an eerie silence, a reminder of the distant echoes of their intense discussion.

Erik managed a small, tight smile that didn't mask his underlying tension. "For the most part, you handled that well," Erik's voice sliced through the silence. "You stood firm, and that's commendable. But now, the real challenge begins. They'll be scrutinizing your every move. You must be ready to make tough choices, even if it means a future that doesn't include the Goshawks. Are you prepared for that?"

A shrug was Hunter's immediate response, his mind a turmoil of conflicting emotions. He had laid down a gauntlet before the very person who'd given him a home as a Goshawks' goalie. There was a sense of victory, yes, but also a nagging apprehension about what the future might hold. The Goshawks' players were his family. Deep down, he was unsure if he could break those ties ... even for Sage.

Reaching the cool expanse of the parking lot, Erik's hand rested on Hunter's shoulder. "You've got this. Just keep your head in the game, and everything else will fall into place."

Hunter pulled out his phone, Sage's number already highlighted. His thumb hovered over the call button. Part of him wanted to share the triumph, to tell her he'd stood up for himself ... for them. Another part hesitated, not wanting to drag her into the complexities of his professional life, especially with her own challenges of a budding photography career, along with her family drama.

As his Uber approached, Hunter locked the phone without making the call to Sage. He needed to process this alone, at least for now. The drive home gave him time to reflect on everything ... the meeting, his career, his future, and especially his relationship with Sage.

He knew one thing for certain; game seven would be crucial, not just for the Goshawks, but for him, for his career. It was time to prove to everyone—the management, the fans, his team, and maybe, most important, himself—that he could balance his personal life with his professional responsibilities.

The apartment door closed behind him, sealing away the outside world. Hunter was home, not just in place, but in purpose. The game ahead was not just another match; it was the arena where he would forge his destiny, on his terms, both on the ice and beyond.

Chapter 49
The Trifecta Part One

June 19th [Game 7 of The Cup Final: Pregame]
Outside the Portland arena, fans of the Goshawks and Savages gathered in anticipation, awaiting the opening of the main doors. Tonight, game seven of The Cup Final, would determine the fate of both teams. Sage could only imagine the pressure Hunter must be under. She hoped her being here wouldn't distract him.

The limo pulled up to a side door marked Private Entrance. Sage, Jessica, Patty, and Luke scrambled out of the car. They were met by a mountain of a man dressed in a dark suit. He handed each of the four, a VIP badge on a lanyard. "You need to wear those at all times."

"Wow, and I thought the private jet was exciting. This is so over the top." Patty was hopping from one foot to the other.

"Settle down, Patty. You act like you've never been out of South Dakota." Jessica pulled the lanyard over her head, adjusting the badge with her picture and name on it.

"It is the first time I've been out of South Dakota!" Patty giggled.

The security guard announced to the group, "My name is Derrick. I've been assigned to your party tonight." Nodding to Sage, he added, "Good to see you again, Miss Larson."

"Thanks Derrick, I'm glad you're the one taking care of us tonight." Sage examined her badge, noting it gave her special photography privileges.

Luke adjusted his new Goshawks' ball cap, a gift from Margret. "I don't know about this, Sage. I'm feeling like a fish out of water. I think I saw a sports bar about a block away. Maybe I should watch the game from there."

Sage turned to Luke. "Don't be silly, we'll all visit the Frosty Nest after the game ... hopefully while celebrating the big win tonight. Besides, it would be rude for you to leave now, especially since Margret included you in the invitation." Sage watched Luke as he pulled the brim of the cap down, to cover his disapproval.

"How long before the warmup skate?" Patty inquired.

Jessica pulled out her phone to check the time. "The teams will be out for the warmup in about fifteen minutes."

"Drat. That won't give us enough time to grab some snacks." Patty's lower lip turned into a pout.

"No worries." Derrick opened the door. "Once you're situated, I'll get whatever you need."

"Thanks so much Derrick," Sage said, stopping inside the door.

"I'm so glad you made it." Margret stood waiting in the hallway. "Derrick, get the girls to their seats." Turning to Luke, she said, "How'd you like to come up top with me and watch the game from the VIP section?"

Luke looked from Margret to his friends. "Aren't we all watching the game together?"

"You'll all be watching the game, but the girls will watch from the stands, and you, Luke, will watch with me upstairs in the VIP room." Margret's smile widened, noting Luke's growing anticipation.

"Do I get to drink beer while I watch the game?" Luke arched an eyebrow.

"We have a full bar setup, with some local specialty beers." Margret poked Luke playfully in the chest with a manicured fingernail.

"Well, if there's beer, I'm in."

Margret then turned to Sage with a knowing sly smile. "Derrick will show you to your seats. Trust me, you're going to love the view. If you need anything, just let him know." After handing Sage three tickets, she linked her arm through Luke's; the two slipped away through a door marked 'Authorized Personnel Only.'

"Wow, what was that all about?" Patty looked at Sage.

"Yeah," said Jessica, holding up her badge to Derrick. "I thought we were sitting in the VIP section."

Derrick smiled as he shook his head. "Follow me girls." He began walking down the tunnel towards the ice.

"Where are we going now?" Jessica groaned.

"Looks like we're headed for *on the glass* seats." Sage picked up her pace to keep in step with Derrick. Behind her, she could hear both Jessica and Patty squealing with excitement.

Upon reaching the rink, Sage was taken aback by the smell of the ice, as the Zamboni raced around for the last pass before the Goshawks' grand entrance.

"This is too much fun," Jessica and Patty said in unison.

"Let's get you to your seats before the warmups start." Derrick guided Sage and her friends towards the ice. He pointed to three prime seats directly behind the goalie net. "I'll be stationed nearby in case you need anything," he said, pointing to an empty seat behind theirs. After ensuring they were settled in, Derrick stood at attention, ready to take their orders. "So, what would you all like to eat and drink?" His gaze moved from one girl to the next.

"Beer," all three sang out.

"Just bring an assortment of food. We're not picky, just hungry," Patty added.

"You got it."

Jessica let out a low whistle as she watched Derrick walk away.

"Stop that," Patty scolded. "We can't take you anywhere."

"I can't help it. He's so hot." Jessica's smile widened.

Sage took in the arena, recalling her last visit when Hunter had kissed her for the first time. Her fingers brushed her lips at the memory. She also remembered the horrific backlash from the press after the game, causing her to shiver.

"Hey, Sage, are you okay?" Jessica rubbed Sage's arm.

Sage turned to look at her friends. "I'm fine. Just cold from the ice."

"I told you we should've worn long johns under our clothes." Patty tugged at her custom-made Goshawks jersey. On her left shoulder she wore number 25 for Axel Berger. On her right shoulder she wore number 56 for Etan Eklund. Both the boys' last names printed on the back.

"Once the game starts, I'm sure you'll be warm enough." Jessica teased. She adjusted her ice blue jersey with the goshawk logo on the front, the back showcasing her favorite Goshawks player, Ryan Mitchell, number 73.

Sage lifted her oversize Goshawks jersey, with Hunter's name and number 1 displayed on the back. Pulling out a large, folded piece of paper from the back pocket of her jeans, she did her best to flatten the creases.

The loudspeakers blared the first beats of 'Poker Face.' "Fans, here are the Las Vegas Savages," the announcer shouted over the music, amidst cheers and a smattering of boos, as the Savages goalie and the rest of the team entered the ice for practice.

"I love Lady Gaga." Patty bobbed her head, clapping her hands to the music.

Jessica turned to Sage with a confused expression. "I thought the visiting team always entered last for the pregame warmups."

"You're right, they do. Looks like the Goshawks are turning things around tonight." Sage shrugged, watching the Savages scurry from the visitor's tunnel.

When the last of the Savages' players took to the ice, the arena lights dimmed as a hush fell over the crowd. The announcer's deep voice broke the silence, "And here are your Portland Goshawks." Blue-tinged spotlights began dancing around the ice, stirring the excitement.

The arena buzzed with an unbridled, kinetic energy, a clear testament to the growing passion of the gathered fans. Their feet hammered out a rhythm against the metal stands, creating a thunderous backdrop. Hands met in unison, clapping, while voices ascended into a collective crescendo of excitement, intertwining with the opening notes of 'The Phoenix' by Fall Out Boy.

The air vibrated with the sound of thousands singing along, a powerful chorus filling the space ... synchronizing in passionate support of the Goshawks. It was more than a pregame atmosphere ... it was a vivid demonstration of unity, with every Goshawks' fan bonded in their unwavering support for their team.

Sage and her friends rushed forward, pounding on the glass, screaming, "Go! Goshawks!"

Ryan was the first player to skate behind the net, almost tripping as Jessica screamed, "Go! Ryan!"

Pivoting, Ryan glided back to where the girls stood. With a fluid motion, he removed one glove, gesturing for Jessica and Patty to follow him to where the protective netting ended. Stooping, he scooped up a puck. Catching Etan and Axel's attention, he beckoned them to join him. Fixing his gaze on Jessica, he called out, "Catch!" before tossing the puck over the glass.

The rookies trailed behind, with Etan bouncing a puck on his stick's blade. As he approached Patty, his smile broadened, giving her an affirming nod. "This one's from me and Axel," he declared, lobbing the puck over the glass. The three then transitioned back into the rhythm of practice, merging with the ongoing drills on the ice.

Sage couldn't shake the feeling of being left out of the fun. As her norm, she reached for her camera; opening the protective window that covered the camera hole in the glass. Having shot from this vantage point before, she appreciated the Portland's arena's commitment to enhancing the fan experience and providing unique photographic perspectives. This camera hole, situated in an unconventional spot behind the goalie's net, was a testament to that effort, offering her an unparalleled view of the action on the ice.

Peering through her lens, Sage focused on Hunter. While her position wasn't ideal for capturing him directly, it allowed her to snap exceptional shots of the Goshawks in action, their sticks sending puck after puck towards his net. Hunter was in top form tonight, a testament to his skill and focus. Despite the barrage of pucks flying his way, only a few slipped into the net, each save a display of his prowess between the pipes.

Sage, engrossed in her shooting, took a brief break to review her captured images. She was oblivious to Ryan's covert signal to Olaf, which led to the Snowman stepping into Hunter's position at the net. As Hunter looked for a spot to stretch, Ryan's voice cut through the air, drawing his attention. Raising his mask to better hear, Hunter's gaze met Sage's, marking their first eye contact of the evening.

Instinct drew him to her as he glided behind his net. Sage retrieved her homemade sign from the seat behind her, pressing it against the glass. The sign declared, 'Hunter, win this battle for us. I'm always with you!' Reading her message, Hunter shouted, "I'm with you too." He gestured for Sage to open the camera hole, and with urgency, he slipped off his catcher glove.

At first, Sage was unsure what he was doing. When Hunter stuck his hand through the hole, she reached down to touch his icy fingertips. She could swear sparks flew between them. After a few moments, Hunter retracted his hand. Sage knelt, placing her ear to the camera hole. Hunter put his lips near the glass. "You made my night by being here."

Chase skated next to Hunter. Looking up, he waved, then yelled, "Hi, Sage." At the same time tapping his stick on Hunter's leg pads, letting him know they needed to exit the ice.

Hunter skated off, giving a quick glance back to Sage, as if willing her to stay. His smile grew wider as she pointed to him and then to his net, shouting, "No! Goals!"

Patty and Jessica came running back to join Sage, displaying their hockey trophies.

"Where's yours?" Jessica asked.

"I got something better than a puck. I got the goalie."

As the girls settled back into their seats, Derrick showed up, his hands filled with Goshawks' designer totes. Behind him, an intern walked with care, juggling three large glass mugs. "I had no idea what kind of beer you gals drank, so I got you some of the local IPA," Derrick announced.

"Wow, thanks." Sage took one of the frosty mugs from the intern.

Retrieving her mug, Jessica examined the Goshawks logo etched into the glass. "Holy Cow, the Goshawks go all out providing chilled monogrammed mugs to their fans."

"They're not from the concession stand, they're from the VIP lounge," the intern corrected her. "I'll be over there in front of the exit. Let Derrick know what you want, and I'll get it for you."

Derrick handed each of the girls a Goshawks bag filled with an assortment of gourmet bite sized treats.

Patty opened her bag, inhaling its contents. "I'm going to gain ten pounds just smelling this food."

Derrick settled into the seat behind the girls, who were now seated, each sipping from their chilled glasses of beer. They turned, raising their mugs in a silent toast of thanks to him, acknowledging his thoughtfulness.

Sage attached her telephoto lens to her camera, looking through it to the VIP box. She watched Margret sitting close to Luke, pointing to different areas of the ice. Luke, beer mug in hand, leaned in close to the Marketing Manager, nodding and smiling.

It was not long before the lights dimmed again. The arena's ambiance shifted. A hush fell over the crowd, anticipation hanging heavy in the air. The moment Hunter's name pierced the silence, the space erupted, chants of "Ice Wall, Ice Wall" reverberating around the arena. A testament to his steadfast presence in the goal.

Following him, the names of the Goshawks' starting line were heralded, each stepping onto the ice to join their goaltender. They aligned on their side of the blue line in a display of unity and strength. Together, they formed a formidable assembly, akin to a warrior tribe poised for the decisive clash.

The call for attention came as the announcer invited everyone to remove their hats and stand for the National Anthem. Sage, caught up in the moment, felt an unmistakable stir of emotion, as fans from both teams united in respect, was a powerful reminder of the sportsmanship hockey fans displayed.

As the anthem's final baritone note faded and the arena returned to darkness, a spotlight carved a path for Hunter. He navigated the stretch of ice between the opposing teams, a solitary figure under the watchful eyes of all. With a gesture that felt like a call to something grander, he extended his arm skyward. Mirroring an action not seen since the last game with Florida, a goshawk made its majestic descent from the heights of the VIP area; a symbol of unity and fierce loyalty, encapsulating the spirit of the moment and the anticipation of the battle to come.

Instead of climbing his arm as before, the goshawk remained steadfast on Hunter's outstretched catcher glove, wings spread wide. The spotlight followed Hunter as he skated a lap around the rink. Upon his return to the center line, Hunter thrust his arm skyward and released a call echoing that of the hawk, signaling the goshawk to glide back to the VIP box. As the bird took flight, an undeniable wave of exhilaration surged through the crowd, the arena alive with the shared excitement of the fans, their voices merging into a spirited echo of the goshawk's 'kak-kak-kak.'

"Wow. Just, Wow!" Patty said as she gripped Sage's arm tighter. "Do they use the goshawk in every home game?"

"As far as I know, this is only the second time they've used the hawk," Sage responded, shifting her attention back to the viewfinder as she snapped photo after photo.

"I would love to figure out how they got the bird trained to do that." Jessica let out a long, low whistle.

As the arena lights brightened, the goalies found their spots in their respective nets, as the rest of the players skated to center ice for the crucial faceoff. The puck dropped, marking the start of what was more than just a game—it was the showdown for The Cup, a moment where every second counted, dreams hung in the balance, and heroes could be made with a single shot.

Chapter 50
Trifecta Part Two

June 19th [Game 7 of The Cup Final: The Game]
"And here we go, folks, the energy in the Goshawks stadium is sizzling tonight as we kick off the last game of the Cup Final in beautiful Portland, Maine. I'm Tom Hughes, and with me again is goaltending legend John 'The Gatekeeper' Hamilton."

"The oddsmakers are divided on tonight's outcome between the Portland Goshawks and the Las Vegas Savages. One thing's a sure bet ... it's do or die time for both teams," John shouted.

"That's right, John. You know the Savages are going to be testing Griffin. He's been the talk of the series with his incredible saves. Without doubt, he's been the backbone of the Goshawks' wins."

First Period

Hunter's heart thundered in his chest, adrenaline surging as he shifted fluidly between the pipes, every sense attuned to the game's pulse. The crisp, sharp scent of resurfaced ice filled his senses, a prelude to the imminent clash. He barely had time to settle before a wave of determined Savages barreled down the ice, their eyes fixed on the net ... on his home. As Hunter positioned himself, vigilant in the crease, the crowd's roar dimmed to a focused silence in his ears.

A breakaway by Douglas, the Savages' first-line forward, had the crowd on edge as he charged the net, maneuvering past Goshawks' defensemen, Ryan and Axel, with alarming speed.

"Douglas breaks through. It's a one-on-one against Griffin, folks. This is the challenge they've been talking about." Tom's voice reverberated throughout the arena.

Hunter, eyes locked on the oncoming threat, dropped to his knees, ready. Douglas unleashed a blistering shot, but Hunter's glove was faster, snatching the puck out of the air, a move that drew a deafening cheer from his fans.

"What a save by Griffin! You could see Douglas thought he had that one. But no, the Ice Wall's too quick tonight," Tom screamed.

"The rest of the Goshawks aren't sitting back either. Look at Rutherford leading the charge, flanked by Eklund and O'Connell. They're pushing into the Savages' zone with purpose."

The Goshawks' offense surged, Etan Eklund passing to Chase Rutherford, who found Finn O'Connell on the left wing. Finn fired, but the Savages' goalie, Mason, matched Hunter's prowess with a spectacular glove save.

"O'Connell with a powerful shot, but Mason's there for the stop. Both goalies are putting on a show tonight." John's voice betrayed his disappointment.

Physical play intensified, the Savages' strategy of aggression and intimidation on full display. A hefty check by the Savages' defenseman Collins, on Etan, drew loud jeers from the crowd, signaling the game's escalating physicality.

"You can feel the tension here, John. That hit on Eklund. It's clear the Savages are using their physicality as a weapon."

As the period wore on, neither team broke the deadlock, with Hunter and Mason turning away every shot. The Goshawks and Savages matched each other, play for play, hit for hit, in a relentless display of skill and determination.

"And that's the end of the first period, folks. Zero to zero on the board, but don't let that fool you. The intensity on the ice is fierce. Both teams are playing like it's the last game they'll ever play," John summarized.

"Right you are, John. It's shaping up to be a legendary finale to the series. The Goshawks may have home ice advantage, but the Savages are showing they're not intimidated."

Skating off the ice, Hunter glanced towards the stands, locking eyes with Sage for a fleeting moment. It was her look—of determination and pride, mixed with a silent promise—that said everything. Tonight, Hunter wasn't *just* playing for his team, or The Cup. He was playing for their future, for a dream that extended beyond the rink's confines. The battle was far from over, but with Sage here, Hunter felt invincible, ready to face whatever the next periods would bring.

Second Period

"Welcome back, folks. The second period's underway, and the Goshawks are looking to capitalize on their momentum. Eklund's looking sharp tonight, wouldn't you say, John?"

"Absolutely! After a scoreless first period, you can bet both teams are itching to get on the board. The Goshawks have the home crowd behind them, which could make all the difference."

An early offensive push by the Goshawks saw Etan taking control, darting through the Savages' defense. A seamless pass from Axel Berger set him up for a precision shot that slipped past the Savages' goalie, lighting up the scoreboard.

GOAL! Goshawks—Eklund

"Eklund finds the back of the net with a spectacular shot! That pass from Berger to Eklund was textbook," shouted Tom.

"And just like that, the Goshawks are up by one," John screamed.

The Savages, undeterred, ramped up their aggression, but at a costly mistake—a cross-checking penalty against their second-line defenseman, Collins—gave the Goshawks a power play opportunity. Etan, once again in the spotlight, didn't disappoint. With the Goshawks pressing the advantage, Etan Eklund unleashed a rocket, his stick flexing almost to the point of breaking, as the puck found its way into the top corner of the Savages' net.

GOAL! Goshawks—Eklund

"With Collins in the box, the Goshawks capitalized on the power play. That's two for the young rookie tonight," shouted Tom.

"He's on fire. The puck hit the net at 99mph. Now that was some force. The Savages are going to have to find an answer to Eklund if they want to turn this game around."

As the second period was coming to an end, tempers flared again, leading to a clash between Finn and Thompson, a Savages' forward. Exchanging blows, each player demonstrating the raw emotion and intensity of this last game.

"Now, O'Connell and Thompson are dropping gloves. You can feel the tension boiling over." Tom's words vibrated through the speakers.

"These are the moments that define a game seven. Every hit, every shot, every save carries so much weight. The linesmen are stepping in, with only seconds left on the clock. It looks like both players will head for their tunnels instead of the box."

"And that's the end of the second, folks. Goshawks lead 2-0, thanks to a pair of goals from the young rookie, Etan Eklund. Savages will have their work cut out for them in the third." The camera zoomed in on Tom, wearing a grin.

"They certainly do. But as we've seen throughout this series, no lead is safe. It's going to be an all-out battle until the third's final buzzer." John said.

———◆◆◆———

Entering the locker room, Hunter collapsed on his bench. Removing his mask, he ran gloveless fingers through his damp hair. Leaning back, closing his eyes, he concentrated on slowing his heartbeat. It felt good to be still. To feel the peace of non-movement, he did his best to block out the chatter from the other players.

"You are playing strong tonight." Viktor stood over Hunter, offering him a towel.

"Thanks." Hunter opened his eyes, accepting the towel, wiping his face, neck and hair.

"Did I see you talking to girl earlier?" Viktor growled as he squatted on his haunches in front of Hunter.

Hunter leaned towards his goaltending coach. "I invited Sage to be here tonight. She's been my rock throughout the playoffs."

The Russian's face grew grave. "Girl has been a rock around your neck, dragging you down."

"No! Sage has always been there for me. She has always believed in me ... even when you haven't." Hunter tossed the damp towel at a stunned Viktor. He then stood and walked into a bathroom stall, locking the door behind him.

When Hunter reentered the room, Viktor was huddled in a corner with the other coaches.

"Hey Jimmy, get me a piece of copy paper and a thick black marker," Hunter called out to an intern. While he was waiting for the young man to return, Hunter turned to Ryan and Axel. "Thanks guys, you are doing a great job in front of the net."

Axel became animated. "I'm always ready to put my body in the way of a bullet for you."

"Yeah, what Axel said. We're there for you, bud." Ryan punched Hunter's shoulder.

When the intern returned with the paper and marker, Hunter grabbed a clipboard, printing five words in bold letters. Hunter stood, displaying the paper in front of his chest. His smile widened as he instructed the intern to get out his phone and take a picture. He then took the phone, attaching the image to a text, sending them both to Margret, tossing the phone back to the bewildered intern.

"Listen up everyone." Coach Harrison stood at the front of the room, hands on hips. "You're all playing a smart game. But we need to push even harder. You cannot afford to get complacent."

He turned to Chase, "I want you and your fellow forwards to stop passing the puck and start shooting it." He then turned to Ryan. "That goes for you defensemen, too. We can't win on Hunter's skills alone. We have to score goals. Now, get out there and fight hard, fight smart."

One by one, the players adjusted their gear. The equipment manager handed Hunter his warmed dry gloves, along with a refilled water bottle. Hunter pulled on his mask, picked up his stick, leading the Goshawks out for their final battle.

Third Period

Entering the ice for the final period, Hunter skated behind his net, tapping his stick on the glass in front of Sage. He then lifted it, pointing to the Jumbotron. Hunter watched Sage's expression change from confusion to delight; as she stared at the picture taken in the locker room, now on display overhead, bigger than life.

The sign read: SAGE, THIS ONE'S FOR YOU.

Hunter struck the glass once more, as Sage screamed, "NO! GOALS!" Fearing a delay of game penalty, he swiftly skated to his net.

The third period began with an extraordinary display of determination from Hunter, his gesture to Sage resonating with Goshawks' fans, as they began chanting, "Sage! Sage! Sage!"

"Well, Tom, I can't say I've ever seen anything quite like that before. It's clear Griffin's playing with a purpose tonight, dedicating this final showdown to someone special."

"It sure adds another layer to this already intense game. And here we go, the third period is underway. The Goshawks are leading by two, but with twenty minutes left, anything can happen."

A rapid advance by Richardson, one of the Savages' enforcers, tested Hunter's resolve early in the period. Richardson's breakaway was a heart-stopper, with Ryan, Chase, and Finn in hot pursuit. Hunter, true to his word, made a spectacular glove save, denying the Savages a chance to narrow the lead.

"Richardson with a golden opportunity, but Griffin's not to be denied. What a save!" Tom shouted.

Tensions escalated when Richardson, out of frustration, flung his stick back, hitting Hunter in the chest full force. The crowd went silent as Hunter fell to his knees, grabbing his chest, the puck still protected in his catcher glove. The Ref's whistle was shrill, but the retaliation was quicker as Ryan and Finn slammed into Richardson, dropping the Savages' player to the ice.

"Whoa, things are heating up! This is turning into a powder keg," Tom voiced his concerns.

Chase skated over to assess Hunter. Lifting the goalie's mask, he asked, "Are you hurt?"

It took Hunter a few moments to answer. "I'm okay. Just got the wind knocked out of me." He stood as a referee skated over. The arena exploded in cheers as Hunter tossed the puck to the ref.

Finn and Ryan, along with Richardson, were escorted to their respective penalty boxes, as Coach Harrison called for a timeout.

After squirting water into his mouth and over his face, Hunter skated to the Goshawks bench.

"Do we need to put Svensson in?" Coach Harrison asked with great concern.

"I'm fine. I just had to catch my breath." Hunter reassured his coach.

"Good. Good." Coach Harrison looked at the rest of his players. "We'll start off with Murphy, Bennett, and Preston." He paused a moment, searching his players' eyes. "Vegas is going to come after us strong. So, keep on your game. I want you ... Chase, Axel and Etan ... on the ice after the first minute ticks off the penalty clock." Turning to Hunter, he asked again, "Are you sure you're up to this? They're going to fire everything they got at you."

"Let Them Bring It!" Hunter sported a cocky grin. Lowering his mask, he skated to his net. Followed by his three teammates.

"It's a 3 on 4 situation, folks. The Goshawks are short-handed, but it doesn't look like they're backing down," John announced.

The Goshawks won the faceoff but lost the puck to a Savages' defenseman. Then it began. Hunter was barraged with shot-after-shot. Until he fell on the puck. He was relieved when the whistle blew, so he could compose himself.

Once again, the Goshawks won the faceoff. Murphy shot the puck to the Savages' zone, giving enough time for a fast change of players. Chase, Axel, and Etan jumped over the bench's railing. Axel caught the puck on his tape, as the Savages' players raced after him.

Axel then made a quick pass to Chase. With a practiced breakaway, Chase skated for the Savages' net, with Etan fast on his heels.

Approaching the Savage's crease, Chase shouted to Mason, "Eyes Up Here!" It proved to be enough distraction for the goalie to take his eyes off the puck, staring into Chase's steely glare. Chase took that millisecond to slide the puck to Etan. With a wicked grin, Chase commanded, "Get a Natty Hatty, rookie."

Without hesitation, Etan took the opportunity to snipe the puck into Mason's unprotected opening, getting not only a shortie, but his first hat trick.

GOAL! Goshawks—Eklund

"Eklund does it again! What a play! Even short-handed, the Goshawks widened the gap. That's 3-0!" Tom's voice was hoarse.

The game halted as hats rained onto the ice. Once more, the Goshawks' fans began singing along to the Fall Out Boy's 'The Phoenix.' The stands filled with fist pumps and feet stomping to the music's beat.

Hunter, who'd never left his net for a teammate's celly, broke with tradition, joining the group hug, nearly toppling Etan to the ice.

"What A Goal!" John screamed.

As they cleared the hats off the ice, Hunter skated to the bench, leaning on the railing. Searching for Sage, he saw her give him a clandestine wave. He responded with a smile and a slight nod.

The rest of the game was filled with frustration from the Savages as the penalties racked up; leaving players on both benches battered, bloodied and bruised. Hunter put Sage out of his thoughts, becoming laser focused on the puck. Axel and Ryan did their best to block shot-after-shot in front of Hunter's net. Sometimes with their sticks, but also with their bodies. Chase, Finn, and Etan also engaged the Savages in a game of keep away.

With only five minutes left on the clock, and Axel in the box for tripping, the Savages pulled their goalie, creating a 4 on 6 advantage for the Savages.

Within seconds after serving his penalty, Axel skated hot into the fray, stealing the puck from a Savages' forward. Axel moved to the Savages' empty net as if his skates were jet-propelled, with three of Vegas' fastest skaters in hot pursuit. The moment his skates crossed the blue line, Axel shot. Time seemed to freeze as the puck rocketed into the net.

GOAL! Goshawks—Berger

Bedlam broke out in the arena.

"Berger finds the empty net! That's 4-0 for the Goshawks. Folks, without doubt, the rookie's goal kills all hope of the Savages kissing The Cup tonight." Tom's words were drowned out by the cheering crowd.

"With the clock winding down, the Goshawks are moments away from claiming victory," John added.

Axel did a little dance, raising his stick in the air. Within seconds, his on ice teammates grabbed him in a group hug. The Goshawks' bench went wild as Axel skated over for the ritual gloved fist pumps. Sticks pounding on the side of the bench's wall. Then Axel skated over to Hunter, bumping his helmet against Hunter's mask.

The final buzzer sounded as the arena exploded in celebration. The Goshawks had done it; they'd won The Cup. Once again, Hunter sought Sage, their eyes meeting across the jubilant chaos. The promise he'd made, to his team, to her, and himself, had been fulfilled. Tonight, the Goshawks hadn't just won a game; they'd secured a legacy.

"There you have it. The Goshawks are the new Cup Champions! A shutout in game seven, a testament to their resilience, skill, and the indomitable spirit of their goalie, Hunter, Ice Wall, Griffin," Tom's voice broke.

"This victory is for the ages." John yelled. "From the brink of defeat in the beginning of the Final ... to champions on home ice! The story of the Goshawks' season, their comeback, and tonight's triumph, it's one for the hockey history books."

Chapter 51

Trifecta Part Three

June 19th [Game 7 of The Cup Final: Celebration]
The stadium vibrated with the deafening cheers of 'Goshawks! Goshawks!' echoing through the rafters. The Goshawks' players cleared the bench like a dam breaking. Helmets, gloves and hockey sticks littered the ice, as the players piled on top of one another in a group hug.

Both teams then lined up for the traditional handshake line. Hunter was taken aback with the graciousness of the Savages' players, as they congratulated him on his shutout.

When Hunter came to the end of the line, the Las Vegas, General Manager pulled Hunter in tight, his lips pressed near Hunter's ear. "Have your agent contact me before you finalize a new contract." He then moved away, giving Hunter a hungry smile and a pat on the back.

The equipment manager and his assistants skated onto the ice carrying a large box. As each player left the line, Ted handed them a series-winner ball cap. Upon reaching Hunter, Ted exchanged a cap for the decorative goalie mask ... he then handed the mask to an assistant for safe keeping.

"Over here, Hunter."

Hunter recognized her voice even through the din of the cheers. Snugging the cap on his head, he turned and skated to Sage, standing on the ice next to Nikki, both capturing the moment with their cameras. Hunter didn't hesitate to take her in his arms, giving her a passionate kiss before placing her back on the ice. "I told you this one was for you."

"I thank you. The team thanks you, and I know the fans thank you." Sage was laughing so hard, she almost lost her footing, even wearing the slip-resistant grips on her boots.

"Hey Hunter, get your butt over here," Chase shouted.

"Don't leave," Hunter commanded, placing a quick kiss on Sage's lips before taking his place with the Goshawks' players.

"Never," Sage whispered, as she lifted her camera, doing her best to steady her hands.

A hush fell over the crowd as a path of thin red carpet unrolled to herald the arrival of prestigious honors. A small table was placed at the end of the carpet. Then, with a reverence suited to the occasion, a figure emerged, bearing a trophy ... a testament to individual triumph amid collective endeavors. Mounted on a rich wooden base, adorned with lifelike silver maple leaves, a symbol of unparalleled valor and skill throughout the playoffs. This was the moment where individual brilliance was acknowledged, a beacon of excellence in the fierce competition of the playoffs.

The Commissioner began his speech, "This year's winner of the playoffs MVP Trophy goes to ..." He paused, scanning the line of players before pointing at the Goshawks' starting goalie. "Hunter Griffin," he announced.

Hunter's delayed response felt eternal until Ryan's nudge sent him skate-tripping towards the commissioner.

"Congratulations, young man." The Commissioner gripped Hunter's hand with a firm shake. "The Pro Hockey Writer's Association has chosen you unanimously as the playoffs' Most Valuable Player."

Overwhelmed, Hunter stood next to the trophy for the obligatory photo op. Lifting it off the table, he felt its weight, a testament to his journey. The crowd cheered as Sage captured the moment, her lens freezing his legacy. With pride, Hunter skated to the Goshawks' bench, entrusting the symbol of his valor to Assistant Coach Scott. He then rejoined his teammates, awaiting the next presentation.

The hush that fell over the arena was charged with anticipation as the lights dimmed once more. A solitary spotlight carved a path across the ice, coming to rest on the far end where The Cup was poised to make its entrance. The announcer's voice, deep and resonant, filled the space, "Ladies and Gentlemen, The Cup." His words drew an awe-struck silence from the crowd.

Hunter watched with pride as the gleaming oversized chalice was reverently carried down the carpet runner, the symbol of ultimate victory and sacrifice. Its presence filled the arena with a sense of history, a sense of immortality. Placed upon the table, it glistened under the spotlight—a beacon of dreams realized, a testament to hard battles fought and won.

"Congratulations to both the Las Vegas Savages and the Portland Goshawks teams for their outstanding season, and this amazing Cup Final," the Commissioner began, his voice resonating through the electric atmosphere of the packed arena. He allowed the applause to calm before continuing. "For the Goshawks, a team only five seasons' young, to clinch this title is not just an achievement—it's a testament to the spirit and tenacity of each player."

The Commissioner waited for the cheers to wane, before he began again. "A special thank you to the Goshawks' players for their dedication, and perseverance in winning the most highly sought after trophy in all of team sports." He nodded towards the Goshawks line, this time pointing to Chase. "I am honored to present this trophy to the Goshawks' captain, Chase Rutherford."

Chase glided forward, his skates tracing a smooth arc on the ice, as the crowd erupted into a roaring ovation. Meeting the Commissioner, he shook his hand, the clasp echoing in the sudden hush that fell over the spectators. "Congratulations, Captain," the Commissioner said, his voice a solemn thread in the celebration's symphony.

After a quick photo op with the Commissioner, Chase lifted the trophy above his head, bringing it down for the first ceremonial kiss as he skated around the rink.

Coming back to his teammates, Chase handed the trophy to Hunter, who lifted it into the air, skating around Sage, as he too placed his lips on the silver surface.

Hunter then handed the trophy to Etan, and said, "You get it next bud, for the series hat trick, your first one as a Goshawk."

"What a night for the two rookies. Every player dreams of lifting The Cup their first year going pro," Tom shouted, as Etan took his turn with The Cup.

"This is a moment they'll never forget." John said.

Hunter, still drenched in sweat, and adrenaline pumping, was approached by a junior member of the press. Microphone thrust forward. Her voice cut through the celebratory din, "Hunter, how does it feel to be named the playoff's MVP?"

He scanned the rink, his gaze locking with Sage's. "It's been a childhood dream," he admitted with a heartfelt laugh. "This journey, with these guys, it's been every-thing."

"The Goshawks had a rocky start the first three games of the Final. How did you turn the last games around.?" probed the reporter.

"One player cannot win a hockey game, it's a team effort." Hunter took a mo-ment to wipe the sweat dripping onto his brows. "For me, it's always been my love for the game, my love for my teammates, and a love for the fans," Hunter responded, his gaze unwavering. "I just couldn't let them down."

"And what about the photo and note displayed before the third period? Did your love for Sage play a role in tonight's focus?"

Hunter remained silent for a beat before he leaned into the mic. "Sage has been there for me throughout the playoffs. She's been my inspiration. She's been my biggest supporter. Sage said, 'No Goals.' I always do my best to give her what she wants." Wearing a smirk, Hunter turned, skating back to the Goshawks' players, as they gathered for a group shot with the trophy.

Chase grabbed Hunter by the arm of his sweater, pulling him into the heart of the group. The rest of the Goshawks' team: managers, coaches and owner, formed a horseshoe ring, with The Cup taking center stage.

Hunter watched Sage weave through the official photographers, knowing she would be the only one to truly capture the memories of this moment to perfection. The second the photoshoot ended Hunter skated across the ice, lifted Sage into his arms, kissing her with passion, the click of cameras following their every move as they exited the arena.

Hunter felt a twinge of concern, certain his public show of affection for Sage would eclipse the news of the Goshawks' victory. But right now, none of that mattered. He just wanted to hold her close, to find a quiet corner where he could express just how much her presence tonight meant to him.

Inside the Goshawks' tunnel, as Hunter put Sage down, he was met by Margret, who gave him an unexpected hug.

"Congratulations Hunter. You were a beast in the net tonight," Margret gushed. "I have a surprise for you." She moved to one side as a middle-aged couple stepped from the shadows.

For the second time tonight, Hunter was greeted by a surprise. "Mom? Dad?" he stammered.

Hunter's mother walked towards him, placing a delicate hand on her son's shoulder. The hug from Hunter's father, so uncharacteristic and warm, overwhelmed him.

"We're so proud of you, son," his dad said.

Hunter's eyes watered as he returned the hug. In his twenty-two years, he had never known his father to show emotion, let alone embrace anyone ... not even his mother.

Stepping back, Hunter looked to Margret with unvoiced questions.

"It was Sage's idea. She persuaded me to invite your parents to the game," Margret answered before being asked.

"I'm glad we won," Hunter said, his solemn expression underscoring his sincerity.

"Me too," Margret agreed, followed by strained laughter.

"I never had a doubt about the Goshawks winning. Because I never doubted you," Sage announced as she wrapped her arms around Hunter's waist. "You really get stinky and sweaty during the games." She joked. Instead of pulling away from his drenched clothing, she moved in tighter.

"I want to thank both you ladies for making this happen," Hunter's father said as he stuck his hand out. "Sage, it's a pleasure to finally meet you."

"The pleasure is all mine," Sage said, shaking Hunter's father's hand.

The Goshawks players entered the tunnel. One-by-one, they passed Hunter's small group, each player tapping Hunter's cap.

"Come on Hunter," Chase called as he entered the Goshawks locker room carrying The Cup. "The sooner we shower and dress, the sooner we can celebrate."

Hunter shouted, "I'll be right there," knowing Chase was exaggerating. He had seen enough locker room Cup victories to know he, along with his teammates, would soon be drenched in champagne. He knew it would be at least an hour before the revelry subsided enough for him to make an exit.

"Go on son. Celebrate with your friends," his mother said.

Hunter hesitated. "Are you sure? Do you have time to wait for me until I'm dressed?"

"Stop by the house tomorrow," his father said. His tone sincere ... wanting.

"Bring Sage and her friends with you, too," his mother added.

"Okay. If you're sure," Hunter stammered, caught up in the surreal moment.

"It will be good to have you home again," his mother said, as she weaved her arm within her husband's, before they turned as one, and walked away.

Ryan opened the door, shouting over the chaos in the locker room. "Hunter. Do I have to come out there and drag you in here?"

"I'm coming," Hunter shouted back. Turning to Margret, he pleaded, "You have to promise me you will not let Sage out of your sight." Turning to Sage, he added, "No more sneaking away."

"I swear on The Cup." Margret grinned, making a playful salute.

"Where do we go to wait?" Sage gave Margret a concerned look.

"My car is waiting outside to take us to the Frosty Nest. Your friends are already there."

Confident that Margret had everything under control, Hunter bent down, pulling Sage into a warm embrace. Their kiss a promise of a swift reunion. As he opened the door to the locker room, a burst of laughter and cheers greeted him ... followed by a cold spray of champagne from a bottle vigorously shaken by Olaf.

Chapter 52

Starting Over

July 2nd

The sun perched high over the sprawling Larson farm, casting a warm glow on the porch where laughter and light-hearted banter filled the air. Hunter draped his arm around Sage, pulling her closer; soaking in the rays as they lounged on the porch steps.

Everyone, including Sage's parents, were dressed in jeans and Goshawks' t-shirts. The girls were all wearing Goshawks champion ball caps. Ryan and the rookies, donning the cowboy hats gifted by Jim, were in a deep debate over who had the best cowboy swagger.

Ryan, sitting on an Adirondack chair with Jessica snuggled in his lap, tipped the brim of his hat to the rookies. "Now, I gotta say, Axel's got the stance down, but Etan, that hat trick last game has got you looking like a real midwestern hero."

Etan, leaning against the porch railing with a mock-serious expression, shot back, "I'll take that, Ryan. Just don't ask me to ride a horse again anytime soon; my backside is still sore from the last time we were here."

Patty, sitting on the railing, sandwiched between the two rookies, raised her glass in a salute. "Well, I think it's safe to say we've all got a bit more hockey than cowboy in us, especially after that big win two weeks ago." Patty looked first to Etan than to Axel. "What I really want to know is ... are you two up for tonight's fireworks?"

Etan looked to Patty. His brow furrowed in confusion. "I thought you celebrated with fireworks on the fourth of July, today is only the second."

"We always celebrate the holiday on the weekend, if the fourth lands on a weekday ... well except if it lands on Friday," Patty reassured him. "Besides, some of us have to work for a living." She playfully poked Etan in the ribs.

"Don't worry, the fireworks are covered." Smiling, Jessica turned slightly, looking deep into Ryan's eyes.

Axel became animated at the mention of fireworks, almost spilling his lemonade. "This will be our first celebration of your Fourth of July. It's going to be too much fun." He leaned behind Patty, high-fiving Etan.

Sage's gaze drifted across the yard where her father was prepping several steaks for the grill. Lilly sat at the picnic table, enjoying the sun, occasionally handing Jim a different spice bottle.

Jim seasoned each piece of beef with expertise. "Okay everyone, let me know how you want your steaks. If anyone says anything other than rare, they'll be the first one mucking out the horse stalls after dinner," Jim shouted to Sage and her friends. His gaze occasionally flickered from the grill to the road.

"Rare!" Came the chorus from the porch. Their voices momentarily distracting Crease from chasing a butterfly. He too barked in agreement, running back to flop down at the foot of the steps.

"I'll sneak you a piece of steak when Jim's not looking," Hunter whispered to Crease, as he scratched the young dog's belly.

The sound of tires crunching on gravel, mixed with the sight of lights flashing caused Jim to halt his food prep. He smiled as he wiped his hands, covering the steaks with a cheesecloth.

The sheriff's car crawled down the drive, followed by a sleek black limo, bringing up the rear was Luke's familiar black Ford. On the porch, everyone's attention snapped to the unexpected procession making its way towards them.

Ryan set his beer down, nudging Jessica. "Looks like things are about to get interesting."

As the vehicles approached, Sage leaned closer to Hunter, squeezing his hand, with a curious expression, she asked, "What's going on?"

Hunter, sporting a half grin, shrugged his shoulders. Giving Sage a quick peck on the lips, he whispered, "Just a little something to make today even more memorable."

They watched as the limo stopped. Nikki was the first to emerge from the front passenger door, camera in hand. He began documenting the unfolding scene.

The quiet murmur of conversation on the porch began anew as the group watched Sheriff Thor Engle exit his vehicle, his loyal Malinois by his side. He exchanged a knowing nod with Jim, who approached the vehicles with Lilly. Looking from the porch to the grill, the sheriff tipped his hat to Sage's mom. "Looks like quite the day you've planned."

Jim laughed. "You might say that Thor. I hope you can stick around for a bit."

"Oh, I'm not going anywhere," the sheriff said, the hint of a knowing smile underlining his words. Giving his Malinois a release command, Hammer turned into a playful pup, interacting with Crease in the yard. Both dogs oblivious to the significance of the moment.

On the porch, the questions kept coming. "Did you know about this?" Patty asked, directing her query to Sage.

"I'm out of this loop," answered Sage, as she watched the limo driver hustle to open the driver's side back door. A distinguished gentleman, dressed in a crisp suit, stepped out, casting a professional glance around before nodding in acknowledgment to the crowd.

"Is that ...?" Etan stammered his question to Ryan.

Ryan moved Jessica off his lap. Switching his cowboy hat with Jessica's Goshawks' cap, he stood, staring at the limo. "I'm not sure, rookie."

"If that's not The Keeper of The Cup, he's his doppelgänger," Axel said, his eyes wide, his mouth agape.

"Why is he here?" Patty asked, hands going to her mouth at the realization of what was about to transpire.

The presence of the guardian of The Cup brought a blend of formality and excitement to the gathering, especially when he began pulling on his white cotton gloves. With a professional flourish, he walked around the limo, opening the back passenger door, revealing The Cup securely fastened inside.

Margret hurried from Luke's truck to the limo. Taking a moment to confer with the honored guest, she slipped him a small box before stepping back. Gesturing to Sage's parents Margret said, "Noah Lizotte, this is Lilly and Jim. The Larson's are our gracious hosts."

Noah nodded, "A pleasure to meet you both."

"As we discussed on the phone, Noah is The Cup's guardian. Where it goes, he goes ... and Hunter has designated this to be his official day with The Cup."

Noah cleared his throat. "Actually, Margret, I don't want anyone to get the wrong impression. I'm the alternate guardian. Our official Keeper of the Cup was unable to travel due to illness. I've been sent in his stead."

"It's a pleasure to meet you," offered Lilly.

"Welcome to our home," said Jim. Noting Noah's gloved hands, he skipped the customary handshake.

"If I may?" Noah gestured towards the open door.

"Of course." Jim stepped aside as Noah unbuckled The Cup's restraints, carefully lifting it from the vehicle. Its gleam captivating all within view.

"Sheriff, thank you for the escort," Noah remarked, as he looked about. His smile grew as Hunter bounded towards him.

"Mr. Lizotte, thank you so much for traveling all the way here." Hunter's words came out deep, filled with humility.

"Where do you want me to set this, Hunter?" Noah asked, adjusting his hold on the trophy.

"Follow me, sir." Hunter escorted The Cup's guardian towards the porch, as Nikki rushed ahead, capturing each moment. Behind the procession walked Sage's parents, followed closely by Margret arm-in-arm with Luke.

With practiced reverence, Noah carried the trophy up the porch steps, placing it gently on a designated table draped in a light blue cloth.

The group on the porch rose, the air charged with expectation. Their gazes flickered between Hunter and the gleaming trophy beside him. Everyone was drawn in by the symbol of triumph that united them. Hunter, feeling the weight of their anticipation, stepped forward, his presence as commanding as The Cup itself.

"I chose today for my time with The Cup," Hunter announced, his words carrying across the porch, as he took Sage's hand. The trophy gleamed under the sun, its presence imbuing the moment with grandeur and significance beyond its usual acclaim.

Reaching inside The Cup's bowl, Hunter retrieved a small, intricately carved wooden box, the lid adorned with a detailed goshawk poised to take flight. Hunter faced Sage, who watched him with wide, expectant eyes. Dropping to one knee, he cradled the box in his hand.

"Sage," he began, his voice thick and sincere. "These past months have been the most meaningful of my life. I thought all my dreams had come true joining the Goshawks and winning The Cup. Then I met you. Though our time together has been brief, it's clear to me that a future with you is my new dream. Where I once saw only hockey, now I also see us ... together for a lifetime."

Hunter opened the box, retrieving a small object from a bed of silk. Setting the box aside, he presented the ring to Sage ... a custom designed setting: a flawless 3-karat diamond flanked on each side by one light and one dark blue sapphire, the black gold band made of delicate replicas of interwoven branches.

"This ring," Hunter continued, his gaze never wavering from Sage's eyes, "carries a piece of my history and my heart. The diamond belonged to my grandmother. The branches woven around the band represent our bond ... of how we continue to grow together, separate but one. The sapphires, the strength and resilience of the Goshawks."

Gently taking Sage's left hand, Hunter asked, his voice etched with commitment, "Sage, I love you so much. Will you marry me?"

Tears welled in Sage's eyes as she nodded vigorously. Finding her voice, she said, "Yes, Hunter, yes! I love you so much too."

As Hunter slipped the ring onto her finger, Sage lifted her hand to admire the sunlight dancing within the diamond. "It's beautiful," she whispered, her voice a mix of awe and adoration.

"Just like you," Hunter replied softly, before cupping her face with his hands, leaning in he placed a long, passionate kiss on her lips. The porch erupted into cheers and applause. Nikki clicked away, his camera capturing every second of their joy.

As the murmur of excitement settled, Luke stepped forward, extending a hand to Hunter. "Well done, Hunter. Sage couldn't have chosen a better man," his voice steady despite the tightness around his eyes—a nod to old dreams set aside for new realities.

Ryan moved next to Hunter. "This is more meaningful than a win on the ice, man," he said, clapping Hunter on the shoulder. "Really happy for you both."

Sage's girlfriends gathered around, gasps and delighted laughter filling the air as Jessica nudged Patty. "I got her ring size for him," she confessed with a wink. "Had to make sure it was a perfect fit."

Patty glared at her. "And you didn't think to clue me in? You know I can keep a secret!"

Jessica laughed, shaking her head. "Not this big, Patty. Not this one."

While Patty and Jessica admired Sage's ring, Margret pulled Hunter aside, lowering her voice to a conspiratorial whisper, "There's talk that the Goshawks' Owner and their GM are thrilled with your season. Expect a call from your agent. The Goshawks are planning to make sure you stay where you belong ... in Portland ... wearing a Goshawks sweater." Margret patted Hunter's chest to emphasize her words.

As they spoke, Crease, unnoticed in the earlier excitement, trotted up with his own way of joining the celebration. He began playfully licking Sage's ring hand, his tail thumping against Hunter's leg, as if trying to get his attention.

"Looks like the real MVP approves too." Axel declared as he scooped up Crease, parading him around the yard like a trophy. Etan joined in, as the rookies played a game of fetch with Crease and Hammer.

Back to his steaks, Jim watched the young people, his expression a complex tapestry of emotions. Finally, he sighed, his look one of reluctant acceptance mixed with genuine warmth. "Who knew a bunch of east coast pro hockey players would now be a part of this family," he murmured to Lilly, who squeezed his hand in understanding.

Late afternoon faded into evening, yet the farm continued to bustle with activity. Beef sizzled on the grill as tendrils of smoke, carrying its savory aroma, mingled with the sweetness of freshly baked goods. Laughter reverberated around the porch, punctuated by the gentle clinking of glasses.

As twilight descended, the golden hues of sunset surrendered to the deepening indigo of early night, casting elongated shadows and softening the day's edges. The horizon, once a line of fading light, transformed into a canvas for an explosion of fireworks, their vibrant colors cascading like celestial confetti. The rookies lifted their glasses in unison, their voices joining in a chorus of oohs and aahs.

Sage leaned into Hunter, her warmth melding with his as they cradled a slumbering Crease. The pup, nestled securely between them, twitched his ears occasionally but remained asleep, oblivious to the muffled bursts of fireworks in the distance.

Sage whispered, "Today, you gave me everything I never knew I always wanted."

Hunter kissed her forehead, his voice filled with promise. "I swear by The Cup to continue to fulfill all your wants and needs."

Acknowledgements

All novels are a labor of love, but the conception of *Shots and Shutouts* was born from a tragic event. One of my long-time and dearest friends succumbed to cancer shortly after being diagnosed. Her daughter is a huge hockey fan; *Shots and Shutouts* was created in hopes of shining a few rays of bright light into the darkness of her mom's passing. Susan, these words were written in hopes of making you smile.

A special shoutout to the most amazing alpha reader turned editor, and one of my cherished friends, Elize Holt. I entrusted her above everyone else to read the first raw pages of my hockey romance novel. Without her eagle eyes, excellent catches, and eagerness to read more, *Shots and Shutouts* would never have come to fruition.

Thanks goes out to my top-line beta readers for their feedback and encouraging words: Carol Max, Sue Carpenter-Diesing, and Lillian Hawkins. I'm excited that reading my story turned you into potential hockey fans.

To the hockey players who inspired this story and further instilled my infatuation for hockey: Linus and Jeremy (my favorite tandem goaltenders), Lucas and Mo (my favorite rookies) ... and of course my all-time favorite player and the reason I first fell in love with hockey, Bert.

Keeping the best for last, my deepest gratitude goes out to my husband, Stephen, for his continued support during these past labor-intensive months of writing, re-writing, and editing. Especially for his understanding and patience, and his constant nagging of, "Is the book done yet?" I deeply appreciated his scrutinizing attention to the technical side of hockey ... and his input of, "What in the world are you trying to say?" whenever I would write a nonsensical hockey scene. I appreciate him keeping me on track ... and only smirking all the years I called a 'five hole' a 'pie hole.' He has been and will always be my favorite and beloved hockey player.

About Author

Dee Marie is an award-winning author, photographer, and artist. Her career in publishing began as a managing editor, eventually advancing to editor-in-chief of an international computer graphics print magazine. She lives in South Dakota with her husband (a former hockey player) and two very loved and very spoiled Labradors.

An avid hockey fan with a special admiration for NHL goaltenders, Dee spends September through June chasing NHL games on her flatscreen. Her passion for the sport shines through in her writing, bringing the excitement and drama of hockey to life for her readers.